W9-AUU-106

More Horus Heresy from the Black Library

HORUS RISING
Dan Abnett

FALSE GODS
Graham McNeill

GALAXY IN FLAMES
Ben Counter

THE FLIGHT OF THE EISENSTEIN
James Swallow

FULGRIM
Graham McNeill

DESCENT OF ANGELS
Mitchel Scanlon

Dan Abnett

LEGION

Secrets and lies

For Jack Abnett O'Reilly and Jesse Coyne for
'Counterterrorism and You: An Operator's Guide. Lesson 1'.
Jesse, you have no idea how much that made me think.

Thanks to Nik, Graham McNeill, Alan Merrett
and Lindsey Priestley.

A BLACK LIBRARY PUBLICATION

First published in Great Britain in 2008 by
BL Publishing,
Games Workshop Ltd.,
Willow Road, Nottingham,
NG7 2WS, UK.

10 9 8 7 6 5 4 3 2 1

Cover and page 1 illustration by Neil Roberts.

© Games Workshop Limited 2008. All rights reserved.

Black Library, the Black Library logo, BL Publishing, Games Workshop,
the Games Workshop logo and all associated marks, names, characters,
illustrations and images from the Warhammer 40,000 universe are
either ®, TM and/or © Games Workshop Ltd 2000-2008, variably
registered in the UK and other countries around the world. All rights
reserved.

A CIP record for this book is available from the British Library.

ISBN 13: 978 1 84416 536 0
ISBN 10: 1 84416 536 1

Distributed in the US by Simon & Schuster
1230 Avenue of the Americas, New York, NY 10020, US.

No part of this publication may be reproduced, stored in a retrieval
system, or transmitted in any form or by any means, electronic,
mechanical, photocopying, recording or otherwise, without the prior
permission of the publishers.

This is a work of fiction. All the characters and events portrayed in this
book are fictional, and any resemblance to real people or incidents is
purely coincidental.

See the Black Library on the Internet at
www.blacklibrary.com

Find out more about Games Workshop
and the world of Warhammer 40,000 at
www.games-workshop.com

The Horus Heresy

It is a time of legend.

Mighty heroes battle for the right to rule the galaxy. The vast armies of the Emperor of Earth have conquered the galaxy in a Great Crusade – the myriad alien races have been smashed by the Emperor's elite warriors and wiped from the face of history.

The dawn of a new age of supremacy for humanity beckons.

Gleaming citadels of marble and gold celebrate the many victories of the Emperor. Triumphs are raised on a million worlds to record the epic deeds of his most powerful and deadly warriors.

First and foremost amongst these are the primarchs, superheroic beings who have led the Emperor's armies of Space Marines in victory after victory. They are unstoppable and magnificent, the pinnacle of the Emperor's genetic experimentation. The Space Marines are the mightiest human warriors the galaxy has ever known, each capable of besting a hundred normal men or more in combat.

Organised into vast armies of tens of thousands called Legions, the Space Marines and their primarch leaders conquer the galaxy in the name of the Emperor.

Chief amongst the primarchs is Horus, called the Glorious, the Brightest Star, favourite of the Emperor, and like a son unto him. He is the Warmaster, the commander-in-chief of the Emperor's military might, subjugator of a thousand thousand worlds and conqueror of the galaxy. He is a warrior without peer, a diplomat supreme.

As the flames of war spread through the Imperium, mankind's champions will all be put to the ultimate test.

~ DRAMATIS PERSONAE ~

Primarchs

ALPHARIUS   Primarch of the Alpha Legion

The Alpha Legion

INGO PECH   First Captain

(MA)THIAS HERZOG   Captain, 2nd Company

SHEED RANKO   Captain, Lernaean Terminator Squad

OMEGON   Lord, Effrit Stealth Squad

The 670th Imperial Expedition Fleet

JAN VAN AUNGER   Master of the Fleet

TENG NAMATJIRA   Lord Commander of the Army

Imperial Army

(Geno Five-Two Chiliad)

SRI VEDT   Uxor Primus of the Geno Five-Two

HONEN MU   Uxor

RUKHSANA SAÏID   Uxor

HURTADO BRONZI   Hetman

KAIDO PIUS   Hetman

DIMITER SHIBAN   Hetman

PETO SONEKA   Hetman

FRANCO BOONE   Genewhip

(Zanzibari Hort)
NITIN DEV   Major General
KOLMEC   Bajolur

(Lucifer Blacks)
DINAS CHAYNE   Bajolur-Captain
EIMAN   Companion
BELLOC   Companion

(Crescent-Sind Sixth Torrent)
WILDE   Lord

(Outremars)
KHEDIVE ISMAIL SHERARD

(Legio Xerxes)
AMON JEVETH   Princeps

(Regnault Thorns)
GAN KARSH   General

Non-Imperial personae
THE CABAL
JOHN GRAMMATICUS
GAHET
SLAU DHA
G'LATRRO

'God has given you one face and
you make yourself another.'
                    – attributed to the dramaturge
                                Shakespire, fl. M2

'Of the fabulous hydra it is said, cut off one head
and two will grow in its place.'
                              – antique proverb

'No one is enough of a fool to choose war instead
of peace. In peace sons bury fathers, but in war
fathers bury sons.'
                    – attributed to the chronicler
                                Herodotus, fl. M0

'War is simply the galaxy's hygiene.'
                    – attributed to the Primarch
                                Alpharius

My name is Hurtado Bronzi.

There, I've said it. I've said it and I can never take it back. The secret is out.

Ah. The rest? Well, if I must, sir. My name is Hurtado Bronzi, a hetman (which is to say, a senior captain) of the Geno Five-Two Chiliad, Imperial Army, glory of Terra, beloved of the Emperor. I am an Edessa-born man, proud of my liberty, Catheric by devotion, a brother to two sisters and a brother. My ears hear only the orders of my estimable Lord Commander Namatjira, my hands know only the purpose of the Emperor and the correct business of a carbine laser, my mouth… well, my mouth knows a great deal more, and knows when not to say it.

Because he has taught us to be scrupulously secretive. No, I will not be drawn to say his name. I said, he has taught us to be scrupulously secretive. That is his way, and we love him for it. The greatest gift he has bestowed on us is to share his secret with us.

Why? Because we were there, I suppose, at Tel Utan and Mon Lo Harbour and now the Shivering Hills. If it hadn't been us, it would have been others.

Why are you whispering? I can hear you whispering. What don't you want me to hear? What secrets are you plotting?

Pain? Is that it? Is that all you have to offer me? Well, yes, it does open secrets. Some secrets, some mouths. What have you planned for me? Ah, I see. Well, if you must. I won't welcome it. What will it be? Eyes? Genitals? The gaps between my toes and fingers? First, you should know–

Nnnhhhhh!

Oh. Merciful–

Mhh. Quite the expert, your little man. Quite the expert. He's done this before, hasn't he? No, wait, I–

Nhhhhghhh!

Beloved Terra! Ahh. Shit. Nhh.

That little bastard. Let me finish, please! Let me finish what I was saying.

Please? Yes?

All right, then. This won't work. This simply won't work. Because I'm telling you it won't.

I will not tell you anything. It doesn't matter what you do to me, really it doesn't. Burn me all you like, my mouth is shut.

Because that's all he asks of us. The only thing. I can tell you who I am, and who I was, but I can't – I won't – betray his confidence.

Gnnhhhhhhh!

Oh shit! Holy fire! Bastard!

Mhhhh…

What? What? Ask what you like. Burn me again, if you must.

My name is Hurtado Bronzi.
That's all you're getting.

PART ONE

REPTILE SUMMER

ONE

Tel Utan, Nurth, two years before the Heresy

THE NURTHENE UTTERED some of the usual gibberish before he died. He pointed at his enemies with his dust-caked fingers and jabbered, spitting out curses on their families and dependants, and particularly miserable dooms on the heads of their children, far away. A soldier learns how to ignore insults, but there was something about the Nurthene way of cursing that made Soneka blanch.

The Nurthene lay on his back on a slope of dry, red sand, where the blast had thrown him. His pink silk robes were stiffening in places where his blood was drying rapidly in the late afternoon sun. His silver breastplate, with its engraving of stylised reeds and entwined crocodilia, winked like a mirror. His legs lay in a limp position that suggested his spine was no longer properly connected.

Soneka trudged up the dry bed of the wadi to inspect him. A terribly dark, terribly blue sky met the

15

red horizon. The sinking sun picked out the facing edges of rocks and boulders with a bright orange sheen.

Soneka was wearing glare-shields, but took them off out of courtesy so that the Nurthene could see his eyes. He knelt down, the small gold box around his neck swinging like a pendulum.

'Enough with your curses, all right?' he said.

The troop stood around him on the slope, watching, their weapons ready in their hands. The desert wind brushed their embroidered, waist-length coats and made them flutter. Lon, one of Soneka's bashaws, had already snapped the Nurthene's falx with his liqnite, and flung the broken stump away over the rim of the wadi.

Soneka could still smell traces of the liqnite spray in the warm air.

'It's over,' he told his enemy. 'Will you speak to me?'

Looking up at him, grains of sand stuck to his face, the Nurthene murmured something. Bubbles of blood formed at the corners of his lips.

'How many?' Soneka asked. 'How many more of you are there in this sink?'

'You…' the Nurthene began.

'Yes?'

'You… you are carnal with your own mother.'

At Soneka's shoulder, Lon raised his carbine sharply.

'Relax, I've heard worse,' Soneka told him.

'But your mother is a fine woman,' said Lon.

'Oh, now you lust for her too?' asked Soneka. Some of the men laughed. Lon shook his head and lowered his carbine.

'Last chance,' said Peto Soneka to the dying man. 'How many more?'

'How many more of you?' replied the Nurthene in a dry whisper. His accent was strong, but there was no denying that the Nurthene had mastered the Imperial language. 'How many more? You come from the stars, in your droves, and you do nothing.'

'Nothing?'

'Nothing, except prove the universal presence of evil.'

'Is that what you think of us?' Soneka asked.

The Nurthene stared up at him. His eyes had gone glassy, like the sky at dawn. He burped, and blood welled up out of his mouth like water from a borehole.

'He's dead,' observed Lon.

'Well spotted,' said Soneka, rising to his feet. He looked back at the men gathered on the slope behind him. Beyond them, two Nurthene armoured vehicles were burning, sweating soot and smoke up into the blue sky. From the other side of the wadi, Soneka could hear sporadic las-shots.

'Let's dance,' Soneka said.

From the rim of the wadi, looking west, it was possible to see Tel Utan itself, a jumble of terracotta blocks and walls capping a long, loaf-shaped hill ten kilometres away. The intervening landscape was a broken tract of ridges and ancient basins and, in the sidelong evening light, the basins had filled with shadows so black they looked like pools of ink. Soneka felt a comparable blackness in his heart: Tel Utan was proving to be their nemesis. For eight months, it had held them at bay, through a combination of terrain, tactics, stoicism and plain bad luck.

The Geno Five-Two Chiliad was one of the oldest brigades in the Imperial Army. An elite force of one thousand companies, it had a martial tradition that stretched back through the time of the Great Crusade and into the era of the Unification Wars that had preceded it. The geno was a proud member of the Old Hundred, the Strife Epoch regiments that the Emperor, in his grace, had maintained after Unification, provided they pledged loyalty to him. Many thousands of others had been forced to disband, or had been actively purged and neutered, depending on their level of resistance to the new order.

Peto Soneka had been born in Feodosiya, and had served, in his youth, in the local army, but he had petitioned eagerly for transfer into the Geno Five-Two, because of their illustrious reputation. He'd been with the geno for twenty-three years, achieving the rank of hetman. In that time, they hadn't met a nut they couldn't crack.

There had been tough dances along the way, of course there had. Off the top of his head, Soneka could mention Foechion, where they had slogged toe to toe for six weeks with the greenskins in lightless, frozen latitudes, and Zantium, where the Dragonoid cadres had almost bested them in a series of running battles and ambuscades.

But Nurth, Tel Utan in particular, was as stubborn as anything they'd ever met. Word was the Lord Commander was getting edgy, and no one wanted to be around Namatjira when that happened.

Soneka pulled his glare-shields back on. He was a lithe, slender man of forty-two years standard, though he could pass for twenty-five. He had a striking, angular head, with hard cheek and jaw lines, a pointed chin and a generous, full-lipped mouth full of gleaming white teeth that women found especially attractive. Like all of them, his skin had bronzed in the Nurthene light. He made a signal, and his bashaws brought the troops in along the rim of the wadi and down into the dry basins beyond. Geno armour followed them, bounding along on their treads, and spuming wakes of red dust behind them as they churned out across the basin floor. Soneka's Centaur was waiting, its engine revving, but he waved it on. This was a time for walking.

There was half an hour of daylight left. Night, they had learned to their cost, belonged to the Nurthene. Soneka hoped to run his troop as far as the forward command post at CR23 before they lost the light. The last tangle with the Nurthene had slowed their advance considerably. Dislodging them from this country was like pulling out splinters.

Soneka's troops looked very fine as they strode forwards. The geno uniform was a bulky, tight-buckled bodyglove of studded leather and armour links, with a waist-length cape of yellow merdacaxi, a Terran silk, much rougher and more hard-wearing than the pink silks of the Nurthene. The ornate leather armour was marked with devices and trimmed with fur, and the backs of their capes were richly embroidered with company emblems and motifs. They carried lightweight packs, munition slings, long sword bayonets, and the bottles of their double water rations, which clinked against the liqnite cylinders they had all been issued with. Standard weapons were laser carbines and RPG sowers, but some men lugged fire poles or support cannons. They were all big men, all genic bred and selected for muscle. Soneka was slight compared to most. Their headgear was spiked helms, either silvered steel or glossy orange, often edged with brims of fur or neck veils of beaded laces. The glare shields were goggle-eyed: bulbous, paired hemispheres of orange metal with black slits across them.

Soneka's troop was coded the Dancers, a name that they'd owned for almost eight hundred years. In those last few minutes of daylight, the Dancers were going to take the worst beating they had ever known.

'SO, WHO'S THAT?' asked Bronzi quietly. 'Do you know?'

Bashaw Tche, busy with the wrapper of a ration, shrugged. 'Some kind of something,' he grunted.

'You're a world of use, you know that?' Bronzi replied, punching Tche in the arm. The bashaw, of the regimental uterine stock and considerably bigger in all measurements than Bronzi, gave his hetman a tired look.

'Some kind of specialist, they said,' he volunteered.

'Who said?'

'The Uxor's aides.'

The Jokers had reached the CR23 forward command post about an hour earlier, and had been billeted in the eastern wing of the old, brick-built fort. Chart Referent 23 was a Nurthene outpost captured two weeks before, and lay just eight kilometres from the Tel. It formed part of the 'noose' that Lord Commander Namatjira was tightening around the enemy city.

Hurtado Bronzi, a sixty-year veteran possessed of boundless charisma and a stocky body going to seed, leaned out of the billet doorway and took another deliberate stare along the red brick passageway. At the far end, where it opened out into a central courtyard, he could see the newcomer standing in conversation with Honen Mu and some of her aides. The newcomer was a big fellow, really big, a giant dressed in a dust-grey mail sleeve and a head shawl, with a soot-dulled bolter slung over his shoulder.

'He's a sizeable fugger, though,' said Bronzi, idly toying with the small gold box dangling on the chain around his neck.

'Don't stare so,' Tche advised, gnawing on his bar.

'I'm just saying. Bigger than you, even.'

'Stop staring.'

'He's only where I happen to be aiming my eyes, Tche,' Bronzi said.

Something was going on. Bronzi had a feeling in his water. Something had been going on for the last few days. Uxor Honen was unusually tight-lipped, and had been unavailable on several occasions.

The man *was* big. He towered over Honen, though everyone towered over her. Even so, he had to be two twenty, two twenty-five maybe. That was gene-build big, *Astartes* big even. Honen was looking up at him, craning up, nodding once in a while at a conversation Bronzi couldn't catch. Despite the fact that she was conferring with a giant, Honen's posture was as tenacious as ever: spiky and fierce, like a fighting cock, full of vigour and attitude. Bronzi had long suspected Uxor Honen's body language was a compensation for her doll-like physique.

Bronzi looked back into the billet hall. His Jokers were busy sacking out, drinking and eating, playing bones. Some of them were cleaning off weapons or polishing armour scutes, wiping away the red dust that had slowly caked on during the long day in the field.

'Think I might go for a little stroll,' Bronzi told Tche. The bashaw, munching, simply stared down at the hetman's feet. Bronzi was still fully armoured, but he'd taken off his boots when they'd arrived. His thick, dirty toes splayed out through the holes in his woollen socks.

'Not cutting a dash?' Bronzi asked.

Tche shrugged.

'Well, fug it.' Bronzi pulled off his embroidered cape, his webbing and his weapon belt, and dumped them on the baked earth floor. He kept hold of his water bottles. 'I just need a refill,' he said.

Bronzi padded out into the passageway, his water bottles dangling from his pudgy fingers. He was disappointed to see that the giant had vanished. The Uxor and her aides were heading away across the courtyard, talking together.

Honen turned as Bronzi wandered into the yard. The air was still warm and the day's heat was radiating out of the shadowed brick. Evening had washed the sky overhead a dark, resiny purple.

'Hetman Bronzi? Was there something you wanted?' she called. The words came pinging out of her mouth like tiny chips of ice.

Bronzi smiled back amiably, and waggled the empty water bottles. 'Going to the pump,' he said.

Uxor Honen pushed through her waiting aides and came towards him. She was such a tiny thing, built like a girl-child, compact and slight. She wore a black body-glove and a grey wrap, and walked on heeled slippers, which served only to emphasise her lack of stature. Her face was oval, her pursed mouth small, and her skin so very black. Her eyes seemed huge. At twenty-three, she was exceptionally young, given her level of responsibility, but that was often the way with uxors. Bronzi had a bit of a thing for her: so perfect, so delicate, so much power emanating from her tiny frame.

'Going to the pump?' she asked, switching from Low Gothic to Edessan. She often did that. She made a habit of speaking to the men, one on one, in their native tongues. Bronzi supposed these displays of linguistic skill were meant to seem cordial while emphasising her formidable intelligence. Where Bronzi came from – Edessa – funnily enough, that was called showing off.

He switched with her. 'For water. I'm out.'

'Water rationing was done earlier, hetman,' she said. 'I think that's just an excuse to be nosey.'

Bronzi made what he hoped was a loveable shrug. 'You know me,' he said.

'That's why I think you're being nosey,' Honen said.

They stared at one another. Her enormous eyes slowly travelled down to his stockinged feet. He saw her fighting a smile. The trick with Honen was to appeal to her sense of humour. That was why he'd left his boots off. Bronzi tried to hold his stomach in and still look natural.

'Hard, isn't it?' she smirked.

'What's that now?'

'Holding that gut of yours in?'

'I don't know what you mean, uxor,' he replied.

Honen nodded. 'And I don't know why we keep you around, Hetman Bronzi,' she remarked. 'Isn't there a mandatory fitness requirement any more?'

'Or a weight threshold?' suggested one of her aides: four blonde, teenage girls, who gathered around Honen with wry smiles on their faces.

'Oh, you may mock me,' Bronzi said.

'We may,' agreed one of the aides.

'I'm still the best field officer you've got.'

Honen frowned. 'There's some truth in that. Don't be nosey, Hurtado. You'll be told what you need to know soon enough.'

'A specialist?'

Honen shot a questioning glance sidelong at her aides. She reached out to them with her 'cept too. They all looked away, recoiling from the touch of the scolding 'cept, concentrating on other things. 'Someone's been talking,' Honen announced.

'A specialist, then?' Bronzi pressed.

'As I said,' Honen answered, turning her attention back to him.

'Yeah, yeah, I know,' said Bronzi, rattling his water bottles together as he gestured. 'I'll know when I know.'

'Get your men settled,' she told him, and turned to go.

'Are the Dancers in?' he asked.

'The Dancers?'

'They should be in by now. Peto owes me a payout on a wager. Are they here yet?'

Her eyes narrowed. 'No, Hurtado, not yet. We're expecting them soon.'

'Oh,' he said, 'then I request permission to take a foray team out, on a ramble, to find out what's keeping them.'

'Your loyalty to your friend does you credit, Hurtado, but permission is not granted.'

'It'll be dark soon.'

'It will. That's why I don't want you rambling around out there.'

Bronzi nodded.

'Are we clear on that? No clever or ingenious misinterpretations of that order forming in your mind this time?'

Bronzi shook his head. As if.

'There'd better not be. Goodnight, hetman.'

'Goodnight, uxor.'

Honen clicked away on her heels, sending out a command with her 'cept. Her aides paused for a moment, scowling at Bronzi, and then followed her.

'Yeah, stare at me all you like, you blonde bitches,' Bronzi murmured.

He padded back to the billet. 'Tche?'

'Yes, het?'

'Get a foray team up and ready in ten minutes.'

Tche sighed at him. 'Is this sanctioned, het?' he asked.

'Absolutely. The uxor told me personally that she doesn't want some fug-fingered ramble blundering around out there, so tell the boys it's going to have to be sharp and professional, which will make a change for them.'

'Not a ramble?'

'I never ramble. Sharp, Tche, and professional. Got it?'

'Yes, sir.'

Bronzi pulled on his boots and redressed his weapon belt. He realised he needed to take a leak. 'Five minutes,' he told the bashaw.

He found the latrine, a stinking cement pit down the hall, unbuckled his armour and sighed as his bladder emptied. Nearby, men were showering in the communal air baths, and he could hear singing from one of the other troop billets.

'You'll stay put tonight,' said a voice from behind him.

Bronzi tensed. The voice was quiet and hard, small yet powerful, like the super-gravity coal of a dead sun.

'I think I'll finish what I'm doing, actually,' he replied, deliberately not looking around, and deliberately keeping a tone of levity in his voice.

'You will stay put tonight. No fun and games. No bending the rules. Are we clear?'

Bronzi buckled up, and turned.

The specialist stood behind him. Bronzi slowly adjusted his stance until he was looking up at the man's face. Terra, he was huge, a monster of a man. The specialist's features were hidden in the shadows of his dust shawl.

'Is that a threat?' Bronzi asked.

'Does someone like me *need* to threaten someone like you?' the specialist replied.

Bronzi narrowed his eyes. He was a lot of things, but timid wasn't one of them. 'Come on then, if you want some.'

The specialist chuckled. 'I really admire your balls, hetman.'

'They were only out because I was taking a leak,' said Bronzi.

'Bronzi, right? I've heard about you. More bare-faced cheek in you than all the arses in the Imperial Army.'

Bronzi couldn't help but grin, though his pulse was racing. 'I could mess you up, son, I really could.'

'You could try,' said the specialist.

'I would, you know?'

'Yes, I have a feeling you might. Don't. I'd hate to damage a friend. Let me be clear. There are things going on tonight that you must not mess with. Don't let me down by pissing around. Don't get involved. You'll understand soon enough. For now, right now, hetman, take my word on this.'

Bronzi kept his stare going. 'I might. I might trust you, if I could see your face or know your name.'

The specialist paused. For a moment, Bronzi thought he was actually going to pull down his shawl and show his face.

'I'll tell you my name,' he said.

'Yeah?'

'My name is Alpharius.'

Bronzi blinked. His mouth went dry. He felt his heart pounding so fast it trembled his torso.

'Liar. You liar! That's a pile of crap!'

A sudden, brilliant flash made the chamber blink white for a second. A deep, reverberative boom reached them.

Bronzi ran to one of the slit windows. Outside, in the dark, he could see the flashes and light blooms of a major battle flaring behind the ridge. The percussive crump and slap of explosions rolled in. One hell of a firefight had just kicked off along the wadi rim less than ten kilometres away from the post. It was concussive, bending the air, bending sound.

Behind Bronzi, men were rushing up, scrabbling around the windows to see out. There was chatter and agitation. Everyone wanted a look.

'Peto…' Hurtado Bronzi murmured. He turned away from the window slit and the rippling light show, pushing his way back through the mob of men to find the specialist.

But the specialist had already vanished.

THE WORLD HAD come off its hinges. For the first few seconds, Peto Soneka thought his company had been caught up in some sort of freak hail-storm. Thousands of luminous projectiles were raining down out of the twilight into the basin, like spits of fire or a cloudburst of little shooting stars. Every one exploded in a searing fireball as it impacted. The overpressure was knocking men to the ground. Soneka reeled as fiery detonations went off all around him like grenades. The bang of the first few impacts had deafened him.

He saw men thrown, burning, into the air by blooming flashes. He saw three of his company's tanks quiver and then explode in whickering storms of shrapnel fragments as the sizzling pyrophoric deluge struck them.

It wasn't a freak hail-storm. Despite the Dancer's scouts and recon, despite their auspex and modar, despite their careful deployment and marching cover, despite the omniscient monitoring of the expedition fleet in high orbit, the Nurthene had surprised them.

The Nurthene were of a tech level several points down the scale from the Imperium. They possessed guns and tanks, but still favoured blades. They should have been easy to overrun.

But from the opening actions of the expedition war, it had become clear that the Nurthene had something else, something the Imperium entirely lacked.

Lord Commander Teng Namatjira had described it, in a moment of infuriation, as *air magick*. The name had, perhaps unfortunately, stuck. Air magick was why Nurth had held off the might of an Imperial Army expedition for eight months. Air magick was why a Titan cohort had been decimated at Tel Khortek. Air magick was why a Sixth Torrent division had disappeared into the desert sink at Gomanzi and never returned. Air magick was why nothing flew above Tel Utan, why every attempt to destroy the place with air strikes, missiles, orbital bombardments and troop drops had failed, and why they were being forced to assault the place on foot.

It was Peto Soneka's first direct taste of air magick. All the horror stories that had leaked back from regiment to regiment and company to company were true. The Nurthene had lore beyond the Terran range. The elements obeyed them. They were casters-in of devils.

A shockwave threw Soneka over on his face. He had blood in his mouth and sand up his nose. He rose on his hands and saw a geno trooper curled up beside him, blackened by heat, smouldering. In the rapid strobe light of multiple explosions, he saw other corpses scattered around him. The sand was burning.

Bashaw Lon came running out of the flashing air. He was yelling at Soneka. Soneka could see Lon's mouth working, but heard nothing.

Lon hauled Soneka to his feet. Sound was coming back, but only in short bursts.

'Get... to... the... we... impossible!' Lon yelled.

'What? What?'

'...much... of... to... the... fugging idiots!'

The hail suddenly ceased. Blinking around at the devastation, Soneka heard snippets of the abrupt quiet too: blurts of crackling fire and the screams of men, cut up and mixed with baffling, numb seconds of profound deafness.

'Oh fug!' Lon cried, suddenly, awfully audible.

The Nurthene were on them.

Nurthene infantry – called 'echvehnurth' – swarmed out of the shadows and pits of the enclosing night, and poured into the firelight. Their swirling pink robes and silver armour shone in the flames. Their falxes whirled. Several of them carried aloft kite-tailed banners showing the water-reed and river reptile badge of the Nurthene royalty.

The falx was an astonishingly proficient and barbarous weapon. Two and a half metres long, it was essentially a hybrid spear, a scythe straightened out. Half its length was a straight handgrip, the other half a long blade with a slight bias hook, the inside curve of which was razor sharp. Spinning and sweeping a falx like a flail, an expert echvehnurth could lop off limbs and heads, and even bisect torsos. The blades went through almost any metal. Only liqnite could break the blades, but it was impossible to use it in combat. Liqnite canisters came out when the fight was done, to neuter the fallen weapons of the enemy. A spray of liquid nitrogen froze the metal brittle so that it could be shattered under foot.

Echvehnurth rushed at them from the ditches of the sink. The first Dancers they met were scythed down by the long, whirling blades like tall corn. Arms and heads flipped into the air. Arterial blood squirted. Truncated bodies fell like sacks. A few carbines fired, but it was hardly a proper reply.

Soneka started running forwards. 'Wake up! Wake up!' he howled. 'Gun them down. Use your guns. Don't let them in!'

They were in already. The night sand was littered with geno corpses and body parts. There was a fine haze of blood in the warm air. Soneka could taste it. His hearing was back, and his ears were filled with the hiss and chop of butchery, and the screams of his men.

He kept running. He fired his carbine one-handed, drawing his sword bayonet in the other. An echvehnurth ran at him and Soneka blew his face off. The man cartwheeled backwards. A falx swung and Soneka sidestepped, kicking its owner's feet out from under him so that he fell on his back. Soneka ran the Nurthene through with his bayonet.

He dropped on one knee, raised the carbine to his shoulder, its barrel resting on the fork of his blade grip, and picked off two more of the charging enemy with aimed shots. Their pink robes trailed out as they crashed backwards. Lon was beside Soneka, along with three other men, firing in sustained bursts. Their shots made bright darts in the air. Echvehnurth toppled and fell, one on fire, another with his ribcage blown wide.

'Dancers, Dancers! This is the Dancers!' Soneka yelled as he fired. 'CR19! We need help here. Immediate. Major incursion!'

'Stand by, Dancers,' he heard an uxor's voice reply. 'We are aware. Retasking units to your position.'

'Now!' Soneka yelled. 'Now. We're being slaughtered!'

One of the men beside him suddenly fell sideways, split in two from shoulder to groin. Pressurised blood escaped in all directions at once. Soneka wheeled and saw an echvehnurth spinning his falx back from the blow to strike again. Soneka slashed with his sword bayonet in an attempt to block.

The long blade of the falx, just a blur of blue metal in the violet twilight, went through Soneka's hand in a line across the base of the thumb, severing his fingers, his thumb and the upper half of his palm, and snapping the grip of his sword bayonet. The blow was so clean that there was no pain at first. Soneka staggered backwards, watching the thin sprays of blood jetting out of his ruined hand.

The falx circled again, tracing a glitter in the air.

It did not land.

Another falx blocked it. Blade struck blade, and the attacking falx shivered away. A dark figure slid into view and killed the echvehnurth with a single, explosive shot.

The newcomer was a huge brute done up in a dark mail sleeve, his head and shoulders swathed in a shawl. He carried a falx in one hand and a boltgun in the other.

He looked down at Soneka. 'Courage,' he said.

'Who are you?' Soneka whispered.

Lon had run to Soneka's side. 'Get this man's hand bound,' the big man told the bashaw. He turned back to the fight, rotating the falx expertly in his left hand like a baton.

He wasn't alone. As Lon wrapped his hand, Soneka saw that a dozen anonymous men had entered the fight, coming out of the darkness like phantoms. Each one of them was inhumanly large, his face hooded in a desert shawl. Each one carried a bolter and a falx.

They moved with a speed that was not human, and struck each blow with a force that was not human. In a matter of minutes, they had carved the heart out of the echvehnurth attack. Their boltguns roared and pumped like thunder, blowing pink silk and silver into blood-caked pieces.

'Astartes,' Soneka gasped.

'Stay with me, het, stay with me,' Lon whispered.

'They're Astartes,' Soneka said.

'You've lost a lot of blood. Don't go to sleep on me!'

'I won't,' Soneka promised. 'Those men… those things… they're Astartes.'

Lon didn't answer. He was staring at the horizon.

'Holy Terra,' he whispered.

Tel Utan had caught fire.

* * *

HONEN MU WATCHED the city burn from an upper window of the CR23 post. Every once in a while, a building cooked off and blew out in a streamer of fire. Rising smoke hazed the clear night sky. Her aides winced and *oohed* at every snap of flame. She could feel their responses through her 'cept.

She nodded, finally. 'May I inform the Lord Commander?'

'You may,' said the specialist, waiting behind her. 'I will make a report to him personally, of course, but you should have the pleasure of transmitting this news to him first.'

Honen turned from the window. 'Thank you. And thank you for your work.'

'Nurth isn't done yet. There is much to do,' the specialist told her.

'I understand.'

The specialist hesitated, as if he slightly doubted this.

'Our paths may not cross again, Uxor Honen Mu,' the specialist said. 'There are two things I want to say. *The Emperor protects* is one of them. The other is a word of admiration for the Geno Five-Two. You have bred good soldiers, in the finest genetic tradition. You ought to know that the old genic legacy of the Chiliads was an inspiration the Emperor acknowledged in creating us.'

'I didn't know that,' said Honen, surprised.

'Ancient history, pre-Unification,' said the specialist. 'There's no reason you should. I must go now. It has been a pleasure making war with you, Uxor Honen Mu.'

'And with you... though I still don't know your name.'

'I am Alpha Legion, lady. Given your 'ceptive powers, I think you can guess it.'

THE SPECIALIST LEFT the post through the back halls, walking through shadow. He moved silently and quickly. Near the north gate, he stopped in his tracks, and turned slowly.

'Hello again,' said Hurtado Bronzi, stepping out of the darkness with his carbine aimed at the specialist's chest.

'Het. My compliments. That was a genuine feat of stealth.'

Bronzi shrugged. 'I do what I do.'

'Can I help you?'

'I do hope so,' said Bronzi.

'Does that thing have to be aimed at me?'

'Well, I don't know. I feel a lot more comfortable like this. I want some answers. I have a feeling only gun-point is going to get them for me.'

'Gunpoint will simply get you killed, het. All you need to do is ask.'

Bronzi bit his lip. 'You've taken the Tel, I see.'

'Yes.'

'Fancy work. Kudos to you. Did it have to cost so many lives?'

'Meaning?' asked the specialist.

'I heard the Dancers got cut to ribbons tonight. Was that part of your plan?'

'Yes, it was.'

Bronzi shook his head. 'Fug, you admit it. You used my friends as cannon fodder and–'

'No, het. I used them as bait.'

'What?' Bronzi's hands shook on the grip of the car-bine. His finger tightened on the trigger until it found the biting point.

'Don't look so shocked. Life is all about secrets, and I'm prepared to share one with you. Honesty is the only really valuable currency. I'll tell you this truth, on the understanding that you trust me.'

'I can do that,' said Bronzi.

'The Nurthene are quite toxic in their power. No conventional assault was going to break them. They are possessed by Chaos, though I don't expect you to know what that word really means. My men needed to get into Tel Utan, and that meant forcing the Nurthene into a distraction. I regret that your friends, the Dancers, were the ideal choice, tactically speaking. They drew the main force of the Nurthene aside so we could enter Tel Utan. I did ask my men to spare and protect as many of the Dancers as possible.'

'That's honest, I suppose. Brutal. Callous.'

'We live in a brutal, callous galaxy, het. Like for like is the only way we can deal with it. We must make sacrifices. And no matter what others say, sacrifices always hurt.'

Bronzi sighed and lowered his weapon a little. Suddenly, it wasn't in his hands any more. It was bouncing off the far wall, broken in two.

'Never aim a weapon at me again,' said the specialist, suddenly in Bronzi's face, pinning him against the wall.

'I w-wont!'

'Good.'

'Are you really Alpharius?' Bronzi gasped, aware that his feet were swinging in the air.

With his free hand, the specialist pulled back his shawl and allowed Bronzi to look upon his face.

'What do you think?' he asked.

* * *

WHEN SONEKA WOKE up, flocks of casevac fliers were dropping into the flame-lit ruin of the basin, wing lamps flashing. The whole night was lit up by the burning doom of Tel Utan.

Soneka looked around, blearily. His hand hurt like a bitch. Air crews were bundling the walking wounded and the stretcher casualties up the ramps of the waiting ships.

Soneka looked up at Lon. 'How many?' he asked.

'Too many,' said a voice.

Three dark figures stood nearby, like a tragic chorus. They were silhouettes in the firelight, their bolters slung across their bodies, their shawls drawn up.

'Too many, het,' said one.

'We regret their loss,' said the second.

'War requires sacrifices. A victory has been achieved, but we take no pleasure in your losses,' said the third.

'You… you're Astartes, aren't you?' Soneka asked, allowing Lon to help him to his feet.

'Yes,' said one.

'Do you have names?' Soneka asked.

'I am Alpharius,' said the first.

Soneka inhaled hard and dropped quickly to one knee, along with Lon and the other geno men.

'Lord, I–'

'I am Alpharius,' said the second figure.

'We are all Alpharius,' said the third. 'We are Alpha Legion, and we are all one.'

They turned, and walked away into the billowing smoke.

TWO

Visages, Nurth, five weeks later

THEY RETIRED, AND spent the last of the summer at Visages, playing bones and other games, sitting out in the heat. Some of the men rode servitors off into the veldt and hunted big game, while others broke the local livestock, and raced them up and down in the dust.

Visages was simply their name for it. Officially called CR345, or Tel Khat in the local dialect, it was a cluster of dwellings in a northern wadi where the ground was littered with broken diorite heads. Some were as large as tank wheels, others as small as beads. No one knew who had carved the faces, or why they had done so in so many contrasting scales, or why the sculptures had been smashed and the heads alone scattered as spoil.

Nor did anyone care.

There was wine, sent as a reward for their pains by Namatjira, and peck in bountiful quantities, courtesy of the same source.

They diced and raced and gambled, played sphairistike, laughed out their pain, and swam in the warm blue pools hidden in the cliff-face caves.

Soneka's hand healed. Field surgeons had cut back the wound, and packed it with basal sensors and motor plugs so that it could later accept a machine graft. He flexed it every day, and sensed fingers that had been and would be again, interim, phantom fingers.

There was a rumour that the Nurth War was ending and they would soon make shift for a new zone. Soneka didn't believe it. He sat around in the Visages billet with Dimitar Shiban, a Trinacrian-born het who had been injured the same week as Peto. The flesh of Shiban's chest and neck was swollen and knotty with buried shrapnel. Like Soneka, he owned a deep hatred of the Nurthene's weaponised magick.

'I have been dreaming lately,' he said one day, as they sat around on an awning-covered terrace. 'In my dreams, I hear a verse.'

They had each sniffed a pinch of peck from the gold boxes around their necks, and Soneka was pouring wine from a gombroonware ewer.

'A verse, huh?' asked Soneka.

'I'll tell you how it goes, shall I?'

'You remember it, then?'

'Don't you remember your dreams word for word?' Shiban asked.

Soneka thought about it, then shook his head with a smile. 'Never,' he said.

Shiban shrugged. 'Fancy that,' he said.

'This verse?' Soneka prompted, sitting back to sip his wine.

'That? Oh, it goes–

From the hagg and hungrie goblin
That into raggs would rend ye,
And the spirit that stands by the naked man,
In the Book of Moones defend ye!'

Shiban broke into laughter as soon as he had finished his rendition.

Soneka looked at him. 'I know that,' he said.

'You do?' chuckled Shiban. 'Really?'

'My mother used to sing it to me when I was a boy. She called it the Bedlame Song. There were other verses that I now forget.'

'Really? What does it mean?'

Soneka shrugged. 'I have no idea.'

SHIBAN'S COMPANY WAS coded the Clowns, and their banner was a howling skull clad in white and rouge vaudevillian greasepaint. Shiban had been hurt by a Nurthene splinter bomb during a wadi fight east of Tel Utan, and he'd been obliged to leave the Clowns under the field command of his head bashaw, a man Soneka came to know as 'Fugging Strabo'.

As in, 'I hope that fugging Strabo is keeping his head', and 'Beloved Terra, let fugging Strabo not be getting my poor boys killed.'

'You worry too much, Dimi,' Soneka told him.

'Oh, so you'd be happy leaving your troop in the hands of your bashaws would you?'

Soneka empathised. Due to the bad mauling the Dancers had taken, the entire company had been retired to Visages, injured and healthy alike. Shiban, however, had been sent north with thirty or so wounded of his Clowns, the rest of the company deemed intact enough to continue operations. Soneka wondered how he would have felt if he'd been forced to leave the Dancers with Lon. He trusted Lon with his life, Shah and Attix too, all the Dancer bashaws. Still, he appreciated Shiban's edginess.

They were sitting, feet up, under the awning in the late sun of an endless afternoon. They were playing the head game, a pastime of their own devising.

A man ran up the dusty slope towards them, a Clown, stripped to the waist, red-faced and sweating from too much exertion in the sun.

He saluted in front of the two reclining officers.

'Sirs!'

'Hello, Jed,' said Shiban. 'Let's see it.'

The Clown, Jed, held out a diorite head. It was chipped and incomplete, about the size of a grapefruit. Soneka really missed grapefruit.

Shiban looked at Soneka. Soneka raised a considering eyebrow.

'Put it in place, Jed,' Shiban invited.

The Clown walked across the hot sand in front of the awning, panting hard, and bent down over the line of heads laid out in the sun. They were arranged in graduating size, seed- and pea-sized at one end, fist- and apple-sized at the other. The head Jed had brought was clearly the largest. He set it down triumphantly at the end of the row.

'Point, Clowns,' said Shiban.

Soneka nodded graciously.

'Get a cup, Jed,' said Shiban, and the Clown ran off eagerly to help himself to the cold wine on the stand behind them.

Shiban took a pinch from his gold box, sniffed, and sat back. He sighed. 'The lho's good,' he said, 'but I miss the combat fix.'

Soneka nodded.

Shiban had a face like a monkey, with a long brow, a long upper lip and a button nose. His tanned forehead was high, and his long white hair poured down off the back of his head like a cascade. The shrapnel bumps covering his throat and chest were the sort of thing a man couldn't ignore. The warty mass was quite fascinating. The medics had drained and lanced some of them, but the rest, they had advised, would work out in time. He looked like he had a goitre of blisters.

As he had told it to Soneka, Shiban had surprised a Nurthene war party in the business of planting bombs. During the firefight that had resulted, the Nurthene had set the bombs off, killing themselves and wounding Shiban and his men. Some of that shrapnel was organic. Some of it was Nurthene bone.

'I hear there's fighting at Mon Lo,' Shiban said.

'I heard that too,' said Soneka.

Another man ran up. It was Olmed, a Dancer. He held out the head he was carrying.

'Place it,' said Soneka.

Olmed took it to the line. His diorite head was bigger than any of them, except the one the Clown had just placed.

'Adjudication!' Shiban called.

The Munitorum aide emerged from the cool gloom of the doorway in the terracotta building behind them, a long-suffering look on his face. The hetmen had been calling him outside all afternoon. This time he brought the digital measure without being told.

'Again with this, sirs?' he asked.

Shiban waggled his fingers at the row of heads. 'My dear friend, we value your impartial judgement.'

The aide trudged out into the sunlight and applied the measure to the heads while Olmed stood, breathing hard, watching, his torso gleaming with sweat.

The aide straightened up and turned to face the het-men, reclining side by side in the shade.

'Oh, don't keep us in suspense,' Soneka said.

'The head is smaller by eight microns than the head at the line end,' the aide sighed, 'but it is larger by two microns than the one behind it.'

Olmed punched the air and did a little victory dance. Shiban tutted. Soneka grinned.

'Point, Dancers,' he said. 'Olmed? Do the honours.'

Olmed nestled his diorite head into position at the head of the line, picked up the head Jed had brought, and threw it with all his strength out into the open field below them, where it was immediately lost again amongst millions of its kind.

'Help yourself to a cup,' Soneka told Olmed. He glanced at Shiban. 'Sundown in, what? Eighty minutes?'

'Everything still to play for,' Shiban replied, confidently.

'I think,' said a voice from behind them, 'you have far too much time on your hands.'

Soneka leapt up from his canvas recliner. Hurtado Bronzi stood in the shadow of the awning, smiling at him.

'Hurt, you old bastard!' Soneka cried, embracing his friend. 'What the hell are you doing here?'

'A matter of twenty crowns and interest growing,' Bronzi replied, grinning.

'This is Dimi Shiban,' Soneka laughed, gesturing across at his companion, who was rising to his feet

'I know Dimi Shiban,' Bronzi said, embracing the Clown het and slapping his back. 'Zantium, eh?'

'I seem to recall you being there,' said Shiban. 'How're you doing, you fat fugger?'

'Well, well.'

'Have some wine,' Soneka offered.

'Oh, all right,' Bronzi replied. His armour was caked in dust. He yanked off his cape and his webbing, and sat down.

'So, this game? It has rules?'

'Many, many rules,' said Shiban.

'And there's money at stake?'

'Money and wine,' said Soneka, pouring a glass for his old friend.

'Two teams,' said Shiban, 'Clowns and Dancers, five men each side. They scour the fields and bring back heads. The heads go in a line, by size. Retrievers win a cup of wine for each head. Incentive, you see? Sundown ends the game. Team with the largest head in the row wins.'

'So just get your boys to roll in one of those big buggers,' Bronzi said, pointing at the boulder-sized heads resting in the sand a hundred metres away. 'Game over.'

'Ah, but this is a game of finesse,' Soneka said.

'Really?' Bronzi smiled, sipping from his wine cup.

Shiban nodded. 'If a team brings in a head that is demonstrably smaller than the largest, but larger than the next in line, the larger head gets thrown out.'

A very broad grin spread across Bronzi's face. 'A game of finesse indeed. Who's winning?'

'I am,' said Soneka.

Bronzi took out his purse. 'Four crowns on Shiban by sundown,' he said.

* * *

SONEKA WON THAT day's head game in the very last minutes before dark, when Bashaw Lon casually wandered in with a head that displaced the Clowns' latest triumph. Lon bent his back and cast the Clowns' usurped head back out into the field where it had been found. Bronzi lost his four crowns. According to the rules of the game, Shiban bought wine for both teams.

'So what are you really doing here, Hurt?' Soneka asked, later on.

'Let me see that hand of yours,' Bronzi replied, and studied Soneka's wound as it was displayed. 'Hnh. You'll be good.'

'Hurtado? I asked you a question.'

'I got a furlough,' Bronzi said, sitting back in the still of the evening. The air went cold very suddenly after dark on Nurth, closing in like lapping black water. They huddled in around the lamps and the peat-fired heaters. 'Five-day pass, signed by Uxor Honen herself. Just wanted to come check on you.'

'That's not it,' said Soneka.

'Why is that not it?'

Soneka smiled, and waved to Lon to bring them a fresh bottle. 'Since when did Hurtado Bronzi not have a secret agenda, huh?'

'You wound me, Peto, you wound me. Can't I come here selflessly to look up an old friend and enquire of his welfare?'

Soneka stared at him, a wry smile on his face, waiting for the punch line.

'All right,' Bronzi admitted, 'there *was* something else.'

'Excuse me, het?' a voice cut in.

They looked up. A Munitorum aide, the very same aide whose time and patience they had abused so thoroughly during the afternoon's game, was standing beside them.

'Yes?' asked Soneka.

'The staff medicae apologises for this interruption. Sir, there is a dead Dancer she would like you to identify.'

CASEVAC HAD BROUGHT the corpse to the cold store at the far end of the Visages camp. The cold store was a long, mud brick building throbbing with refrigeration units. Soneka and Bronzi wandered up in the chilly dark, aware of the stars draping overhead like dust on a desert shawl.

The frozen, stiff bodies of geno dead were piled up inside like firewood. Each one was wrapped in a plastek shroud. Pairs of bare, pallid feet stuck out of the ends of the stacked shrouds, decorated with toe-tag labels. The hets walked in past them, ignoring the gross stink of embalming chemicals.

The corpse in question was waiting for them in the next room. Not yet preserved, it was laid out on a stainless steel gurney, with drip-trays slotted in to catch the noxious seep. It had been dead in the desert for several weeks, and it had bloated. The face was lost in one raw, black graze, the uniform frayed and faded, the torso limp and slack where gut gas had previously bloated it.

Soneka and Bronzi stood in the chilly light, and shivered as they regarded it.

'That's no Dancer I know,' said Soneka. His words made smoke in the sub-zero air.

'Oh, but he's certainly one of yours, het,' the staff medicae insisted. Medicae Ida was a tall woman, wearing a long surgical gown, the apron front of which was smeared with stains. She'd been a combat uxor in her youth, but age and experience had seen her graduate to the medicae branch as her perceptive skills dulled. Bronzi wondered if Ida missed her uxorhood, missed her command of geno men. It seemed so, from her tone.

'He's not,' Soneka insisted, peering down at the corpse.

'Well, I don't know how you can tell that, sir,' Ida said. 'His face is missing.'

'He'd know,' said Bronzi.

'Where was he found?' Soneka asked, placing a hand on the corpse's wax-cold shoulder. A surgical cloth had been spread over the abdomen to obscure the ravages of the autopsy.

'The Tel Utan wadi,' Medicae Ida replied.

Soneka shook his head. 'He's not one of mine. I'm not missing anyone. The lists were in weeks ago.'

'But he is wearing Dancer insignia,' Ida insisted. 'Here, the collar pins, and here, the brooch.' She pointed. 'He is dressed as a Dancer.'

'Have you tissue-mapped him?' Soneka asked.

'Not yet,' Ida admitted.

'Then you'll see the truth. This isn't one of my men.'

Senior Medicae Ida sighed. 'I know that, het. I just wanted you to confirm it, before I–'

'Before you what?' Bronzi demanded.

'Before I alert the Chiliad uxors. Hetman Soneka, is there any reason you can think of why one of your men would have no heart?'

'What?'

'No heart?' Ida repeated emphatically.

'What the fug did he have in there then?' Bronzi asked, nodding at the corpse's covered chest.

'A cadmium centrifuge,' replied Senior Medicae Ida gently. 'The subject has undergone some extreme and non-standard organ modification. His liver was... well, I've never seen anything like it.'

'What is going on here?' asked Soneka.

'I don't know.' Ida replied. 'I was hoping you might.'

'There's something else,' she added. She pulled back the surgical cloth.

For a moment, all they could see was the scissor-snapped sternum and the splayed ribs, caked black with blood.

'Here,' she said, pointing.

On the dead flesh of the corpse's hip there was a small brand, partially obliterated by a shrapnel puncture.

'What is that?' asked Soneka, squinting at it. 'Is that a snake?'

'Maybe,' said Bronzi, bending down to look for himself. 'A snake... or some kind of reptile.'

SONEKA TOLD THE medicae to place a guard on the corpse and send someone to wake up the post commander. He went back outside with Bronzi.

'Insurgent?' Soneka asked.

Bronzi nodded. 'Has to be. That mark.'

Soneka didn't reply. Crocodilia and other forms of aggressive reptile were the most persistently recurring of all Nurthene emblems.

'Have they the art to change a man inside like that?' Bronzi asked.

'I don't know,' Soneka replied, 'but since that night outside Tel Utan, I could believe them capable of anything.'

Bronzi wiped his mouth with the back of his hand. 'Listen, Peto, the reason I came here today, it's about that night. I wanted you to know that I didn't hang you out to dry.'

'I never thought you did, Hurt.'

'Really, though. I was all for taking a force out to support you. I was warned off.'

'I can imagine,' said Soneka.

Bronzi looked at him strangely. 'What does that mean?'

Soneka walked a few steps away and stared out into the great bowl of the moonlit desert. Sky and land alike, both dark, had a sheen across them, a haze produced by airborne dust. 'My men were used as a tactical sacrifice to break Tel Utan open. Lon and a few others know, but I've told them to stay tight-lipped. I've kept the information quiet for reasons of morale.'

'How do you know this?' asked Bronzi.

'Because the men who sacrificed us told me to my face,' said Soneka.

'And me,' Bronzi replied. 'You saw them, then? The specialists?'

'The Alpha Legion,' said Soneka. He looked at Bronzi. 'So many stories, over the years, and then to meet them, the most secret and cunning of all the Astartes.'

'I was this close to him,' Bronzi said, 'as close as I am to you. He warned me off, and told me why, and then told me to keep my mouth shut about the whole thing.'

'Who?'

'Alpharius!'

Soneka smiled. 'They were all called Alpharius, Hurt.'

Bronzi shook his head. 'This was the primarch, Peto. I swear it! I saw his face.'

'I believe you,' said Soneka. 'Terra, but what kind of war are we fighting here?'

'A war of lies and disguise and dissembling,' Bronzi answered. 'Why else would that Legion be involved?'

'I'M NOT ENTIRELY sure of the significance,' said Koslov, the post commander. He was a brigadier in one of the Crimean support regiments charged with running the campaign's rear party operations.

'Neither are we,' said Bronzi, 'but the fact remains that we have the body of an unidentified combatant showing signs of non-standard anatomical work and a brand mark like a reptile.'

'We know that subversive and covert tactics are being employed in this zone,' said Soneka.

'How do you know that?' asked Koslov.

'That's classified,' Bronzi said carefully.

'If the Nurthene have infiltrated our companies, high command needs to know about it,' Soneka went on. 'The body needs to be examined, so that others like it can be identified. This could break the war, man. This could be one of the key reasons those devils have us on the back foot all the time.'

Koslov took a deep breath and stood up behind his camp desk. The habitent was sparsely equipped, and lit only by a pair of lumen packs.

'Far be it from me to argue with two frontline hets,' he said. 'What do we do?'

SONEKA AND BRONZI agreed that Honen Mu was the first point of contact. If infiltration was widespread, they had to tread carefully. They had to start with someone they knew they could trust; someone, as

Bronzi pointed out, who had dealt with the specialists and therefore understood the gravity of the matter.

Koslov granted them access to the Visages post's main vox transmitter, and personally activated the command-grade cryptogrammics using a biometric key he carried around his wrist.

'The channel is secure,' he told them, and left the chamber.

Bronzi picked up the speaker horn and threw the transmit switch.

'CR23, CR23, this is Joker Lord broadcasting in encrypt, stop.'

The vox speaker emitted a series of dull, metallic clicks, and then settled into a deep background hiss. Bronzi repeated his signal.

Ten seconds passed and then the answer came. 'Joker Lord, Joker Lord, this is CR23 reading you encrypted, stop.' The voice was cold and clear, as if the speaker was standing in the next room. Apart from a slight trebly quality caused by the cryptogrammic coding, they couldn't have asked for a stronger, purer link.

'CR23, I need to speak to Uxor Mu urgently, Code Janibeg 5, stop.'

'Confirm code, please, stop,' the vox answered him. The connection was so clean, the words sounded as if they were polished.

'Confirm Code Janibeg 5, stop.'

'One moment, Joker Lord, stop.'

Another wait. Two minutes of liquid hiss this time. Bronzi glanced at Soneka.

'Joker Lord, Joker Lord. This is Honen. Bronzi, this had better not be one of your entertainments, stop.' The tone was sharpened by the digital overlay of the cryptogrammics, but there was no mistaking Honen Mu's spiky attitude.

'It's not, uxor. Trust me and listen. I've got a body here. I'm pretty convinced it's a Nurthene infiltrator, surgically altered. I think we've been compromised. Requesting your advice, stop.'

A pause. 'Give me more information to work with, Bronzi, stop.'

'Uxor, I think this stiff needs to be examined by tech-adepts, a full work-up. We could be looking at a huge security breach. I'm thinking, maybe to scare up a lifter to my position, and I'll baby-sit the specimen up to the fleet, stop.'

'Stand by, Joker Lord, stop.'

Bronzi lowered the speaker horn. 'She's wary,' he said.

'Can you blame her, Hurt?' Soneka asked. 'The number of pranks you've pulled over the years?'

They were both beginning to sweat, despite the night chill. The massive voxcaster rig kicked out a fug of heat exhaust, and the air in the chamber was close.

They waited for over five minutes, so long that Soneka began to pace. Then the vox cycled up again.

'Joker Lord, Joker Lord, this is CR23, respond, stop.'

Bronzi picked up the horn and waited until all five green lights on the console had re-lit, indicating full-strength cryptogrammics.

'CR23, this is Joker Lord, stop.'

'What is your position, Bronzi, stop?'

'CR345, uxor, stop.'

'Listen to me, Bronzi. I can't risk an air extraction from where you are. There are some details I can't go into, even via encrypt. Suggest you get transport and move fast and light. I'm checking the charts now… Yes, leave

Tel Khat and head west along the Sarmak Trail. If you don't mess around, you should be able to get to CR8291 by dawn. I'll divert a cavalry squadron to pick you up there and escort you in. Did you get all that, stop?'

Bronzi nodded, even though she couldn't see him. 'Understood, uxor, stop.'

'Is this workable, Bronzi, stop?'

'Absolutely, stop,' Bronzi replied.

The link leaked out an ambient hiss for a moment. 'CR23? Bronzi? I need you to tell me who knows about this, stop.'

'Say again, stop?'

'Who knows the details of this incident, het, stop?'

Bronzi frowned. 'Me, the post commander, the duty medicae, maybe a couple of staffers, stop.'

'Understood, thank you. I'm sorry, Bronzi, but we need to keep this close for now. Are you ready to move, stop?'

'Yes, uxor. Joker Lord out.'

The lights went out and the hissing died away. Bronzi threw the voxcaster's power-down switches and got up.

'All right then,' he said.

'Why didn't you mention me?' Soneka asked.

'What?'

'When she asked who knew, why didn't you mention my name?'

'Because you're staying here,' Bronzi told him.

BRONZI HAD A few words with Koslov, and a pair of Crimean noncombatants were sent to bring a transport up from the hard standing behind the main dwelling cluster of Visages. Then Bronzi strode off to the billet he'd been given. Soneka followed him.

'What do you mean I'm staying here?' Soneka asked as Bronzi quickly repacked his haversack.

'Don't start.'

'Bronzi?' There was a warning tone in Soneka's inflection. Bronzi stopped what he was doing and looked around at his old friend.

'Was it just me, or did Mu sound seriously weird?'

'She was just being wary. I said that.'

Bronzi shook his head. 'Something's up. I need you to be my joker, Peto.'

'What?'

'My ace in the hole. If anything goes wrong, you'll still know what I know. That's why you're staying here.'

'Nothing's going to go wrong,' said Soneka.

Bronzi laughed. 'How many years have we been soldiers, Peto?'

'Enough to know that covering your arse is never a waste of time,' Soneka replied. He shook his head. 'We're worrying about nothing.'

'No,' said Bronzi. 'We've found ourselves in a war of lies, disguise and dissembling. We're worrying about *everything*.'

Soneka didn't look convinced.

'Come on,' Bronzi rumbled. 'That's why the Geno Five-Two has survived this long. We fight smart, we always have. Brains have got us out of more scrapes than balls.'

'In your case, I'd hardly trust either.'

Bronzi winked. He wasn't going to rise to the bait. He lashed up his haversack and swung it onto his shoulder.

'Don't go alone,' Soneka said.

'I won't. I'll take Dimi Shiban with me. I can trust him, and he knows how to handle himself if there's an outbreak of stupid.'

'Good. All right.'

'Let's be off, then,' said Bronzi.

THE TRANSPORT KOSLOV provided was a Scarab-pattern carrier, a medium-sized armoured speeder with a troop hold for stowage and a stern-mounted auto turret. Its long, gently curved hull had been sprayed in a desert tan, but as it slid towards them out of the night on its powerful suspension fields, it looked like a desert phantom, cold and moonlight blue. The delivery crew dismounted, leaving the engines running. Medicae Ida loaded the wrapped body into the hold and made it secure.

'I can provide a driver,' Koslov offered.

'No need,' Bronzi replied, tossing his haversack in through the open hold hatch. 'I can handle one of these babies.'

'You're infantry,' Koslov said.

'I'm a Renaissance man,' Bronzi replied. 'There are few things in this galaxy I can't turn my hand to.'

'And entirely mess up,' Soneka said.

Shiban ran up to join them out of the cold darkness. He was lugging a pack and a twin-barrelled las carbine.

'What's this about?' he asked.

'I'll tell you once we're moving,' Bronzi said. 'All secure, doc?'

Medicae Ida jumped down from the hold and sealed the hatch behind her.

'I've secured it in ice blocks, but it will deteriorate. Get it into stasis as quickly as you can.'

'The organs?'

'Individually packed in vacuum sealed bags in the hopper under the gurney.'

'Thanks, doc,' Bronzi smiled. Shiban was already climbing aboard through the cabin hatch.

Bronzi looked back at Soneka. 'I hate goodbyes,' he said, 'so fug off.'

Soneka laughed. Bronzi turned away, and then swung back round to face Soneka. His face was solemn. 'Look, Peto, there is one thing. One thing I just want to say.'

'What is it, Hurt?'

Bronzi looked him in the eyes, all seriousness.

'Peto, have you got that money you owe me?'

THE SPEEDER KICKED up dust like a gauzy bridal train and slipped away into the cold desert night. Koslov, Ida and the noncombatants turned away and walked back into the post.

Soneka stood out in the chilly darkness, under the enveloping cloak of the sky, and watched until all traces of the speeder had vanished into the endless black.

THEY RAN THE SCARAB into the west, along the old trail, using only auspex and the low-light viewers wired to the dashboard. The viewers showed the world like a green moonscape, but they had only a one hundred and ten degree forward spread, so when Bronzi or Shiban turned their heads too far left or right, the ghostly view vanished in a wash of fizzle and telemetry junk.

The Scarab coasted well, and made eighty kilometres per hour over the clearest terrain. Bronzi loved grav-effect transports, and always tried to secure them for his Jokers when dismount assaults were on the cards. He let Shiban drive for the first three hours, through the tipping point of midnight. The stars came out over the desert rim with a rare magnificence, heightened by their viewers.

'You ever going to tell me what this is about?' Shiban asked.

'No,' said Bronzi.

THREE HOURS BEFORE sunrise, Bronzi took the stick. The world ahead of him was a jumbled, fast-moving path of lime-cast furrows, with the occasional emerald crag looming for a moment before it was lost behind them. Shiban sat back, reclining in the shotgun seat, and took a pinch from his box. Then he played with the auto-turret controls, impelling the sense-net to target the stern guns at passing rocks and crumbling slopes of sand rock.

'Set it on auto-serve and get some kip, Dimi,' Bronzi suggested.

Shiban yawned, and promptly fell asleep, rocking in his leather cradle.

Bronzi envied him. It had been years since he'd been able to manage the old geno trick of crash-sleep, the hypno-suggestive shut-down that allowed a man to catch a wink under any circumstances. Bronzi had been trained that way, but the knack had left him.

He kept his hand closed around the bucking stick and watched the ghost-green world outside flash by.

THE SUN CAME up, a slow, terrible firestorm rising from the south. All of the landscape's shadows stretched out, long and painful, and Bronzi took off the viewer. White light filtered in through the cabin's chipped and crazed windows, and he decided to rely on auspex alone. Twenty kilometres now. The cursor on the cab's lightmap display moved slowly towards its destination.

Soneka woke with a start. Nothing special there. The dull, afterglow of pain in his hand had woken him that way every morning since he'd arrived at Visages.

He sat up on his bunk. Dawn light, already hot and bright, speared in through the gaps around his rattan blind. He'd been having the strangest dream. He'd been playing the head game with Dimi, and Lon had brought him a good piece. He'd taken the diorite head out of Lon's calloused hands, and looked down at it to judge it.

The carved face had been Hurtado's. It had grinned up at him.

'Tell me this, Peto,' the head had said, 'all these broken heads, are any two faces alike, or are they all different?'

'I don't know, Hurt. Get out of my dream.'

'It's important. Do they all look the same? Are they all different? Doesn't that matter? Doesn't it?'

Soneka had lobbed the head away into the wide scree field of broken heads. He'd done it with his left hand. His left hand had had fingers and a thumb.

'Fug,' Soneka said, coughing. He had dust in his throat. That was par for the course at Visages.

He looked down at his incomplete hand and felt the missing fingers waggle.

He had slept naked. He pulled on his breeches, socks and boots, and went out into the early light bare-chested. A hard rind of sun was cresting the edge of the crags. The sky was off-white, like old ivory, and the landscape was a pink wash, broken by hard black shadows bending to evade the sun. It was going to be a hot one. He could already feel the air baking. The local livestock, some of them still saddled from the previous day's racing, wandered free, grazing the patchy grasses. Soneka walked towards the well, rubbing his face with his good hand. He needed a shave; a shave and a grapefruit.

The livestock all looked up at the same time. They stared in the same direction, some of them still chewing, and then broke and scattered.

Geno instinct pulled Soneka back into the cold shadows of one of the terracotta huts. He looked around, suddenly very alert. Where were the sentries, the perimeter guard, the overnight patrols?

The pink wash of the landscape moved. Semi-visible figures scurried forwards out of the desert rim.

Soneka swallowed hard. He turned and ran back through the shaded maze of dwellings towards the post commander's habitent. He wanted to raise the alarm, but he didn't want the enemy to know he'd raised the alarm. Koslov had a silent signal device that trembled every post resident's wrist cuff.

Soneka slipped into the hot darkness of the habitent. Koslov sat at his camp desk, staring at Soneka in surprise.

'Commander!' Soneka whispered. 'Emergency alert now!'

Koslov didn't move. He continued to stare back at Soneka with the same look of mild surprise.

'Commander Koslov?'

Koslov's eyes did not follow Soneka as he moved forwards. They continued to stare at the tent flap where Soneka had entered. Koslov didn't move at all.

Soneka threw himself sideways.

The falx swung by the echvehnurth concealed behind the inner tent flap missed the hetman by a matter of centimetres. The blade *chokked* through the groundsheet into the dirt beneath. Soneka rolled and came up on his feet. The Nurthene yanked his long blade free and charged him.

'Alarm! Alarm!' Soneka began to shout. 'Enemy in the camp!'

He dived headlong over the desk to avoid the lunging blade, and fell into Koslov. Koslov toppled backwards off his seat, his camp table collapsing under Soneka's weight. Blood ebbed slackly out of Koslov's nose and mouth. He continued to stare, in mild surprise, at the roof of the tent.

Soneka rolled off the still-warm corpse, and fumbled frantically to release Koslov's service pistol from its holster.

The Nurthene whirled his falx so high it ripped a slit in the tent roof. He swung it down. Soneka threw himself to one side. The descending blade cut clean through Koslov's left shoulder.

'Alarm!' Soneka yelled again, diving away. Outside, he heard shouting, and the sudden, sporadic bark of las weapons.

Soneka threw a saddle bag at the advancing Nurthene, and the whispering falx struck it aside. He scrambled backwards, hurling a writing case. The falx splintered it, and a shower of pens, nibs and blotting patches spilled out. Soneka ducked again, and the falx tore a wide gash in the tent wall.

Geno training took over. As he landed, Soneka groped for a weapon, any weapon, and found a writing quill that had fallen out of the writing case. Soneka seized it, tested its weight automatically, and threw it like a dart, underhand.

It embedded itself, nib first, in the echvehnurth's left cheek. The Nurthene yelped and lurched backwards. Soneka leapt up and grabbed the haft of the falx. He kneed the Nurthene in the groin. Now the bastard really staggered. He howled. His grip on the falx weakened.

Soneka tore the weapon out of the echvehnurth's hands and swung it. The echvehnurth's head rolled clean off his shoulders in a puff of blood. The body folded up, and the head bounced off the ground sheet beside it.

Gripping the falx, Soneka strode across the habitent to the master alarm control. He smacked it, and sirens began to wail all across the Visages post.

He walked back to Koslov's body, staked the falx blade down in the ground, and pulled out the service pistol, a heavy las model.

Two Nurthene raiders burst in through the habitent mouth and Soneka shot them both in the face. They walloped over on their backs, their silver plates dotted with droplets of blood.

Pandemonium had erupted outside the command tent. The waking Imperial troops, roused by his shots and the blaring sirens, were scrambling to fight off the Nurthene intruders. The dawn air whizzed with gunfire and the *swukk* of impacting blades. Soneka heard awful wails of pain.

With the pistol in his good hand, he went outside into the baking air. A Nurthene ran at him, falx raised. Soneka blew the man's throat out with a single shot and dropped him on the sand. All around him, las carbines rattled on auto. The shouts and yells were deafening. He ran towards the cold store.

Bodies littered the ground outside the mud brick building: Imperial soldiers, mostly half-dressed, sliced into pieces. He went inside, and shot down the two Nurthene he found there. One fell forwards against the stacked, frozen bodies in their shrouds, and wrenched off his breastplate as he slid down. The breastplate landed in front of Soneka, rattling to a stop. He saw the engraved reed emblems and the snapping crocodilia.

'Get. Out,' a voice gasped. 'Run.'

He turned. Medicae Ida stood behind him. She clutched at the falx that stapled her through the chest to the cold store wall. Her gown was soaked in blood. Her own, for the first time.

'Medicae!' Soneka yelled.

'Too late for me,' she wheezed, and died.

A Nurthene raider burst in behind them, and Soneka spun around, firing a shot that silenced the man forever.

More followed, falxes raised. Soneka began to shoot. By his weapon's digital display, he had twenty shots left. Nineteen, eighteen, seventeen...

BRONZI BROUGHT THE Scarab to rest and hit the dampers. The sun was up, fierce and bold.

'Wake up,' he told Shiban as he unstrapped his harness. Shiban groaned.

Bronzi jumped down out of the speeder and looked around. His stomach was grumbling. Where the hell was Honen's promised cavalry? The cratered desert spread out all around him in the burning light of the rising sun.

He saw a figure toiling up the trail towards him, a tall figure wobbled by the heat haze. Bronzi waited, two minutes, three. The figure came closer, becoming properly visible.

It was a Space Marine in full battle plate. The armour was purple, trimmed in silver, with green markings on the immense shoulder plates.

'Great god,' Bronzi murmured.

The towering Astartes came to a halt ten paces from Bronzi and the speeder. Soft red light glowed like embers in its eye slits as it read and targeted him.

'Bronzi, we meet again,' the helmet speaker crackled.

'Sir?'

The Astartes held its massive boltgun close against its armoured chest.

'I warned you. You really do know how to stir up trouble, don't you, Hurtado?'

Bronzi blinked. 'I don't understand. This is important! This is–'

'None of your business, but you've made it your business, which is a colossal mistake, and a shame, because you're a decent fellow. There's only one option.'

'What the fug are you talking about?' Bronzi cried, wishing, very suddenly, he'd brought a weapon with him.

'Back right off, you son of a bitch,' Shiban declared, moving out from behind the cover of the hovering tank, his double-carbine raised to his shoulder and aimed squarely at the armoured figure.

'Dimi, don't!' Bronzi yelled.

'No one threatens my friends,' Shiban growled back. He edged forwards, his weapon fixed steadily on the figure in purple armour.

The Astartes turned its visor slowly to regard Shiban. The soft red ember-light flickered in its eye slits.

Far too fast for Bronzi to follow, the Astartes wheeled and fired its bolter. Dimitar Shiban, who remembered his dreams word for word, left the ground and exploded as he travelled backwards, showering blood and meat in all directions. His twisted carcass hit the ground and lay still.

'Oh god! Oh Terra! No!' Bronzi yelled.

The Astartes switched its aim back to Bronzi. Bronzi sank to his knees in the dust.

'Please…' he murmured.

'As I said,' the Space Marine remarked, stepping forwards, its bolter aimed, 'there is only one option.'

'Why are you doing this?' Bronzi pleaded.

'For the Emperor,' the Astartes replied.

THREE

Mon Lo Harbour, Nurth, two days later

THOUGH JOHN GRAMMATICUS was over a thousand years old, he had only been Konig Heniker for eight months, and he was still getting used to the idea.

According to his file, and as far as any Imperial methods of scrutiny were concerned, Konig Heniker was a fifty-two year-old man from a region of Terra known as the Caucasus, and he served in the Imperial Army as an intelligence officer attached to the Geno Five-Two Chiliad.

Grammaticus still thought of himself as *essentially human*. He had been born human, raised as a human, and he had been human when, to all intents and purposes, he had died for the first time. Definitions became a little more complicated after that. One thing was certain: at some non-specific point after his first death, probably as the result of a slow process rather than a sudden change of heart, he had stopped being quite so steadfast in his devotion to the interests of his birth species.

He was still unashamedly fond of the human race, and was a stout apologist for its less edifying qualities, but he had been with the Cabal for a long time, and they had shared the Acuity with him, at least in part. These days, he saw what his birth race had once been wont to call 'the long view'.

Grammaticus was one of the last few humans still working as an agent of the Cabal. Over the centuries, the Cabal had recruited a good many human go-betweens, but most of them were long dead, forgotten or disavowed.

The Cabal had been recruiting human agents for as long as there had been humans to recruit, a fact Grammaticus always found particularly hard to reconcile. At the very start of human history, before writing, before Ur and Catal Huyuk, before Mohenjo-daro and Thebes, before the construction of the lost monuments, the Cabal had visited Terra and encountered a breed of unprepossessing, unpromising mammalian hominids busy making its first axe marks on the trunks of ancient woodland trees to mark out its first boundaries.

The Cabal had seen some particular quality in those mammalian hominids. They had recognised that the hominids would one day rise, inexorably, to play a pivotal role in the scheme of all things. Mankind would become the greatest weapon against the Primordial Annihilator, or it would become the Primordial Annihilator's greatest weapon. Either way, the Cabal decided that the unprepossessing mammalian hominids developing on that backwater world were not a species to be dismissed.

Grammaticus knew that this fact frustrated most of the Cabal's inner circle. They were Old Kinds, every damn one of them, and regarded all the upstart species of the galaxy as inferior ephemera. It pained them to accept that their destiny, all destinies, lay in the purview of creatures that had been simple, single-cell protocytes when the Old Kind cultures were already mature.

Gahet had once told Grammaticus that the Cabal had made its first subtle advances towards the human species long before the advent of the Age of Terra. Gahet had said this bitterly, and more bitterly still had admitted the Cabal's repeated failure to apply influence on human development.

'You've always been feral, stubborn brutes,' Gahet had said, 'shockingly dogmatic in your self-worth. We tried to direct you, and influence your course. It was like…'

Gahet had paused, allowing his mind to select an appropriately humanocentric simile. 'It was like commanding a tide to turn back,' he finished.

Grammaticus had smiled. 'We *are* a headstrong people, aren't we?' he had replied, with no little pride. 'Did you not think it might have been easier to cull us before we grew teeth?'

Gahet had nodded, or at least, he had flexed his secondary nostrils in a mannerism that equated to a nod. 'That was not our way then. We all deemed such notions as gross barbarism. All of us except Slau Dha, of course.'

'Of course. And now?'

'Now I regret we did not abort you when we had the chance. Destruction has become our only tool in latter days. I miss the subtle methods.'

Almost all of the humans recruited down the years had proved to be unviable or flawed. Most had been disposed of. Grammaticus believed that he had succeeded where so many others had failed because of his gift.

John Grammaticus was a high-function psyker.

'THE UXOR WILL see you, Het Heniker,' the subaltern in the fur shako announced.

'Thank you,' John Grammaticus replied, and got up off the wooden chair at the end of the corridor. He walked down the hall towards the briefing room door, straightening his double-breasted jacket and cape. He undid the collar buttons of his shirt. It was almost noon and the terracotta palace was sweltering. Situated fifteen kilometres outside Mon Lo Harbour, the palace had been commandeered as a control station for the advance. Its ancient walls held the day's heat like an oven. Reed screens soaked in water had been fixed over the windows to keep the palace interiors cool and fresh, but they were beginning to dry out.

John Grammaticus had no physiological need to perspire, but he permitted his body to do so. Every other human around was sweating freely, and he didn't want them to notice that he wasn't like them.

He knocked at the door.

'Come!'

He went in. The chamber was long and broad, with pillars flanking the walls to support the tiled ceiling. The tops of the pillars had been carved to resemble the fronds of reeds, or snapping crocodilia, both common features in Nurthene architecture. A folding steel table had been set up in the centre of the room, and Uxor Rukhsana stood at the head of it, her four aides ranged on either side of the table beside her.

'Uxor,' Grammaticus said. 'Good to see you.' He tapped his throat. 'I apologise for the unbuttoning, but this objectionable heat.'

'Quite all right, Konig,' she replied. Her aides all nodded accordingly. They were all female, all aged between thirteen and sixteen, uxors in waiting. Their ovaries had already been harvested for the Geno Five-Two Chiliad stock banks. They were now honing their 'cept powers, and acting as a support buffer for their assigned uxor.

Grammaticus found the operational structure of the Geno Five-Two Chiliad quite fascinating. Formed during the savage continental wars that had engulfed Terra at the end of the Age of Strife, the geno had proved to be a most effective and adaptable force. No wonder the Emperor had permitted them to endure after Unification. No wonder he had looked upon their system and stolen from it.

The geno practised genic mustering. Grammaticus had been thoroughly briefed on this. Genic mustering had been an essential tool during those caustic years of atomic hurricanes and drifting rad clouds. The core of the regiment was the uxors, a bloodline of latent psychically sensitive females. The females had their eggs harvested at puberty, and from them the heavy-built uterine soldiery of the unit were vat-grown, using the genetic codes of several proven, robust agnate gene-pools notorious for their martial merit. The geno grew tough warriors, but they complemented their brute strength and kept the pool clean by importing smart, proven field commanders from other forces. The hetmen were always non-stock individuals who excelled at tactics and strategy.

The uxors, at the top of the Chiliad's command tree, were no longer capable of carrying children of their own to term. This, in ways not entirely understood, freed their minds, and allowed them to operate as perceptives, operational coordinators who could appreciate, as Gahet had put it during the briefing, 'the behaviour of their children'.

At best, the uxors were weak psykers. Each one was capable of a rudimentary talent known as the 'cept, enough to enable their forces in the field and supply them with some insight. They burned out quickly. By twenty-six, twenty-seven, they were done as uxors, and restricted to other duties. During their active phase as perceptives, they were always accompanied by aides, uxors in training, whose raw psychic talent bolstered the 'ceptive power of their uxor even as they learned from her.

None of the females in the chamber possessed a fraction of John Grammaticus's talent.

As he sat down at the end of the table opposite Uxor Rukhsana, he reached out. Instantly, he tasted feeble, immature 'cepts, chitter-chatter minds, the moist, unwholesome mental architecture of the pubescent aides. The technical inability to conceive made most uxor-aides gruesomely promiscuous. Grammaticus was repelled by the lurid, shallow thoughts that washed towards him. The aides were all thinking about the next soldier boy they'd hump, or how fabulous it was going to be to become an uxor.

Rukhsana was different. Grammaticus looked down the table towards her. For a start, she was a woman, not a girl; a startlingly appealing woman. Her lips were full, her long, straight, blonde hair centre-parted, her eyes heavily lashed and exotically grey. A master sculptor could not have improved upon her cheek bones. She was also twenty-eight, and at the end of her uxor service. He could feel that she hated this fact. She was broken by the thought that she would soon be something else: a medicae, a Munitorum commander, a cartomancer, an *uxor emeritus*.

Her powers were ebbing. Her 'cept was waning and weakening.

'What do you have for me, sir?' she asked.

Quite a voice. Even the aides took notice. Husky. No, silky, like honey. Grammaticus knew he was a little in love with her, and allowed himself to relish the fact. It had been a long time, seven hundred years, give or take, since he had permitted himself to respond to a human female in any way other than physical need.

'Well, I have plenty, uxor,' he replied, taking out the document case from under his arm and opening it.

'You've actually been in Mon Lo Harbour?' asked one of the aides, looking right at him. Grammaticus felt a wash of admiring lust.

'Yes... what's you name?'

'Tuvi, sir,' the girl said. She was the most mature of Rukhsana's aides, about nineteen. Tuvi clearly found the idea of a daring intelligence officer quite intoxicating.

'Yes, Tuvi. I made cover as a merchant called D'sal Huulta, and spent the last four days gathering evidence in the inner quarters of the town.'

Amongst other things, he thought.

'Wasn't that terribly dangerous?' asked another of the aides.

'Yes, it was,' said Grammaticus.

'How were you not unmasked by the infidel enemy?' asked Tuvi.

'Be quiet,' Rukhsana told her girls. 'Intelligence operatives are hardly required to give away their tricks.'

'It's all right, uxor,' Grammaticus smiled. He looked at Tuvi and said, 'El-teh ta nash el et chey tanay.'

'What?' Tuvi replied.

'It means,' Grammaticus told her, '*I speak the local language as a native does*, in Nurthene.'

'But–' Tuvi began.

'My dear, I'm not going to tell you how, so please don't ask. If I might continue?'

Tuvi looked as if she was going to say something else.

'Let the man speak, Tuvi,' Rukhsana snapped. 'Heniker?'

'Oh, of course. Well, the location itself… as we know, the Nurthene have no orbital or interplanetary technology, nor have ever possessed such means. However, the area known as Mon Lo Harbour, though flooded and used for maritime shipping, was originally constructed as a setting down point for starships.'

Uxor Rukhsana blinked. 'For starships?' she echoed.

He was taking a slight risk in sharing this information, but John Grammaticus's mind was finely trained to sort and appraise data. He knew exactly what he could give up and what he couldn't. He believed it mattered very little if the Imperials found out that Mon Lo had once been an extraplanetary set-down. It was a halting site, in fact. The Cabal used to visit here, long ago. That's why they knew about the Nurthene culture.

'For starships, uxor.'

'Are you sure?' Uxor Rukhsana asked.

'Absolutely,' Grammaticus replied. 'I have excellent sources.'

'And when you say "originally", Konig, what does originally mean?'

'It means something between eight and twelve thousand years ago, enough time for sea-levels to change, for flood plains to rise, and for a massive, stone-cut extraplanetary harbour to fill with water and become a harbour of a more traditional nature.'

It was eleven thousand, eight hundred and twenty-six years, in fact, and the construction work had taken eighteen months. Grammaticus felt it wise to fudge the precision of his knowledge.

The aides started speaking all at once.

'That would place construction during the Second Age of Technology,' said one.

'Around the time of the First Contact Event, and the first Alien Wars,' said another.

'Is there any evidence as to which xeno form might have been responsible?' asked another.

'Do the Nurthene know of its provenance?' asked Tuvi.

'Tuvi frames the best question,' said Grammaticus, shutting down the chatter. 'Do they know? Well, I don't believe they do. They possess myths and legends, as all cultures do, and some of them contain elements that might be interpreted as containing some race-memory of xeno contact or intervention. But until the 670th Expedition came along, the Nurthene believed they were alone in the galaxy. Remember, the Nurthene don't even realise they were originally colonists from Terra.'

'That is the true misery of this war,' Rukhsana nodded. 'They do not recognise us as kin.'

Grammaticus felt her discomfort. Kinship meant so much to the geno uxors. Indeed, he found this aspect of the Emperor's Great Crusade especially troubling. In its youth, mankind had spilled out across the stars, colonising thousands of worlds, forming the first human stellar community. Then the Age of Strife had come down, like the blade of a guillotine, and for the better part of five thousand years, warp storms had rendered interstellar travel impossible. The out-reaches of Man had become cut off, beleaguered, isolated. In that turmoil, many offshoots had entirely forgotten who they were or where they had come from. Such was the case with Nurth.

When the Emperor, a figure long foreseen by the Cabal, had finally unified the anarchic fragments of Terra, he had undertaken a Great Crusade – oh, how telling was *that* title! – to seek out, and reconnect with, the lost outposts of the human race. It was astonishing how often the lost worlds resisted those overtures of reconnection. It was unconscionable how many times the roving expedition fleets had been forced to go to war with the very cultures they had set out to rescue and embrace, just to bring them to what the Emperor had euphemistically called *compliance*. It was always, so the official line went, for their own good.

John Grammaticus had met the Emperor once, close on a thousand years before. The Emperor had been just another feudal warlord then, leading his thunder-armoured troops in an effort to consolidate his early Strife-age victories, and pave the way to eventual Unification. Grammaticus had been a line officer in the Caucasian Levvies, a significant force inveigled by truce and pact to support the Emperor's assault on the territorial holdings of the Panpacific Tyrant, Dume.

After a bloody conquest at Baktria, Grammaticus had been one of a hundred Caucasian officers invited to a Triumph at Pash, hosted by the retinues of the thunderbolt and lightning army. During the festivities, the Emperor – even then he had been known only by that objectionable epithet – had grandly toured the tables to personally thank his foreign allies and the leaders of the mercenary clans. Grammaticus had been one of hundreds present to receive his grateful handshake. In that moment of contact, he had seen why the Emperor was a force to be reckoned with: a psyker of towering, unimaginable strength, not really human at all by any contemporary measure of the fact. Grammaticus, who had never met anyone else like himself, had shuddered, and felt like a drone insect in the presence of its hive king. The Emperor had felt Grammaticus in the same passing second of contact. He had smiled.

'You have a fine mind, John,' he had said, without having to ask Grammaticus his name. 'We should talk, and consider the options available to beings like us.'

Before any such conversation could happen, Grammaticus had died, that painful, stupid first death.

Looking back, Grammaticus wondered if he would ever have been able to influence the Emperor's course if he'd lived. He doubted it. Even then, in that tiny moment of connection, it had been clear that the Emperor was never going to turn away from the road of catastrophic bloodshed he was set upon. One day, he would unleash upon the galaxy the most dreadful killing machines of all: the Astartes.

How ironic it was that Grammaticus's current task was to broker cooperation with one of those fearsome Astartes Legions.

Gahet had once remarked to Grammaticus that the Emperor was the only human who would have ever made a viable addition to the Cabal's inner circle. 'He sees the long picture of it,' Gahet had said. 'He understands the vast, slow cycle, and is content to allow it to run its course. He appreciates the epochal dynamic of true and thorough change.'

'Have you ever met him?' Grammaticus had asked.

'No, John, I haven't.'

'Then you have no idea what a bloodthirsty bastard he really is.'

Gahet had smiled. 'That's as may be, but he understands that the Primordial Annihilator is the true enemy of everything, so perhaps we need a bloodthirsty bastard on our side?'

'Konig?'

'I'm sorry, uxor,' Grammaticus said.

Rukhsana smiled down the table at him. 'You were quite lost in thought.'

'I was. I apologise. Where was I? Uhm, it is my belief that the extraplanetary harbour was built by some xenos kind several hundred years before this world was colonised by the original human outships. As far as the Nurthene are concerned, it has always been here.'

'So it is an intriguing aside, and not pertinent to our combat evaluation?'

'Indeed not. But for all their parochial mindset, the Nurthene have an appreciation of extraplanetary matters. They have lived in fear of first contact, of discovery by beings from other worlds. In their doctrine, our arrival proves to them the universal presence of evil. There is no dealing with them.'

'None at all?'

'No, uxor.'

He wanted to tell her that they were dealing with a human culture that had succumbed to the corruption of the Primordial Annihilator, but he knew she simply wouldn't understand what Chaos meant. Very few humans did. Grammaticus did, because he had shared the Cabal's Acuity. He had a feeling, deep in his gut, that the Emperor knew all too well.

So why hadn't he told any of his children? Why hadn't he forewarned them about the deathless abomination they would encounter if they ventured out into the stars?

The briefing turned to matters of fortification and placement. Gramaticus had brought the plans he had carefully hand drawn.

Discussion began on the best practice of attack on Mon Lo. Tuvi surprised him by suggesting the most perceptive tactical solutions. She would be a full uxor soon, with a pack of aides of her own. Rukhsana let her lead the plotting, nodding contentedly at her stepdaughter's excellence.

As the talk went to and fro, Grammaticus decided, wilfully, it was time to switch places. He put himself behind Rukhsana's eyes – she was far too preoccupied to resist or even notice – and looked back down the table at himself.

He saw what she saw: a well-made man of mature years, strong in the back and arms, with a very handsome face and grey hair. The man wore a scarlet dress coat with ornate double frogging down the front, and he was perspiring very slightly.

Not bad, thought John Grammaticus, not bad at all. It wasn't the body he'd been born with, but at least it pretended to be from the Caucasus, which was where the first John Grammaticus had been born, towards the end of the Twenty-Ninth Millennium.

'If we are going to commit to an attack,' Tuvi was saying, 'we need to know more about the enemy disposition in these lines, and along the north wall here, and here.'

'I wasn't able to collect data,' Grammaticus replied, 'but you're right. I'll be going in again tomorrow. In three days, I should have the information you need.'

'Good,' said Rukhsana. She paused. 'You're going inside again?'

'I think it's necessary, uxor.'

'Then may the Emperor protect you,' Tuvi said, and several of the aides echoed her.

Oh, I'm quite sure he won't, Grammaticus thought.

'That's all for today,' Rukhsana told her aides. 'Be off with you. I'll finish the brief myself.'

Grammaticus sensed annoyance and disappointment as the aides filed out.

The door closed behind them. There was a long silence.

'Where were we?' Uxor Rukhsana asked.

'You were about to undress,' he said in demotic Scythian.

'Was I indeed?' she laughed, answering in the same language. 'I had no idea you were fluent in my native tongue, or knew me to be of Scythian extraction. You're very clever, Konig.'

You don't know the half of it, he thought. I'm fluent, instantly, in every tongue, every language I encounter. It's my particular talent, and my curse.

'I'm sorry to be forward,' he said, again in Scythian, 'but I've seen the way you look at me.'

'And I've seen the way you look at me, sir.'

'Is it so bad?'

Rukhsana smiled. 'No, Konig, it's flattering. But I'm no aide-cadre hussy. I'm not about to disrobe for some sordid little tryst in this briefing room. I'm not sure I'm going to disrobe for you at all.'

Grammaticus allowed a smile to cross Heniker's face. 'My dear uxor,' he said, 'the simple doubt expressed in that sentence is all I could ever ask for.'

IN THE OLD times, in the time of inchoation, races built their fastnesses in places of safety, and left the darker places unexplored. It had been the primitive instinct of man to behave this way. It had kept him safe from the wolf and the sabre-cat. Grammaticus wished his species had kept hold of this instinct, and not forsaken it. The darker places were darker places for a reason. He was fairly certain it was the eternal influence of the Emperor that had quashed that particular taboo.

He thought of Terra's old maps, with their quaintly phrased notations of warning, *here be dragons*. That had always been a shorthand motto of man's ignorance of the darker places of his universe.

'What did you say?' Ruhksana asked, rolling over sleepily.

'Nothing,' he replied.

'You said something about dragons, Konig.'

'I may have.'

'There are no dragons, Konig.'

It was late afternoon. The palace compound had sweltered out another day, so close to the sea everyone could smell it, yet so far away its cooling influence did not reach.

The sex had been exceptional. The emotional intimacy had almost reduced him to tears. He hated allowing himself to get so close. Seven hundred years was a long time, long enough for him to forget the consequences of proper connection. He had felt her hunger, her appetite to prove she was still something of significance even though her uxorhood was sloughing away like dead skin.

He had allowed himself to love her, and allowed her to reciprocate, and now he faced up to the consequences of that decision.

'Konig?'

She didn't even know his real name. He wanted to tell her.

'Do you have to go back in?' she asked, rolling over and lying sidelong. Her lithe, naked body made him stir, but he resisted the temptation.

'Yes.'

'I'm sure we can do the rest of the tactical plan with drone spotters and the fleet appraisal.'

'You can't. You need me in there.'

+ John. +

'Oh no,'

'Oh no, what?' she asked, sitting up.

He rose to his feet. 'Nothing, my love.'

'My love. *That* sounds very serious.'

+ John. +

Not now.

'You've gone quite pale, Kon. Are you all right?'

He paced away from the bed, bare-foot, towards the wash room. 'I'm fine. Absolutely fine. I just need a sip of water.'

Rukhsana rolled onto her back and stared at the ceiling. 'Don't be long,' she called.

Grammaticus entered the wash room, closed the door behind him, and paused for a moment, head down, leaning his hands on the edges of the stone basin. 'Not now, really not now,' he moaned softly. The stone was cool under his palms. He poured some water into it from the jug. All the while, he could feel the old, chipped mirror hanging on the wall behind him.

He turned around.

Gahet looked out at him from the mirror's cloudy surface.

+ You have taken a wrong step, John Grammaticus. The intimate bond you have made with this female is impairing your mission. +

'Go away.'

+ John, you are risking everything. You know what's at stake. What are you doing? +

'Being human for a change,' Grammaticus replied.

+ John, we have eliminated agents for less. +

'I'm sure you have, not in the old days, but in these latter days. I'm sure you have.'

+ I am not threatening you, John. +

'Yes, you actually are,' he told the mirror.

+ The galaxy must live. +

'Right, right, and can't I be allowed to live *in* it a little?'

Gahet's face faded slowly.

Grammaticus rinsed his face in cold water from the stone basin.

'Bastards,' he spat.

BEFORE DAWN, IN a cool, mauve twilight, the escort arrived to take Grammaticus back to the insertion point. He had already been up for an hour, ritually packing and re-packing his small bag. He told the escort to wait with the vehicle, and finished his chores, sipping tepid black caffeine and eating some preserved fruits and spelt bread left over from the night before.

She surprised him by waking up.

'Were you planning on leaving without a goodbye?'

'No,' he lied.

'Good.' Rukhsana brushed a strand of long, blonde hair off her face and looked him up and down. He had dressed in a simple desert suit of soft brown kid-skin, with Army-issue boots and a canvas jacket.

'You don't look much like a native.'

'That part comes later.'

All she was wearing was the sheet from the bed. 'Well, goodbye, then. The Emperor protects.'

'Let's hope so,' he agreed.

'Try to come back,' Rukhsana said. 'I'd like to see you again.'

'I'll come back,' he replied, not lying this time, 'because I *want* to see you again.'

Uxor Rukhsana smiled and tilted her head slightly to one side, regarding him. 'There's something about you, Konig. It's as if you see right into me.'

'That's because I do,' he said.

THE ESCORT, A young geno company bashaw and three sleepy troopers, were waiting for him in the rear yard of the palace compound. The ride was a light speeder, the hull of which had been sand-blasted back to bare metal by the environment.

'Sir,' the bashaw saluted as Grammaticus walked out of the lit doorway into the darkness of the yard with his bag over his shoulder. It took a second to place the man's background accent... Yndonesia, Purwakarta Administrative District, perhaps one of the Cianjur hives.

'What's your unit?' Grammaticus asked in Bahasa Malay. The bashaw blinked in surprise and smiled.

'Arachne, sir,' he replied. 'I didn't know you were a Pan-Pac, sir.'

'I'm not. I'm from all over.'

They got in and rode out of the yard, and through the descending levels of the ancient desert palace, via checkpoints, gateways and night-watch barricades where sentries lurked beside sputtering braziers, their rifles hooked through their folded arms. Papers and biometrics were routinely checked.

The Nurthene had a subversive streak. Experience had taught the Imperial Army that the Nurthene had spies of their own, saboteurs too. It felt odd to be a spy checked on the way out.

Outside the palace perimeter, the speeder picked up velocity and coasted along the bombed-out avenues and dust-dressed streets of the township surrounding the compound. The sun was threatening to rise behind the passing ruins. Grammaticus sat back in the rear seat, trying to relax, trying to compose his focus into identity immersion, feeling the breeze of motion against his face. He began to regret making a connection with the young bashaw. The officer, sitting up front, kept leaning around and talking to Grammaticus about places in Cianjur that Grammaticus had never visited, nor had any wish to visit. Grammaticus had been in Cianjur once, long ago. He'd been there as part of an army that had burned the place down, five hundred years before the hive the bashaw had grown up in had even been planned.

He closed his eyes and thought of Rukhsana.

It's as if you see right into me. There was too much truth in that. His mind saw into everything. It made him think of the thing he tried never to think about: that day, long ago, meeting the Emperor, shaking his hand, tasting the power, and seeing, behind the glamour of that handsome, noble, healthy face, seeing...

Just for a nanosecond.

Seeing…

'Are you quite well, sir?' the bashaw asked. 'You went rather pale all of a sudden. Is it motion sickness?'

'No. I'm fine. Absolutely fine,' Grammaticus replied.

THEY CAME UP out of the ruins, and followed the rutted dispersal tracks around the back of the dug-in Imperial lines. The sun was rising, crisping the lower edge of the sky. In the lea of the earthworks, for kilometre after kilometre, gun emplacements made sulking silhouettes against the dawn, and millions of bivouac tents covered the ground like blisters, breakfast fires glowing. They passed standards and banners hanging limp in the slowly heating air.

'That's my lot,' the bashaw called out as they shot past a particular standard. Grammaticus turned his head to look, and saw Arachne, a mousy but surprisingly large bosomed girl, if the banner's image was any guide, weaving her complex web of fate and destiny.

THE INSERTION POINT was an outfall of the city's antique sewer system some eighteen kilometres west of the palace. It had been exposed by shelling about three months earlier, and was well guarded. Apart from the geno sentries, automated gun-servitors watched it, unblinking, day and night. The Nurthene guarded the other end just as proficiently, but Grammaticus wasn't going all the way to the other end.

The bashaw introduced him to the point officer, a ruddy-faced hetman called Maryno. Maryno wanded the servitors to default/passive, and stood watching with the bashaw as Grammaticus slithered down the shattered embankment into the maw of the outfall.

Darkness, as had so often been the case in his life, embraced him.

TEN KILOMETRES AND ninety minutes later, he pulled himself out of a run-off vent not far from the rising walls and banked towers of Mon Lo Harbour.

He had already switched off his lamp, and left it in the bag, along with his canvas jacket and army boots, stuffed behind the loose bricks of a culvert.

His journey along the dark chute had provided him with almost enough time to complete his identity immersion. He was no longer Konig Heniker. He was D'sal Huulta. In all, he had taken very few real measures to disguise himself: a wrap of pink silk over his desert suit, felt shoes in place of the army boots, a desert shawl expertly pulled around his head. His skin was tanned, though not as dark as the average Nurthene, and a strict Nurthene observer of the *Pa'khel* would have worn his hair tied in a net under his shawl, and anointed his scalp, armpits, groin and belly with scented oil.

Grammaticus never went to such extremes, even though his Imperial spymasters recommended he should. He knew that his mind was more than capable of smoothing over most epistemological blemishes. Besides, the anointing oils smacked of a ritual offering to the Primordial Annihilator, something he was not prepared to undertake.

He fastened the hooked knife worn by all Nurthene to his under-belt, then strapped on the broad over-belt with its three pouches for fluid, mineral salt and currency. He washed his hands in the trackside dust to blacken his fingernails. Apart from the knife, he carried no weapon, except, of course, for the ring.

The sun was crawling up into the sky, having revealed itself during his trek through the dank underworld. He felt its searing heat on his head and shoulders, but he was near the sea, close enough to both feel and smell it. Fresh winds came in from the harbour shore, snaking in across the desert outland. He sniffed moisture. He began to walk towards the banked towers and enamelled walls of the port city.

Others were doing the same. War or no war, life went on. Straggles of traders and merchants, some with trains of pack animals, were heading into Mon Lo from the hinterland, hoping to do business at the city markets. Migrant workers were walking to the port in search of employment. Refugees and displaced citizens were coming to the gates, fleeing the Imperial advance. Grammaticus fell in with them.

As he walked, Grammaticus began the psychic litany in his head, the final progression towards immersion in another dialect and culture base.

I am John Grammaticus. I am John Grammaticus. I am John Grammaticus pretending to be Konig Heniker. I am Konig Heniker. I am Konig Heniker pretending to be D'sal Huulta. I am D'sal Huulta. I chey D'sal Huulta lem pretending. El-chey D'sal samman Huulta lem tanay ek. El'chey D'sal samman Huulta lem tanay ek...

'Who are you, fellow?' one of the echvehnurth warriors at the city gate asked as he approached. The echvehnurth had been resting his falx against his silver breastplate, but now he raised it. Some of his companions did likewise. Others were stopping and searching some water merchants heading in out of the desert through the ancient arch.

'I am D'sal Huulta,' Grammaticus replied in Demotic Nurthene, making the obeisance of all-the-sunlight to the echvehnurth. 'I am a merchant.'

Falx held ready across the left shoulder to strike, the echvehnurth stared at Grammaticus. 'Show me your palms, your face, and your brands.'

Grammaticus made as if to do so.

+ I'm safe and you've seen all you need to reassure you, + he sent at the same moment.

The echvehnurth nodded, and waved him into the city, already sweeping the incomers for his next subject.

Grammaticus had shown him nothing.

Mon Lo was waking up. As a city girded to the expectation of assault, it never truly slept, but its habits followed a circadian ebb and flow.

The outer walls were well defended by squadrons of echvehnurth, by iron mortars and bombasts, and by platoons of the regular nurthadtre ground troops. They loitered in unruly, spitting gatherings around the heavy steps of the city's thick walls, or stood on the wall's fighting platforms, watching the distant, unmoving enemy through spyglasses.

Deeper in the city, the rhythmic pulse of life was easier to discern. Markets woke up. Merchants announced their wares. Morning devotions were declaimed by strong-lunged priests. Water-carriers called their services as they wandered the plazas and the winding, cobbled streets and lanes.

Grammaticus retraced his steps, trying to recall the specific layout of the place as he had experienced it the first time. Passing merchants and elders nodded and made the all-the-sunlight gesture to him as they acknowledged his status.

He made the gesture back.

Grammaticus wanted to get into the northern suburb, an area called Kurnaul, so he could get a good look at the city's north wall. Tuvi would appreciate his efforts. He stood aside to let a grox-cart trundle past. Street washers cleaned the cobbles with bristle brooms and pails of water, using spades for the animal dung. They sang as they worked.

The faience tiled walls of the port city glimmered around him in the morning sun, showing reeds and reptiles in mosaic. The Nurthene had no street names, just pictorial emblems. He looked at a particular symbol, a great monitor lizard delineated in cherry red tiles, and knew, with a trained certainty, that he had never seen it before. He'd made a wrong turn. Mon Lo was so complex, so interwoven, it was hard to recall the specific plan. It was like Arachne's web; mousy, big-bosomed Arachne.

He was the needle, he fancied, her needle, moving through the net of fate.

He halted and took a moment to consider. His internal compass was out. He checked with the rising sun and established where east was. He slowed his breathing, and allowed himself to perspire for a minute, just to stabilise his body. He had his bearings again. He'd just gone a street too far west, that was all. Karnaul district was over to his left.

Except it wasn't. He halted again, refusing to allow panic to dig in.

A water-carrier came up to him and offered a ladle of water.

'No, thank you,' Grammaticus said.

'God love you anyway,' the carrier replied, moving on.

Grammaticus shuddered. What the water-carrier had actually said literally translated as, *The Primordial Annihilator immolate your living soul.*

What's wrong with me, Grammaticus thought? Last time I was here, I slipped easily from street to street. This time, I'm behaving like an amateur. My head is swimming. This is… this is stupid.

He crossed through two more busy streets, looking for familiar landmarks. It felt as if Kurnaul district was further away than ever. It was as if something was distracting him, baffling his abilities.

On impulse, he reached into the bag of mineral salts hooked to his broad over-belt, and closed his fingers around the memeseed hidden in the salt inside. The seed was the size of an earlobe, set into a small silver clasp. Gahet had given it to him. The seeds, fruited from some xenotype tree on a world somewhere in the Cabal's range of influence, were psychically sensitive. If they grew warm, or desiccated in any way, it was a sign that psychic activity was close by.

Grammaticus looked at the memeseed. It was always a little warm and dry, because it reacted to his own talents. In his hand, the seed was positively hot, like a burning coal. It had shrivelled in its setting.

He was in trouble. The memeseed screamed a warning that something was nearby, perhaps something hunting him.

'D'sal? D'sal Huulta?'

Grammaticus looked over his shoulder and saw a portly merchant waving to him. The man had been standing in conversation with a group of his brethren on the steps of a counting house, but he left them to hurry over. Grammaticus quickly put the memeseed away.

What is his name? His name? You've met him before.

'D'sal, my good fellow,' the portly merchant declared, making the all-the-sunlight gesture and adding a bow. 'I have missed your face at the market these last few days. What news of the fire-brick deal we sketched out on our last meeting? Has your supplier delivered?'

H'dek. H'dek Rootun. That was his name.

'H'dek, my good fellow, I am pained to respond that my supplier has become a goat's maw,' Grammaticus answered politely, 'taking more than it gives. It turns out I can't deliver on that fire-brick deal. I apologise.'

H'dek waved his pudgy hand. 'Oh, don't worry! I quite understand. In these times of hardship and oppression, with the alien siege at our door, things like this happen.'

He looked at Grammaticus more earnestly. 'You have my fetish, my gene-print? Yes? Good, we can deal in future! I look forward to receiving your envoy.'

'I am always your servant, H'dek,' Grammaticus mumbled. He made the sign of all-the-sunlight, and added the gesture of the moons-entire as he ended the meeting.

He strode on down the length of the street feeling as uneasy and lost as before. Then he hurried into an open square, where the foot traffic was lighter, hoping the freedom of the space would give him room to clear his head, and perhaps even identify the source of the psychic activity the seed had detected. Clarity obstinately refused to come.

Grammaticus paused, and slowly raised his eyes.

He was standing in the Pa'khel Awan Nurth, the square of the pre-eminent temple in Mon Lo. High above him on the temple's tympanum, a bas-relief frieze showed the four properties of the Primordial Annihilator: death, ecstasy, mortality and mutability, blending together into one, huge, ghastly symbol of unity.

What gross mistake had led his feet here, what clumsy mis-turn? This was the last place in the city he would have visited voluntarily.

The tympanum symbol seemed to pulse, to throb, pressing his eyeballs back into their sockets. Sunlight flared and buzzed. He gagged, and forced hot reflux back down into his gut. His previous visit hadn't been anything like this. It was as if the city had become aware of him, and his role as an intruder, and had become a web, spun to trap him. Someone, something, was playing with him.

The vomit wasn't going to stay down. He hurried off into an alley away from the temple precinct, and bent over in the shadows to release the acid liquid. It rushed out of him in a geyser. He barely had time to drag his head shawl off.

He sank to his knees, trembling and spitting.

Two figures, two men who were just dark shadows, were moving down the alley towards him. They weren't rushing, but there was a purposeful, urgent stride to their gait. Grammaticus got to his feet and made off in the opposite direction, with equal purpose, not quite running.

Three more figures rounded the opposite end of the long, winding alley, and came towards him. What were they? Militia? Echvehnurth? Agents of the Pa'khel Awan, the temple's zealous doctrinal clerics?

The alley had a couple of side turnings along its length. Grammaticus took the first, and broke into a run as soon as he was out of sight of the figures closing in on him. He reached a dead end, a closed courtyard behind some tall, fine town houses. He heard footsteps approaching behind him. He tried the doors, and found all of them bolted, except a heavy gate of painted wood, where green reptiles intercoiled and made helical patterns. Grammaticus pushed the gate open and ducked into the blessed cool and darkness of the room beyond it. He closed the gate, and drew the bolt across to hold it. He waited, listening to the muffled footsteps and voices outside.

A gigantic hand, gloved in steel, reached out of the darkness and picked him up by the neck. It turned him around and slammed him back against the wall, holding him by the throat.

Grammaticus was being throttled, his feet kicking off the ground. The steel hand pressed him back against the wall. Terracotta brickwork ground into his back.

'I have a suspicion,' a deep voice said, coming out of the darkness, 'you've been looking for me, John Grammaticus.'

It knew his name.

'Th-that's possible,' Grammaticus gasped, 'though it m-might depend upon who you are.'

'My name? You know my name, you treacherous bastard. My name is Alpharius.'

FOUR

**House of the Hydra, Mon Lo Harbour, Nurth,
continuous**

THE POUNDING BLOOD vessels in Grammaticus's head
felt as if they were about to burst. His windpipe had
closed.

+ Let me go, + he sent, desperately.

The steel-gloved hand released its grip, and Grammaticus fell awkwardly onto the tiled floor. Hurt and
dazed, he forced his mind to work fast. His eyes were
becoming accustomed to the cold blue darkness of the
chamber.

He could see the giant shadow of his captor, and the
hot, red glow of a visor, but he could not read a mind.
Something was screening it. Nevertheless, his urgent
commands were getting through.

+ Step back, and keep your hands away from your
weapons. +

The giant shadow above him took a step backwards.

'Stop him doing that,' the shadow's deep voice
growled.

There was someone else in the room, in this bolt-hole that had not been safe at all. Grammaticus saw the second person as a hooded figure, though he could not actually see the man with his eyes. The figure was hooded *in his mind*.

Grammaticus tried to rise. A piercing liquid squeal, like a wet finger sliding on glass, stabbed into his neo-cortex. Pain fired through his autonomic nervous system and sizzled down his spine. He grunted and fell back against the wall.

'He is fierce. Strong and well protected,' the hooded figure said out loud.

'Too much for you?' asked the giant shadow.

'No.'

'Then keep him down.'

The squeal increased in power. Grammaticus convulsed.

'We're going to have a conversation, John,' the giant shadow said, bending down and looming close. 'I want some truth out of you, or so help me, I'll simply crush your psyk-cursed skull. Yes? Are we clear?'

Grammaticus nodded. The agony was immense. He could feel blood running out of his nose and over his top lip.

'Good. Shere is going to release you. That will be nice, won't it? When Shere releases you, no mind tricks. Are we still clear?'

'Yes,' Grammaticus hissed, his throat bruised and sore.

'Let him go, Shere,' the giant commanded.

The squeal went away and took the worst of the pain with it. Grammaticus slumped forwards onto his hands, gasping.

'Lights,' the giant's voice ordered.

There was a brief pulse of telekinetic effect, and several dozen wax candles arranged around the room spontaneously lit, a decent pyrokinetic display. The light from the candles was soft and yellow. It showed Grammaticus a shuttered greeting room, typical of Nurthene houses, with a faience tiled floor and mosaic walls that snagged the candlelight like water. It also showed him his antagonists: an armoured trans-human giant and a standard human in black whose face Grammaticus couldn't see, even though the man wore no physical mask or hood.

'Your name is John Grammaticus?' the giant asked.

'If you say so.'

'I can get Shere to start again, if you prefer.'

Grammaticus shook his head. Spots of his blood dappled the tiles around him. 'Yes, my name is John Grammaticus. You already knew that.'

'Look at me,' the giant commanded.

Grammaticus looked up. The giant was clad in power armour, the metal and ceramic wargear of an Imperial Astartes. The armour was a rich purple with silver edging. Green heraldry had been marked on the shoulder plates. The helm was the very latest, baleen-snout version. Dull red light shone inside the visor slit. To the left of the towering Astartes stood the mind-hooded figure, small by comparison.

'No, *me*,' said the Astartes. 'Look at *me*. Ignore my psyker. Better.'

'I–' Grammaticus began.

'Quiet,' said the Astartes, raising a massive index finger. 'You're going to tell me what I want to know, not what you want to say.'

Grammaticus nodded.

'You've been looking for me. That's why you keep coming into this city. You knew I'd be here.'

Grammaticus nodded again.

'How did you know that?'

'Because we invited you here,' Grammaticus replied.

'You invited me here? Who's "we"?'

'The Cabal I work for.'

The Astartes turned to look at the hooded figure. 'Once again,' he said.

The squeal speared into Grammaticus's head and made him shriek.

'What is the Cabal?' the Astartes asked.

Grammaticus sobbed. He could barely answer. 'They… I don't know… they are eternal and… and they…'

'That's not really very good,' said the Astartes. 'Maybe I should just shoot you.'

'The Cabal is… the Cabal is the only hope!' Grammaticus pleaded.

'Go on.'

'Please!'

'Stop it now, Shere,' the giant instructed.

The squeal died back.

'Whose only hope?' asked the Astartes.

'Mine. Yours. Mankind's,' Grammaticus sighed.

'You're talking about the Imperium?'

Grammaticus shook his head. 'Broader than that. The species.'

'The Imperium is the species,' the giant replied.

'You don't really believe that, do you?' Grammaticus asked. 'The worlds you've seen, the worlds you've been obliged to bring to compliance… worlds like this one, sapling shoots of human culture, cuttings from the root plant. The human race is far, far more than the militant tribe that is spilling out from Terra to accomplish the Emperor's vision.'

The Astartes drew his boltgun. Grammaticus did not actually see it happen. One moment, the hefty weapon was holstered at the giant's hip, the next it was in his steel fist, aimed at Grammaticus's head.

'Are you insane?' the giant asked. 'Are you blind? Look at me. I am an Astartes warrior, oathed to this moment and sworn to serve the Emperor. Why would you say something that sounds so perilously close to treason?'

'I apologise if that's how it sounded. I meant no disrespect.'

The boltgun remained aimed at him. 'You said this Cabal of yours invited us here. Explain that.'

Grammaticus swallowed. 'Of all the Astartes Legions, the Cabal believes the Alpha Legion to be most receptive to its message.'

'Why?'

'In all truth, sir, I do not know. I am simply a go-between. The Cabal wanted the Alpha Legion to become involved in the compliance war here on Nurth, so that it could see the evidence for itself.'

'See what, John?'

Grammaticus straightened slightly and looked boldly at the muzzle of the gun aimed at his face. 'What was at stake. The real enemy. Not the Nurthene, but the Primodial Annihilator that holds sway over them.'

The Astartes slowly lowered his weapon. 'You're talking about their warp-magick?'

'It's not–' Grammaticus began. 'May I stand, sir? This floor is cold.'

The snouted helm nodded. Grammaticus rose to his feet. The Astartes still towered over him.

'It's not magick. It's not some fanciful trickery. It's the visible manifestation of a deep power – a universal, pervasive abomination.'

'Chaos,' the Astartes replied. 'If that is what your masters wanted us to see, they have wasted your errand. We already know of Chaos, and have numbered it in the litany of xenos hazards.'

Grammaticus shook his head sadly. 'The simplest name for it is Chaos. You've numbered it in the litany of xenos hazards, have you? Then you know it only as a child knows the world. It has always been and will always be, and compared to it, nothing – not mankind, not the Imperium, not the Emperor's mighty design – is of any consequence. Unchecked, it will poison and stagnate the galaxy. Fuelled and driven, it will destroy everything. The Cabal wanted you to see it properly, to see it with your own eyes, so that you would take its message seriously.'

He paused. 'And it needed you to see it quickly.'

'Why?' asked the giant.

'Because a great war is coming.'

'A war against what?'

'Against yourselves,' said Grammaticus.

The giant Astartes stared at Grammaticus for a moment. Grammaticus heard the dull *click* of his helmet vox operating. A private conversation was taking place. Grammaticus waited. The candle flames trembled. A tiny green house lizard scuttled across the tiled floor and up a wall.

The giant turned back to look at Grammaticus.

'What is the message your Cabal wants us to take so seriously?' he asked.

'I don't know. I was simply sent here to propose a dialogue.'

The Astartes looked over at the mind-hooded man. 'I am called for,' he said. 'Take him to the parlour and stay with him. Do not allow him to play any tricks.'

The psyker nodded.

The Astartes went over to the wooden gate, unbolted it, and stepped out into the sunlight. Just before the gate closed, Grammaticus saw that the intercoiled green reptiles painted on the wood were dragons, each one with three serpentine heads. *Hydras*.

'This way,' said the psyker to Grammaticus.

HE FOLLOWED THE psyker through the rooms of the house, rambling chambers and hallways that followed no more logical a scheme than the streets of Mon Lo. All the rooms were dark and shuttered, and dust sheets covered the few pieces of furniture. This was a place of convenience, Grammaticus decided, a safe house. He had been meant to open that painted gate all along.

The psyker led the way with a single fluttering candle.

'You contrived to bring me here?' Grammaticus asked. 'You baffled my mind and got me lost, so I could be directed to this house?'

'Not on my own,' the hooded man replied. 'You are a powerful being. We've been aware of you, these last few weeks, operating here, shadowing us, watching us. We thought it was time to ask why.'

'You're not Astartes.'

The man turned and looked back at him but, despite the candlelight, Grammaticus could still not resolve his face. 'The Alpha Legion uses any and all instruments to get its work done. I am honoured to serve them.'

The psyker took Grammaticus into a dark sitting room where several low couches and upholstered stools had been brought into use, their dust sheets folded and put away. A golden ewer of Nurthene wine, some small silver-dished mazers, and an earthenware bowl of preserved fruit stood on an inlaid table.

The psyker nodded slightly and the many candles arranged around the room's surfaces spontaneously lit. The sudden light made a couple of little house lizards skitter into the shadows.

'I do hate lumen and glow-globe light,' the psyker said. 'It kills the darkness. Candles illuminate it.'

'And darkness is just another instrument of the Alpha Legion?' asked Grammaticus.

Though he could not see the man's face, Grammaticus understood that the psyker was smiling. 'You really *have* been watching us carefully, haven't you?' the psyker said.

'It's my job,' Grammaticus replied.

'Help yourself to wine, to a bite of food,' the psyker offered, sitting down on a couch and putting the candle he was carrying down on a low table.

Grammaticus poured some wine into one of the silver drinking bowls. He needed something to wash his mouth with, but would have preferred water. As he sipped from the mazer, he focused his limbic system to negate the effects of the alcohol.

He took a seat opposite the psyker. 'You're called Shere, right?'

'Yes.'

'You're a gifted pyrokine. It's a technique that never manifested in me.'

Shere shrugged. 'You get what you get, John. I'm far more impressed by your particular talent. Logokinetic skill. That's rare.'

'You can read that in me?'

'Of course,' said Shere, 'but I can't understand it. Is it any language, or just specific groups?'

'I've never encountered a tongue I couldn't master.'

'Including xenos?'

Grammaticus smiled. 'They're not so hard. It depends on the organ they use for speech. I can understand some, but am unable to respond in kind because I lack the necessary biology to manufacture reciprocal sounds. And some are just abstruse. The eldar have a particular verb form that always trips me up.'

'And you can tell where a person is from, just by their speech?' Shere asked, deftly switching from Low Gothic to Sinhala.

'Nice try,' said Grammaticus in fluent Sinhala, 'but your palatal voicing gives you away. You are speaking Sinhala well, but I read Farsi vowels underneath, and something else. You are Uzbek or Azerbaijani.'

'Uzbek.'

'And the something else, the long diphthongs, that's a trace of Mars, isn't it?'

'I spent eight years growing up in the habitats of Ipluvian Maximal. You're very good. I presume, as a result, you are very good at reading the truth?'

Grammaticus nodded. 'I am. It is particularly hard to lie to me, a fact which I hope you'll mention to your masters when you report this conversation back to them. I excel at recognising truth, so I am not unwittingly conveying someone else's lies to the ears of the Alpha Legion.'

Shere chuckled. 'You may recognise the truth, John. We have no guarantee you are transmitting it.'

'That's a decent point, I suppose,' Grammaticus replied, taking another sip from the mazer cradled in his fingers.

'How did you invite them?' Shere asked. 'They'll want to know.'

'It's taken about a decade,' said Grammaticus. 'Agents like me have been planting seeds and suggestions for a while now. Using Imperial codes and cyphers, we've logged reports and bulletins into the Crusade's data-architecture, certain things that we thought would tantalise the Alpha Legion. We diverted a few orders, reversed a few command communiqués. Little by little, we made sure that when the time came for the 670th Expedition to request assistance in prosecuting the Nurthene campaign, it would be the Alpha Legion that responded to Lord Commander Namatjira's plea.'

'Great Terra,' Shere breathed, 'that's astonishing. The level of influence, of access… the strategy, the patience. Incredible! Such subtle manipulation!'

'That's the Cabal's way, Shere,' Grammaticus replied, 'strategy, subtle influence, the long view. They're very good at it. They've always been very good at it.'

'They could have simply asked.'

Grammaticus laughed. It hurt his bruised throat. 'That's not their way! Besides, would the Alpha Legion have said yes?'

'Not in a thousand years,' Shere agreed. 'Look, I'd be careful how I explained that to them, if I were you. The Alpha Legion prides itself on knowing everything. They prize knowledge above all things, and hate the idea of anyone knowing more than they do. That's how they win their battles. In fact, the only thing they hate more is the idea that they're being manipulated.'

'So noted, thank you. I had already foreseen that as a stumbling block.' Grammaticus put the empty mazer down on the tray by the ewer. 'You're no slouches when it comes to manipulation, though. You got me, today. From the moment I entered Mon Lo, you were misleading me, clouding my mind, pulling me to where you wanted me to be.'

'Well, not quite,' said Shere.

'Don't be so modest, you admitted it to me just now.'

Shere looked up at Grammaticus in the candlelight. His lack of a coherent face was hard to look at, but Grammaticus could read alarm. 'John, I'm not being modest. Yes, we led you here, but only once we had located and identified you. That was just before you entered the temple square, on Red Monitor Street. Before that, we weren't aware of you at all.'

'No,' said Grammaticus, 'it was before that. I–'

Shere got up. 'John, are you telling me that you were being influenced from the moment you entered the city today?'

'I–'

'This is important, John! Was something on to you right from your point of entry?'

Grammaticus swallowed. His guts suddenly felt as if they were full of ice. 'Yes,' he said.

'Damn,' Shere murmured. 'That wasn't us. That wasn't us. They made you.'

'Shere, I–'

'Be quiet, please. We may have just been seriously compromised.'

Shere walked over to the parlour door and bent his head, talking urgently into a vox microbead. Grammaticus waited, his head spinning slightly. An awful creep of realisation was coming over him. The Cabal

and the Alpha Legion had not been the only forces
playing games that morning.

Shere looked over at Grammaticus, his conversation
over. 'We're moving,' he said. 'We're getting out of here.'

'What's going on?'

'It's as bad as I feared. The city's gone quiet. The Nurthene identified you and used you as a lure to draw us
out.'

'I'm so sorry,' Grammaticus said.

'Your apology hardly counts for anything. Come on.'

Footsteps were thumping up the hallway outside.
The door opened and three men came in. Two were
standard humans, dressed in mail sleeves and head
shawls, carrying crude pattern lascarbines. The third,
attired identically to the other two, was a gene-big
beast lugging a bolter.

'We're quitting the house,' the gene-giant told Shere.
'Is this the wretch who blew our operation?'

Without waiting for confirmation, the gene-giant
turned and advanced towards Grammaticus.

'Leave him, Herzog! Please, sir!' Shere called out.
'He's valuable. Pech told me to watch him and keep
him safe.'

'Shame the rodent couldn't do the same for us,' the
gene-giant growled. 'All right, let's head out. Double
time.'

They flanked Grammaticus and hurried him down
the hall. Scared as he was, Grammaticus sorted the
data that had just come his way. The gene-giant was
called Herzog, apparently. Grammaticus could smell
the whiff of Astartes about him. The other two, the
mail-sleeved standard humans, suggested to Grammaticus that the Alpha Legion used all sorts of
non-Astartes operatives to accomplish their missions,

not just specialists like the psyker Shere. What had
Shere said? *The Alpha Legion uses any and all instruments
to get its work done.* Grammaticus risked a quick surface
read of the men's minds, and saw they were soldiers of
the Imperial Army, though there was something definitely non-standard about the biological samples he
was getting. He dared not risk a deeper probe.

And that other thing Shere had said: *Pech told me to
watch him and keep him safe.* He could only have meant
the armoured giant, but the giant had identified himself as *Alpharius*. Was that another lie? How did the
names connect?

They reached the ground floor of the house. Herzog
raised a hand to activate his link.

The shutters opened. They banged aside, one by one,
opening each window in turn, spilling hot, hard daylight into the closed house. Grammaticus flinched at
each opening, feeling the residual pulse of the telekinetic power responsible. A trio of minute green house
lizards danced in over an open sill.

'Damn,' Herzog murmured.

More lizards skittered in, running like water over the
sills, some falling onto the floor with little *plips*. Inside
five seconds, they were pouring in like a flood, thousands of them, rushing over the window ledges and
under the doors, flowing as if dumped out of handcarts.

'Back up! Upstairs!' Herzog ordered.

They thumped back up the staircase. The tide of
lizards behind them quickly covered the tiled floor of
the hall and began to pour, like green water disobeying
gravity, up the stairs.

Grammaticus could feel a malevolence in the air, a
pervading touch of cloying heat and rage, the trademark of an angry, potent psyker.

'We're in trouble,' he whispered. The others ignored him, except for Shere, who glanced in his direction. For a brief second, Grammaticus saw Shere's face, the face of a startled young man with fine features. Shere was so unnerved he was letting his psyk-hood slip.

Rivers of pattering lizards were pouring in through the upper windows too. The shutters on the first floor had been yanked open. Tiny, sinuous green shapes rippled across sheet-wrapped furniture and spilled along the tiled flooring.

'Oh hell's teeth,' one of the mail-sleeved operatives gasped.

'Second floor!' Herzog ordered. 'Make for the bridge!'

Herzog's mind was unguarded by distraction. Grammaticus skimmed its surface and saw that the bridge was a brick walkway linking the house to its neighbour. He started to run. They all started to run. Behind them, the swarming lizards filled the hallways, making no sound except for the *plick-plack* of their billion sticky feet.

The running men, led by the Astartes, reached the second floor. The torrent of lizards was running up the walls, coating the ceiling with a carpet of scurrying bodies.

'Arkus! Delay them!' Herzog yelled out.

'Why me?' one of the mail-sleeved operatives wailed.

'Just do it. Broad burn!'

The operative turned, adjusting his lascarbine to the widest emission setting. He started to fire, blasting unfocused washes of energy back down the stairs, singeing and crisping the wriggling mat of advancing lizards. Tiny, smouldering bodies dropped off the ceiling and walls. The hand-painted wallpaper crisped.

Arkus kept firing, cooking thousands of squirming shapes, adjusting his aim rapidly to check each front of the swarming plague in turn.

It wasn't enough. It was never going to be enough. They reached him, and he screamed and jiggled as they rushed up his legs and his body, covering him. He started to flail wildly, enveloped by tiny, biting, snapping green shapes. He lost his footing and fell, crashing down the staircase into the main body of the green torrent. In seconds, his form was lost from view, submerged in the writhing flow.

Ignoring the grim demise of his operative, Herzog ran down the hallway, his moving weight creaking the old floorboards. He reached a door, and halted, preparing to kick it in.

Before he could, the door splintered in towards him, throwing him backwards. A snout, two metres long, shoved its way through the shattered opening. Shere yelped.

The crocodilian was a massive thing, the sort of creature that simply had no business existing on the second floor of a domestic house. It rammed its way forwards, its colossal skull swinging left and right as it came on. Its huge, scuted body and immense tail trailed back across the bridge into the neighbouring building. The house shook under its gigantic mass as it moved.

Herzog tried to drag himself back out of its path. Shere retreated, slipping over on the scurrying house lizards that were darting underfoot. Grammaticus grabbed him and hauled him to his feet, smacking the wriggling, biting things off Shere's robe with his bare hands.

The remaining operative fired twice at the advancing monster. The crocodilian lunged forwards, extending its white-scaled neck, and took the operative like a grazer at a waterhole, snatching him up in a huge V of jaws. The man tore open, screeching, as the jaws shook him apart like a straw doll.

Herzog, on his back, fired his boltgun, and blew out one of the crocodilian's eyes. It thrashed in pain, slamming its vast body to and fro into the walls of the bridge and the corridor, shattering plaster and shaking the building. The mangled corpse of the operative tumbled out of its jaws and it snapped forwards, seizing Herzog by the leg. Mail rings cracked and pinged away as the gigantic teeth bit down.

Herzog roared.

Grammaticus had never heard an Astartes cry in pain before. He decided he never wanted to hear the sound again. He pushed Shere aside against the moving wall of lizards and adjusted his ring. It was an Old Kind digital weapon, a gift from Gahet.

He triggered it. An incandescent blue beam lanced out from it and exploded the crocodilian's braincase in a wet blast of meat, bone and tissue.

'Come on!' Grammaticus yelled.

Herzog pulled his leg free of the ruptured jaws, and got to his feet. Limping, he led Gramaticus and Shere across the bridge. They had to clamber over the apparently endless bulk of the dead crocodilian. It was still twitching.

They reached the stairs of the neighbouring house and headed down. Herzog's leg was badly lacerated from the bite, and he was faltering. Behind them, they could hear the advancing patter of the lizard tide. The first few green shapes were appearing above them, scurrying out across the ceiling, some falling like drops of water down the stairwell around them.

'Where did you get that?' Herzog yelled at Grammaticus.

'What?'

'That weapon!'

'Does it matter?'

'You could have used it on us earlier,' Shere said, scrambling down the stairs beside Grammaticus.

'The fact that I didn't might persuade you that I'm serious,' Grammaticus replied.

They snatched open the main street door of the house, and came out into bright sunlight, and into the middle of a gun battle. Two Astartes warriors in purple power armour – one of them, Grammaticus was certain, the giant who had questioned him earlier – were exchanging shots along the dusty, sunlit street with gangs of nurthadtre ground troops. Crowds of braying Nurthene civilians were urging the nurthadtre on, hurling cobbles and other missiles. Half a dozen mail-sleeved operatives, anonymous in their desert shawls, were supporting the outnumbered Astartes. Las-rounds and ballistic loads streaked up and down the narrow thoroughfare.

'Pech?' Herzog called out.

The armoured giant glanced around. So, not Alpharius then, Grammaticus thought, unless 'Pech' was some nickname or surname unknown to the Cabal.

'Get out, Thias!' the giant yelled. 'We'll hold them here and rendezvous as soon as we can!'

'For the Emperor, Pech!' Herzog shouted, pausing to add his bolter fire to the fight for a moment.

'Let's go!' he declared, turning to face Shere and Grammaticus.

They began to run again, covering the sun-heated cobbles, the sounds of the firefight behind them echoing along the overhanging walls.

'Where to?' Grammaticus found the courage to ask.

'To wherever is safe,' Herzog replied. He was still limping badly.

'I don't think there's anywhere safe for us in this town,' Shere grunted.

'No, neither do I,' agreed Herzog, 'thanks to him.' He glared at Grammaticus.

'This was not my doing,' Grammaticus insisted as he ran. He checked his stride suddenly, flinching as he sensed the stomach-churning ripple of psyker activity again.

Shere had felt it too. 'What—' he began.

The street ahead of them split as if torn open by a fierce earthquake. The road surface burst upwards, and cobblestones flew like hail.

A vast monitor hauled itself up out of the ground in front of them, pulling its bulk free of the cloven street and the earth beneath. Cobblestones, hardcore and soil spilled out around it as it emerged. Its skull alone was the size of a lifepod. Its tongue, long, dry and forked, flickered in and out of its extravagantly massive maw. The tongue was as pink as Nurthene silk. The monitor was covered in cherry-red scales. They could smell the carrion stink of its jaws, feel the tremor of its advancing steps.

'Here be dragons,' Grammaticus whispered.

'What?' Shere yelled.

Here be dragons. It was no longer a quaintly phrased notation of warning, no longer the shorthand motto of man's ignorance of the darker places of his universe. Dragons were real, not ambiguous scrawls on fading maps.

Grammaticus could see into it, past the giganticised body it wore, past the scale and flesh and muscle of the varanidae-genus form it had chosen, or been instructed, to take. He could see the absolute fury of its daemon heart.

Herzog began to fire, slamming bolt after bolt into the red monster's head. Blood splattered from the snout, and two or three teeth were blown out of their sockets. The dragon lunged.

Shere screamed and lashed out with his pyrokinetic talent, and flames swirled along the reptile's back and flanks in wild, flaring streams. The immense beast began to thrash as its scales scorched. Flames travelled down its length, engulfing it in a molten inferno too bright to look at. Its whipping, burning body and tail convulsed furiously and smashed into the surrounding buildings, bringing down their facades in thunderous torrents of brick and dry mortar.

Dust rose in solid, gagging walls. Grammaticus lost sight of Herzog and Shere. He began to run. Behind him, the death throes of the burning dragon sounded as though they were demolishing the entire city.

Grammaticus kept running. He didn't look back.

FIVE

Mon Lo Harbour, three days later

'WHY IS THE city screaming?' asked Namatjira. No one had an answer for him, nor had they an answer to his next question, which was, 'Why is this offensive turning into a total farce? Anybody? Anybody?'

They shifted uncomfortably, the high officers of the Imperial Army regiments at the Mon Lo front. Namatjira had summoned them to attend him in the largest meeting hall of the terracotta palace, and they were wary of his displeasure. Lord Commander Namatjira had a famously choleric temper.

He also had one of the finest martial records of any Army commander in the Great Crusade: one hundred and three successful campaigns of compliance, the last twenty-four of which had been achieved as commander of the 670th Expedition Fleet. Nurth was to have been the expedition's twenty-fifth, making it officially Six-Seventy Twenty-Five, or the twenty-fifth world brought to terms by the 670th Fleet.

That achievement now looked to be in serious jeopardy.

Namatjira was a tall, dismayingly handsome man, with heroic features like the noblest classical statue, and skin so black it possessed a smoky sheen. He wore a frock coat of chrome plate armour over a deepwater blue uniform, and black riding boots with ornate chrome spurs. A floor-length cloak of painted silk hung off one of his shoulders, and a soldier standing to his left carried his fur shako with the reverence ordinarily accorded to a holy relic.

The soldier was a veteran of the feared Lucifer Blacks, so-called because of their coal-dust velvet coats and jet body plate. The Lucifers, an Ischian-raised elite brigade as old and celebrated as the Byzant Janizars or the Sidthu Barat, were all but extinct. Most of their strength had been depleted in the last years of the Unification Wars and, lacking the structural resilience of the Geno Chiliad, they had never rebuilt. During the Crusade, they had served a ceremonial role, providing companion retinues for distinguished commanders like Namatjira.

Five other Lucifers stood behind the Lord Commander, their hands on the pommels of their sabres. One carried a standard from which dangled the many laurels and sun disks, all stamped out of sheet gold, that enumerated Namatjira's triumphs. Another held the golden lead of the Lord Commander's pet thylacene, a regal, lithe beast with a dappled and striped mahogany pelt.

'Anybody?' Namajira asked.

There were almost a hundred high officers and uxors in the chamber, the senior unit commanders of the serried forces deployed at Mon Lo, some three-quarters of a million men. The two dozen uxors represented the

Geno Five-Two, and stood solemnly amongst various dress-uniformed officers of the Zanzibari Hort, the Crescent-Sind Sixth Torrent, the Regnault Thorns, the Outremars, and a clutch of support and auxiliary detachments. No one seemed especially willing to risk framing a response.

Towards the rear of the gathering, Honen Mu watched the Lord Commander carefully. She had only arrived in Mon Lo the day before, bringing with her the geno forces freed up by the conclusion of the Tel Utan offensive. She'd arrived in time to see the dispiriting disaster Mon Lo was turning into, and was therefore thankful that Namatjira could not direct his wrath at her. What was happening at Mon Lo had not occurred on her watch.

She pitied Nitin Dev. A major general in the Zanzibari Hort, and a damn fine warrior in Mu's experience, Dev held overall field command of the Mon Lo theatre.

Namatjira looked directly at Dev. 'Major general?' he asked. 'Anything to say?'

There was a pause. Lord Commander Teng Namatjira seldom toured a fighting zone in person, except to join the victory celebrations at the end of a compliance war. He preferred to orchestrate his campaigns from orbit. For him to make the drop to the surface, to risk exposure by visiting the sharp end of things, was a very big, very telling detail.

'No, my lord,' said Dev. 'I haven't.'

'Really?'

'Yes, my lord. I cannot add anything to what you already know.'

Honen Mu narrowed her eyes in admiration. The major general had balls of steel. Many times, she'd seen officers whine and dissemble and make excuses when brought to task by their superiors. Dev was making no attempt to wriggle out of this. He was taking it face on.

Namatjira gazed at the major general. Dev stood stiff and straight-backed, his eyes as glossy and black as the tight folds of the durband that secured his spiked helm to his head. Without expression, Dev half-drew his sabre with his right hand, his left hand clutching the top of the scabbard, and waited. Dev was showing he was prepared, at a simple nod from the Lord Commander, to snap his sword blade against the braced scabbard, to symbolise his disgrace and discharge, forfeiting forever his rank and rights. It was a brave offer.

'Perhaps later, Major General Dev,' Namatjira said, mildly. Dev resheathed his sword. The Lord Commander stepped forwards and the gathered officers parted to let him through. He strode down the chamber through the midst of them, heading towards the windows at the far end. His Lucifers followed him. The thylacene padded with them, lean as a coursing hound, its tongue lolling from its long, rapacious jaws.

'Eight months,' Namatjira said as he walked, 'eight months we've had to slog at this world, and still the sorcerous bastards confound us. I thought we'd finally broken the deadlock when Tel Utan fell. I thought we were about to prise victory from their dead hands at last. But now this, this *nonsense*. It's as if we've taken a backwards step. No, a *dozen* backwards steps. It feels like this bloody war is only just getting started and, Terra knows, it's cost us enough already. It's cost us blood, it's cost us men, it's cost us time. They're barbarians! This should have been over and done inside two weeks!'

He stopped in his tracks halfway down the chamber. The Lucifers halted smartly and stood with him, eyes front. The thylacene pulled up sharp on the golden lead and sat. Namatjira turned slowly, running his gaze across the gathered commanders on either side of him.

'It has been my recent privilege,' he said solemnly, 'to have shared communication with the First Primarch. Do any of you know where Lord Horus is, just now?'

No one answered.

'I'll tell you,' said Namatjira. 'Great Lupercal is fighting on a rock called Ullanor. He stands at the Emperor's side, at our most glorious Emperor's side, and together, for the benefit of our future, they are making war upon the greenskins. The bestial monsters have gathered in unprecedented numbers, and the Emperor has met their attack head on. Can you imagine that? Ullanor may prove to be the single most important combat in the history of our new Imperium. We may, in time, regard Ullanor as *the* defining victory of the Crusade, the moment mankind confirmed his mastery of the void, the moment our xenos adversaries turned tail and fled forever.'

Namatjira hesitated before continuing. He was still turning slowly, watching them all, his eyes shining with passion. 'And in the thick of it, the First Primarch finds enough time to contact the Crusade commanders, to check on their progress and encourage their efforts. What do I tell him? What? Do I tell him, *Good luck with the greenskin horde, we're having a terrible problem with a bunch of subhuman peasants?'*

He let the words hang. He raised his hand and gestured towards the ceiling with outstretched fingers. 'Out there, immortal combats are being waged in the name of humanity. The stars are quaking with the Emperor's might. Yet this is the *best* we can do?'

He started walking again, and reached the window. The chamber was high up in the palace, and afforded a good view out towards the city of Mon Lo.

The officers and uxors gathered in behind him. There was no doubt, even from that distance, that the city was screaming.

ACCORDING TO HONEN Mu's sources, the port city had started its eerie screaming during the early morning, three days previously. Within half an hour, the besieging forces had realised something momentous was afoot. Dark clouds, like the stain of vapour from a slumbering volcano, had spread above Mon Lo, and a wind had picked up. Oddly, despite the wind, the cloud cover in the broad sky above had slowed down, as if the planet had become retrograde on its spin. All of the astrotelepathic resources of the fleet had gone blind, or suffered sudden trauma shock. Word was, a powerful psychic force had been born in Mon Lo, the last bastion of the Nurthene.

The city had begun to emit a howling scream, a scream audible to both the regular soldiery camped outside, and the minds of the fleet's wounded sensitives. The screaming, both acoustic and psychic, sounded like the anguish of the damned.

The uxors and their aides had suffered particular discomfort, but everyone had been affected. Vox links had been impaired, and many Army units had been rendered nervous and undisciplined. Assuming that some calamity had stricken the city, Major General Dev had ordered an immediate attack to take advantage of the situation. The attack had stalled when significant portions of the besieging force had simply refused to advance.

Other stories had surfaced: plagues of lizards and frogs had been seen around the city's sewer outfalls, and petals of sloughed snakeskin had blown into the Imperial lines on the wind. Forward observers claimed to have seen giant things, great saurian shapes, moving around in the dust storms that had whipped up outside the city walls. Orbital scans revealed that the basin of Mon Lo harbour had turned pink overnight, perhaps due to algae infection, and that the pink stain was spreading out of the harbour area into the open sea.

Still, through it all, the plangent screaming had continued.

QUITTING THE MAIN chamber, Namatjira retired to his private quarters. He left one of his Lucifer Blacks to announce a list of the persons he wished to meet with personally.

'Attend! Major General Nitin Dev,' the Lucifer called out in his thick, Ischian accent, 'Colonel Sinhal Manesh, Colonel Iday Pria, Princeps Amon Jeveth, Uxor Rukhsana Saiid, Uxor Honen Mu.'

Honen Mu froze. *What?*

'DO YOU KNOW what this is about?' Honen Mu asked Rukhsana as they walked briskly along the hall to the Lord Commander's quarters. They didn't know one another especially well, having served in different theatres during their careers. Honen was much younger and much shorter than the long-limbed Rukhsana. She was also much stronger, perceptively, and rather despised Rukhsana, though she didn't mean to. The older uxor was in the last days of her command, and her 'cept powers were eroded. To Honen Mu, Rukhsana embodied the inevitable frailty that awaited all uxors.

'I have no idea, Mu,' Rukhsana replied.

'This is a mess, though, isn't it?' Honen Mu replied, scampering her little feet to keep pace with Rukhsana.

'Oh, quite a mess indeed. I understand you had some success, though. Tel Utan?'

Honen Mu shrugged. 'I was lucky.'

'Define luck, sister.'

Honen Mu glanced up at Rukhsana. Rukhsana's strong features were almost entirely veiled by her long, blonde hair.

'That is, I'm afraid, confidential,' Honen replied.

They had left their respective bands of aides waiting in distant anterooms. At the end of the corridor, a stern Lucifer opened a door and let them into the Lord General's suite. Namatjira sat on a low couch, with data-slates and furls of reports scattered around him. The thylacene lay at his feet, and he scrunched at its scalp and neck with his fingers, making it tilt its head back and purr. Major General Dev lurked in the background like a reprimanded schoolboy. Lucifer Blacks flanked the room.

Princeps Amon Jeveth was leaving as the uxors arrived, heading back to his Titan legio with a fierce scowl on his face. Colonels Manesh and Pria were standing to attention as they weathered Namatjira's abuse.

'Not good enough,' Namatjira was saying. 'Not good enough, sirs. Your forces baulked and refused to obey a direct order. I want to see some damn discipline!'

'Yes, sir,' they mumbled.

'Proper damn discipline! You hear me? *You hear me*? I aim to bring this compliance to a swift and brutal end, and when that end comes, I want your men in at the kill, no questions. I tell you to advance, you advance! Do not fail me the way you did Dev.'

'Yes, sir.'

'Get out of my sight.'

The officers hurried away. The thylacene opened its huge jaws and yawned languidly. Namatjira studied a data-slate one of the Lucifers handed to him, and then looked up.

'Uxors,' he smiled. 'Come close.'

They came forwards, side by side. 'First of all,' he said, 'I want to build the full picture here. Rukhsana, I'm told you were responsible for reconnaissance and scouting at Mon Lo?'

'That was my role, sir.'

'You had agents in the field?'

'I did, Lord Commander,' Rukhsana said. 'Most of them were long-range observers and spotters.'

Namatjira consulted the data-slate. 'But you had at least one intelligence officer inside Mon Lo the morning this hubbub began?' He waved his hand distractedly in the direction of the window.

Rukhsana pursed her lips and looked down. 'Yes, sir, I did. Konig Heniker.'

'Heniker? Yes, I know him. He's a reliable man. What happened to him?'

'He had entered the city covertly once already, sir, and briefed me afterwards. His intelligence was of good quality. He inserted that morning, very early, intending to collect data on the Kurnaul and north wall areas. He never came back.'

'Ah, I see,' the Lord Commander sighed. 'Thank you, Uxor Rukhsana.'

Honen Mu stiffened. The 'cept link between uxors was never that strong, especially between a fading veteran and a blossoming youngster, but Honen Mu could feel it all the same, a cloying dampness in the mind. Rukhsana was lying or, if not lying, shielding some truth.

She looked at Rukhsana. The other woman did not meet her eyes. She turned to go.

'You might as well stay, Uxor Rukhsana,' Namatjira told her. 'You'll hear of this soon enough.'

He looked at Honen Mu. 'Uxor Honen. My compliments. You, of course, know something these others do not. Tell them, because it's about to become common knowledge.'

Honen Mu cleared her throat. 'Tel Utan was taken thanks to the secret contrivance of the Astartes Alpha Legion,' she said.

Major General Dev's mouth dropped open. Rukhsana blinked.

'That's right, the Astartes have sent forces to assist us,' Namatjira said. 'Not before time. Lord Alpharius has committed units to help us break this struggle. We will meet with him tomorrow, openly.'

Namatjira rose to his feet and looked at them. 'In his messages to me, the Lord Alpharius has confided that the First Primarch personally urged the Alpha Legion to assist with this compliance. Furthermore, he has recognised that there is something about Nurth that defies conventional attack, and claims to possess special techniques that will remediate the Nurthene's ghastly wizardry. Those techniques seemed to work at Tel Utan, as Uxor Honen will testify. Let's hope they work here too.'

Namatjira looked around at Major General Dev. 'So it's all right, Dev,' he smirked, 'the Astartes are coming to rescue your reputation.'

'I'll take care of my own reputation, thank you, sir,' Dev replied.

'Good man, well spoken. Mu? You're the only one of us who has dealt with the Legion face to face. What do you make of them?'

'I have found them to be highly effective, sir,' Honen replied. 'They are Astartes, after all.'

Namatjira nodded, but seemed unconvinced. 'I cannot help wishing,' he remarked, 'that it was a different Legion coming to our side. One of the first, the old breed. Lord Alpharius and his warriors are comparative newcomers, with only a few decades' experience. I know, I know, they're Astartes, and our beloved Emperor does not found a Legion without full confidence in its abilities, but still…'

'What is it that troubles you particularly, sir?' Honen asked.

Namatjira frowned. 'They're not like the other Legions. They don't fight like the other Legions. They practise war in the most insidious way. Guilliman has said to me, on more than one occasion, that he finds their methods underhand and discreditable. They are sly and devious, and unnecessarily opaque.'

'Perhaps,' Dev ventured, 'that is why Lord Horus thought them ideally suited to this devilish war?'

Namatjira nodded. 'Perhaps. All I know is, they were already operating here, undisclosed, before I knew anything about it. Name me one Lord Commander who would be pleased to discover other men fighting his wars for him, without invitation, consultation, or consent?'

'It certainly lacks respect,' replied Dev, 'for them to have got involved without your knowledge, sir.'

'Respect be damned!' said Namatjira. 'What about strategy? How can I properly orchestrate a war if I don't know what a part of my force is up to? The potential for contradiction and misunderstanding is unacceptable. It amounts to manipulation, and that's the Alpha Legion's trademark. I do not appreciate being played.'

He sat back down and stared thoughtfully at his pet. 'It makes me wonder about this present fiasco. I do hope it's not significant that the moment the Alpha Legion embroils itself in my affairs, things go to hell in a land speeder.'

THERE WERE PREPARATIONS to be made. The Lord Commander dismissed them, and Major General Dev left the room with the two uxors.

'Dinas?' Namatjira called when the door had closed behind them.

One of the Lucifer Blacks moved quickly to his side. The Blacks did not walk, they padded, as silently and fluidly as cats. As if recognising an alpha male, the thylacene got up and moved out of the man's way.

'Uxor Rukhsana?' the Black asked.

Namatjira grinned. 'You noticed it too?'

Dinas Chayne looked identical to the other Lucifer Blacks in the room. The brigade made no great show of rank or duty markings. Only an expert in Late Strife Era regimental ephemera would have recognised the trio of embossings on his left shoulder plate that identified him as a bajolur-captain. 'It was obvious in her body language, sir,' Chayne said. 'The set of her head, the position of her feet.'

'Hiding something?'

'Undoubtedly.'

Namatjira nodded. 'Yes, I thought that. Place her under scrutiny. These are depressing times, Dinas, when we have to watch our own shadows.'

'There are shadows in our shadows, sir,' Chayne replied, citing an old Ischian proverb. 'This war has become a business of counterfeit and duplicity. We manipulate, and are in turn manipulated.'

The Lord Commander shook his head sadly. 'It is the latter I seek to avoid. Place her under scrutiny.'

'Uxor?'

Rukhsana stopped in her tracks and looked back. The palace hallway was busy with mustering troops and servants hurrying with platters of food. A servitor was lighting the night lamps. Honen Mu stood a few steps behind Rukhsana, staring at her.

'Was there something else, Mu?' Rukhsana asked.

'I'm sorry you lost your agent,' Mu said.

'So am I.'

'Is… is everything all right?' Honen Mu asked.

'What do you mean?'

The tiny girl shrugged. 'I don't know you, uxor, but I am your friend. I sensed a tension in you back there.'

Rukhsana combed her long, straight hair back behind her ears with her fingers. 'We were called to attend an angry Lord Commander, uxor. I think tension may have been inevitable.'

Mu nodded.

'Are you accusing me of something?' Rukhsana asked.

'Of course not. I was simply offering my support, uxor to uxor. If support were necessary.'

'It's not. But, thank you.'

They nodded to each other.

'Tomorrow, then.'

'Tomorrow.'

Honen Mu stood and watched Rukhsana walk away until she was lost in the crowd. Then she turned and went to locate her waiting aides.

They rose like hungry fledglings as she entered the anteroom, snapping and yabbering all at once.

'Settle!' Mu ordered.

'What's happening?' Nefferti asked.

'What did the Lord Commander say?' Jhani wanted to know.

'Settle!' she repeated, snapping with her 'cept.

They fell quiet. 'Tiphaine?' Mu said. The oldest of her blonde aides looked up brightly.

'Yes, uxor?'

'Go and find Boone for me.'

'Boone? Really, uxor?'

'Just go and do it, girl,' Mu snapped. Tiphaine darted away, slamming the anteroom door behind her. The other aides began whispering and chattering to one another.

I will not see the Chiliad disgraced, Mu thought to herself, I simply will not permit it. If there is canker in our ranks, I will root it out before it comes to light. The Geno Chiliad, worthy Old Hundred, will clean its own house. I will not leave it to others to purify us of con-tamination.

'Uxor?' Jhani called.

'What?'

'There is a hetman waiting to take audience with you. He has been waiting three hours.'

'A hetman? Which hetman?' Mu asked.

'Soneka of the Dancers,' Jhani replied.

* * *

MU WALKED INTO the side room where her aides had left Soneka waiting. Rush lights flamed in the wall brackets, and myrrh had been left burning in small scoop bowls. The shutters had been lifted, so that the cold and clear night air could be admitted. Through the window, Mu could see the distant outline of Mon Lo, shimmering in the darkness. The dull echo of its screaming came in on the wind.

'Peto,' she said.

He rose to his feet from a low couch. He had been cleaned up a little, but there was no disguising the fact that he was thin and unshaven. His clothes were ragged and ill-used, and he had been given a non-issue canvas jacket to wear.

'Uxor,' he nodded.

She went straight over to him, and hugged him, her small embrace barely encircling his upper arms.

'Oh, I thought you were dead!' she cried into his chest.

'So did I,' he admitted.

She stepped back to look at him. 'I was told Tel Khat was a massacre! A surprise attack… they said no one made it out of the Nurthene ambush.'

'Virtually no one did,' he replied. 'I got lucky. With Lon and Shah and about a dozen others, I fought my way out. It was a terrible day. We were…' he paused. 'We were almost dead, every step of the way. We fled into the hills behind the Tel, and laid low in the cave pools for a day and a night. When the place went quiet, we dared to come out. The Nurthene had gone. Everyone we found had been butchered. So we trekked across country, made it to CR668, and picked up a transport there.'

Mu sat down on one of the couches and reached out with her 'cept. Nefferti came in immediately.

'Food and wine, girl, right now,' Mu ordered.

Nefferti ran off to do her uxor's bidding.

'They've brought me food and wine already, Honen,' Soneka said, sitting down on the couch opposite her.

'You're starved. You need more,' she replied. 'You say Lon made it? Shah?'

He nodded. 'Both of them, eight other troopers. We lost Attix, Gahz, all the other bashaws. It was a slaughter.'

He wiped his good hand across his mouth. A faltering smile appeared from under it, as if by some conjuring trick. 'The Dancers have danced their last, I'm afraid, uxor.'

She hung her head. 'At least you're alive.'

'At least that.'

He drew a breath and stared at her. 'What happened about the body, Honen?' he asked quietly.

'About the what?'

'The body.'

She hesitated. 'I don't know what you mean, Peto.'

He frowned at her. 'Yes, you do. The thing Bronzi voxed you about from CR345.'

'Voxed? When was this?'

His eyes grew narrower. 'About a week ago, the day before the massacre. Bronzi spoke to you on encrypt for several minutes.'

Honen Mu returned his look cautiously. 'I swear on the Emperor's life, Peto, I have no idea what you're talking about. I took no call from Hurtado.'

She looked at him as if he were slightly mad.

Peto Soneka felt an odd sensation, as if the world were gently swallowing him up. The last five days had been little short of hell, but he'd weathered everything by focusing on one thought. Bronzi's words.

My ace in the hole.

'Where's Bronzi?' Soneka asked.

'Look,' said Honen Mu. 'There seems to have been an unfortunate lapse in the channels of communication. Why don't you start from the beginning, Peto?'

There's been no lapse, Soneka thought. We spoke to you. I heard your voice on the vox set. You were the only one who knew. And the next day Tel Khat was annihilated. Oh shit, you're part of it.

The chamber door opened behind Mu.

'Uxor? You sent for me?'

Mu looked around. Franco Boone stepped into the room. He ambled forwards, smiling at Mu, then blinked in surprise as he recognised Soneka.

'Dancer het? God's grace have me, I thought you were dead, man!'

'Apparently not,' Soneka said, forcing a smile onto his face. Franco Boone, the genewhip? What the hell is he doing here? Unless… he's part of it too.

'We were just talking,' Mu said. 'Peto was telling me how he'd survived the ambush.'

'I'd like to hear that myself,' Boone grinned. 'Juicy stuff, I bet. What happened, Soneka? I heard it was bloody.'

He sat down on the couch beside the uxor, looking at Soneka eagerly. Boone was a powerfully built man, with a nose like an axe's blade and a small tuft of black beard on his chin. He was uterine, but his abnormally high IQ, an atavistic aspect that was occasionally generated by the Chiliad's genic pool, had qualified him for the special role of genewhip. Genewhips were the strict regulators of the Chiliad's ethos, specially empowered to maintain levels of conduct and morale, and to enforce discipline and punishment. In another age, Boone might have been called a political officer.

Peto Soneka decided it was time to shut up.

'It *was* bloody, sir. But I've been out in the desert a long time,' he said, 'and I fear a lack of food has addled my brain, not to mention the wine the uxor's aides have been plying me with. Forgive me, I am all out of sorts. I'll tell you the story some other time.'

'Peto?' Mu said. 'What was that other matter? Something about Bronzi and a body?'

Soneka shook his head. 'I'm sorry. I think I may be slightly delirious. I keep doing that. Lon'll tell you. I keep talking about dreams as if they're real. It's the fatigue. Forgive me, uxor, I need sleep.' He rose to his feet. 'I'll find a billet and dream this off. Tomorrow, you may get more sense out of me.'

'Peto? Are you sure you're all right?' she asked.

'Good rest to you, uxor,' he said, and closed the door behind him.

Soneka strode away down the hall. He was perfectly wide awake. His world was unravelling from a point he didn't think it could possibly unravel from.

Just for the time being, he realised, there was no one he could trust.

'WOULD YOU LIKE to explain that curious moment?' Boone asked, once Soneka had gone. Boone helped himself to a cup of wine from the tray Nefferti had just brought in.

'I'm not sure I can,' said Honen Mu. 'I think Soneka was a little too tired for his own good. He was saying something about Bronzi.'

Boone smiled. 'And a body, as I heard it.'

'I know. It makes no sense. The poor man, he must be so strung out.'

'Soneka wasn't why you summoned me, then?' Boone asked, leaning back and sipping his wine.

'Not at all.'

'So why am I here, exactly?'

Mu told him of her encounter with Uxor Rukhsana.

'She was clouding something with her 'cept,' Mu said. 'Something she didn't want the Lord Commander to know. If there's treachery within the Chiliad, we have to deal with it ourselves, for the sake of our regimental honour. This must not become an exterior issue.'

Boone nodded.

'You don't seem surprised, Franco.'

'Someone's been playing games with us since we arrived on this damn planet,' Boone said. 'I've been aware of it, all the genewhips have. Insurgency. The enemy is trying to pick us apart from within, by means of guile and subterfuge. Subterfuge is like an iceberg. All the real weight is hidden under the surface. Let me look into it. I'll find out what Uxor Rukhsana is hiding.'

RUKHSANA ENTERED HER quarters and bolted the door behind her. She went into the bedchamber and froze.

John Grammaticus slowly lowered the laspistol he had been aiming at her.

'Terra's sake!' she mumbled.

'Sorry.'

'I'm going out on a limb for you here, Kon.'

'I know. You didn't tell anyone?'

She made a face at him. 'No.'

'No one knows I'm here?'

'No!'

He nodded and sat down on the end of the bed, the pistol across his lap. 'I'm sorry, Rukhsana,' he said.

He'd been saying that a lot, ever since he'd sneaked back into her chambers two nights previously. The man she knew as Konig Heniker had been dirty and dishevelled, and clearly distracted by an experience he didn't want to discuss. He'd told her, briefly, that things had gone wrong in Mon Lo, and that he'd had to extricate himself quickly. He hadn't been willing to add much more, except to say that his cover had been compromised and he didn't know who he could trust besides her.

'I believe I've been quite patient, Kon,' she said.

He looked up at her. 'You have. You certainly have.'

Rukhsana shrugged. 'This feels more and more like something I shouldn't be doing. Concealing you here, denying all knowledge of you... it feels like treason.'

'I suppose it might.' Grammaticus knew that he was asking a lot of her, and he was uncomfortably aware that she was only his ally because of the intimacy they had shared. She was now risking her career. She was risking execution. He had never meant for her to become involved in his business. The bond between them had grown out of honest attraction. He had not courted her just to use her.

But you're quite prepared to use her now, aren't you, he thought to himself, and despised his own weakness.

Almost all of his instincts screamed at him to get out, to get off Nurth and fade into the background, to segue back through the fleet from one false identity to the next, the way he'd got in. But that would mean abandoning the mission, and he simply couldn't bring himself to do that, because he knew how vital it was. A chance remained. He was still ideally placed, despite the set-backs, to accomplish the goal. With time, the sort of time he might buy from a sympathetic uxor, he could broker the contact and put the Cabal's scheme into play. It would require sacrifices. Grammaticus wanted to make certain Rukhsana wasn't one of them. He owed her that much.

Which meant he had three choices: abort and get out, use her cruelly, or bring her in on the truth.

'I can't hide you much longer, Kon,' she said.

'I know.'

'Why don't you go to the Lord Commander?'

'I can't.'

'When are you going to tell me what this is about?' Rukhsana asked.

Grammaticus rose to his feet, stared at her, and carefully considered his choices.

SIX

Mon Lo Harbour, Nurth, the next day

THE SKY WAS sapphire, the dusty earth cinnamon. Under the alien sun, the expedition's Imperial Army forces formed a corridor. To one side, the Geno Chiliad, the Zanzibari Hort; to the other, the Outremars, the Sixth Torrent, the Thorns. Ranks of armoured warriors stood ready, ninety deep, their banners and standards fluttering in the wind. Battle tanks and armoured speeders elevated their weapon mounts in salute. Horns bawled into the morning. Kettle drums clattered incessantly. Amon Jeveth's Titans formed a towering backdrop, backlit by the scalding Nurthene sun.

Overhead, the slow skies turned. The wind made a reptilian hiss, and the noise of the drums almost drowned out the sounds of screaming coming from the city ten kilometres away.

Namatjira was wearing gold plate armour, with a fan of ostrich feathers around his head, and a ten-metre cape of peacock eyes held out behind him by his slaves. Liquid gold had been delicately painted onto his face by his cosmeticians, and it had dried to form a tissue-thin mask. He held a silver Mughal mace in one hand, the sunlight glinting off its many jewels, and a golden ritual saintie in the other. The torso of his armour was engineered with two extra pairs of cybernetic limbs, and these spread to clutch a pair of daggers and a pair of sabres. Six arms extended, Namatjira resembled the death goddess of ancient Sind myth.

The Lucifer Black companions surrounded him, swords drawn, holding stiff, ritual poses of defence. The thylacene lay at Namatjira's feet in the dust, licking its coat. A marsupial tiger from Taprobane, it was one of the many lost species back-ginered from DNA samples during the Unification Era. Namatjira's pet was called Serendip. It gazed out at the day's heat with hooded, disinterested eyes.

Major General Dev stood at Namatjira's right hand in bronze battle armour, his durband crimson and his spiked helm silver. Dev carried a gurz and a long-handled sword. Next to him stood Lord Wilde of the Torrent, his platinum wargear glittering with rubies and emeralds. Lord Wilde's augmetic eyes were glowing green slits in his white ceramic face mask. He personally carried the vexil-standard of the Torrent, a four-metre golden pole surmounted with a diamond-checked tail and the gilt crest of the Pontus Euxinus. Third in line was General Karsh of the Regnault Thorns, his ritual chrome armour so thwart with spikes and recurve barbs that he seemed more the embodiment of a vicious trap than a person.

To Namatjira's left stood Khedive Ismail Sherard of the Outremars, a congenital dwarf dressed in graphite grey robes and a brow-circlet of titanium. His stature belied his level of influence in the Army and the hierarchies of Terra. Though the Outremars had supplied just five thousand foot soldiers to Namatjira's expedition, far fewer than the Chiliad, the Torrent or the Thorns, they were the backbone of the Imperial Army, accounting for almost seven per cent of the Army's overall numbers.

Outremar troops served in almost all expeditions and martial hosts, and their khedives, all dwarfs of the same blood dynasty as Sherard, were famed for their tactical insight and discipline. The Grand Khedive, Sherard's great uncle, was one of the Emperor's foremost advisors and confidants. Khedive Sherard stood on a small grav disk, suspended half a metre above the sand. The train of his grey robe, cut with a batwing edge, was held out behind him by eunuchoid slaves, each slave pulling taut a point of the batwing so that it seemed as if Sherard was spreading great pinions to ascend into the sky.

Beside him stood Sri Vedt, who held the rank of Uxor Primus of the Geno Five-Two units attached to the expedition. She was sheathed in a red burqua, and escorted by thirteen of her most senior uxors, including Honen Mu and Rukhsana Saiid.

Forty burnished servitors held long poles supporting billowing white canopies above the expedition commanders, shielding them from the sun's bite.

A transatmospheric craft slid down out of the blue, roared over the assembled multitude, and settled with a whine of dampers at the end of the long troop corridor. The drums stopped playing. The horns stopped braying. There was silence apart from the crack of the canopy sheets and the distant screaming of Mon Lo.

A figure emerged from the craft and began to walk down the corridor towards the waiting commanders.

Namatjira nodded and, as one, the vast host of men dropped to their knees. Banners, flags and standards sloped forwards in deference.

The lone figure came closer, trudging down the sand of the corridor, nodding in respect to the men bowed down on either side of him.

The figure wore silver-edged purple power armour. He was fully a third taller than the tallest geno warrior in the muster.

There was an awed hush. It took almost eight minutes for the Astartes to walk down the entire corridor to Namatjira. In that eternity, the only things that moved were the wind-caught banners, the slow-turning clouds, and the Astartes himself.

Ten metres short of Namatjira and his commanders, the Astartes stopped. Slowly and deliberately, he removed his left gauntlet and dropped it onto the hot sand. Then he unlocked his helm, drew it up over his face, and dropped that as well. His head, revealed, was noble: hairless, powerful, copper-skinned. His eyes were as bright as the sapphire sky.

He drew his gladius with his right hand, and sliced its edge across the palm of his bared left hand. Tossing the short sword aside, he knelt, holding out his left hand to Namatjira. Blood dripped from the deep palm wound onto the sand.

'Respected lord,' he said, his head on his chest, 'worthy and appointed master of the Six Hundred and Seventieth Expedition, I pledge my forces and my allegiance to you, recognising you as the proxy of our beloved Emperor in this theatre. It is my honour to add the Alpha Legion's strength to your fighting force. United, may we annihilate our common foe. To this end, I offer tribute in blood.'

Namatjira spread all six of his arms and allowed the Lucifers to take his weapons from him. One of them also removed the golden glove sheathing Namatjira's real left hand. Namatjira stepped forwards, his slaves releasing his long cape of peacock eyes so that it floated out behind him on the breeze. He stroked his bare left hand down one of the spikes of Karsh's armour, then held it out, dripping, to meet the proffered hand of the kneeling Astartes.

Their bloody palms pressed together and gripped tightly.

'I receive your tribute,' Namatjira replied, 'and respond with my own blood. The expedition rejoices that you have joined us. Welcome. I am Namatjira and this is my pledge. For the Emperor.'

The hands parted. The Astartes rose to his feet. He towered over the Lord Commander.

'I am Alpharius. For the Emperor, my lord.'

'REALLY? ARE YOU?' Grammaticus murmured to himself. Two kilometres away, he was observing the great meeting through a high-power scope from the flat roof of the terracotta palace's kitchen block. He kept low, carefully avoiding the eyesight range of the palace sentries, the jamming module attached to his belt non-invasively blocking the field sensors and the stationed gun servitors.

His scope was a quality piece, an eldar long-gun sight, another gift from the Cabal. It resonated the images back into his eye, almost as though he was standing at Namatjira's shoulder.

He could not hear their words from that distance, of course, but he read lips as well as any high-function logokine.

I am Alpharius. For the Emperor, my lord.

Grammaticus's perception was so acute and specialised that he could even lip-read accents. 'Alpharius' was speaking in common Low Gothic, with a rising spur on the middle syllables of *Alpharius* and *Emperor* that hinted at a Gedrosian or Cyrenaican basal slant. But the cursal lip motions suggested something akin to Mars hivecant, or even Odrometiccan.

The Cabal had briefed him well, but the problem was that virtually nothing was known about the Last Primarch. Unlike all the other primarchs, Alpharius had never publicly identified his homeworld. Furthermore, no definitive portraits of him were extant. The Cabal had procured many images, but they were clearly contradictory. It was as if Alpharius had many heads.

The face Grammaticus was watching through the powerful viewer agreed, at least, with a few of the historical portraits. There was a certain likeness in the cast of features to both Horus Lupercal and the face the Emperor wore, which made sense if the gene-legacy theory was true.

Even from a distance, Grammaticus could accurately gauge height and mass. The being he was observing was substantially larger than either Herzog or Pech, the bona fide Alphas Grammaticus had encountered in Mon Lo.

Maybe, *maybe* this was the genuine article.

The thought of Mon Lo washed angst back into him, unbidden. His hands began to fidget and shake. The dragon had been in his mind, and in his dreams, ever since his escape. Of course, he wasn't afraid of it *because* it was a dragon or, at least, he was no more afraid of dragons than any rational human being might be. The real, deep fear that chilled his soul was knowing what the dragon *represented*.

He dulled his mind as he felt another psychic pass. Shere was still alive, out there, scanning for him from time to time like a passing spy drone. Grammaticus curled his mind away like an armadillo every time one of Shere's probes came close.

The sun beat down. In the distance, he could hear the screaming. This was no life for a thousand year-old man. Grammaticus was beginning to think he had been a fool to accept the Cabal's gift of reincarnation. He began to wish, honestly and absolutely, that his first death had been his only death.

I wish you'd left me there, bleeding out on the asphalt at Anatol Hive. Why did you bring me back, and sleeve me in new flesh? Why? For this?

The Cabal made no answer. They had made no approach to him at all since his return from Mon Lo. From the moment he'd stolen his way back into Uxor Rukhsana's quarters, he'd spent hours gazing into mirrors and dishes of water, waiting for Gahet, or one of the others, to contact him via flect conduit.

They had not come to him.

My life has been long, he considered, but it is too short for this.

He trained the scope back towards the distant meeting.

SILENT IN THE hard sunlight, Dinas Chayne scaled the terracotta wall and slipped his black armoured form over the parapet onto the roof of the kitchen block. The most recent sensor sweep of the area had picked something up.

Or rather, it hadn't.

There are shadows in our shadows, sir. He remembered his own words.

Chayne had been on his way to search Uxor Rukhsana's quarters while she was out attending the great meeting when the security post had flagged the anomaly. The sensor sweep had revealed a vague blank on the roof of the kitchen block, a dead spot that the sensors seemed unable to read or probe. The adepts manning the security post had dismissed it as an imaging artefact, but Chayne had not been so quick to judge. In his opinion, the reading suggested someone or something well-veiled, a presence announced by its very absence.

Dinas Chayne was a wary man. He had been a soldier longer than he had been an adult. Born on Zous, one of Terra's myriad lost colonies, a planet that had been locked in a brutal global war for almost a century, Chayne had grown up on the losing side. Its economy bankrupted by the war effort, its industry shattered by saturation bombing, its menfolk decimated, his birthnation had begun to turn, in desperation, to its remaining assets. It conscripted its womenfolk and its children. Aged eleven, Chayne had found himself wearing the uniform of the National Youth, carrying an autorifle, and en route to a border outpost to fight. The youngest soldier in his company had been seven. The troop leader had been a boy of fourteen.

They had held the outpost for twenty-six months. The troop leader had been killed after three weeks, two days shy of his fifteenth birthday. Perhaps seeing something only children could see, the troop turned to Chayne for leadership. Barely twelve years old, Chayne had taken command. By the time he turned thirteen, he had killed sixteen men in open combat, and was a hardened, emotionally extinct veteran of that hopeless conflict.

Then the fleet of the Imperial expedition had arrived in close orbit. The war was crushed out in six days, and Zous itself brought to compliance in six weeks. It was one of Namatjira's earliest actions. The brutalised child soldiers were gradually rounded up during the subsequent cleansing campaign, and the fiercest of them paraded before Namatjira for his amusement.

The Lord Commander had always said that there had been something in Chayne's face that had marked him out from the other pugnacious, filthy war-urchins. Dinas Chayne wasn't quite sure what that meant, but he had been placed in the ward of a Lucifer Black officer, to be raised as his surrogate son.

Aged eighteen, Chayne had joined the Lucifers. Twenty years later, he served as the bajolur of Namatjira's companion bodyguard, and was one of the most decorated and respected warriors in the regiment.

Namatjira had a good eye for natural born warriors.

Chayne crouched low, drawing his short, curved sword of folded Toledo steel. The palace sensors were feeding directly into his visor, conjuring subtle green tactical displays in front of his eyes. There was the blank, the absence. Twenty metres left, at the rim of the roof.

He coiled like a cat, and pounced.

The rim of the roof was vacant. There was no one there. Nothing.

No, *not* nothing. On the low parapet, there was a scrap of paper, held down by a small white stone.

The scrap read: *Better luck next time.*

'HEY, WE'RE MISSING everything,' said Lon, nudging him.

Soneka woke. 'What?'

'We're late. It's started. We should get out there, het. The regiments have assembled to greet the Astartes.'

Soneka sat up. He was in the hospital wing of the terracotta palace, where he'd taken a cot to be with the last of his men, the last ten Dancers. The wing was sweltering hot and smelled of stale urine.

'You all right, het?' asked Shah.

'Yes, I'm fine.'

'We may not be a company any more,' said Lon, 'but I say we go out there and stand in the line like men. Like Dancers.'

'Yeah!' agreed Gin.

'You got the flag?' asked Lon.

Shah nodded. He'd been carrying the Dancers' tattered standard like a bedroll since Visages.

'Good,' said Lon. 'Let's go. You coming, het?'

Soneka was busy getting dressed. He was sweating. He couldn't find his socks.

'Yes, I'm coming, all right?'

'The Astartes have already landed,' said Sallom, gazing out of the chamber window. 'Hell, there's an awful lot of flag waving and how d'ye do going on out there.'

'Well, it's Astartes, isn't it?' said Shah. 'What do you expect?'

Soneka reached his good hand under his stained pillow in search of his socks. His fingers struck something hard.

'Did one of you put this here?' he asked.

'Put what where?' asked Lon.

Soneka held up a small, diorite head, one of the many hundreds of thousands that had given Visages its name.

The last of the Dancers all shrugged.

'Must have been me, then,' Soneka decided.

HE ALREADY REGRETTED the note. The note had been stupid. Cocky. Yes, cocky was the word. Gahet had forever been reproving Grammaticus for his arrogance and his over-confidence in his logokine powers. A Cabal agent should never bait the killers stalking him, especially if those killers were good at their job. Grammaticus knew enough about the Lucifer Blacks to realise they were *terribly* good at their job. He'd been a fool to taunt them like that. What had he been thinking?

That I'm immortal and nothing can kill me? Mon Lo had shown him how spurious that assumption was. *You just can't resist it, can you, John? That's all it is. You can't resist showing off?*

They're not that good, Grammaticus thought. Not compared to me.

'You can't come in,' the aide was insisting. 'Uxor Rukhsana is away at the Grand Welcome. Her quarters are private.'

Grammaticus stepped back into the shadows of the colonnade and listened. He had been slipping his way back to the sanctuary of Rukhsana's private quarters, the only place he felt safe. The palace was quiet, with almost everyone outside for the arrival of the Alpha Legion. Coming back along the hallway, he'd heard the voices ahead.

Three cowled and robed men stood at the door of Rukhsana's quarters, confronting the aide. Their leader was saying, 'You don't understand, aide. I am Tinkas, surveyor of fabric for the expedition fleet. It's my duty to systematically assess and evaluate all properties captured or commandeered by the expedition. I am in the process of surveying this palace. The work must be done, by order of the Fleet Master.'

He showed the aide some kind of paperwork.

Don't let them in, Tuvi, Grammaticus willed.

The girl wavered. 'This really isn't a good time, sir. My uxor's privacy is–'

'I simply need a moment to scan and assess. It's quite un-invasive. A measurement or two. We're not interested in the contents of the chambers. We will be discreet.'

Tuvi, they're not who they say they are. Be cautious! I've met Tinkas, and he doesn't wear a robe nor is he anywhere close to that height. You're being deceived.

'Well, I suppose,' Tuvi said.

Damn it, Tuvi! Grammaticus began to move. As the hooded men shuffled into the uxor's quarters past the aide, Grammaticus headed back down the colonnade and climbed out through the last archway. He clambered up onto the roof, and crossed the tiles, running low, heading for the far side of the block.

'Give us a moment,' the surveyor of fabric told Tuvi, and she nodded, waiting outside.

The door pulled shut behind her. Franco Boone pulled back his cowl. 'Two minutes,' he told his fellow genewhips. 'Two minutes before that little bitch suspects something. Quick and clean, no messing about.' The men, Roke and Pharon, spread out and began to search the apartment area.

'Boone!' one of them hissed. Boone hurried into the bedchamber. Pharon was holding up a canvas jacket, soiled and dirty.

'Since when does an uxor wear something like this?'

'Bag it and hide it under your robe,' Boone replied. 'We'll test it for genic elements.'

'Here!' the other genewhip called urgently. Boone went into the dressing room, and found Roke staring at a dresser top crowded with bowls and dishes of water.

'What the hell is this about?' Roke asked.

'Is that you, Rukhsana?' Grammaticus called, walking out of the wash room into the bedchamber, naked. He froze at the sight of Boone and his men, and grabbed at the bedspread to cover himself.

'Who are you?' Grammaticus yelped.

Boone hesitated, startled. 'Uhm, surveyor of fabric, we–'

'Genewhip Boone? Is that you?' Grammaticus growled.

'Do I know you, sir?' Boone asked, quite taken aback.

'I should think so!' Grammaticus snapped. 'Kaido Pius!'

'Oh, good grief! Yes! Sorry, Hetman Pius,' Boone stumbled. 'Sorry, sorry, didn't recognise you with your clothes off.'

'What the hell are you doing in my uxor's chambers, Genewhip? Sniffing around?'

'We had a lead, a lead about a–'

'A what?'

Boone paused. He smiled. 'All right, you got me, het. My hands go up. I wanted to check on Uxor Rukhsana because of information received.'

'What sort of information?'

'That she might be carrying on.'

'She is,' smiled Grammaticus. 'With me. It isn't just the aides who like to put it about, you know?'

'Shouldn't you be out at the Great Welcome, het?' Pharon ventured.

'Yes, I should,' Grammaticus grinned. 'But it's much more fun being in here. Shouldn't *you* be out at the Great Welcome?'

The genewhip looked at his feet.

'Well, I believe we've just embarrassed each other,' Grammaticus said. 'Me being here and you… coming in here unauthorised. So what say we forget this ever happened?'

Boone nodded. 'That's a splendid notion, het.'

'Is that my jacket?' Grammaticus asked. 'Toss it over here. I've been looking for that.'

Pharon threw the jacket to him.

'All good?' Grammaticus asked.

'All good,' Boone nodded.

'Good. Now get the hell out of here and I'll forget you ever tried this.'

'You won't tell the uxor?' Boone asked.

'Would I?'

Boone and his men left fast.

Grammaticus sighed and sat down on the bed. In looks and build, he was nothing like Kaido Pius, het of the Carnivales. It was amazing what a confident, clear tone of voice could do. Such was the strength of a logokine. A logokine's voice could tell you what you were seeing in defiance of your eyes and your better judgement.

But it had cost him. Exhausted, Grammaticus flopped back on the bed and stared at the ceiling. He knew a blackout was coming.

He embraced it, even though he knew there would be dragons in it.

OUTSIDE, THE GREAT Welcome was dispersing. Namatjira, with all ceremony, was leading Alpharius and the senior commanders towards his pavilion to discuss forward planning. The vast troop marshals were spilling back towards their billets and positions.

Coming out into the sunlight, Franco Boone paused. Walking back through the palace, he'd had a mind to find Uxor Mu and remonstrate with her for sending him on a fool's errand. How clumsy to have embarrassed a distinguished het like that!

Now he was in the open, a mist of doubt filled his head. The encounter in the uxor's quarters took on a disquieting, dream-like gloss. He found he could barely remember the actual exchange.

'Something the matter?' asked Roke, walking at his side.

'Kaido Pius, right?' Boone asked.

Roke nodded. 'Bare-assed. Takes all sorts, I suppose.'

'Rukhsana *is* a tempting prospect,' put in Pharon, the other genewhip.

Boone nodded. There wasn't a man in the Chiliad who'd disagree with Pharon's appraisal. 'But it *was* Pius, wasn't it?'

Roke and Pharon looked at the senior genewhip and laughed.

'Are you getting peck that's stronger than we get?' Roke chuckled.

'The question stands,' said Boone. 'Was that Kaido Pius?'

'Yes, Franco!' Pharon laughed.

'Then explain that to me, would you?' Boone asked, pointing.

Through the crowds of dispersing troopers, a hundred metres away, the Chiliad company of Carnivales was breaking ranks to head for their station. Pikes and banners had lowered, the men moving in easy groups, chatting, laughing, taking pinches of peck from their golden boxes.

In the midst of the huddle, joking with his bashaws, was Kaido Pius.

'PETO? PETO!' KAIDO Pius cried in delight. He pushed past his bashaws to embrace Soneka.

'Good to see you,' Soneka gasped, clenched in a serious bear hug.

'Good to see you? Good to see you, he says!' Pius cried to the bashaws. 'We thought you were dead!'

Soneka smiled, and embraced each of the bashaws in turn. 'I very nearly was,' he said.

'You got out of Visages, then?' Pius asked.

Soneka nodded. 'I did. Just.'

'Where have you been hiding yourself?'

'The hospital wing. I'm staying there with Lon and the others. Hey, Lon, Shah! Come over here!'

Pius shook his head. 'Shameful, that's what it was. When we heard about Visages, we were shocked. My boys have drunk to the Dancers' memory several times.'

'Thanks for that, Kai,' said Soneka. 'Glory, it's good to see you.'

Pius looked at Soneka. 'Come back with us to our billet. We'll drink and talk of old times.'

'Later, Kai, I'll come and find you. Where are you posted?'

'Line fifteen north, under Uxor Sanzi's 'cept.'

'I'll join you later, all right?'

'We'll look out for you, Peto!' Pius cried, already disappearing in the moving mass. Soneka was pushing on, through the shambling ranks, past the banners of the Threshers and the Arachne.

He could see another banner, up ahead, above the moving tide of troopers.

The Jokers.

Soneka pushed his way forwards until he reached the ranks of the Jokers. He had a terrible, queasy feeling.

'Hurtado?' he whispered.

Fifty metres away, through the flowing throng, Bronzi turned and looked back at him. The Jokers' het was flanked by Tche and Leng, his massive bashaws.

For a moment, through the moving crowd, their eyes locked. Soneka and Bronzi.

'Hurt? You're alive! For Terra's sake! Hurt!'

Bronzi frowned. Then he turned away and was lost in the tide of bodies.

'Hurt?' Soneka stood still, as the river of soldiers flowed around him. He wondered if he should follow Bronzi.

He decided that was probably a very bad idea.

SEVEN

Mon Lo Harbour, Nurth, the evening of the day

DINAS CHAYNE HAD been intent on scouring the palace for the author of the insolent, provocative note. He had not risen to its bait, or allowed himself the distraction of anger, but it had usefully focused his mind. Chayne held a frightening grip over his emotions, a skill he'd mastered between the ages of twelve and thirteen. He did not allow emotions to rule his behaviour, ever. Instead, he channelled them as fuel for his actions.

He returned to the security post to review all the feeds from the palace's sensor lattice, but one of the adepts had brought him a coded message from the Lord Commander, summoning him with immediate effect. The Lord Commander was holding his first meeting with the Master of the Alpha Legion in his pavilion, and wanted the Lucifer Black bajolur to witness and observe the proceedings.

'Have this run through full genic and biometric testing,' he told the adept, handing him the note. 'Report to me, directly on my link. Misplace this evidence, and I'll have you shot.'

The adept hurried off to do Chayne's bidding, a sick and anxious expression on his face.

Chayne made his way to the pavilion. A vast edifice of void-shielded silk marquees, it had been erected on a low tel south of the palace precinct. The first streaks of evening were discolouring the sky, and the shadows had gone soft and long, as if they were melting. Thousands of filament lights, in crystal shades, had been strung like climbing ivy around the structure of the pavilion, and they twinkled in the dusk like the lights of a distant hive. They reminded Chayne of the god-walls of the Imperial Palace on Terra, the mountainside bastions and soaring ramparts illuminated by billions of slit windows, and the great beacons of light that sent vast beams of radiance into the top of the sky. That was a monument no man could see without experiencing an emotional response, not even Chayne. In the older days, it was said that the antique Great Wall of Zhongguo could be seen from near orbit. The Imperial Palace could be seen from Mars.

Chayne entered the pavilion via the security portal, and submitted himself for checking and searches. On Sameranth, two years earlier, a security detail at the pavilion portal had waved him through, not wishing to interfere with a Lucifer Black. Chayne had ordered the detail's immediate execution. A Lucifer Black uniform could be stolen or copied. No one could be given access to the Lord Commander until he had proved he was who he appeared to be.

Chayne paused briefly in one of the outer tents to converse with Eiman and Belloc, two of his most trusted Lucifers. He explained the business of the note to them, and told them to return to the palace and continue the search. Their conversation, to an outsider, would have seemed odd. There was nothing convivial or comradely about it. Brief statements and instructions were exchanged or given. Lucifer Blacks related to one another in a dry, utilitarian shorthand, dealing only in facts. They expected one another to fill in any speculative blanks, and make their own conjectures.

Chayne had already decided what the note meant, and was fully confident that Eiman and Belloc had grasped the implications too, from the bare facts he had relayed. As had been suspected, a process of espial was active at Mon Lo, within the weave of the Imperial fortifications. The spies were good, able, intelligent and well equipped. Their loyalties were unclear. Chayne had suspected the Nurthene, but no Nurthene would have left a note in Low Gothic, unless the Imperials had massively underestimated the enemy's capacity for psychological warfare.

The note meant many things, but most of all it meant over-confidence, and that was a fatal weakness in any person. A weakness of emotion. It was quite a feat to be able to sneak out from under the piercingly vigilant lattice of an Imperial security system, but it was altogether something else to acknowledge that you had been there, to leave a trace, a signature, a calling card. Why evade detection, seamlessly in this particular case, if you then admit that evasion by taking credit for it? Two motives occurred to Chayne: someone wanted to goad him and play games with him, or someone was so sure of himself, the gamesmanship was part of the sport.

Either way, over-confidence. A fatal flaw.

The note itself, that little scrap of paper, would tell him everything he needed: the choice of language, the use of language, the phraseology, the psychology of meaning, the pen weight, the handwriting, the paper source, the type of stylus, the ink residue, the gene residue, the fibre trace, the note's position, the type and origin of the stone left to weigh it down.

The spy, Chayne's prey, had betrayed himself in a hundred different ways, simply by being cocky. And that cockiness was the biggest lead of all.

Chayne removed his black helmet, slid it under his arm, and entered the main chamber of the glowing pavilion. Inside, lords of mankind were speaking with demigods.

'KON, MY LOVE?' the dragon crooned, and licked his forehead with its red tongue.

John Grammaticus forced his way out of the dragon's biting jaws and woke up. Rukhsana smiled down at him, stroking his cheek.

'Damn. What time is it?' he asked.

'Night has fallen, Kon. Lord Alpharius is dining in the pavilion tent with the Lord Commander.'

Gramaticus sat up quickly, blinking. 'Damn! I have to go. I have to be there.'

'Be here with me instead, Kon.'

'I wish I could.'

He began to get dressed. She sat back, sullen and rebuffed. She glanced around.

'I think someone's been in here,' Rukhsana observed.

'Yes. The genewhips,' he said, nodding.

'Terra!' she asked. 'What were they looking for?'

'Me,' he smiled.

* * *

A SLOW SMILE extended across Namatjira's lips. 'I'm no expert,' he said, 'but you can't all be Alpharius.'

Alpharius, or at least the giant who had presented himself as Alpharius to the Lord Commander at the Great Welcome, tipped back his head and laughed.

'Of course not, lord. My Legion is one body, and we share everything. Identity can be used as a weapon, so we turn one face against the enemy. However, we are friends here.'

Surrounded by his Lucifer Black companions, Namatjira stood at one end of the tented chamber, the senior commanders of the expedition grouped around him in a crescent. The filament lamps covered the pavilion ceiling like stars, and lumen banks underlit the tent walls. Striped and spotted animal pelts had been laid out across the floor as rugs, overlapping and luxurious. Serendip, Namatjira's thylacene, had laid itself down on a speckled hide at the end of its slack, gold lead.

Facing them were four Astartes in purple plate. Foremost, Alpharius, his helmet still doffed, his copper skin lustrous in the golden light. The other three had joined him for the meeting, though no one, as Chayne would later discover to his consternation, could say from where.

Chayne slipped in through a flap at the rear of the chamber, behind Namatjira's entourage. Through a slit in the folds of the pavilion's walls, he could see gangs of liveried servants awaiting the order to hurry in with trays of sweetmeats, wine and fruit. Chamberlains were holding them at the ready.

'I am Alpharius,' said the copper-skinned giant, repeated the pledge-claim he had made at the Great Welcome. 'I have brought with me Ingo Pech and Thias Herzog, my first and second captains.'

Two of the Astartes behind him stepped forwards, removed their helmets with a click-hiss of collar locks, and bowed. They were shaven headed and copper-skinned too. A simple human glance would have read all three as identical triplets.

Chayne did not make a human glance. He appraised them, quickly and efficiently. Not identical triplets, not non-identical triplets, or even uterine brothers. The immediate similarities were strong but superficial. Alpharius was considerably taller than both of his captains. What was more, there was an evident ethnic derivation in the build of his cranium, a slope of the forehead, a mass of the brow. Chayne had been in the presence of Horus Lupercal, and he'd seen that distinctive physiognomy before. There was something about the eyes too. Alpharius's eyes were cold blue, and shone with an arctic intelligence that made Chayne shudder slightly.

Of the other two, Herzog was ever so slightly the taller. Chayne gauged their heights using the angles of the guy wires and sheet planes of the pavilion behind them. Herzog and Pech were not related either. Chayne counted eighteen points of dissimilarity between the comparative angles of their skulls, their eyes, their lips, the structure of their cheeks, the muscles of their necks, their noses and, most especially, the fingerprint-precise lobes of their ears. Herzog was older by twenty years. Pech was smaller, but stronger and smarter. There was a very slight but telling shadow around Herzog's scalp that suggested his hair was of a darker natural colour, and that he shaved his head to resemble his primarch and his fellow captain. Herzog's eyes were blue, like his primarch's, but Pech's were gold-flecked brown.

'Welcome, captains,' Namatjira said.

The Astartes nodded.

'And the other?' Namatjira asked.

The fourth Astartes had remained at the back of the group, his helmet in place.

'That is one of my common troopers,' Alpharius said. 'He is simply here as an escort. His name is Omegon.'

The warrior bowed, without removing his helmet.

The first lie, Chayne thought. Omegon is no common trooper.

Chayne estimated Omegon's stature, once again using the geometries of the tent structure as a scale. The Astartes was at least as big as the primarch himself.

Who are you, Chayne wondered? What are you pretending to be?

'Let us talk of Nurth, my lord,' said Pech, 'and of how we finish this war.'

Namatjira smiled. 'This *compliance*,' he corrected.

'It is a war, sir,' Pech replied, 'as I'm sure the stalwart soldiers of the Imperial Army would attest. Let us not dress it up in political terms. Let us not skip over their sacrifices.'

Major General Dev and Lord Wilde of the Torrent coughed to suggest their gratitude at Pech's acknowledgement of their efforts. Some of their huscarls and high officers clacked their swords against their shields in approval.

Namatjira snapped up a hand quickly for silence.

'Of course it's a war, sir,' the Lord Commander said, acid in his tone. 'Men die. *My* men die. But this is still an Action of Compliance, or are you questioning the Emperor's design?'

Pech shook his head. 'No, lord. I appreciate that the Emperor upholds a teleological scheme for the future of man, and I will endeavour to uphold it.'

'He chases a utopian ideal,' Herzog put in.

'He wishes to unify and perfect humanity through the intense application of martial violence,' said Pech.

'We have no quarrel with that approach,' said Herzog. 'It is the only proven way man's destiny has ever been advanced.'

'Even if utopian goals are ultimately counter-intuitive to species survival,' Pech added quickly.

'Any political ambition that is inherently impossible to achieve is ultimately corrupting,' said Herzog.

'You cannot engender, or force to be engendered, a state of perfection,' said Pech. 'That line of action leads only to disaster, because perfection is an absolute that cannot be attained by an imperfect species.'

'Utopia is a dangerous myth,' said Herzog, 'and only a fool would chase it.'

'It is better to manage and maintain the flaws of man on an ongoing basis,' said Pech.

'We say this only to recognise the blood debt of the Imperial Army, that suffers and dies, resolutely, in the pursuit of that goal,' said Herzog.

There was a long silence. Just as the blades began to batter the shields again, Alpharius said, 'I encourage my men to explore the philosophy of bloodshed, lord. I like them to understand the intellectual structure that informs their killing. The Emperor, my love and my life, seeks to set mankind in place as the uppermost species of the galaxy. I will not dispute that ambition, neither will my captains. We simply recognise the pro-crustean methods with which he enforces that dream. A utopian ideal is a fine thing to chase, and to measure one's achievements against. But it cannot, ultimately, be achieved.'

'Are you suggesting the Emperor's design is… wrong?' Namatjira asked.

'Not in the slightest,' replied Alpharius.

'My Lord Alpharius,' said Lord Wilde in his piercing, blade-keen voice, 'how do we combat the Nurthene… magick?'

'My Lord Wilde,' said Alpharius, 'we don't. We extinguish it.'

THE TRAYS OF food were heavy. There was no telling how much longer they'd be forced to stand there in the tented wings of the main pavilion space. The worst of it was, he simply couldn't hear. The voices in the main tent were muffled. Grammaticus realised he should have brought a listening aid.

He thought he'd be close enough to hear the proceedings for himself. He needed a revised plan quickly, or the significant risk he was taking would be for nothing.

'Sir?' he whispered.

One of the chamberlains came down the line to him.

'What's the matter, boy?' the chamberlain asked. Some of the other platter-laden servants in the line looked around.

'How much longer, sir?' Grammaticus asked.

'As long as it damn well takes,' the chamberlain replied.

'Sir,' said Grammaticus, 'this sauce is curdling. It needs to be set on the heat again, or it will spoil. I dare not, for my life, serve bad food to the Lord Commander and his guests.'

The liveried chamberlain nodded. 'Back to the kitchens with it. Be quick. They'll be calling for us soon.'

'Yes, sir,' said Grammaticus, and left the line, running with his platter towards the back flap of the tent's service entrance.

Outside, in the dark, he paused, and dumped the platter and its contents into a spoil bin.

No one noticed him. Outremar guards were distantly patrolling the edge of the pavilion's perimeter. He slipped into the dark blue shadows of the desert night.

Grammaticus pulled off the servant's tabard and discarded it. He hadn't disguised himself as one of the feast servants in any detailed way, trusting his logokine to get him by. But knowing he would be under scrutiny for several minutes, he had stolen a tabard to wear over his tight, armoured bodyglove to reinforce his logokine disguise.

He took a pair of low-light goggles from his thigh pouch and put them on. The world around him was instantly rendered in fuzzy, caustic shades of red and ochre light. He read the rows of taut cables that stretched from the side of the pavilion like millipede legs, anchoring it to the ground. Between these physical lines, he made out the web of intangible ones: the sensor beams and harmonic tripwires that protected the skirts of the great tent. Invisible to the naked eye, these thin beams would set off a multitude of alarms if tripped. Grammaticus adjusted his goggles to pick them up, tuning them to a harmonic value he'd cribbed from Rukhsana's code book without her knowledge or permission.

He skirted forwards, along the flank of the pavilion, looking for another way in, ducking under and stepping over the rigid cables and the ghost beams alike. In several places he had to stoop or even crawl to avoid breaking the luminous strands. Most projected diagonally down from small emitters attached to the lip of the tent's roof, but others followed the ground, or ran parallel to the pavilion, snaking between emitters spiked in the sand. The goggles guided him. This endeavour was a great deal more demanding than evading the field security lattice on the kitchen block roof. The beams were active and live. Three times, he froze, realising he was about to interrupt a beam with a leg or a shoulder.

There was no obvious vent or egress. Grammaticus found an open spot and knelt down. He put his ear against the skin of the tent, using its taut acoustics to bring the voices inside to him.

He could hear voices in conference. Lord Namatjira's tone was easy to detect, as was Lord Wilde's. Grammaticus identified the voice that had to belong to Alpharius, and listened to the way it sounded for the first time. There was a quality to it that was quite distinctive.

They were talking about the Nurthene magick and how to combat it. It both amused and distressed Grammaticus to hear the condescension in the primarch's tone as he explained the notion of Chaos to the Lord Commander and his retinue. What he was saying was such an over-simplification. The Alpha Legion barely understood the nature of Chaos, yet here was its leader presuming to teach even less well-informed souls about it. The Alpha Legion were the ones who had to learn, and soon.

Grammaticus was concentrating so hard on listening that he detected the Lucifer Black behind him with only seconds to spare.

Grammaticus stood up and turned. The Lucifer, who had come up behind him quite silently, was raising his sabre to strike.

'Fool!' Grammaticus hissed. 'It's me!'

The Lucifer stopped in his tracks, and quickly lowered his sword.

'Chayne?' he asked. 'Sir?'

'Yes!' Grammaticus snapped. 'Return to your patrol.' *Chayne*. Grammaticus logged the name in his memory for future reference.

'Apologies,' the Lucifer replied. 'I obey.'

The Lucifer turned to melt away into the night. He hesitated.

Shit, thought Grammaticus. His logokine skills had wrong-footed the Lucifer Black for a moment, but *only* a moment. Clearly, the elite companions possessed iron-willed, unsuggestible minds. The Lucifer had already questioned the encounter, and realised he had been tricked.

The Lucifer Black was armoured. Grammaticus was not. Grammaticus couldn't count on landing a clean, quick kill-blow, nor could he risk using his digital ring-weapon. The energy flare would set off every alarm within ten metres.

As the Lucifer turned back, Grammaticus threw a wolf-paw jab that crushed the vox-hub bulge on the side of the Lucifer's jet-black helmet, preventing him from signalling an alert. The Lucifer began to shout, but his voice was muffled by the helmet's padded snout. Grammaticus rammed another jab in under the chin of the helm and crushed the man's larynx, rendering him mute.

Grammaticus briefly hoped that the larynx punch might also prove to be a killing strike, but the Lucifer was made of stronger stuff. His sabre was still drawn, and he slashed at Grammaticus. Grammaticus blocked the blade with the adamantium strips woven into the forearm sleeves of his bodyglove, and drove the palm of his right hand flat into the Lucifer's breastplate, a tension-reflexive strike that the eldar called the *ilthrad-taic* or breathless touch. The Lucifer lurched, his breastplate cracking. As he stumbled backwards, Grammaticus looped his left hand around the Lucifer's right wrist, and whip-snapped it, forcing the sabre out of the man's grip. It landed on the sand, a bare centimetre short of one of the ground level sensor beams.

The Lucifer was not yet done. Grammaticus had been forced to close tightly, and the Lucifer head-butted him. Grammaticus lurched backwards, pain engulfing the centre of his face as the helm crunched into him. He staggered, and barely avoided an overhead beam. The Lucifer fumbled and drew his sidearm, his broken right wrist forcing him to use his left hand, across his body. As soon as the laspistol came clear of its holster, Grammaticus threw a spin kick that sent it skidding away into the night beyond the tent. He flinched as the tumbling weapon passed between two strands of the invisible security web.

This had to end, fast, before something got tripped. They were so tightly boxed in it was like fighting inside a spider's web, and any wrong move would bring the spider pouncing down on them.

The Lucifer threw a steel-shod fist at Grammaticus, who ducked left, and chopped a passing body-blow into the Lucifer's ribs. Grammaticus's hands, trained and subcutaneously strengthened though they were, were already sore and bloody from punching armour. Grammaticus tried to get behind the Lucifer, but the

Lucifer caught him and clenched him in a choke hold. It would have finished the fight, except that the Lucifer was struggling with just one working hand.

Grammaticus grunted and corded his neck muscles to ward against the Lucifer's choke. Training and experience told him there was one clean way out of the hold, a body throw that would hurl his opponent up and over him. But his goggles saw a sensor beam running right in front of them. If he threw the Lucifer, his opponent's body would land across the beam.

He kicked back hard instead, and the back of the Lucifer's head struck against one of the taut, diagonal guy wires of the pavilion. The impact snapped the Lucifer's head forward, and he involuntarily butted the back of Grammaticus's skull. Grammaticus winced, but the choke-hold broke. He swung around, dazed by the blow, and shot out a straight-fingered jab.

The middle and index fingers of John Grammaticus's right hand punched through the left lens of the Lucifer's helmet and popped the eye behind it. The Lucifer, gurgling through his useless throat, fell backwards against the tent side and slid down in a heap.

Grammaticus paused, crouching low, ready to sprint away if the impact raised an alarm.

No alarm came.

Grammaticus began to straighten up.

The Lucifer flopped forwards, matter dripping like glue from his ruptured eye socket, and began to crawl across the sand.

Grammaticus realised the Lucifer was dragging himself towards one of the ground level beams, his armoured hand clawing out to break it.

He threw himself onto the Lucifer's back, grappling with him, trying to pull the arm back. The Lucifer was monstrously strong. He dragged Grammaticus with him as he crawled across the sand, straining to reach the harmonic tripwire.

Vicing an elbow around the reaching, straining arm of the man underneath him, forcing it to pull short, Grammaticus drove another jab into the man's spine. Something cracked. Still, the Lucifer heaved himself forwards, ten centimetres from the beam, five, the outstretched fingers shaking as they groped for the invisible cord.

Grammaticus saw the Lucifer's discarded sabre lying on the sand beside them. He grabbed it, simultaneously wrenching the man's reaching arm back and up with all of his strength. He hacked with the sabre, and took the Lucifer's limb off mid forearm.

The Lucifer convulsed under him. He reached out towards the beam with his stump, but he was well short of touching it. Grammaticus hastily clamped his left palm around the severed stump and compressed to stop the jetting arterial spray from hitting the beam and accomplishing what the Lucifer's outstretched hand had not.

The armoured body under him went into spasm. Grammaticus pinned it down with his legs and kept the stump clenched tight. He felt the hot blood surging against his palm.

'I'm sorry,' he whispered.

The Lucifer trembled. Grammaticus put the tip of the sabre against the nape of his neck, in the tiny gap between helmet lip and collar armour, and pushed. The blade slid clean through the neck and bit deep into the sand beneath.

The Lucifer went still. Grammaticus waited until the pressure pulse against his palm finally ebbed away,

and then let go of the stump. The truncated arm
flopped onto the sand.

Grammaticus rose to his feet. The stench of blood
in the night air was overpowering. Some of it, a little of it, was his own. His fists were swollen and
mangled. Blood seeped from his battered face, and
pain made him see double. His skull throbbed from
the blows it had taken. He was sure his nose was
broken.

He tried to steady himself. He felt sick. There was no
chance of him continuing with his surveillance now.
The Lucifer would be missed soon enough. Grammaticus had to get away, fast.

He moved away from the body, stepping over the
tracery of sensor beams his goggles revealed, and stumbled away into the desert and the enfolding night.

DINAS CHAYNE PAUSED. Alpharius was busy talking to
Namatjira and the assembled lords about 'warding
countermeasures'. Chayne wasn't listening any more. A
signal light was flashing on the jet-black cuff of his
suit.

He slipped back behind the gathering and made his
exit through the service tent.

Outside, under the Nurthene stars, he put his helmet
back on and triggered the vox.

'Chayne. You signalled?'

'Vital trace from Zeydus lost.'

'Report his last position.'

'West side of the pavilion, twenty metres north of the
West Porch.'

'Route two men to that position. From the reserve,
not the ones stationed with the Lord Commander.'

'I obey.'

Chayne moved off down the west side of the huge pavilion, carefully stepping over and around the light-beams his visor showed to him. He drew his sabre.

'Trouble?' a voice asked from behind him.

Chayne whirled. The tip of his blade made a tiny *ching* as it grazed against the chest plate of the Astartes who had appeared, miraculously, behind him.

The huge armoured warrior looked down at the sabre tip pressing against his chest armour.

'Nice,' he said. 'Very quick. Dinas Chayne, isn't it?'

'You know me?' Chayne asked.

'The Legion likes to know everyone.'

'You're Omegon.'

The Alpha chuckled, his laughter carried oddly by his helmet speaker.

'You're good, Dinas Chayne. We heard this about you. Yes, I'm Omegon. I saw you leave the tent in a hurry.'

'You saw me?'

'I was watching you. You, you were watching me. Don't pretend you weren't now.'

'I won't.'

'We love the same things, I think, Dinas.'

'Such as?'

'Caution. Secrecy. Stealth.'

'How do you know my name?' Chayne asked. 'The names of the Lucifers are never published.'

'Oh, come on, Dinas. Do we look like amateurs to you?'

'No.'

'You can put that away, I think,' said Omegon.

Chayne withdrew his sabre. The tip had actually buried itself in the Astartes's chest plate and it took a tug to remove it.

'Any other man I'd have killed for less,' said Omegon, looking down at the dent, 'and, by the way, that's all you get.'

Chayne shrugged.

'Why did you leave the pavilion in such a hurry?'

'One of my men is down.'

'Let's see, shall we?'

The Alpha legionnaire led the way. Chayne realised, with alarm, that the Astartes was cheerfully striding through the serried sensor beams, breaking them without setting any of them off. Chayne followed, hopping and stepping over the harmonic tags.

'Something on your mind?' Omegon called over his shoulder.

'You are invisible to our security lattice,' Chayne replied.

'Like I said, Dinas, do we look like amateurs to you?' He paused. Two men were approaching, the two Lucifers Chayne had sent for. Chayne raised a hand to indicate they should stay back.

Omegon crouched down. 'Is this your man?' he asked.

Zeydus lay face down beside the tent wall in a patch of blood-stained sand. His left arm had been severed above the wrist, and he had been pinned to the ground with his own sword. The hilt of it was almost flat to the nape of Zeydus's neck.

'Yes,' said Chayne. He bent down beside the Astartes.

'Quite a fight,' said Omegon, pointing idly. 'His assailant crippled his vox to mute him. Right wrist is snapped, probably a disarming move.'

Omegon wrenched the sabre out and rolled the corpse. 'Muted him too, larynx punch. The eye's gone as well. Spine's snapped, between the third and fourth vertebrae. See? Someone did a good job here.'

Chayne nodded. Zeydus had been one of his best.

'I thought you Lucifers were meant to be tough?'

Chayne bridled.

The Astartes laughed. 'Relax. I know you're tough. I just meant, whoever did this, he did it with his bare hands.'

'What?'

'That blood there, on the vox bulge. That's the assailant's. He crushed it with his fist.'

'You can read that?'

'Rudimentary typing via optics. Yes, I can read that. We should take a sample for proper genic analysis. But on first look, I'd say your man was taken out by an unarmoured human.'

Chayne straightened up.

'Tell me, Dinas,' said Omegon, looking up at him, 'who do you know that could do a thing like that?'

'No one,' Chayne replied. His reply was honest, but he had his suspicions.

ALL ALONG THE earthwork of the Imperial fortifications, huge watch fires crackled, and a million campfires twinkled between them. Overhead, a cloud-scudded night sky turned slowly, retrograde.

The night air was hot. Around their campfire, under their lank banner, the Carnivales were laughing, and passing the bottle.

'So Lon made it?' Kaido Pius asked.

Peto Soneka took a swig from the bottle that came by and nodded. 'He did, like I said.'

'Good old Lon,' laughed Tinq, one of Pius's bashaws. 'Nothin'll ever kill Lon.'

Soneka nodded, took another pull from the bottle, and handed it on. Behind him somewhere, men were playing loud Gnawa on hand drums and ghimbris. Someone had thrown incense flakes into the camp-fires, and sweetened the smoke.

'Ah, but it's good to see you, Peto,' Puis said, taking a swig of liquor and then belching triumphantly.

'You too, Kai,' Soneka laughed.

'What will you do?' asked Bashaw Jenz.

Soneka shrugged. 'I dunno. Find another outfit that can use a few officers? I'm not worried about myself. I just want to make sure Lon and the others get placed all right.'

'Room for you all here,' said Pius.

Soneka shook his head. 'No room for two hets like me and you in this outfit, Kai,' he chuckled. 'We'd end up fighting to the death.'

'Maybe,' admitted Kaido Pius.

'You know it.'

'Maybe.'

'You know it, Kai. Terra, you're a good friend and gen-erous to a fault. I thank you for that. But I'm gonna hold out, maybe rebuild the company, maybe petition the uxors for a new one. Fug, what is this we're drinking?'

'Jenz's homebrew,' Pius replied, regarding the bottle he was clutching groggily. 'It's basically pure alcohol–'

'With a secret mix of herbs and spices,' Jenz added. 'My gene-da's special recipe!'

'You gene-da clearly had sanity issues,' Soneka told him.

Pius snorted.

'I've been meaning to catch up with Hurt,' said Soneka. 'I haven't seen him since I got here. He's around right? The Jokers are here?'

Pius nodded. 'Yes, Bronzi's here.'

'The Jokers are camped at line ten south, I think,' said one of the bashaws.

'What about Dimi Shiban?' Soneka asked, trying to make the question sound natural. 'You seen him?'

No one had. Despite the liquor in his system and the blazing fires, Soneka felt cold.

'Well, my friends,' he said, getting to his feet unsteadily. 'I have to drain now, secret mix or no secret mix.'

Pius and his men laughed and booed Soneka as he meandered away from the campfires in search of the latrine trench. The raucous Maghrebi rhythms of the Gnawa fell away behind him, and the hot, scented smoke thinned into cold, spare desert air.

'That's Soneka,' said Roke, passing the night-vision scope to Boone.

Boone took a look for himself, training the scope down the embankment towards the field of campfires.

'Yup. So he's hanging out with Pius, is he?'

'He's got no one else to hang out with,' said Roke sourly. 'All of his Dancers are bones in the desert.'

'We should have ourselves a word with Peto Soneka, I think,' said Boone.

'Why?' Roke asked. 'We're watching Pius, aren't we? Pius is the one you've got the twitch about.'

Boone shrugged. 'I know. But Soneka was acting real funny last time I saw him, and now he turns up here, breaking bread with the very man we're watching. I got a twitch, all right, Roke. Come on.'

Boone signalled to Pharon, and the three genewhips moved off quietly down the slope.

* * *

SONEKA STOOD ON the clapboards over the latrine pit, undoing his fly with his one good hand, wrinkling his nose at the rising stink of ammonia. He swayed as he urinated. Behind him, the Carnivales huddled around the crackling fires laughing and shouting. Amber smoke hazed up into the soft darkness of the backwards sky.

Something made Soneka look around. He buttoned up quickly, dearly wishing he could clear his swimming head.

A man was walking towards him along the edge of the latrine gutter, a silhouette backlit by the dancing campfires of the billet behind them.

'Who's that?' Soneka called out. 'Who is that?'

He hoped Kaido would hear him, but the men around the campfires were making too much noise.

'How's it going, Soneka?' the man asked.

The man was in shadow, but his teeth glinted in the distant firelight as he smiled.

Soneka knew him. Pharon, one of the genewhip's bulls.

'I'm fine,' said Soneka. He turned to walk away in the opposite direction and found Roke blocking his path.

'What is this?' Soneka asked, though he was sure he knew all too well. He began to sober up very quickly.

'You and Pius, you're tight?' asked Roke.

'Of course,' said Soneka warily. 'We've known each other a long time.'

'You know him well, then?'

'Yes,' said Soneka. The line of questioning was not going where he had expected it would. He braced himself for whatever verbal trap they were trying to lead him into.

'So you know about him and Uxor Rukhsana, then?' asked Pharon.

'What about them?'

'You know,' Roke leered.

'Kai and Rukhsana?' That almost made Soneka laugh. 'You've got that wrong. If they were carrying on, we'd all know about it.'

'Why?' asked Roke.

'Because… because if Kaido Pius had nailed a piece of ass that fine, he'd be bragging about it to everyone.'

'Maybe Kaido Pius isn't who he seems,' Pharon said, coming in closer behind Soneka. 'We met Kaido Pius earlier today, at least, we think we did.'

'I don't know what you're talking about,' said Soneka. 'Have you boys been at the homebrew tonight?'

'What's going on with Pius?' Roke asked, unamused.

'What's he into?' asked Pharon. 'You know him. What's he got involved in? Are you involved too? Is that why you're being so evasive?'

'I'm… I'm not.'

'What's the story, Soneka? How come you survived Visages when every other bastard there got cut to ribbons? Someone looking out for you? Someone tip you off?'

'Listen, you–' Soneka began.

'What's all this stuff about a body?' Roke asked. Soneka sank his shoulders, as if about to cave and confess to something. As Roke leaned in, Soneka caught him by the arm and pushed him into the latrine pit. There was a splash followed by furious, spluttered curses. Pharon lunged at Soneka, and took Soneka's left elbow in the teeth for his trouble.

Soneka began to run. Pharon came after him, hurling as much abuse as his floundering partner down in the pit.

Soneka scrambled up the embankment in the dark, and found the billet road. Torch beams chased him.

'Stay right there, Soneka!' a voice called out. Soneka knew it. Genewhip Boone. He started to run away from the beams and heard the crack of a laspistol. A bright puff of dust lit up the ground near his feet.

'Next one goes in your head, Soneka!' Boone yelled. 'Stay right where you are!'

Soneka didn't slow down. He sprinted along the billet road, looking for cover. Blazing lights suddenly came on and blinded him. He skidded to a halt, shielding his eyes against the glare. He heard the rumble of a turbine engine. A door opened.

'Get in!' a voice yelled.

Soneka blinked. Behind the headlights, he saw Bronzi glaring at him from behind the wheel of a battered staff speeder.

'Just get in, Peto,' Bronzi repeated, 'for fug's sake.'

Soneka got in and the speeder ripped away into the darkness, leaving the pursuing genewhips far behind.

EIGHT

Mon Lo Harbour, Nurth, continuous

'WHERE ARE WE going?' asked Soneka after a while. Bronzi was driving in silence, steering away from the Army billets and out along a crude track that ran into the scrubland south of the terracotta palace.

'Bronzi?'

'Don't ask questions, Peto,' Bronzi replied.

'I think I will. This–'

'Is bigger than you, Soneka, so shut the fug up. You're supposed to be dead.'

'You don't seem too delighted to discover I'm not.'

'Of course I am,' said Bronzi. 'You're my tightest friend. Of course I'm pleased you're not dead. But this complicates things.'

'What things?'

'Just shut up, all right? Just consider this to be your old mate rescuing you from the unpleasant attentions of the genewhips.'

'How did you know they were onto me?'

177

'Because I've been shadowing you all day.'

They left the established track, and went cross country, following dry watercourses between the dusty tels. Bronzi ramped up the speeder's lift. The vehicle's main lamps picked out the thorn scrub and dunes in their path in a frosty glare. The further they got from the lights and fires of the vast Imperial encampment, the bigger and blacker the night sky became, and the lonelier it felt.

After twenty minutes, Bronzi decelerated, and aimed the speeder along a deep wadi. At the end of an arid creek stood an old ruin, a place that might have once been a temple or, just as easily, a bier for livestock. Someone had lit a fire inside.

Bronzi stopped the speeder and killed the drive.

'Get out,' he said. 'Follow me. Don't be an idiot. I can protect you, but only so far. Please bear that in mind.'

'What are you saying?'

'I'm saying they wanted to kill you to keep things tidy. I asked them to give you a chance. So this is my reputation on the line, along with your life. Don't fug this up for either of us by being stupid.'

They walked across the sand from the speeder to the ruin. Soneka could smell fuel bricks burning. The flame light inside the place flickered and danced the shadows.

They went inside. A small fire of fuel bricks and dry thorn sheaves was blazing in the middle of the baked earthen floor. A man sat beside the fire on a lump of tumbled stone, cleaning his fingernails with a dagger.

'This is Thaner,' said Bronzi.

Thaner looked up at them, his face expressing very little interest towards either of them. He wore the uniform of a bajolur in the Outremars. His face was blemished down the left side by an old las burn. Even without the burn, his face would have been mean and tight.

'You took your sweet time,' he said.

'Yes, well, I got it done,' Bronzi replied.

'You're Soneka?' the man asked, still fiddling the tip of his blade along his fingernails.

'Yes.'

'You came out of Visages alive?'

'Yes.'

The man pursed his lips. 'That makes you either tough as a bastard or very lucky.'

'Little of both, maybe.'

Thaner rose to his feet and sheathed his dagger. He brushed dust off the front of his uniform.

'I'm going to ask you a few questions,' he told Soneka. 'You give me the right answers, things will be thoroughly civilised. You give me the wrong ones, no amount of tough bastardy or luck is going to see you out of here.'

Soneka smiled. 'Did they change the rules? I don't remember there ever being a time when an Outremar bajolur got to threaten a geno het like that.'

'Yes, they changed the rules, all right,' said Thaner. 'Trust me.'

'I have no reason to trust you,' Soneka replied.

'Yes, you do,' said Bronzi. 'Me.'

The fire crackled.

'I'm waiting,' said Soneka.

'Who have you told?' Thaner asked. 'About the body at CR345?'

'No one.'

'Come on, you're not fooling me. Who have you told?'

'No one,' Soneka insisted. 'Not even my men, the ones I got out of Visages with. Bronzi knew. I knew. Everyone else who knew about it died at Visages. Except Dimi Shiban, and I don't know what happened to him.' Soneka looked at Bronzi. 'What happened to Dimi, Hurt? You'd be the one to know that. What happened to him?'

Bronzi stared at the floor and didn't answer.

'So you haven't told anyone, that's what you're saying?' asked Thaner.

Soneka nodded.

'What about Uxor Mu?'

Soneka shrugged. 'All right, yes. I spoke to her about it when I got in yesterday. But she already knew.'

'Did she?'

'Bronzi and I voxed her from CR345 and–'

'When you told her,' Thaner cut in, 'did she act like she knew about it?'

'No.'

'No,' Thaner nodded.

Soneka cleared his throat. The flickering fire was beginning to play tricks on him. He kept tensing, as if seeing things out of the corner of his eyes, shadows in the shadows around the edges of the ruin. There was something – someone – out there.

'Look,' he said, 'I don't know why she decided to deny it. I assumed she was confused, or had her own agenda. I–'

'She denied it because she didn't know about it,' said Thaner.

'But Bronzi spoke to her. I heard her voice.'

'No, you didn't,' said Thaner.

'I did!'

'You really didn't,' said Bronzi quietly. He put his hand on Soneka's arm. 'It was an intercept. We weren't speaking to Mu at all.'

'That's not possible,' said Soneka. 'She used the codes, the encrypts, all the–'

'They're way ahead of us,' said Bronzi. 'Peto, they know all the codes. They listen to us.'

Soneka turned to look at Bronzi. 'Who's "they", Hurt? What the hell is this?'

Bronzi glanced at Thaner.

Thaner shook his head.

'One of you had better start making sense,' Soneka growled.

'Peto…' Bronzi warned.

'I'm serious with this, Hurt! Someone explain this now. What happened to the body? Did you deliver it?'

'Yes,' said Bronzi. 'I made the rendezvous. I handed the body back to the people who'd made it.'

'I don't know what that means,' snapped Soneka. 'I don't know what the fug that means, Bronzi. What happened to Shiban? Where is he? Is he dead?'

Bronzi stared at Soneka. There was a hard look in his eyes. 'He was dead before he got on the transport,' he said.

'I don't know what that means either,' Soneka growled.

'That wound he took, the shrapnel wound here,' Bronzi said, gesturing towards his throat. 'Some of it was bone, Nurthene bone.'

'I know. That happens,' said Soneka.

'You don't know, Peto,' said Bronzi, uncomfortable. 'It was in him. It was in him and it was just a matter of time before it turned him. They knew that. They shot him. They would have had to anyway.'

'You keep saying *they*. Who the fug is *they*?'

'We don't have to tell you anything we don't w–' Thaner began to say.

Peto Soneka had always been quick. The snub-nosed laspistol was in his hand and aimed at Thaner before either he or Bronzi had a chance to react.

'Start explaining this mess now,' Soneka ordered. 'Right now.'

'Oh, Peto, come *on*–' Bronzi moaned.

'You shut up. Don't think I won't aim this at you too.'

'Put it away,' said Thaner.

'I want answers first,' said Soneka.

Thaner sighed. Keeping his hands clearly open, so Soneka could follow what he was doing, he reached down to his midriff and untucked his tunic. He pulled the garment up, along with the vest beneath, and exposed the corded muscle of his right hip. Soneka could see the brand mark quite clearly.

'Oh… *shit*,' Soneka murmured.

'The body was one of our people,' said Thaner, lowering his tunic. 'It got recovered from the field before our retrieval teams could locate it. We needed it back.'

'It was dressed as one of my men,' said Soneka.

'It was a Hort sergeant called Lyel Wilk,' said Thaner, matter-of-factly. 'He was operating as one of your men.'

Soneka had a million questions, and knew every single one of them had an ugly answer. None of the questions would form in his mouth. He was struck dumb by the sensation of the universe as he knew it grinding out of joint around him. Since that bloody dawn when Visages had been sacked, and most especially since his meeting with Honen Mu the night before, total dislocation had been looming. Now everything he trusted tore away and revealed nothing: no answers, no explanations, no single thing he could trust or recognise.

Simple panic seized him. He aimed the pistol at Thaner's head and squeezed the trigger. Something crunched into him from the side and the shot went wild as he fell. The something was Bronzi. Bronzi had punched him.

Before Soneka could begin to process that information, Thaner had kicked the pistol out of his hand. It skittered away into the crawling shadows. Thaner put a second kick into Soneka's gut to keep him down. It was a brutal blow. The air crashed out of Soneka's lungs and he felt a deep, internal pain that could only be organs rupturing.

'He's no use to us,' Soneka heard Thaner tell Bronzi. Thaner drew his dagger.

'Don't!' Bronzi warned.

'He's a liability. We can't use him.'

Gasping, agonised, Soneka writhed. He saw Thaner coming towards him, dagger held low for the old jab and twist.

'We've taken him this far,' said a voice. 'Why don't we show him the rest? If he still objects, you can put that in his heart, Thaner.'

Soneka's lungs began to work. He sucked in air, choking, tears streaming down his cheeks.

'Peto?' Bronzi was calling. 'Peto, look at me. Peto?'

Soneka looked up. Bronzi had pulled up his own shirt. His right hip was a good deal more upholstered in flesh than Thaner's, but the brand was exactly the same.

'Oh glory,' Soneka wheezed. 'No… not you too, Hurt…'

'It's the mark of the hydra,' the voice said. 'It's the mark we bestow upon our friends, the friends we can trust.'

Soneka heard heavy footsteps crunch across the hard-baked floor towards him. A shadow fell across him, blocking out the light of the fire.

Even in silhouette, Soneka recognised it. An Astartes in full plate.

'Alpha Legion…' Soneka whispered.

'Exactly.' The Alpha legionnaire knelt down over Soneka. 'I believe you're a good man, Peto – honest and trustworthy. I think we could be friends. I have no wish to kill you, but I will, without compunction, if you maintain this stance of resistance.'

'Then stop lying to me,' Soneka moaned, his voice shrunk by pain.

'I'm not, Peto.'

'What's your name?'

'Alpharius.'

Peto Soneka started to laughed. It was a ragged, painful sound. 'Lies, lies, more lies. I know for a fact that Lord Alpharius is in the grand pavilion right now, meeting with Lord Commander Namatjira. You're lying to me, so you might as well kill me now and get it over with.'

'Give me your blade, Thaner,' said the Astartes.

'FOR THE PROSECUTION of Mon Lo, I will require full access to, and use of, your astrotelepaths, sir,' said Alpharius.

'Why?' asked Lord Namatjira.

The assembly was seated at the low couches, as servants brought in the feast. Namatjira marvelled at the nimble finesse with which the Astartes manoeuvred food into their mouths using their huge gauntlets. Despite their bulk and crude size, these beings were dextrous and refined.

'Psychic power is a key weapon in denying the Nurthene menace,' said Pech.

'This menace...' Namatjira said. 'You have spoken already of this force of Chaos, but I fear it sounds like dark age nonsense and superstition.'

Alpharius smiled, expertly shucking a piece of shellfish that was dwarfed by his motorised glove. He slid the pink flesh into his mouth. 'You have seen it at work, my lord. How do you account for it? Lord Wilde insists on referring to it as magick.'

'It's not magick,' said Herzog.

'And yet it is,' said Pech. 'It is the very quantity that mankind has called magick since the very start of his history.'

'What Ingo and Thias mean,' said Alpharius, 'is that there is a primal power in our galaxy that defies comprehension. It is foul and it is powerful, and it exists sidelong to our frame of reference. It resides in the warp.'

'And this, you say, is *Chaos*?' asked Namatjira.

'We use the word Chaos, but that term is very imprecise. It is a primordial force, and may be used by those who have fallen under its influence.'

'You've seen it before?'

'Yes, my lord, once or twice. It is a cosmic bane, a toxic effect that flows freely in some places. It subverts the mind and the will, it corrupts.'

'Will it corrupt us?' asked Namatjira.

'Of course not!' Alpharius laughed, shelling another piece of seafood. 'It is not some kind of plague. But it is deeply ingrown in the Nurthene society. It gives them access to many skills that we would consider occult. Psykers are our best defence against Chaos. They will allow us to extinguish the enemy's advantage here. For the same reason, I would like the Geno Chiliad to be deployed at the front of our assault when it comes.'

'For what same reason?' asked Namatjira.

'The Chiliad uxors are rudimentary psykers. That will lend us an advantage.'

'So be it,' said Namatjira. He looked at Alpharius. 'I'm trusting you, lord primarch. I'm trusting you to make a clean fist of this debacle.'

'Your trust is not misplaced, sir,' replied Alpharius.

Dinas Chayne appeared behind Lord Namatjira, and whispered in his ear.

Namatjira nodded. 'My apologies, lord primarch. Much as I find this conversation fascinating, I must withdraw now. There are matters to attend to.'

Alpharius nodded. 'I understand. I too, must go. Omegon has signalled me. Thank you for this feast, sir. It was a true and warm welcome.'

They rose. A hush fell.

'Everyone,' Namatjira called out, 'everyone, please continue to enjoy this evening. Let nothing spoil your hard-won relaxation. My Lord Alpharius and I must withdraw to consider the days ahead. Eat and drink to your surfeit!'

Approval ran around the vast tent.

'It has been my pleasure to meet you all,' said Alpharius. 'I am convinced that, together, we will finish this compliance in under a week. Ladies, gentlemen, feast well.'

He raised his cup and drank deeply.

A servant took Alpharius's empty cup from him. 'Lord Commander?' Alpharius nodded graciously to Namatjira.

'I have learned a great deal tonight, Lord Alpharius. My view of the cosmic order has been altered. I hope we may speak further on this subject.'

'Of course.'

'Terra rest you and the Emperor protect you,' said Namatjira.

They left the pavilion in opposite directions. The carousing continued behind them.

By the south porch, Namatjira exited into the cold night. His Lucifers were waiting for him.

'Report,' said Namatjira. 'Have you uncovered anything on Uxor Rukhsana?'

'No,' said Chayne. 'But there is definitely a foreign agent at work in our midst. The spy has slain one of my men, right outside the pavilion. He's too close and too good. We need to purge our ranks at once.'

Namatjira nodded. 'See to it. You have my full sanction. By the way, what did you make of the Astartes, Dinas?'

Dinas Chayne looked back at his lord and commander coldly. 'Every single one of them was lying,' he said.

AT THE WEST porch, Alpharius, Pech and Herzog strode out into the night. Omegon was waiting for them. He had dismissed the perimeter guards so they could be alone. The four hulking armoured figures fell into step and began to cross the open dunes towards their lander in the cool, violet darkness.

'How was I?' asked the Astartes who had played the role of Alpharius all night.

'Imperial,' Pech replied.

'Masterful,' said Herzog. 'But then, you do have a certain advantage, Omegon. Besides, I think you enjoy playing the part of primarch.'

'Don't we all?' chuckled Pech.

'So, Sheed,' said Omegon, glancing at the Astartes who had worn the name Omegon in his place that evening. 'What's the story?'

Sheed Ranko, master of the Alpha's Terminator elite, was an especially large Astartes, who doubled well for both Omegon and Lord Alpharius in diplomatic circumstances. He shrugged his massive, plated shoulders. 'Grammaticus was here, trying to spy on the meeting. He took out a Lucifer Black.'

'He's good, then?' asked Omegon.

'He's very good,' Herzog assured.

'But he's hurt,' said Ranko, 'busted up. I typed his blood.'

'Get a match?' asked Pech.

'Yes. Konig Heniker. Apparently, one of the Army spies. Deep cover agent, specialist.'

'He's Grammaticus?'

Ranko nodded. 'I think so. He's a sly one, and very capable. The Lucifers are scared of him, and very little scares those wily bastards. We have to find him, and before they do. I've told Shere to hunt for him.'

'What are we waiting for?' asked Herzog.

'Where's Alpharius?' Omegon asked.

'Out in the dune wastes,' Sheed Ranko replied. 'Tidying up another loose end.'

NINE

Mon Lo Harbour, Nurth, just before the evening dawn the next day

By SHEER STRENGTH of will and the straining muscle power of his arms, John Grammaticus forced open the jaws of the dragon that was swallowing him and tumbled out of its furnace maw onto the cold sand.

He was too weak to fight any more, but that was all right. The dragon had gone away, as all dream things do when a person wakes.

Grammaticus lay shivering for a while in the basin behind the lonely tel. The injuries he'd taken the night before were worse than he had realised. His hands were torn raw, and most of his fingers refused to bend, either because they were too swollen, or because they were broken. His forearms were striped with blue bruises from deflecting the Lucifer's sabre blows, despite his sleeve armour. His face was sore and throbbing, swelling out around the bridge of his shattered nose and half shutting his eyes. His nostrils were black with caked blood and the back of his head was a contusion too tender to be touched.

He'd been in pain the night before, but he'd also been warm, and fuelled by adrenaline. Sleeping rough had reduced his core temperature and robbed him of every sensation except nausea and aching hurt.

After his confrontation with the Lucifer, Grammaticus had fled into the desert. There had been no sense or safety in heading for the terracotta palace. Grammaticus knew he was now being hunted by at least two formidable enemies, the Alpha Legion and the Lord Commander's companion retinue. He'd found a place to shelter out in the dune sea, and had gone to sleep speculating on how best to resume his mission.

However, in the freezing dawn, shivering and hurt, Grammaticus was starting to believe his mission was no longer viable. What little chance there might have been to redeem himself and finish his work had probably vanished. He feared he was too hurt and too compromised to risk continuing. Perhaps it was time to abandon the mission and get out. The Cabal would just have to find another way of accomplishing its designs.

He got up, unsteadily. Thin light was beginning to pour over the horizon as dawn sliced its way into the sky. It would be bone-chill for another hour or so, then the sun would rise fully, like a bleach spot on pink blotting paper, and the land would bake. And then he would be dead.

But John Grammaticus had not fled blindly into the empty desert quarter. He read charts as well as he read lips. Before immersing himself in the Mon Lo offensive, he'd spent three days reconnoitring the desert edge twenty kilometres south of the palace. He'd methodically dug in contingency bolt holes, each one ready to play its part in whatever exit strategy he might be forced to use.

Yes, he decided, it was time to go now, more than time. He'd done his best, and he'd failed. He'd been a fool to stay on as long as he had, especially after the business with the dragon. His expectations had reduced to three, simple possibilities. He could escape, alive, and attempt to persuade the Cabal his failure on Nurth was not an eliminating offence. He could escape, and hide from the Cabal for as long as his wits held out. Or he could die in the desert. The Cabal was not the forgiving master it may have once been, but the first option seemed the best, nevertheless. He prayed he was still useful enough as a toy to be spared.

He walked west for a kilometre, glanding a little boost to wake himself up and sharpen his senses. The chemical boost helped numb the throb in his arms, his knuckles and his skull. As his mind cleared, he took stock, and verified his position using landmarks that he had patiently memorised during his reconnoitre: a pile of six, flat stones; a pronghorn skull, decades old; a patch of scrub that looked like a map of the Crimea.

In just under fifteen minutes, he found the pool.

It lay at the bottom of an especially deep wadi, a slick of left-over winter rain that the long summer had not yet quite evaporated. The pool was less than a metre deep at its centre, and the water had reduced down to a brackish, brown silt. It was unpotable, but pure enough to clean himself with. He winced as the mineral salts in the water burned and sterilised his wounds.

He groaned through gritted teeth as he sluiced the liquid against the back of his skull with his wounded hands.

The first rays of the rising sun began to stab into the cold blackness of the gulley like laser spears. Grammaticus gingerly traced the wadi wall around to a place marked with two lumps of onyx. He dug the sand away clumsily with his damaged hands and pulled out the kitbag he'd buried there.

It was a standard Army clip-lock satchel, woven from waterproof canvas. Inside were two litre bottles of rehydration fluid, a pack of ration bars which he began to eat immediately, a medicae capsule, a collapsible knife, a laspistol with two spare charge clips, three chemical flares, an autolocator, a clean bodyglove, rolled up around a plastek-wrapped sheaf of documents, and a write-enabled data-slate.

He sat down, munching on one of the ration bars and taking the odd swig of fluid from one of the bottles. He sorted through the documents: two pre-prepared alternate identities, along with two sets of blanks that he could make up quickly using the genic traces loaded into the data-slate.

He ran through one of his exit strategies. The food and fluid would get him as far as his next cache of supplies, eight kilometres south. Then he'd use the autolocator to call in a rescue ship from the fleet. The flares would help the ship find him. They'd be all too keen to pick up a precious Geno Five-Two hetman lost in the desert edge, and that was precisely what one of his pre-prepared documents said he was. He'd been careful to make up a set using the ident of a het missing and lost during the last few weeks. Peto Albari Soneka, het of the Dancers, missing in action since the CR345 raid. Grammaticus idly practised a Feodosiyac accent. He could carry that off, no problem.

By the time anyone realised he wasn't Peto Soneka, he'd have vanished behind two or three other stolen identities and become lost in the data labyrinth of the fleet. Then, what? A berth on a supply vessel heading towards the core regions? Something simple. Something unfussy. A hundred ships came and went every day, servicing and supplying the huge demands of the advancing 670th Fleet. He'd be gone on one of them before anyone knew it, and on some backwater colony, ninety light years away, he'd step off and disappear forever. *Forever.*

He thought about using the medicae capsule to tend his injuries, then considered that dirty wounds would reinforce any survivor story he attempted to weave.

Grammaticus sighed and began to repack his bag. He tried not to think about Rukhsana Saiid any more. Gahet, that old bastard, had been quite right. That had been a wrong step. It hadn't impaired his mission so much as it had impaired her chances of survival. It was likely that she would pay the price for his disappearance. Once again, he despised his own weakness. He had used her so badly, so knowingly, and yet the sad truth of it was that he had genuine feelings for her. Perhaps, once he was back in the fleet and functioning under a new identity, he might arrange to have her recalled. He'd get her out and take her with him. Of course, that risked exposure… perhaps too *much* exposure.

'I am a coward,' he told the desert out loud, tears on his cheeks.

'You are,' the desert replied.

Grammaticus leapt to his feet, his heart pounding. He fought to get his broken fingers to take hold of the laspistol, and aimed it.

At nothing.

He snatched around, chasing the source of the voice, the pistol braced.

+ Show yourself! + he sent.

'I'm right here, John.'

He looked down at the stained pool. The Cabal was using it as a flect. It wasn't Gahet this time. This time, they'd sent Slau Dha.

'You've been quiet a long time,' Grammaticus said boldly, despite the fact that the vision of Slau Dha terrified him. 'I called for you, and no one answered. Now you come?'

Slau Dha nodded. His reflection was extraordinarily pure, like a hologram cast up from the pool's water. The autarch gazed at Grammaticus through the slits of his glinting, bone-white helm. He was as slender as he was tall. The white feathers of his giant wings caught the advancing light. A few metres in front of the towering white figure stood G'Latrro, Slau Dha's little Xshesian interpolator.

'What do you want, lord?' Grammaticus asked.

Slau Dha murmured something.

'He wants to know why you're giving up, when we're so close to our goal,' G'Latrro translated into Common Ppfif'que, quite unnecessarily. Grammaticus spoke the eldar tongue well enough.

'I'm compromised. You must understand that. I can't get any closer. I can't do what you want me to do.'

Slau Dha did not reply. He continued to stare at Grammaticus.

'You are terminating your mission?' asked the little Xshesian in Ppfif'que.

Grammaticus switched to the eldar tongue, ignoring the hunched insectoid and looking directly at the autarch. 'I said, I can't–'

'He knows what you said, John,' said G'Latrro. The Xshesian had to move its mouthparts rapidly and nimbly to approximate human speech sounds. 'He thought the Cabal had trained you well. Briefed you fully. Shared its Acuity with you.'

'You did, but–'

'He thought you understood how vital this gambit was.'

'I do, but–'

'Why are you giving up, John?'

Grammaticus shook his head and tossed the laspistol back onto his pack. 'I'm no good to you. This situation is no longer viable. I've tried to get close to the Alpha Legion, and I can't. They're too wary. You should deploy another agent, and try elsewhere. Another Legion, perhaps?'

'Are you planning for us now, John Grammaticus?' G'Latrro chose not to translate Slau Dha's question. Instead, he relayed it straight. The question was simple, but framed in the eldar accusative form, it felt like a death threat.

'I would not presume, lord,' said Grammaticus, shuddering.

'Two years, sidereal, that's all we have before it starts,' G'Latrro said, relaying Slau Dha's whispers. 'A decade, maximum, before it ends. This is our window. Our one chance to turn your feckless race into an instrument of good.'

'You've never liked humans much, have you, "honoured lord"?' Grammaticus asked.

'Mon-keigh,' the autarch said, contemptuously.

'You are weed-species, afterbirth, runts,' the Xshesian glossed.

'No, tell me what you *really* think,' Grammaticus said.

Slua Dha muttered. 'You are the blight of the galaxy, and you will be its doom or its deliverer,' G'Latrro relayed.

'I do so love our conversations,' Grammaticus smiled. 'It's so rewarding to speak to a being who perceives my entire species as a momentary aberration in the galaxy's evolution.'

'Aren't you, just?' asked Slau Dha, in thickly accented Low Gothic.

'You know what? Fug you, you uptight eldar bastard. Piss off and hide in whatever corner of the cosmos you deem safe. Leave me alone. Stop flecting up and abusing me.'

Grammaticus spat. His spittle landed in the pool and caused a ripple that spread out and broke around Slau Dha's armoured shins.

'John?' asked G'Latrro. 'Whatever made you think he was flecting himself here?'

Grammaticus backed away quickly, stammering. 'No, no… no!' The autarch took a step towards him, past the cowed Xshesian, roiling the pool's sediment with his feet.

Grammaticus lunged for his pack, but the eldar, as had been the case since the start of time, was far too fast. A blur of white, it reached him in a second and seized him by the throat. Long, bone-armoured fingers bit into Grammaticus's neck and pinned him down.

'Please! Please! Aghh!'

Slau Dha tightened his grip on Grammaticus's throat.

'Do not plead, mon-keigh.'

'Ghnn! You came… you came here *in person*?'

'Yes, John,' said G'Latrro, coming up behind them. 'Lord Slau Dha came here in person because it is *that* important.'

* * *

'TWO YEARS, THAT's all we have,' said the insectoid, relaying the white giant's almost inaudible whispers. 'Two years, John. The Cabal has seen this clearly, compounding our farseer and visionist talents. Even the Drahendra have seen this, and you know how slowly they move.'

Grammaticus nodded. The Drahendra was the most silent and inscrutable faction represented in the Cabal. Sentient, energised dust, virtually extinct, the last of them existed as membrane skins around dying gas giants. Even they perceived the rapid reshaping of universal destiny.

'We're all going to die. Only mon-keigh kind can alter the pattern.'

'I wish he'd stop calling us that,' Grammaticus told G'Latrro, rubbing his bruised throat.

'It will be called a heresy,' Slau Dha replied through his interpolator. The insectoid's mouthparts twirled feverishly. 'It will halt your species' growth in its tracks. Even your glorious Emperor will be lost in it.'

'Lost?'

'He will die, John.'

'Oh glory. You're sure?'

'It has been farseen. He will die forever. And his eternal death is the one thing we wish to prevent. Tiny thing though he is, you Emperor is a pivotal player in this.'

'And Horus?'

'A monster. Not yet, but soon. A monster to engulf all monsters.'

'Can't you stop it? Engage with another Legion, perhaps?'

'John, we have tested them all, one by one. The Dark Angels first, centuries ago. There is too much inherent corruption in them. The gene-seed weakness in all of the older Legions has been exacerbated by the need to keep them up to strength for the Great Crusade. They have all, one way or another, weakened themselves. They are vulnerable. But the Alpha Legion, the last, the latest... they are still pure enough. Green, receptive to change.'

'Surely...?'

'John, listen to him,' said G'Latrro. 'He let the Cabal into the Black Library, so they could read this truth. He broke all the ancient edicts to make that happen. It is predetermined. The Cabal has exhausted hundreds of other agents trying to recruit the Astartes.'

'Human agents?'

'Yes, John. Human agents. Agents of all species. John, the Alpha Legion is our last hope. They are late-comers. Their gene-seed has not been diluted by the Terran and Alien Wars. John, we must–'

Slau Dha spoke, cutting his interpolator off. 'Your first death,' he said, speaking in the eldar tongue, knowing Grammaticus had no need of an interpreter.

'My first death,' Grammaticus answered in kind. 'Anatol Hive. I never asked you to save me, autarch. You chose to do that, remember? You chose to re-sleeve me in flesh and make me your agent. Don't you dare start calling in favours that I never asked for.'

There was a long silence.

'I must, John,' Slau Dha replied.

He began to whisper again.

'This is no longer about the mission,' G'Latrro translated. 'The mission is still vital, but another factor has entered the scheme, an unpredicted one.'

'What?' asked Grammaticus.

'It is something previously invisible to the Cabal's Acuity. The Cabal chose Nurth as an ideal opportunity to demonstrate the effects of the Primordial Annihilator to the Alpha Legion. It turns out it is, perhaps, too *much* of a demonstration.'

'I don't understand,' said Grammaticus. 'What do you mean?'

'This is why I have come in person,' said Slau Dha quietly.

'We have lately discovered,' said G'Latrro, 'that the Nurthene possess a Black Cube.'

TEN

Mon Lo Harbour, Nurth, later that morning

CHASED BY HER aides, Honen Mu strode out into the bright sunlight that was bleaching one of the terracotta palace's wide inner yards. She walked like she always walked, as if she was late for something important and nothing would stop her.

Other uxors, along with senior hets, were gathering in the yard, chatting in small groups or reading data reports. The morning briefing with Sri Vedt and Major General Dev was due to start in half an hour, and expectations were high. With the full strength of an Astartes taskforce now in play, commanded by the Legion's primarch, no less, everyone anticipated a swift escalation in operations, a major assault, most likely, and soon. It was common knowledge that the Lord Commander was entirely pissed off with the Mon Lo theatre, and expected the Alpha Legion to take it quickly and cleanly, and so end his troubles.

Her aides were all gabbling at her. The day was bright, but cold, thanks to a blustery wind blowing in off the desert. The sky seemed to be moving backwards even more slowly than before. The vapour stain above Mon Lo was as dark and immobile as ever, but the screaming seemed to have diminished a little, or had at least been baffled by the desert wind. The sound lurked at the edge of hearing, like tinnitus.

Honen Mu came to a halt. 'Shut up,' she snapped with her 'cept, and her aides shut up. 'One at a time now,' she instructed.

'Two attempted incursions along the earthwork overnight,' said Tiphaine. 'One at CR412 around midnight, repulsed by a contingent of the Outremars after a patchy firefight, the other at CR416, seen off quickly by the Knaves Company.'

'Losses?'

'None on either occasion, uxor,' said Jhani.

'Force estimations?' Mu asked.

'Both incursions were made by nurthadtre raiders,' Leeli said, 'numbering no more than thirty individuals. Lightly armed skiritai units, desert rogues, each force probably led by an echvehnurth elite. They melted back into the desert as quickly as they could.'

'They are testing our lines, probing for weaknesses,' said Jhani.

Honen Mu looked at the girl snidely. Jhani hung her head. 'Which, of course, you had already appreciated, uxor,' she murmured.

'Anything else?' asked Mu.

'There are sketchy reports that a spy was driven away from the pavilion last night,' said Tiphaine.

'Define "driven away",' said Mu.

'An insurgent agent got close to the pavilion during the Lord Commander's meeting with the Astartes,' said Nefferti. 'He was discovered, and fled, probably into the desert.'

'This is unconfirmed?' asked Mu.

'It is simply a rumour. The Lord Commander's staff seem unwilling to admit that such an outrage occurred.'

'No wonder, an agent getting that close…' said Mu.

'The rumour also suggests that said agent may have taken out a Lucifer Black,' said Erikah.

Honen Mu redirected her gaze at Erikah. The girl did not shy away from Mu's hard stare. Mu liked Erikah's strength. Far younger than Tiphaine, Mu's senior aide, the youngest of them all, Erikah showed great promise. She reminded Mu of herself: unabashed, strong, wilful.

'The enemy agent killed a Lucifer?' Mu asked.

Erikah nodded. 'Right outside the tent wall and no one inside heard anything. Of course, the Lord Commander's staff is denying this, but you know how word gets around.'

'I happen to know a bajolur in the Outremars who said he saw the body being whisked away,' said Leeli.

I can imagine how you happen to 'know' the bajolur, thought Mu. 'Shit,' she whispered. 'A Lucifer got burned?'

'Though the Lord Commander's staff has refused to comment on the rumour,' said Tiphaine, 'operational security has been beefed up to Code Order Six as of midnight last night.'

Mu nodded. Code Order Six was the highest of the standing security impositions.

'We have learned that the Lord Commander has authorised the Lucifer Black companions to conduct a full security purge on all Army units,' said Jhani. 'Every-one should make themselves available for interrogation by the companions at short notice. The Lord Commander is clearly keen to root out the spy in our midst before any assault begins.'

'That's exactly what I would do,' Mu sighed. I need to clear things up before that happens, she thought. I need to clean the Chiliad ranks quickly and effectively, before the damn Lucifers find our regiment wanting. I know in my bones that a weakness resides within us. Rukhsana, Rukhsana, that silly bitch, she's hiding something, and I will find it before our entire Old Hundred is shamed and disgraced.

She looked up at the sky, and watched it slide back on itself, slowly and unnaturally, like a pict feed of ice collapsing into melt water played in reverse. The desert wind tugged at their cloaks.

'Uxor?' asked Nefferti.

'Wait here, please,' Mu said, and strode off across the yard. Her aides lingered where they had been told to linger, whispering and nattering.

'Genewhip,' Mu said.

Franco Boone looked around at her. He had been standing in conversation with uxor Sanzi and her aides.

'Uxor,' he nodded. 'I was just about to come looking for you.'

'A word,' said Mu.

They walked away from the gathering throng, to the south side of the yard, under the shade of the colon-nade.

'Something stinks,' said Boone, keeping his voice low.

'Go on,' she replied.

'Let me ask you this,' said Boone. 'Uxor Rukhsana? You told me she was covering something. Could it be an affair with Het Pius?'

Mu gazed at him. 'Maybe, I don't know why she'd hide it. Who would care?'

Boone shrugged. He took hold of the golden box hanging around his neck and took a pinch of peck. 'The thing is,' he said, sniffing, 'we went to scope out Rukhsana's lodgings, to follow up on your lead. We found Het Pius there, bold as brass and twice as naked.'

Mu laughed. She felt relieved. If that was all it was, if that explained Rukhsana's behaviour, then she had been worrying for nothing. 'There's your answer,' she said. 'I apologise for putting you to such trouble.'

Boone's dark look had not gone away. 'The trouble's only just started, uxor,' he said. 'As it turns out, it couldn't have been Pius, unless Pius can be in two places at once. Whoever it was, they fooled me and two of my best bulls good and proper.'

'I don't understand,' said Mu. Suddenly, despite her cloak, she felt how cold the wind was and shivered.

'Neither do I, lady,' said Boone. 'I spent last night surveilling Pius. Guess who I saw with him?' Boone scratched the tip of his axe-blade nose, and gave her a significant look.

'You'll have to tell me, Franco,' she replied.

'Soneka.'

She stared at the genewhip. 'Well, of course. They're old friends.'

Boone shook his head. 'Soneka's got *suspicious* written all over him, Mu. He got out of Tel Khat alive, and came to you with stories, what was it? About a "body" and Hurt Bronzi? Soneka, Pius, the pieces don't fit.'

'I'm sure they do,' she assured him.

Boone shook his head again. 'Not in any way I feel comfortable with, uxor.'

Mu pursed her lips and glanced up at the slow sky, squinting at the light. 'Peto's story was a fabulation,' she said, 'he admitted it himself. He was delirious after his ordeal and–'

'We approached him for a quiet word,' Boone cut in. 'Just a quiet word. He fought us off and fled.'

Mu didn't reply.

'He's hiding something,' said Boone. 'Soneka's in league with Pius, or whoever it is that's pretending to be Pius. I'd laugh it off, but we're in the deep and stinky here. The companions are closing us down. A purge. If they dig up any real dirt, our heads will roll, literally. You know how forgiving Namatjira can be. He'd merrily eviscerate the geno if it meant making an example of a traitor.'

Mu looked at Boone so directly that he was forced to avert his gaze. 'Franco, Peto Soneka is not the problem. He's a good man, a damn good man, who's been through hell these past weeks. He was shaken and delirious when we spoke to him. He's no spy. He ran because you scared him. I'd stake my life on it.'

Boone finally found the bottle to look straight back at her. 'He ran, Mu. He fought us off and ran. He vanished, and as of this morning, Bronzi's missing too. His bashaws don't know where he is. They haven't seen hide nor hair of him since dawn yesterday. He's dropped off the scope. I swear, they're in it together, Mu... Soneka, Pius and Bronzi, three of our best hets. We're not talking junior gee-tards here. They're encrypt-cleared hets; they know the Army's entire playbook. If it turns out they've gone over, the scandal will finish the regiment.'

Honen Mu pulled her cloak around her to fend off the worst of the wind. 'Franco, would you please come with me?' she asked.

She led him along the colonnade to a shadowy stone stairwell that led up onto the flat roof of one of the buildings overlooking the yard. Up on the roof, the wind was stronger and the light brighter. Two men were waiting for them at the edge of the roof space. They got to their feet as Mu and Boone approached.

Boone blinked in consternation and drew his sidearm. 'Hurtado Bronzi, Peto Soneka... consider yourselves under detention and–'

'Put that away, Franco,' said Mu. 'They're here under their own recognisance. They asked me to arrange this meeting, so that they could speak to you directly.'

Boone lowered his gun, but did not put it away. 'I'm waiting,' he said.

'Genewhip,' Bronzi said, making a casual but respectful namaste in Boone's direction. 'My old friend Peto has an apology to make to you. Haven't you, Peto?'

Soneka nodded. 'I was a fool to run last night, really, a complete fool. I was a little bit crazy. My mind was all over the place. I'm sorry for that, Genewhip Boone.'

'Not good enough,' said Boone.

'He's telling the truth,' said Bronzi. He fished out a sheaf of documents from his belt pouch. 'Look, see? Medicae reports. They signed off on him this morning after an exam. Combat fatigue.'

'Likely story,' Boone snorted, bringing up his sidearm again.

'Look, I spent the last day and a half looking for him,' said Bronzi, 'because he's my best friend and I didn't want to see him swinging in the wind. He's messed up, that's all.'

'Really?' asked Boone.

'His company got hammered at Tel Utan. Then the remnants of them were slaughtered at Tel Khat. It's no surprise Peto's suffering from combat fatigue,' said Mu.

'That kind of trauma would make anyone run if genewhips started pressing the wrong buttons,' Bronzi added. 'Your men were suggesting that the Tel Khat Massacre was all his fault.'

Boone lowered his weapon. 'I suppose…' he began. He snatched the papers out of Bronzi's hand and skimmed them. The sheets flapped in the wind.

'I don't want Bronzi or my uxor making any excuses for me,' said Soneka. 'I can stand on my own two feet. I'm sorry I cut rough with your bulls, genewhip. Terra, I really am.'

'I didn't want to see Peto hang when he hadn't done a thing, Boone,' said Bronzi. 'Like I said, I spent the whole of yesterday out looking for him, and when I found him, I persuaded him to turn himself in, to make peace with you and smooth this trouble out.'

'With my full sanction,' said Mu. 'Hurtado brought the matter to me early this morning, and explained the facts.'

'Hurt convinced me that it was better to turn myself in and face you,' said Soneka. 'I realise I should never, ever have run. That made me look guilty as hell.'

Boone holstered his weapon. He glared at all three of them, and thrust the paperwork back into Bronzi's hands. 'All right. All right, but I'm still not happy.'

'Of course you're not,' said Soneka.

'That's why we'd like to offer you something in return,' said Bronzi, 'by way of recompense for your trouble, and in gratitude for your understanding.'

'Like what?' asked Boone sourly.

'Kaido Pius,' said Soneka. 'Hurt and I are his oldest friends. We can get stuff out of him that you genewhips would never manage, about him, Uxor Rukhsana, whatever dirt there is.'

'Just give us a day or two,' said Bronzi. 'We'll report back and give you everything we've found.'

Boone looked at Uxor Mu. 'I don't trust either of them.'

'I trust them with my life,' Mu said. 'They are two of my best hets. Let them loose, Franco. They'll find the canker in our midst. If they play us for fools, I'll kill them myself.'

'She would,' said Soneka.

'She really would,' Bronzi agreed.

Boone grinned. 'No doubt of that, but if you two bastards are tight with Pius like you say, why would you sell him out?'

'If Kaido's betrayed the Chiliad,' said Soneka, 'it wouldn't matter if he was my brother. I'd skin him alive.'

'Company first, Imperium second,' said Bronzi. 'Geno before gene.'

'All right,' said Boone. 'Two days, then I bring hell down on your heads.'

'That's fair,' said Bronzi.

'Totally fair,' Soneka agreed.

Boone turned to leave, and then turned back. 'Soneka? I'm truly sorry for your anguish. A company is a hard thing to lose.'

'Indeed it is, genewhip,' Soneka replied.

BOONE LEFT THEM on the roof and returned to the yard. Honen Mu regarded the two hets. She brushed wind-blown hair out of her eyes.

'I have to go to the briefing,' she said.

They nodded. 'Thank you for doing this,' said Soneka.

'An uxor looks out for all her charges,' she replied, and then paused. 'Don't let me down. Don't make me regret sticking my neck out today.'

'We won't, Honen,' said Bronzi.

'All right,' she said. 'I want the Chiliad's house swept clean in twenty-four hours, before the companions start picking at our loose threads. Start with Rukhsana. Like I said, she's covering something. That's why I sent Boone after her in the first place.'

'If we find anything, you'll be the first to know,' said Soneka.

'And we can all go and tell Boone together,' smiled Bronzi.

'As a matter of interest, do you think Pius is compromised?' Mu asked.

'Kaido?' asked Bronzi. 'Not for a moment.'

'And Rukhsana?'

Bronzi shrugged.

Mu turned to go. 'Oh, Peto,' she said, 'your medicae papers not withstanding, are you fit for posting?'

'We only got the papers to convince Boone,' said Soneka. 'I'd actually rather be working.'

She nodded. 'With Shiban gone, the Clowns need an acting het, especially if we're about to go in. I'll get the warrants drawn up, a temporary assignment for you and your bashaws until I can bring in a permanent new het. Maybe you can go up the line and make an overture later today? They desperately need licking into shape before we go hot. There's–'

'Fugging Strabo,' said Soneka, nodding. 'I know.'

She smiled. 'Good. Excellent. Well, carry on.'

She walked away, her heels clacking on the cinder roof, and disappeared down the stairwell.

Bronzi looked over at Soneka and grinned. 'Shiban's mob. That's–'

'Ironic,' Soneka finished.

Bronzi chuckled and stroked his belly. He looked out from the roof at the distant, hadean vista of Mon Lo.

'You think we fooled them?' asked Soneka.

Bronzi held up his hand. The middle and index fingers were crossed.

'I mean, I'm new to all this,' said Soneka.

'I'm hardly a veteran,' Bronzi replied, 'but, yes, I think we're good. We'd better get on with it.'

He turned to go. Soneka put out a hand to stop him. It was his ruined, truncated hand, and for some reason, Bronzi found this terribly telling.

'I'm not prepared to countenance anything that betrays the geno,' Soneka said, 'and absolutely nothing that would hurt Mu.'

'Then we're on the same page, aren't we, Peto?' said Bronzi. 'Let's get on with it.'

IN THE SHUTTERED darkness of his private cell, Dinas Chayne sat in meditation. The cell, deep in the subterranean layers of the palace, was damp and cold, but Chayne had not lit the small iron firebasket, nor any of the tapers.

He liked the cold. The cold had been his friend on Zous as a child warrior, especially during the last, long, hard winter of his thirteenth year. The cold had sharpened his wits, and forced him to steel himself. The cold was a tool that a man, or a boy, could use to temper himself.

Breathing slowly, Chayne took apart the facts, and built them back up one by one. Uxor Saiid. The Alpha Legion. Omegon. The note. His dead Lucifer. The astonishing skill of the elusive spy. The astonishing arrogance of the elusive spy. *There*, the arrogance suggested that the spy was confident in his cover.

Where does a spy hide? In plain sight. How does he operate? Without drawing attention to himself, by being what he is naturally, to avoid question and comment. The best way of doing that was to be exactly what you claimed to be. It made the cover story so much easier to run.

The best cover a spy could have was to be a spy.

Chayne had already decided to pay a visit to Uxor Saiid. He'd had his men watching her since the Lord Commander's order, to no great result. Now that Namatjira had sanctioned a security purge, Chayne felt duty bound to stop being reactive and bring her in for interrogation.

The morning briefing would end in thirty minutes. She'd be on her way back to her quarters. He would meet her there in person, and show no mercy. She was the key, somehow. She'd covered something during her meeting with the Lord Commander. She'd covered for *someone*.

Chayne had photographic recall. Breathing ever more slowly, his heart rate down to an inhuman level, he replayed the moments of the meeting.

'Rukhsana,' Namatjira had said. 'I'm told you were responsible for reconnaissance and scouting at Mon Lo?'

'That was my role, sir.'

'You had agents in the field?'

'I did, Lord Commander,' Rukhsana had replied. 'Most of them were long range observers and spotters.'

Namatjira had consulted the data-slate. 'But you had at least one intelligence officer inside Mon Lo the morning this hubbub began?' He had waved his hand distractedly in the direction of the window.

Rukhsana had pursed her lips and looked down. 'Yes, sir, I did. Konig Heniker.'

'Heniker? Yes, I know him. He's a reliable man. What happened to him?'

'He had entered the city covertly once already, sir, and briefed me afterwards. His intelligence was of good quality. He inserted that morning, very early, intending to collect data on the Kurnaul and north wall areas. He never came back.'

'Ah, I see,' the Lord Commander had sighed. 'Thank you, Uxor Rukhsana.'

Dinas Chayne opened his eyes in the dark. It was so obvious, so obvious! He'd been a fool to miss it.

The best cover a spy could have was to be a spy.

There was a knock at the door behind him. He ignored it. His men knew better than to disturb him during meditation.

Another knock came. The alert cursor on the cuff of his armour, stacked on the floor in front of him, began to wink.

'Who is it?' Chayne called.

'Eiman, sir. We have something.'

'Wait.'

It took forty-six seconds for Dinas Chayne to fully clothe himself in his jet-black armour.

He opened the door. Eiman was outside, along with Treece. They were fully armoured, and stood flanking a nervous young man, the adept from the security post that Chayne had handed the note to the night before.

The adept was clearly terrified at the thought of disturbing a Lucifer Black.

'Tell me,' said Chayne.

'Sir, I have completed the tests you ordered. I have run a comparison check on the handwriting base of all expedition personnel. I have a match, sir. It's–'

'Konig Heniker,' said Chayne.

The adept blinked in astonishment. 'Yes. How could you possibly know that?'

Chayne pushed the adept out of his way and began to stride along the corridor. Eiman and Treece fell in behind him.

'Instructions?' snapped Eiman.

'Eight men,' said Chayne. 'Close down Uxor Saiid's quarters and bring her to me. Her spy is *our* spy.'

THEY CROSSED THE upper courts of the palace, through bustling streams of servants carrying sacks of manioc and blondleaf to the kitchens, past a marching band rehearsing on a small quad, past a group of artillery officers being briefed on a sunlit terrace. They hurried up the stairs to Rukhsana's quarters.

The day's heat was building, and the warmth was beginning to ooze from the brickwork. Slaves were soaking the reed window screens with water.

They knocked sharply at the door of Rukhsana's accommodation.

An aide answered the door, and called for her uxor as soon as she saw who it was. Uxor Rukhsana came at once.

'What's this about?' she asked, puzzled.

'So sorry to disturb you, uxor,' said Soneka. 'I think there's been some kind of clerical glitch. I've just been issued temporary command of the Clowns, and I'm on my way up the line to meet with them. The thing is, there's a been screw up. The warrants I've been given say that the Clowns have been transferred to your purview.'

'That's not right,' Rukhsana said. 'The Clowns come under Honen Mu's 'cept.'

'I know, I know,' said Soneka, shrugging, 'but she's off somewhere, and I need to get this sorted urgently. If you wouldn't mind accompanying me, you could authorise the warrants, and I could get on with my job.'

Rukhsana frowned. 'Soneka isn't it?'

'That's right, uxor.'

'And Bronzi?'

'Good day to you, uxor,' Bronzi smiled.

'Something's obviously gone very wrong,' she said.

'Would you mind?' Soneka asked.

'Of course not,' she said. She fetched a long desert shawl from the anteroom and told her aides to wait. 'I'll be back shortly,' she said to Tuvi.

The hets escorted Rukhsana along the upper colonnade of the palace, overlooking the terraced yards. The sun was biting through the slow, unwinding clouds.

'So much confusion these days,' she said, pulling on her shawl.

'Oh, it's terrible,' Bronzi agreed.

'It's the scale of the operation, I suppose,' Rukhsana said. 'I sometimes wonder if Tactical and Provisional is entirely on top of the job.'

'Must be a nightmare, logistically,' Soneka said pleasantly. 'Look, I really do appreciate this, uxor,'

'I heard about the Dancers, het,' she said. 'I am truly sorry. They were a great company.'

'War happens,' Soneka replied, with an appreciative nod. 'I'm just glad to be getting back on the horse.

Gives me a sense of purpose. Besides, we're going to need every unit on top form in these coming days, and without Shiban, the Clowns are unravelling.'

'Peto will whip them into shape,' Bronzi grinned.

She hesitated. 'Forgive me, Het Bronzi, I'm not entirely sure why you're here?'

'Moral support,' Bronzi said, making a polite namaste. 'Peto was anxious about disturbing you this morning.'

She looked at Bronzi, as if not entirely convinced.

'Strange,' she began, 'he doesn't look like the sort to lack–'

She fell silent. Something had caught her eye. She pushed past them both, went to the stone rail of the colonnade, and gazed down into the terraced yards below.

'What's going on down there?' she asked quietly.

They joined her at the rail, and looked down. Below them, on the far side of the upper yard, eight figures in black armour were hurrying up the staircase to the summit levels, rushing like shadows in the shade of the tiled mantle roof.

'Some nonsense, I'll be bound,' said Bronzi.

'Those are Lucifer Blacks,' she said.

'Yes, I think they are,' said Soneka. 'Sorry, could we get along? My driver's waiting.'

'They're heading towards my quarters,' she said.

'I don't think so,' Bronzi replied confidently. 'They're probably responding to an alert from the watch station up in the tower.'

'No,' she said, firmly. She turned to stride back the way they'd come. Soneka was blocking her, a calm, reassuring smile on his face.

'It's nothing, uxor. Let's go, shall we?' he said.

She glanced to her right. Bronzi had closed in too.

'What is this?' she asked, realising that she was trapped between two very capable geno hets.

Soneka looked at Bronzi.

Bronzi nodded quickly.

'What the hell is this?' she demanded.

'Heniker,' said Soneka.

Rukhsana froze.

'Heniker sent us,' said Bronzi. 'The companions are on to you. He sent us to get you out.'

'Please,' said Soneka. 'There's very little time.'

She stared at them both.

'Heniker?' she asked.

Bronzi nodded. Without hesitation, she allowed them to lead her away down the colonnade. The three of them began to run.

TUVI AND THE other girls flinched as the doors to the chamber flew open. Lucifer Blacks burst in, training their weapons.

'I demand to know–' Tuvi began.

'Shut up,' said one of the companions, pointing his weapon directly at her.

Dinas Chayne entered the room, moving forwards between his braced and aimed men.

'Rukhsana?' he asked, his voice issuing from his grim helmet's loudspeaker. The aides cowered in terror. The youngest of them whimpered.

'Where?' Chayne hissed.

They were all too scared to reply. Chayne made a quick gesture, and four of the companions broke forwards to search the adjoining rooms.

Chayne looked directly at Tuvi, who was comforting the youngest aide, a girl, barely thirteen years old.

'You are the leader. Where is your uxor?' he asked.

Tuvi swallowed and returned his gaze defiantly.

'She's not here,' Tuvi said. 'She was called away on geno business.'

'Called away?' asked Chayne, taking a step towards her and lowering his weapon.

'A het came. A het who needed her authorisation or something,' Tuvi replied.

'Which het?'

'I'm not sure,' said Tuvi.

'It may have been two hets,' said one of the other girls.

'It may have been,' said Tuvi, 'I didn't really see.' Tuvi was an ambitious girl, but she was also careful. Until she understood exactly what was going on, she didn't want to give out any more information than necessary. Despite her youth and her hunger for command, she also firmly believed in the adage *Company first, Imperium second, geno before gene.* She had been raised that way.

Chayne reached out with his left hand, and took hold of her face. She moaned quietly and closed her eyes. It looked as gentle as a lover's touch, but the compression pain he was exerting was immense.

'How long ago?' he asked quietly.

'Ten minutes. N-no more than ten.'

'Who did she go with?'

The grip had made Tuvi quickly re-evaluate her priorities. 'S-Soneka,' she said.

AT GROUND LEVEL, to the east of the palace sprawl, Army pioneers had excavated a deep ramp, and removed the side wall of a giant ceremonial chamber to provide a vast depot for vehicles. The excised wall section had been replaced by load-bearing, pneumolithic girders, and fortified with flakboard and ballistic pumice. Trucks and transports toiled in and out along the ramp all day long in a haze of dust, under the direction of artificer banksmen and other security personnel. The engine fumes gathered in the roof space, slowly sucked away by powerful vent systems that had been bolted under the vaults. Lumen rigs hung from brackets all the way down the chamber. The place echoed with rivet guns and pressure drivers.

'That one,' said Bronzi, hurrying back to them. Soneka and Rukhsana came out from behind a turreted trans-trak painted in Thorn livery, and crossed with him to an armoured scurrier dressed in desert pink. Bronzi popped the hatch and they climbed in. Bronzi clambered forwards into the tight cockpit space.

Bronzi had checked the vehicle out for use at the depot station. If he'd used his own biometric key, or Soneka's, or even the uxor's, klaxons would have been sounding already. Instead, he'd used the key they had given him.

Soneka closed the hatch behind them, and strapped in beside Rukhsana. She was pale with panic, but containing her agitation.

'Go, Hurt,' Soneka said.

Bronzi gunned the engines and brought the scurrier to life. It rose on its twenty sets of calliper legs and spurred forwards, leg units running in syncopation, racing it across the earth floor like a giant centipede.

They passed out under the gate. A banksman flashed their biometric signature, and waved them enthusiastically on with his luminous wand.

They ran up the ramp, followed the rampart wall to the west exit, and headed out into the desert.

THE SCURRIER'S MODE of ambulation provided a soft, rolling sensation of travel, despite the high speeds Bronzi was making across the dunes. The wind was raising a spume of fine dust from the crest of every slope. Bronzi checked the navigation display. It was only a kilometre or two. Not far, not far at all…

'Is Konig all right?' Rukhsana asked Soneka.

'Konig?'

'Heniker,' she said.

'Oh, sorry. I only really know him as Heniker.'

'Is he all right?'

'Yes, he's fine.'

'Really fine?'

'Yes.'

She thought about that. He could tell she didn't trust him at all.

'How are you involved?' she asked.

'I can't tell you.'

'I think you can,' she insisted.

'I can't, really,' he said. 'I'm sorry, uxor, it's an Army intelligence thing.'

She stared at him hard. 'Army intelligence? Is that so?'

'Yes.'

'But–'

'But what, uxor?'

It wasn't an Army intelligence thing. It was a Cabal thing. She realised that she was going somewhere to die. She tried to swallow the dry knot in her throat.

'I'm only doing this because I love him,' she said.

'Heniker?'

'Yes, Heniker.'

'I didn't realise,' Soneka said. He looked bothered and uncomfortable. 'I'm sorry, I really didn't. Look, we–' he began.

'Get set, we're there!' Bronzi called out.

The scurrier rippled down a bank of soft sand into a deep wadi, and came to a halt. The sun was at its zenith, burning like a low-set las. The light was hard and there were no shadows.

'What were you saying to me?' asked Rukhsana.

'I'm sorry,' said Soneka, 'that's all. There's no time to say anything else. We're out of time.'

'So am I, I think,' she replied.

He watched her as she unbuckled and got up.

'I never meant to hurt you, Rukhsana,' he said. 'Please, this is for the best.'

'I hope so.' She smiled at him, a brave, intoxicating smile despite the shadow of terror in her expression. 'But I don't hold out *much* hope,' she added.

Bronzi opened the hatch, and they climbed out into the baking hole of the wadi basin. There was no one around. Bright sunlight burned the sand and the tops of their heads.

'Come on,' said Bronzi, glancing around impatiently.

'While we're waiting,' said Rukhsana, 'why don't you explain that lie you sold me? As a last favour, so to speak. I'd like to know what I'm getting into. Tell me about Konig. How do you know Konig?'

'It's like I said,' Bronzi replied, awkward and unsettled.

'Oh, Hurtado, please credit me with some intelligence,' she said. 'It's *nothing* like you said.'

There was a soft, sifting sound, the sound of sand pouring away onto sand.

Four Astartes, concealed beneath the dunes around them, rose to their feet, the sand sliding off the contours of their armour as if they were rising up out of concealed trap doors.

'Is this her?' asked one.

'Yes, lord,' Bronzi replied.

Soneka realised that Rukhsana had begun to tremble badly.

'We'll take her from here,' said another of the Astartes.

'Oh, glory,' Rukhsana whispered. 'Please...'

'It's all right,' Soneka told her urgently. He looked at the giant warriors coming towards them. 'It will be all right, won't it?'

'You've done your job, friend,' one of them told him, 'and we thank you for it. We'll take it from here.'

'But–' Soneka began.

'We'll take it from here, operative,' the giant reassured him. The Astartes put out a huge paw around Rukhsana's tiny shoulders, and led her away across the sand.

She looked back, once. 'Peto!' she called.

'I'm sorry. I–' he called out.

But she was gone in the deep shadows of the wadi's base.

One of the Alpha legionnaires strode over to them.

'Good work,' he said.

Bronzi nodded.

'Will she be all right?' Soneka asked.

'Of course,' the Astartes said, his voice deep. 'She's with us.'

'That's not what I was asking,' Soneka said.

'Will *we* be all right?' Bronzi asked, looking up at the giant.

'Did you do what we told you to do?'

'Yes.'

'Did you use the biometric?'

'Yes,' said Soneka.

'Then stick to the story, and it will be fine,' replied the legionnaire. 'Trust me, and thank you.'

He turned to go, and then looked back, his huge form stark in the sunlight. 'You did the right thing. If things turn bad, we'll get you out. You're us now.'

He walked away. In under two minutes, the Alpha legionnaires had vanished into the desert, leaving no trace.

Bronzi looked at Soneka. He grinned, but Soneka could tell the grin was forced. 'Scary bastards, right?'

'Scary bastards,' Soneka agreed. They began to trudge back to the scurrier.

'Something on your mind?' Bronzi added.

Soneka shook his head.

'You don't like this, do you?'

'Of course I don't,' Soneka said.

THEY GOT BACK into the scurrier and headed back towards the palace. Half a kilometre from the west exit, a shadow flickered across them, and the scurrier's target alarms started to ping.

'Scurrier, scurrier,' the vox crackled. 'Come to a halt and open hatches. We have you at weapons lock.'

Bronzi threw the leg brakes and killed the spinal drive. The scurrier rocked to a standstill.

'Get out. On the deck. Now!' the vox demanded.

Bronzi looked at Soneka. 'Sure you know how to play this?' he asked.

Soneka nodded.

They unlocked the hatch and got out, falling on their faces in the glaring sunlight, a few metres from the vehicle with their hands behind their heads. A blizzard of sand was being kicked up around them by a circling Jackal gunship. A second gunship settled nearby on roaring turbofans, like a giant skeletal raven. Its occupants ran towards them.

'Get up!'

Soneka and Bronzi got up, hands locked behind their necks in submission. Lucifer Blacks surrounded them, weapons aimed. The air was so thick with winnowing dust from the hovering gunship that Bronzi and Soneka were coughing hard.

'Het Hurtado Bronzi and Het Peto Soneka?' the nearest Lucifer demanded.

They nodded, hands knotted behind their heads.

'You are under arrest, by order of the Lord Commander.'

'Is this about Uxor Rukhsana?' Bronzi shouted, above the wash of the gunships.

'Of course it is.'

'Then can you tell me,' Bronzi yelled back as the companions started to herd them towards the gunship, 'where the fug has she gone?'

ELEVEN

Mon Lo Harbour, Nurth, that evening

'So?' ASKED NAMATJIRA, looking up from his desk.

'We've let them both go, sir,' said Dinas Chayne.

'Why?'

'Their story checks out. The hets went looking for Uxor Rukhsana, chasing the same suspicions as us. They got her into a vehicle, to take her away from the palace for private interrogation. The geno like to protect their own, sir.'

Namatjira put the quill he had been using back into its power well, and rose to his feet, tapping his left index finger against his pursed lips. It was a modest gesture, designed to give the impression that he was pondering, but Chayne knew it was a mechanism the Lord Commander employed to curb his temper. He watched as Namatjira wandered towards the chamber window, into the pool of soft light cast by the setting sun. The light made his long, gold-embroidered robe glow.

'But the vehicle,' Namatjira asked, 'wasn't it swiped out on a blank biometric? To avoid detection?

Chayne shook his head. 'The biometric was Bronzi's. For some reason, it didn't read cleanly in the scanner. I am advised that this is occurring quite often, scanning glitches, caused by the pervasive dust. Now we've checked it, it evidently was Bronzi's.'

'And Rukhsana?' Namatjira asked. He patted his thigh, and his thylacene got up from the rug and trotted over to him. 'What about her?'

'She broke free and fled into the dunes.'

'She broke free from two frontline hets?'

'I believe they underestimated her resolve, sir,' said Chayne. 'When we questioned them, the hets both seemed frankly embarrassed that she had escaped. They were searching for her when we found them.'

'Do you believe any of this, Dinas?'

'I have no reason not to, lord. The facts match up perfectly. However, I will admit that I am uneasy whenever that happens.'

'You have them under scrutiny?'

'Yes, lord.'

Namatjira sank down into a crouch, and tenderly scrunched the thylacene's ears with both hands. It closed its eyes in pleasure. 'What about Rukhsana?'

'We're questioning her aides, but they don't seem to have been aware of any indiscretion, and we're searching for the uxor, obviously.'

'Can she survive in the desert?'

'Without supplies or protective clothing, no, not more than a day. I expect all we'll find of her is her bones.'

* * *

BRONZI POURED ZNAPS into two glass cups and handed one to Soneka. Bronzi held out his glass to clink, and Soneka did so reluctantly.

'Here's to the skin of our fugging teeth,' said Bronzi, trying to make light of it. He'd been trying to make light of it for a long time. Soneka's mood was low, and Bronzi hated that.

'Here's to Rukhsana,' Soneka replied. 'May some power protect her from the fate we delivered her into.'

Bronzi shrugged, and drank to that instead. 'They'll treat her well enough, Peto,' he said. 'They only want answers.'

'They are not sentimental creatures, Hurt,' Soneka replied. 'They use any means they can to achieve their goals. They let my Dancers get slaughtered, just to throw the enemy off guard. What on Terra makes you think they'll use Rukhsana any less clinically?'

Bronzi couldn't come up with an answer.

Soneka took another sip and regarded his glass. 'This comes so easily to you, doesn't it, Hurt? Why is that?'

Bronzi sniffed. 'I don't know. It's the Astartes, I suppose. To be chosen by them, to be singled out by them for service, that's an honour in my book. The Astartes are the image of the Emperor, whom I adore, and to whose work I have devoted my life. To serve them is to serve Him. There is no finer duty.'

'Whatever happened,' Soneka asked, 'to Company first, Imperium second, geno before gene?'

Bronzi made a sour face, and lifted his meaty shoulders. 'That's just something we say, isn't it?'

'I thought it was something we believed,' Soneka replied.

Bronzi finished his drink and poured another. 'The Emperor is the Emperor,' he said, 'and the Astartes are his chosen, the brightest and the best. I'm comfortable working for them.'

'Provided they're on our side,' said Soneka.

Bronzi snorted. 'What does that mean?'

Soneka shook his head. 'Nothing. I have a gut dislike of this sordid intrigue, Hurt. I'm a soldier, not a spy, and lately I've been wondering which of those words best describes the Alpha Legion.'

Bronzi shook his head and decided it was high time to change the subject. He looked Soneka up and down, approvingly.

'Formal looks good,' he said.

'Been a while,' Soneka replied, adjusting the cuff of his dress uniform.

'When are you off?'

'Ten, fifteen minutes.'

'The Clowns are lucky to have you,' said Bronzi.

The chamber door behind them opened without any knock. Mu marched in, followed by Franco Boone.

'Drink?' Bronzi asked lightly. She glared at them both. Boone walked past Mu and helped himself.

'That was your idea of delicate, was it?' Mu asked.

'Well, we proved she was up to something, didn't we?' Bronzi answered.

'You were arrested and interrogated by the Lucifers,' Mu growled.

'Who, please remember, let us go without charge,' Bronzi countered.

'How did Rukhsana escape?' Mu asked.

'How would you have escaped us, Honen?' Bronzi asked playfully. 'Because, you know you would have.'

Mu hesitated.

'Uxors can be quite tenacious when they want to be,' Bronzi continued, taking the bottle out of Boone's hand and pouring himself another drink.

'Have you come to arrest me?' Soneka asked the genewhip, 'Or can I go meet my new unit?'

'You're all right,' Boone said. 'I'd have liked a cleaner end to this matter, but it's worked out decently. Rukhsana was a bad seed, but the Chiliad has saved face.'

'How?' asked Mu, in a mocking tone.

'These two were caught in the act of chasing her,' Boone said levelly, knocking back his drink, 'clear proof that we were trying to clean our own house and root out corruption. In the circumstances, their arrest was probably the best thing that could have happened. It may have been by accident or downright incompetence, but Bronzi and Soneka have protected our regimental reputation.'

'Company first, Imperium second, geno before gene,' Bronzi chuckled. Soneka shot him a hard look.

'What?' asked Bronzi.

Soneka put down his glass and lifted his pack. 'I have to go,' he said.

'I'll walk you down,' Mu said.

'March in fortune, Peto, and take the Clowns with you,' said Bronzi.

Soneka nodded, and left the chamber with Mu.

'Fancy another?' Bronzi asked Boone.

Boone stared back at the het, hard-eyed. 'Pius? He's clean?'

'As the proverbial,' Bronzi replied. 'Whoever Rukhsana was in bed with, he was playing games with you. A subliminal veil, a mind trick, maybe? I don't know. Pius is solid.' Bronzi waggled the bottle. 'So?'

'Go on then,' said Boone.

* * *

They walked down into a lower courtyard where the last of the Dancers were waiting beside a fat-wheeled transport in what remained of the daylight. Soneka nodded to Lon, and let Shah take his bag and stow it in the transport's panniers. The driver started up the truck's engine.

'Is there anything you're not telling me, Peto?' Mu asked, looking up into his face.

'Like what?'

She shrugged. 'Hurtado is a rogue, and I wouldn't put anything past him, but you, het, you're as straight as a die. You always have been. I don't believe you're capable of subterfuge. If you are, it must come with effort, so spare yourself that effort. Is there anything?'

'No. No, not at all.'

She nodded. 'Good. Get on your way. Whip the Clowns into shape, and march in fortune. I'll look for your preliminary report tomorrow.'

'Yes, uxor.'

'If they give you any grief, call me in to straighten them out.'

'Thank you. It won't be necessary.'

'Don't let the Dancers haunt you, Peto,' she said. 'You're not carrying some curse that will infect the Clowns too. New start, fresh page. Get the Old Hundred fit, and ready for the hell that's about to break.'

'I will.'

Mu smiled. She paused, and then stood up on tiptoe to kiss his cheek. 'I know you will,' she said.

Soneka climbed into the transport, and it rolled away down the yard towards the gate.

The tiny, childlike figure of Honen Mu stood in the lengthening shadows and watched until it was out of sight.

* * *

'SO WE'RE CLOWNS now, are we?' asked Lon over the grumble of the transport's engine.

'Seems so,' said Soneka. They rocked in their seats as the vehicle lurched along the uneven track.

'You all right there, het?' asked Shah.

'Yes,' said Soneka. 'Why?'

'You keep rubbing at your hip. You got a sweat sore or a dust blister?'

'No,' Soneka said, shaking his head. 'It's just this damn formal jacket chafing.'

Soneka turned aside and looked out of the dirty window vent at the passing desert, which was staining with a startling maroon hue as the sun finally slipped out of the sky.

The hydra brand on his hip was still raw and fresh.

THE CAVE WAS cool, and remarkably angular. Rukhsana presumed it had been cut out of the rock with meltas or some kind of precision drill. It was a cube, ten metres by ten, lit by a series of lumen orbs placed around the base of the walls. The light they gave out splashed up the dark walls and made her feel as if she was under water or on some airless moon. The air smelled of dust and cold stone. The air smelled of hopelessness.

She was shivering and terrified, and the terror magnified her body's reactions, reinforcing the drop in its core temperature. She tried to slow her breathing.

They had seated her on a wooden stool, her hands cuffed behind her back, in the middle of the cave. Then they had left her alone.

It felt as if hours had passed, but she suspected that it was merely a few minutes.

A figure came in through the cave's only egress.

He was larger than it was possible for any regular human male, a giant: an Astartes giant. He was dressed in a simple dark bodyglove that somehow emphasised his huge build and muscular strength more pointedly than any suit of power armour could have. His head was bare, noble, hairless, powerful, copper-skinned. His eyes were as bright as a sapphire sky.

He came across the cave floor slowly, and stood in front of her. She looked up at him.

'Uxor Rukhsana Saiid?' he asked. The sound of his voice made her think of slow, glowing embers. His words issued as gently as honey dripping from a spoon.

'Yes.'

'I am Alpharius, Primarch of the Alpha Legion.'

'I know who Alpharius is,' she replied, feeling a tremor of panic in her chest that she could barely control.

'Do you know why you're here?' he asked.

She nodded.

'Say why, please.'

'Konig Heniker,' she said. 'You're looking for Konig Heniker, and you think I know where he is.'

'Do you, uxor?'

She shook her head, dearly wishing her hands were free so that she could press them against her chest and persuade her heart to slow down.

'We'll see. Do you know what Konig Heniker's real name is?'

Rukhsana looked up at the giant sharply.

'I see you do not. No one could fake a response like that. Your beloved Konig's real name is John Grammaticus.'

'John?'

'Grammaticus. John Grammaticus. What about the Cabal, uxor? What do you know of the Cabal?'

'I don't know what that is,' she replied.

'I see you do. Just as you couldn't have faked the first response, you couldn't conceal the second. You know about the Cabal.'

Rukhsana bit her lip. 'He mentioned it, that's all.'

Alpharius stared down at her. His expression was almost benign. 'Help me help you, uxor. Where is Konig Heniker?'

'I don't know, I really don't. He was with me for a while, but he vanished, yesterday, just after the Grand Welcome. I don't know where he is.'

'We'll see,' said Alpharius. He nodded. A much smaller, robed figure entered the chamber and came to stand at the primarch's side. Rukhsana blinked and tried to focus. Though she could see the robed figure plainly, she could not resolve its face.

'This is Shere,' said Alpharius. 'He will help you exorcise your doubts.'

'Brace yourself,' he added.

THE CENTRAL SECURITY centre of the terracotta palace was a large, low ceilinged chamber filled with whirring and flashing cogitators, and bustling adepts. The heat-stink of the machines was acrid and harsh. Cooling systems had been rigged along the walls.

At nightfall, the duty rotated. Adepts arrived in their russet cloaks, and took over from the rostered operators on duty, signing in their biometrics as they took over machine stations.

He sat down at his appointed machine, his biometric accepted. The departing operator he was replacing bade him goodnight.

'Salutation, Adept Ahrum,' the screen display read.

That was good. That's who he was.

Adept Ahrum typed in his access codes. Data flowed in a sudden gush across his lithographic screen. He pulled his russet robe closer, and leaned in to study the graphics.

'Attend!' the senior adept on the chamber's central dais cried out, and all the operators stiffened.

'Carry on,' said Dinas Chayne as he walked into the room and went to join the senior.

Adept Ahrum risked a glance over his shoulder. Chayne stood in quiet discussion with the senior adept on the dais. He was barely five metres away.

Adept Ahrum decided to continue with his work.

He typed quickly, using his stolen biometric clearance to pull up confidential material. Uxor *Rukhsana... official scrutiny... actions of the Lucifer Blacks in the last fifteen hours...*

Oh Rukhsana... oh, my love, what have I done to you?

'You,' said a voice at his shoulder.

Adept Ahrum looked up quickly. Dinas Chayne was standing over him.

'Sir?' Ahrum asked.

'Why are you accessing this material?' Chayne asked.

'I was told to, sir, by my superior. It is a request from the Uxor Primus of the Geno Chiliad.'

'Trying to clean house, I suppose,' said Chayne.

'I imagine something like that. The Chiliad are very conscious of the fact that they have been found with a traitor in their ranks.'

Chayne nodded. 'All right. Carry on. Process your findings to the Uxor Primus, but copy me the details first.'

'Sir?'

'That's an order.'

'Yes, my lord.'

Chayne turned away and went to resume his conversation with the senior adept.

Adept Ahrum continued to type. He pulled up the interrogation report submitted by the companions that afternoon. There were two names.

He depressed his station key and rose to his feet. Both the senior adept and Dinas Chayne looked over at him.

'Adept?' the senior adept asked.

'Request permission to access the docket archive.'

'On you go, Ahrum,' nodded the senior adept, and turned to continue his conversation.

Adept Ahrum left the chamber. In the hallway outside, he threw off his russet robe and ditched his biometric. John Grammaticus tucked them away in an alcove out of sight and walked away down the corridor in the lamplight.

Two names. *Soneka. Bronzi.*

DINAS CHAYNE CUT the senior adept off suddenly.

'That man. That station,' he said, pointing to the vacated cogitator.

'Ahrum, sir?' asked the senior adept. 'He's a sound fellow, good at his work. What is your problem, sir?'

'Something about him. Something familiar,' murmured Chayne.

'Sir?'

'I'll be right back,' said Chayne, and left the station. Outside, the hallway was empty.

TWELVE

Mon Lo Harbour, Nurth, black dawn

THE FIRST PERSON to realise that something was terribly wrong was a subahdar in the Zanzibari Hort called Lec Tanha. Tanha had woken early, before first light, with a sore head and an ardent wish to continue sleeping. A solid sort, dependable, he had pulled on his boots and his cape, and climbed the bank of the earthwork from the camp to oversee the watch change.

He took a restorative pinch of peck. It was an eerie time of day, with the first daylight milking into the sky. A loose wind was blowing, scudding the land between the vast earthwork and the besieged city with a spectral fog that moved like crop smoke.

Tanha checked his sidearm, took another little furtive pinch, and conversed with two of the duty officers. He entered the observation redoubt, a fortified platform on the lip of the earthwork. The redoubt was open to the sky, and the wind riffled Tanha's hair. He took out a set of field glasses, and aimed them at Mon Lo.

'What's that?' he asked, sniffing.

'What's what?' replied the redoubt's vox-officer.

The distant, wind baffled screaming still sounded like tinnitus. There was a scent on the wind that smelled like wormwood.

'That smell,' Tanha said.

'Damned infidels are burning something,' said the vox officer. 'Incense?'

'No,' said Tanha. 'Something else.'

He looked up and listened into the windy air. A distant sound was mingling with the tinnitus. Tanha put his hand against the sand-bagged edge of the redoubt's parapet. He felt a deep, ominous trembling.

'Get the major general on the vox,' he said quickly.

'What,' the vox-officer replied. 'At this hour?'

'Get Dev on the line now!' Tanha ordered.

The vox-officer scrambled to his set. Tanha raised his field glasses again and looked down into the wreathing fog bank.

Subahdar Lec Tanha saw what was coming towards them.

He managed to speak, in a desperate, fearful stammer, the first two syllables of his wife's name.

Then he died.

A KILOMETRE TO the west, and exactly thirty seconds later, Dynast Cherikar, a senior commander of the Regnault Thorns Second Division, turned sharply to his tribune, Lofar.

'Can we usually hear the sea from here?' he asked.

The tribune shook his head. 'No, sir.'

'But you heard that? A wave striking a beach?'

Lofar looked dubious. 'I heard something,' he conceded. They were walking the top of the earthwork, on a standard morning patrol. Cherikar turned and looked towards the east. A great cloud, like mist or spray vapour, had enveloped the top of the earthwork a kilometre away. It was hanging in the air, like a pale hill that had not been there before.

'What is that?' Cherikar asked. Lofar did not reply. The duckboards under their feet had begun to shake.

The dynast and his tribune instinctively raised the spikes of their armour, barbing themselves with the psycho-receptive steel quills that gave their regiment its name. Studded all over with lethal blades, they drew their weapons, and turned to meet the onslaught.

The beautiful, mechanised blade systems of their ancient warsuits did not save them, nor did the weapons in their hands.

'GET UP!' Tche roared. 'Get up now!'

'Go away or I shall kill you,' Bronzi told his bashaw, and turned over in his bed roll.

Tche kicked his hetman squarely in the arse, which was presenting a reasonably generous target area.

'Get up!' Tche shouted.

Bronzi got to his feet, rubbing his offended backside, blinking in the half-light of the frame tent. His mind was addled, trying numbly to distinguish bits of memory that were real from pieces of dream that were not.

He was reasonably sure that geno bashaws didn't usually wake their hets with a boot in the seat of the pants.

'What?' Bronzi asked.

Tche stared at him. There was a token of anxiety in the bashaw's eyes, the sort of look that no man as big and well-muscled as Tche should ever have the need to display. 'Get up, het,' Tche repeated.

Bronzi was already heading for the tent flap, hopping as he tried to run and put on his boots simultaneously. He could already hear it, plain as day.

The murmur.

From a distance, war made a particular sound. The quake of the ground, the throb of engines, the rattle of weapons, the thump of detonations, the holler of voices; it all blended together into a kind of ominous murmuring, the feral grumbling of a monster waking over the next hill.

Hurtado Bronzi had heard the murmur dozens of times in his life. It had always augured days that he was lucky to live through, or hours that he could never forget.

Outside, first light was on them. Commotion ran through the camp as the Jokers scrambled to readiness. Bronzi looked up at the sky. The slowly turning clouds were staining pink, like blood in water or Nurthene silk. He could smell wormwood on the wind's bad breath. To the east, what looked like a vast, slowly creeping dust storm had shrouded the Army lines, obscuring even the dark shoulder of the earthwork.

Bronzi pushed through his swarming men, yelling out orders, and calling for a vox. Bashaws spread out from him like shrapnel from a grenade, conducting and relaying those orders in unequivocal tones, putting rigidity and structure into a company caught on the back foot.

Still calling for a vox, Bronzi hauled himself up the ladder of one of the observation derricks. Halfway up, he looked down at Tche, and called his name. Tche tossed his scope up to him. Bronzi caught it one-handed, uncapped it, and scanned east.

Adjacent to the Jokers' encampment, an Outremar infantry group was assembling from its tents and billets with the same kind of mad scramble that beset the geno. Beyond that, yes, now he saw it.

Veiled by the dust, the sporadic *flash-flash-flash* of explosions looked like someone flicking a signal lamp behind a dust shawl. The blasts were ripping off as quickly and frenetically as firecrackers. He could hear heavy weapons chattering and the bass drum beat of artillery positions waking up. Drums too, real drums, beat wild and rapid tattoos. A few seconds later, las-batteries in reboubts to the south-east began spitting incandescent shooting stars north into the dust cloud, adding their squeals to the communal murmur.

Bronzi saw movement in the filmy edges of the advancing dust storm, and resolved it into shapes, figures.

'Holy fug,' he whispered.

Once, during his childhood in Edessa, Bronzi had witnessed a blight swarm on the move. For centuries, great tracts of Osroene and the Mesop Delta had been seeded with genic cereals as part of the Emperor's program to improve food yield for the regenerating world, and surge years of insect over-breeding were triggered every few decades by over-abundant harvests. The swarm had darkened the sky, turning day to night, a dense river of locusts seventy kilometres long.

He had never forgotten the sound of a trillion wings, a purring noise like the murmur of war. He had never forgotten the sight.

He was reminded of it forcibly.

The Nurthene were spilling out of the roiling haze in huge numbers, a blight swarm of charging infantry and racing cavalry sweeping in over the earthwork and down across the Imperial lines like an avalanche. Echvehnurth warriors led the host, their whirling falxes glittering in the curiously dull light. A tide of nurthadtre followed them. Through the dust and broken light, their pink silks looked black, like the bodies of milling, teeming locusts. Bronzi saw swaying standards of reeds and crocodilia, banners of lizard skin trailing like friable green metal, nodding totem staves depicting scale, tooth and biforked tongue.

There was no regimentation, no order of battle. Nurthene cavalry charged along in the midst of the massed foot troops. He saw individual lancers, whooping and howling, mounted on galloping monitors the size of grox. Giant caimans, dull as coal, their scutes and teeth plated in gold, trudged forwards, bearing howdahs full of echvehnurth archers on their broad backs. Primitive gunpowder rockets whooped out of the host like fireworks, exploding amongst the Army encampments. Fletched darts fell like rain.

The murmur was no longer a murmur. It had become a roar.

Bronzi leapt off the derrick ladder and landed amongst his men. Whichever Army component had been camped east of the Outremar infantry group's billet had already been swallowed up by the Nurthene storm, and Bronzi had seen enough to know that the Outremars were falling in droves, falling like genic crops beneath a hungry blight swarm, as the storm swept on across their position. Bronzi reckoned that he had less than five minutes before the Nurthene assault reached him.

'Akkad formation!' he bellowed to his bashaws. 'Six lines, cannons to the front! Mortars to the ridge there! Relay this! Relay it!'

The Jokers moved like an intricate mechanism, forming structures across the land south of the earthwork. Two lines of alternating pike and carbine rifle solidified along the northern edge, behind the livestock corrals and the latrines. Cannon crews grimaced as they struggled to heave their heavy weapons, ammo crates and tripods to new positions. Men ran past him, lugging the iron tubes of mortars across their shoulders.

'Forwards! Forwards!' Bronzi yelled at the rifle cadres. He was waving his sabre above his head. Tche appeared, and passed Bronzi a vox-horn.

'Jokers, Jokers, Jokers!' Bronzi yelled. 'Mass incursion at CR88 and eastwards. Reporting mass assault at this time! We are preparing to resist! Support requested!'

'Joker lord, we are aware,' the vox replied. 'Stand ready. March in fortune. We are redeploying strengths to your position.'

'Standing by,' Bronzi snapped. He tossed the vox-horn back to Tche. 'Get the fugging banner aloft!'

Bronzi looked back at the doom rushing to engulf them. He realised it wasn't the crowing enemy forces that he really feared, despite their numbers, but the slow dust cloud that came with them and disgorged them, towering ten times higher than the earthwork ramp.

It was like a mountain about to fall on him.

THE CHAMBER OF the terracotta palace secured for central operations had turned into an undignified scrum of shouting, gesticulating personnel. A crowd of uxors and senior officers had invaded the place, demanding information as they jostled to get a look at the main strategy display, a hololithic chart table that dominated the centre of the room. Some of them were half-dressed, their eyes puffy with sleep; some were still buttoning tunics or fastening robes. Around the chamber walls, the vox adepts of Tactical and Provisional called out reports from their cogitator stations in voices that overlapped the queries of the crowd.

'Incursion reports CR88 and eastwards!'

'Massive numbers!'

'Support stations engaging! We have–'

'No response from CR89 and CR90!'

'Get a station report from the 4th Hussars!'

'Reporting losses at CR91 and–'

'Say that again! Again!'

'Losing your feed, CR90–'

'CR93 reports contact!'

'Silence!'

Major General Dev entered through the west door. 'Take your places and behave according to your ranks,' he snarled. Uxors and officers alike, cowed by his tone and his authority, fell silent and straightened respectfully.

Dev's adjutant took the major general's helm and sword from him, and Dev stepped forwards to the table, peering at it.

'They took us by surprise?' he asked.

'Completely, sir,' said the senior adept.

'Assessment?' the major general asked, leaning on the edge of the chart table and peering down. The glow from its surface underlit his face.

'We're still waiting for orbital appraisal,' the senior adept replied. 'There is an atmospheric peculiarity that–'

'I'm not waiting for orbitals,' said Dev sharply. 'Someone give me a decent assessment!'

'A major incursion has breached the earthwork in an eleven-kilometre line between CR88 and CR96, Wadi

Ghez, so-called the Little Sink,' said Sri Vedt, the Uxor Primus, tracing her finger across the hololithic chart. 'I cannot appreciate precise numbers, but it feels like tens of thousands.'

'I would concur with the Primus,' said Uxor Bhaneja. 'Their forces struck eight minutes ago, and overwhelmed the earthwork by sheer dint of numbers.'

'And took us by surprise?' asked Dev. 'A force that size? They just sneaked up a division of warriors and dropped them on us? Doesn't that seem unlikely?'

'They are cloaked by a vapour cloud,' said Uxor Sanzi. 'That must surely be more than the dust produced by their movements. The cloud struck the earthwork first, with a kinetic force akin to a tsunami.'

'More air magick?' suggested a Torrent officer.

'Do not,' said Dev, raising a finger to him, 'do not let the Lord Commander hear you utter those words.'

The Torrent officer made a quick namaste and backed away.

Dev glanced towards the uxors around the table. 'Thank you for your frank appraisal, uxors. How accurate should I consider them to be?'

'Our 'cepts are sharp,' said Uxor Sanzi.

'We feel this,' added Uxor Bhaneja. 'I have a Company at CR90, the Jacks. I 'cept that they are already dead.'

Dev nodded. 'I am sorry for your loss, Uxor Bhaneja.'

Bhaneja nodded back and, tearful, accepted Sri Vedt's consoling embrace. 'Everyone will be mourning losses before the day is out sir,' said Sri Vedt.

'We are mobilising the armoured cavalry at CR713,' Dynast Kheel of the Thorns announced, 'and the Outremar reserves at Tel Sherak.'

'Sri Vedt has directed four geno companies to move along the line to support the forces at CR88,' said Honen Mu. 'More are needed, in my opinion.'

'Provided they bring their armour support,' put in a Hort officer. 'Armour's what we need–'

'Armour will not suffice,' Mu responded. 'A muscular infantry riposte will be quicker to deliver. These are low tech warriors with blades and black powder bombs, and–'

'Stop wasting time with debate!' Kheel growled, rounding on the tiny uxor. 'This is a shambles! There is no unification of command!'

Honen Mu looked Kheel straight in the eyes, or at least what she could see of them beneath the bulging thorns of his visor.

'I believe, Dynast,' she said levelly, 'that Major General Dev is in charge.'

'That was my understanding too, Kheel, so stand down and bite your tongue,' said Dev with a brush of his hand. 'Senior, where are the nearest Titans?'

'Princeps Jeveth has already ordered the three Titans closest to the incursion forward to engage,' the senior adept replied.

'Bless that old goat for not waiting for an order,' Dev nodded. 'We need to bring the weight of the Hort and Torrent forces in to dam this flood.'

He began to track deployment lines across the glowing chart, conferring with the adepts and officers. Sri Vedt watched, approving of his decisions, gently correcting any detail she 'cepted as unwise.

Mu wondered if it was complacency that had cost them. Besieging forces often suffered from that flaw. The expedition had bested an entire world, and driven the last of its resistance back into one city to die. No one had expected the Nurthene to go back on the offensive.

No, it wasn't complacency, she decided. She reminded herself that the Nurthene did not think the way Imperial humans did. Their actions were determined by values quite alien to Mu and her kind. Driven to the brink of defeat, the Nurthene had not resigned themselves to an inevitable fate.

They had fought back, the way any cornered beast would.

We have underestimated the creatures of this world too many times in this campaign already, Mu thought. Please, let us not be about to do that again.

THE STINK OF wormwood was oppressively strong, and the roar of the approaching host had become so great that Bronzi could no longer hear the voices of the men around him raised in prayer.

He glanced left and right, surveying his lines. The Jokers had done him every credit. Despite the extremity of the moment, and the haste with which they'd been obliged to assemble, the company had formed up perfectly. They were ready, pikes and carbines held at their shoulders.

Bronzi was prepared to bet that the Jokers were going to be the first Army unit to meet the enemy assault that morning with any kind of coordination or discipline. How the Jokers gave account of themselves in the next thirty minutes would therefore be critical. There was no possibility of the geno company men defeating the assault, but if they delayed it, or slowed it down, it would most likely decide how the rest of that damnable day would go.

A full company of Outremar regulars, flying the Samarkand banner, had rushed up into position on the Jokers' right flank, taking up a line across the billet road and a broad valley to the south that faced the desert. A second Outremar unit, smaller, but armed with weapon servitors, was moving up behind them, and the vox said that a Sixth Torrent armour unit with infantry support was a minute or two behind the Jokers.

The Jokers' left flank was the earthwork wall. Skilful placing by Bronzi and his trusted bashaws had spread the Jokers along the higher banks and mounds of the uneven terrain in the billet grounds. They were getting decent tactical instruction over the vox, and the 'cept was with them. Bronzi could see how his men were tightening and adjusting their structures slightly as Mu's wisdom touched them.

Bronzi nodded to himself. His company was as ready as it would ever be. He raised his sabre and held it aloft. There was a sharp crackle of gunlocks releasing.

The tidal wave of enemy warriors was less than a quarter of a kilometre away, the dust storm rolling with it. Dozens of Outremar soldiers fled before it, chased out of their overrun position. They ran frantically towards the geno line, past rows of abandoned tents and empty dug outs. The poor fools were doomed, Bronzi realised. They were in the line of fire, and he could not afford to stay his men for long enough to allow the Outremars to reach safety.

War forced choices on a man, unpleasant choices. At Tel Utan, the Alpha Legion had demonstrated how clinically such choices should be made. Compassion was a liberal folly that spared a life so that a hundred others might die as a consequence.

Bronzi looked up at the company banner, hanging limp and heavy in the dry air. He studied the figure on the banner, the cosmic joker, the trickster god Trisumagister, capering in his motley, a belled wand in one hand, a spillglass in the other. The Joker god knew all too well how wanton and feckless fortune could be, and how quickly time ran out for those who dallied with her affections. Bronzi believed he knew Dame Fortune just as well. You paid for her time, and took her service, and knew that she would be with another man the moment the fancy took her.

The sky overhead had darkened so much that it had turned the colour of arterial blood.

'Geno!' he yelled.

Full-throated, the men echoed the word.

The time was on them.

Bronzi rotated his sabre in the air, making quick, cutting sweeps. The first signal.

On the low ridge to his right, the company mortar teams began to drop shells into their angled tubes and step back, heads turned aside. A plosive, hollow *plunk-plunk* racket began. Mortar bombs whizzed up and over onto the enemy formation, expertly ranged. Bronzi observed the thumps and flashes as they struck with a nod of satisfaction. Each blast cast up white smoke and flailing bodies.

He sawed his raised sabre back and forth. The second signal.

The tripod-mounted cannons and crew-served weapons began to chatter and pulse tracer and blinding las at the oncoming foe. Sections of the leading ranks were demolished. Smoke and bloody steam furled back across the Nurthene press and chunks of shredded meat rained down on them. Bronzi saw echvehnurth elite judder and disintegrate as the heavy fire ripped through them. He saw a galloping monitor tumble over, disembowelled, crushing its rider under its rolling back.

Bronzi chopped his sabre straight down. The third signal.

The rifle lines opened fire. The lingering peal of muzzle cracks sounded like snapping twigs. Firing row by row, coordinated by the yelling bashaws and Mu's 'cept, the ranks of riflemen aimed, fired, re-aimed, fired.

The effect was devastating. Five hundred Anatolian lascarbines, hefty pulse repeaters developed from the ubiquitous Urak-1020 combat gun that had been the workhorse of every Strife-Age warlord's army, trained and fired by professional soldiers drilled to perfection, blazed at the Nurthene. The Jokers were especially famed for the quality of their marksmanship, a fact that Bronzi took a great deal of personal pride in. Every Joker rifleman was a crack shot by Army standards. There wasn't a damn one amongst them who couldn't hit a moving gamebird at nine hundred metres. Bronzi regularly fielded requests from other regiments asking for the loan of a rifleman or two to conduct training programmes. He bitterly regretted that Giano Faben and Zerico Munzer, his two best marksmen, were not at his side that morning. He'd loaned them as tutors to a Gedrosian regiment on Salkizor fifteen months earlier. The last he'd heard, they were en route back to him by pack ship, training tour over.

Giano and Rico were missing all of the fun, the lucky bastards.

The fusillades expertly slaughtered the first eight ranks of the Nurthene host, bringing down infantry and reptile riders alike. Though a handful of the flee-ing Outremars had been clipped too, Bronzi was gratified to see that his men's vaunted skill had spared most. Frantic Outremar survivors were dashing into the geno lines, weeping and screaming for sanctuary.

Tche looked at his het.

'Keep them firing,' Bronzi mouthed over the din. 'Sustain order until there is no distance left.'

Tche nodded.

Bronzi lifted his sabre and held it out straight in front of him at head height. The fourth signal.

The pikemen, laced in between the rows of rifles, took a step forwards with their left feet, and declined their weapons into a murderous fence. Strengthened by sheathes of gravimetric force, the telescopic pikes extended until each one was ten metres long. The pike-men kept the arches of their right feet braced over the grav counterweights in the spikes at the bases of their hafts.

The las-spines on the tips of the pike blades began to sizzle with cising power.

Run onto that, you bastards, Bronzi thought, then you'll discover how badly a geno company can maul you.

As if obeying his will, the Nurthene host did exactly that.

The front edge of the vast blight swarm spilled across the last few metres of open ground, losing men to the sustained rifle volleys at every step. Ten metres, five, two, and still they came, despite their losses. For every Nurthene casualty, there were two more men behind to take his place, and die in turn, and be replaced by four.

The Nurthene reached the pike fence.

The first of them were split apart, sectioned and
chopped. The next waves became impaled, bodies
skewering onto pike blades like living souvlaki. The
geno pikemen leaned into the weight and multiple
impacts, some grunting as their elongated poles
hoisted whole bodies off the ground, writhing like
speared fish, others struggling and collapsing as the
crude mass of corpses pulled their pikes down.
Gravitic counterweights shorted out under the
demands put on them, and hafts splintered as the
gravimetric sheathes supporting their outlandish
lengths evaporated. Pikemen started to use broken sections of their weapons to jab and flay at the pressing
tide.

Now we're in it, Bronzi thought.

The concussion of the Nurthene charge meeting the
geno line sent a ripple of shock back through Bronzi's
ordered files. For a moment, the Jokers held, like a
dam before floodwaters, but the pressure built rapidly.
The Nurthene piled in, hundreds upon hundreds of
them, packing tighter and tighter against the geno bar-
rier. In the gaps where the pike fence had broken,
Nurthene warriors lunged and shoved and stabbed.
Jokers fell down, cut open by whirring falxes, or toppled against the rows behind them. Carbines fired,
point blank and scattershot. Pressed back by the layer
of the dead and dying in the buffer of the front ranks,
the Jokers tried to maintain structure. The dead of both
sides formed a ghastly ridge, which the Nurthene
urgently scrambled over.

'Blades, blades!' Bronzi yelled.

Bashaw Fho, one of his senior men, turned to relay
the order. An iron dart punctured his head and he
dropped on his face. Nurthene arrows were suddenly

coming down like torrential rain. Every man in Bronzi's field of vision was struck by a dart. Bronzi felt one slice his right thigh and another embed itself in his left boot.

He roared and threw himself forwards, sabre in one hand, Parthian revolver in the other.

Sense departed. Instinct took over. He fired his pistol, and saw an echvehnurth's head spray apart. He stroked with his sword, and took the top off a skull. Something hit him in the gut. Winded, he wheeled, and eviscerated a Nurthene with his blade. He shouldered another aside with his bulk, and shot the devil in the head to make it count. Turning, he stabbed another through the chest, and had to twist hard to pull his sword free.

Twenty seconds in and his gun was out. He threw it at a Nurthene and snorted as it bounced off the man's skull. He drew his other sidearm, a shot-loaded back-up piece with a pepperpot snout of six barrels.

The Nurthene cavalry came crashing through the dense forest of fighting bodies with an indiscriminate momentum that trampled both Nurthene and Imperial underfoot. The reptile riders bucked and lurched above the heads of the infantry, like horsemen driving their steeds across a swollen river. Pikes caught some, hooking them out of their saddles, and the riderless beasts ploughed on, snapping and thrashing. More iron darts whizzed down out of the haze, dropping men by the dozen. The churned soil bristled with embedded arrows as if it was sprouting some strange new crop.

The first of the monstrous caimans lumbered into view out of the swirling vapour. Bronzi had never seen animals so enormous: dull-eyed heads the size of

ground speeders, bodies the bulk of Imperial tanks.
Their tails seemed to go on forever. From the ornate
howdahs and fighting platforms on their massive
backs, Nurthene archers in blue silks and silver mail
fired salvo after salvo of iron darts from small, double-
curved bows.

The caimans were inexorable. Their black scales
shrugged off small-arms fire and snapped pike hafts,
and they simply ran over anything that got in their
way.

Bronzi sheathed his sabre, and took aim with his
pepperpot. The clothes on his back felt heavy, and he
knew it was due to the weight of the blood soaking
into them. He lined up on the howdah of the nearest
crocodilian, and discharged all six barrels at once.

Bronzi made up his own cartridges, tight packing
them with twists of monofilament wire, adamantium
shot and pebbles of xygnite putty. Six of them were
enough to explode and shred the howdah and everything in it. Flying shot and wire injured the animal
too. It rocked, and shifted its slow bulk in a slovenly
pain response. Bronzi broke open his pepperpot, the
smoking cases ejecting automatically, and rammed in
six more with shaking fingers.

The caiman was turning towards him, flicking men
into the air with its vast snout. Bronzi clacked the stock-
less weapon shut and re-aimed, the ball of his right
thumb wedged into his cheek. He fired again, and the
tiny, lethal debris of his rounds blew out the creature's
throat and right shoulder in a shower of meat and
blood. It crashed over, its snout gouging into the ground
like a ploughshare and its hindquarters kicked out in
spasm. The tail whipped around and three dozen bodies, caught in its stroke, flew into the air.

He was about to reload, but there was no opportunity. Two echvehnurth came at him with their falxes. He managed to block the first swipe with his spent weapon and then let go of it to wrestle with the Nurthene. The man was screaming at him, but Bronzi had hold of his falx, and jerked him close to dish out a head butt that crushed the man's nose. The Nurthene became more pliant and Bronzi used his grip on the falx to heave the warrior around as a shield. The other echvehnurth had committed a swing of his falx at Bronzi, and the blade cut through his kin's back instead.

The falx belonged to Bronzi suddenly. He pulled it out of the dead fingers, rotated it, and thrust it at the second echvehnurth. The long blade plunged in through the man's left cheek, and the tip came out of the back of his head. Bronzi jerked the unfamiliar weapon free, and slashed wildly at a third echvehnurth who was closing to his left. The blow missed, but the echvehnurth toppled over dead anyway.

Tche grabbed Bronzi by the shoulder. His pistol shot had slain the enemy warrior.

'Back, het!' Tche yelled. 'We have to get back!'

Bronzi knew Tche was right. It was turmoil. All semblance of row and order had vanished, and the Jokers were being broken up into melee units as the Nurthene poured in. The mortar positions had been abandoned and overrun, and over to the right flank, the Outremars seemed to have collapsed entirely.

The rolling wall of dust that came in with the Nurthene like a shroud was washing softly in across the Jokers' stand.

They had done all they could. It felt to Hurtado Bronzi that they had been fighting for thirty or forty minutes, but in fact it had been little more than ten. The 'cept was urging the geno fighting men to fall back and reposition.

'Do it!' Bronzi yelled to his bashaw. 'Disengage and fall back!' He was nursing a fancy that his men could pull away and regroup as skirmishers to harry the Nurthene flanks.

But the dust was enveloping them, and there were Nurthene warriors everywhere. He realised that they would be lucky to get away alive.

THERE WAS NO sign at all of Lord Namatjira's infamous rage. He patiently studied the minute by minute reports Tactical was providing in a composed, reflective manner. It was a curious trait, one that had undoubtedly contributed positively to Namatjira's ascent to the highest military rank. In the grip of a genuine crisis, a glacial calm surrounded him. Lord Namatjira had no time or energy to waste on tirades or recriminations. Those would come later, after the fact. In the heat of open war, a cold, analytical focus was required.

'Our first line of resistance, which included the Jokers geno company, has been smothered,' Major General Dev told him. 'Outremar 234, Outremar 3667 and the Hort Eighteenth have all been lost or put to rout.'

Namatjira nodded. Major General Dev and the senior offices waited for him to speak. From all sides came the low murmur of the adepts and the hum of cogitators.

'The Titans?' Namatjira asked.

'Six minutes from contact,' Lord Wilde replied. 'They should turn this around.'

Namatjira turned and strode out of the chamber. His retinue followed him. Chayne paused, and nodded to Dev, indicating that he should follow.

Bounding with the vitality of a much younger man, Namatjira took the stairs up to the observation deck two at a time, holding up the skirts of his rakematiz robes. His Lucifers jogged double time to keep up.

They came out into the open air, into the curdled dawn. A large, low-walled terrace in the upper part of the palace precinct had been turned over to distance observation. Heavy scopes and detection grids had been erected along the parapet, and tall clusters of vox masts stood like pollarded trees in the centre of the terrace area. The observation crews made respectful namastes as the Lord Commander appeared.

'Carry on', he told them, with a solemn nod that seemed almost respectful. He walked across to the east-facing section of the parapet, and two adepts bowed and stood aside from a high-gain optical scope mounted on a tripod servitor.

'I wanted to see for myself,' Namatjira said quietly as Dev joined him.

'Yes, lord.'

Namatjira peered into the scope's viewer, and carefully adjusted the resonance as he turned it slowly from left to right.

The crest of the earthwork rampart filled the skyline to the north-east. To the south, in the broad road gully that Imperial pioneers had constructed beyond the palace walls, a steady line of transports and tanks were churning east along the track, heading into the incoming storm. A flock of Jackals whined overhead in tight formation, and turned south-east to begin strafing passes. Despite the scope's powerful resolution,

Namatjira couldn't see the enemy, but he could see the vast veil of rolling vapour that mantled them and filled the sky.

'Extraordinary,' said Namatjira, straightening up. He looked at Dev. His eyes were bright, almost excited.

'When a man finds war commonplace, it is time for him to retire from service,' said Namatjira. 'This reminds me why I am content to serve the Emperor for a while longer.'

'Sir?' asked Dev. 'Why is that?'

'Because it's a challenge, Dev, a revelation. The enemy has done the unexpected, and that tests us. In all of the predictive scenarios, did we ever consider that the enemy might launch a full-scale counter-offensive?'

'No, sir. Petty raids and line assaults, perhaps, harrying attacks along our picket, but nothing like this. We didn't realise they had the manpower left.'

'They have taught us a lesson about expectation,' said Namatjira. 'We have them besieged, we have them outnumbered, and we hold a clear advantage in technology. Yet they have invaded us.'

'An act of desperation,' suggested Dev. 'We are about to take their world from them. This is a last stand, perhaps, a last effort to drive us out.'

'And a brave one,' Namatjira replied, 'yet it plays to our advantage.'

Dev hesitated. 'Our advantage, sir?'

'They have broken the siege. They have come out into the open and demanded a pitched battle. We will give them that. We will annihilate them. Nurth will be an Imperial dominion by nightfall. After months of grinding, nuisance war, they have handed us a swift and comprehensive final victory.'

Dev nodded.

Namatjira glanced up at the slow-turning sky. 'It's almost as if that is their intention,' he mused. 'For all the losses we may take, initially, to their brute assault, they must know our superior firepower will ultimately slaughter them. It is almost as if they are committing suicide as a race. It is almost as if they want to die, in one last firestorm, rather than linger on to ignominious defeat.'

Namatjira turned back towards the stairs. 'Commit the Hort and the Torrent in full order to follow the Titans in and crush the enemy. No quarter, major general.' He paused. 'By the way, where are the Alpha Legion?'

'I... I don't know, sir,' said Dev.

'Signal them, major general,' said Namatjira. For a second, a tiny flash of his carefully suppressed rage showed itself. 'Inquire as to their status and ask, respectfully, if they intend to join us.'

THERE WAS A distinct possibility that Hurt was already dead.

Soneka stood on the brow of a dune hill eight kilometres west of the battle, and felt the presentiment sink in. He felt it in his marrow. Hurt was dead. Tactical had informed him that the Jokers had been caught right in the path of the enemy onslaught. He had twice requested permission to draw the Clowns in along the southern service track to support the front line, but had been denied both times. The Clowns were to hold their position. 'At this time, we do not know if the enemy will attempt to penetrate our line in other locations.'

Soneka knew that made sense. The Army had to maintain a defence formation right along the earthwork wall, or be guilty of the most basic military sin. Besides, at the rate the dust cloud was creeping in, the Clowns would be in it too, in no more than an hour.

Yet he dearly wished he could go to his friend's aid.

He'd had less than eight hours to get to know his new command. The transport had delivered Soneka and his bashaws to the Clown billet long after dark the night before. The Clowns had already begun their fire-side revels, and had welcomed their temporary commander with vocal enthusiasm. It had turned into a late night under the stars, fuelled by the Clowns' bottomless supply of znaps.

Soneka had spent two hours talking with Strabo, *fugging Strabo*, who turned out to be a far more competent and likeable man than Dimi Shiban had suggested. Strabo had done his best to keep the company functioning and viable in the absence of a senior genic het. By the end of their chat, Soneka had felt a grudging admiration for the bashaw, who had evidently been holding the Clowns together with a glue composed of charisma and coercion. They spoke of Shiban, and Soneka related some of the things that had passed between him and Dimi at Tel Khat. He chose not to tell Strabo the truth of Shiban's demise. How could a man explain that a fine officer like Dimiter Shiban had been executed by the Alpha Legion, and not have it sound like treason?

Soneka stared out across the dawn landscape. Where the sun should have risen, the ominous pall of vapour hung across the skyline. The sky had congealed into a slick of brown and amber clouds, all wandering slowly against the wind and common sense. The vapour was brighter than the sky, a creamy mass like a deep desert dune caught in noon sunlight. Soneka could smell something on the wind, a resiny smell like myrrh or wormwood.

He had been thinking about Shiban a lot in the last few days. Should he have noticed some change in him, some tell-tale sign that Shiban was not himself? How did one detect the trace of Chaos? The Alpha Legion, if they were to be believed, had some infallible method.

If they were to be believed. Soneka tutted to himself. *After all this, and I'm still not inclined to trust them.*

Drinking with Strabo the night before, Soneka had remembered an idle conversation he'd had with Shiban at Visages. It had meant nothing at the time, but in hindsight, Soneka wondered if it was some kind of sign or symptom.

'I have been dreaming lately,' Dimi had said. 'In my dreams, I hear a verse.'

'A verse, huh?' Soneka had replied.

'I'll tell you how it goes, shall I?'

'You remember it, then?'

'Don't you remember your dreams word for word?' Shiban had asked.

'Never,' Soneka had said.

Shiban had shrugged. 'Fancy that.'

'This verse?' Soneka had prompted.

'That? Oh, that goes–

From the hagg and hungrie goblin
That into raggs would rend ye,
And the spirit that stands by the naked man,
In the Book of Moones defend ye!'

'I know that,' Soneka had said.

'You do?' Shiban had replied. 'Really?'

'My mother used to sing it to me when I was a boy. She called it the Bedlame Song. There were other verses that I now forget.'

'Really? What does it mean?'

Soneka had shrugged. 'I have no idea.'

He still had no idea, except for the awful feeling that it had been the shards of Nurthene bone lodged in Dimi Shiban's throat shaping the words, and not Dimi Shiban at all.

Those shards of bone had been polluting his friend, corrupting him. The Alpha legionnaires had seen it instantly, and turned their weapons on him. Chaos had laced its poison claws into Dimi Shiban's soul.

If that was true, why did Soneka know the verse? Why had his mother known it to sing it to him?

'Sir?'

Soneka snapped out of his thoughts and looked to his left. Lon was approaching, carbine swinging from its long strap.

'Any news?' Soneka asked.

Lon shook his head. 'Command repeats its instruction to hold here. Two units of Outremars are moving in from the east to cement this as a rearguard defence position.'

Soneka nodded. 'Thank you. Let's make ready to slot them in.'

'Oh, and Strabo wants you, sir,' Lon added.

Soneka looked back along the ridge of the dune. The Clowns were assembled in file order, facing the gauzy wound in the dust cloud where the sun should have been climbing. Their shouldered pikes glinted in the toxic light, and the company banners hung like moribund kite sails. Strabo was picking his way up the cinnamon dust of the dune towards them, followed by two riflemen, and a tall man wearing the uniform of a geno het.

Soneka did not recognise the het.

'Sir,' said Strabo, arriving and saluting. 'This het has just reached our position and requests a moment of your time.'

'His name?'

'Uhm–' Strabo began.

'Shon Fikal,' the het said, sticking out his hand. Soneka took it and shook it. The name meant nothing.

'Could we have a word in private?' Fikal requested.

Soneka nodded. He looked back at Lon. 'Have the Clowns present,' he ordered, 'Akkad formation, with Lycad reserve lines. When they get here, draw the Outremar forces around to the south, and have them draw in along our left flank. Then we'll meet with their officers. Relay that to all, especially–'

'Fugging Strabo?' Strabo asked.

Soneka grinned. 'Yes, especially him.'

Lon and Strabo laughed, and turned back down the hill to the waiting company.

'Shon Fikal?' asked Soneka, drawing the het aside, 'and what company does Shon Fikal serve?'

The het shrugged. 'You may know me better by another name, sir,' he said. 'Konig Heniker.'

Soneka stared at him. His hand began to move towards his holstered sidearm.

'No need for that,' said Heniker. He looked Soneka in the face. 'My real name is John Grammaticus, and I need to get a message to the Alpha Legion. It's my understanding that you can arrange that.'

'Your understanding?'

'Don't be coy. Is it true or not?'

'Possibly,' Soneka replied carefully.

'Let's hope so. And quickly. This is the Black Dawn, and we have very little time left.'

* * *

Bronzi reached a tel two kilometres south of the fighting line with about half of his company. They were all exhausted and caked in dust. It had taken thirty minutes of brutal skirmishing to break through the edges of the host pouring across them. Their heads were ringing from the demented melee, and Bronzi knew he wasn't the only one who couldn't clear his mind or stop his hands from shaking.

Two Outremar units had made it to the tel, fragments of demolished strengths, along with a score of Torrent gunners who had been forced to abandon their artillery and flee. Bronzi took charge of the lot of them, reporting numbers and position to Command. He had his bashaws check that the bewildered gunners were armed, even if it was simply with a knife or a broken wheel spoke.

Through his scope, Bronzi could see a long fan of Imperial armour drawing up across the desert from the west, trailing individual wakes of dust from their churning tracks. They were Zanzibari Hort, in full force, pushing up from the marshalling fields at Wadi Suhn. He wondered why they seemed to be hanging back. It was Major General Dev's habit to plunge his fast armour into enemy infantry cohorts like heavy cavalry, and they were certainly gathering in significant enough numbers to make a difference, but they seemed to be dawdling a kilometre or so west of the enemy rush.

The explanation appeared.

Dull giants loomed out of the west through the ochre dust, trudging slowly up out of the great Ahn Aket wadi. They rose into view out of the desert sink, burnished monsters that walked like gods. Jeveth's Titans had reached the fighting line.

There were three of them. The driving dust was such that their distant shapes were obscured from view several times, despite their scale. Bronzi could hear the occasional metal creak or squeal of their vast, lumbering chassis. They strode through the waiting formations of Hort armour at a relentless pace dwarfing the heavy tanks and gun platforms and, line abreast, advanced on the Nurthene host.

The first of them began to fire.

Bronzi winced and lowered his scope. The pulsing flashes of the Titan's limb mounts were dazzling bright, and left a neon after-image on his retinas.

'Great Terra,' he murmured.

Fat beams of luminous energy began to rake out of their cannons, and were quickly supported by huge, pumping bolts of light like shooting stars, and sooty blurs of hard ordnance. The Titans seemed to smoke from head to foot, but it was just dust coming off them. The sustained recoil vibration of their weapon arrays was so great that the dust and sand accumulated during their trek to the front was shaking off their vast, plated forms in powdery swathes.

Bronzi could hear the shriek and wail of their las weapons, and the brisk thunder of their machine cannons. The sounds rolled to him, out of synch with the flashes and light bursts. He'd seen Titans at war before, and the sight never failed to fill him with awe. He was always unprepared for the astonishing rapidity of their rate of fire, the zipping, torrential pulse and spit of green, amber and white light that unloaded from their forearms and shoulders.

The ground ahead of their slow advance began to ripple and distort as it sprouted sudden forests of blooming dust, thrown-up earth and writhing

fireballs. A juddering, flickering carpet of destruction
spread out before them, billowing dark smoke and
vapourised sand back into the edges of the pale fog
that the Nurthene had brought with them. Bronzi
could feel the relentless plosive concussion of the
onslaught quaking his viscera. The ground was
shaking.

The men around him started to cheer and bellow,
but Bronzi could feel their dismay. It was not a scene
that a man could witness without an involuntary
shiver of fear.

He wondered how many of the screaming enemy
had perished in the first second, how many in the second, or the third. It was impossible to see, even with
his scope. He could resolve nothing except the churning smoke, the serried flicker of furious impacts, the
sudden chains of fireballs, igniting and expanding and
overlapping. For a split second, he glimpsed a dark
shape that had to be a giant caiman rise up out of a
flurry of detonations, and then crash back like the hull
of a sinking ship.

The smell of wormwood had gone. In its place was
the reek of superheated gases, of fycelene, of molten,
vitrified sand and of burning flesh.

The Titans ploughed on, stepping through the
seething, burning devastation they had wrought, like
men walking through low mist. Their bombardment
did not relent. Behind them, the Hort armour began to
spur forwards, and Bronzi heard the distant slap and
howl of tank guns beginning to hammer.

The Titans reached the edge of the Nurthene storm
cloud, and waded into its pale fog. For the first time
since dawn, that ominous pall began to recoil and fold
back on itself, as if the three huge war machines were

a fresh breeze out of the desert, slowly blowing the stain away.

SONEKA LED HENIKER, or whatever his name was, down the wadi to where the company's support vehicles sat. He felt a deep unease, as if he was embarking on some unconscionable betrayal. He also knew it was far too late to consider such niceties. He'd made a choice, and he had to live with it.

'They're looking for you,' he said.

'Who is?' asked Heniker.

'Everyone,' Soneka replied.

'I know. I also know who I want to be found by.'

'The Astartes?'

Heniker nodded.

'Why?' asked Soneka.

'It's complicated. The simple answer is that I believe they will listen to me. Your masters in the Imperial Army would simply execute me as the Nurthene agent they believe I am.'

Heniker looked at Soneka with a strange smile. 'Except, they're not your masters, are they?' he asked. 'Not any more. I mean, you don't answer to them first, do you?'

Soneka did not reply.

'How did that happen?' Heniker asked. 'Have you been an operative for a long time, or was it a recent thing? Did they co-opt you or coerce you?'

'That's enough.'

'I'm simply interested, interested in how they work, how their mechanism functions.'

'You're not asking the right man,' Soneka told him. 'Just wait here.'

Heniker nodded and remained where he was. Soneka walked over to an open-topped staff-track, and told the driver to go for a walk.

'Sir?'

'I need to use the vox,' said Soneka. 'Clearance only.'

'Yes, sir,' the man said, and jumped out of the cab. He wandered away in the direction of a group of drivers sitting in the shade of a transport.

Soneka switched on the track's vox unit and let it warm up. He kept glancing over at Heniker, but the man showed no sign of disappearing. When the vox was up to power, Soneka reached into his pocket and took out his biometric. He looked at it for a moment. It would be an easy thing to slot it in, contact Mu, and make a report. An easy thing, Company first, Imperium second, geno before gene. Was it really too late for that now?

He sighed, put the biometric down on the top of the set, and typed a seven digit channel code into it instead. The vox whispered for a moment, and then a voice answered.

'Speak and identify.'

'Lernaean 841,' said Soneka.

The vox murmured. As Soneka watched, the encryption lights on its display lit up, one by one.

'Speak.'

'Is this link secure?' Soneka asked.

'You can see that for yourself.'

'Is this link secure?'

'Yes, Peto. Be assured of it. Do you have information for us?'

Soneka swallowed. 'I have Konig Heniker.'

There was a pause.

'Repeat, Peto.'

'I have Konig Heniker,' Soneka said.

'In your custody?' asked the vox.

'In my company. He surrendered himself to me ten minutes ago. He says he has a message for you, vital, apparently.'

There was another pause.

'What is your location, Peto?'

Soneka read out his chart referent.

'Bring him to us.'

'I can't just–'

'Bring him to us.'

'Listen to me, I am on active station. My company is in the field. Have you seen what's going on out there?'

'We have.'

'I can't just leave my post, I have a duty–'

'Yes, you have,' the vox said. 'There is no alternative. Trust us. Bring Heniker to CR583 immediately. We will cover you.'

'I–' Soneka began.

'Is that understood?'

'Look, it's not as if I can–'

'Is that understood?'

'Yes,' said Soneka quietly.

'Please confirm that this is understood.'

'Yes, it is,' said Soneka.

'Please confirm the chart referent.'

'CR583.'

The link went dead. The encryption lights faded out, one by one.

Soneka sat back and exhaled hard. He keyed off the set, retrieved his biometric, and got out of the track.

'Well?' asked Heniker. 'You look unhappy.'

'Don't talk to me. Just shut up and follow me.'

They slogged back up the soft drift sand of the wadi, and Soneka made Heniker wait while he called to Lon.

'What's up?' Lon asked, jogging over.

'I've got to go.'

'What?' Lon laughed. 'Go? Go where?'

'I can't explain. It's… it's classified.'

Lon stared at him. 'Classified? What are you talking about, het? Are you Army Intelligence all of a sudden?'

'Something like that.' Soneka jerked his head in Heniker's direction. 'Listen, Lon, I think this guy's got information,' he whispered. 'I think he might even be one of the spies everyone's gossiping about.'

'What?'

'Just listen. I need to deliver him to the genewhips or someone.'

'How long are you going to be?' asked Lon.

'Half an hour. I don't know. You're in charge. Tell Strabo you're in charge, my authority.'

'You've only been with the Clowns a few hours,' Lon began.

'Then they're not going to miss me much, are they?' Soneka replied. 'This is important. I'll be back as quickly as I can.'

The bashaw looked unhappy. Finally, he shrugged his heavy, heterosis-magnified shoulders. 'Whatever you think best, sir,' he said.

'Thank you.'

'Does Uxor Mu know about this?' Lon asked.

Soneka shook his head. 'I can't trust the vox, not even encrypted.'

'And if she asks for you? If Command asks for you?'

'Tell them to stand by. Tell them I have left my station to deal with a critical matter, and that I will report to her as soon as I can.'

Lon nodded.

'March in fortune,' Soneka said.

'You too, het.'

SONEKA REQUISITIONED A light atav from the supply line, and they headed south-west across a patch of open desert that resembled a dried seabed. The daylight had taken on an even more unsettling cast, and the sky had turned the colour of beaten copper.

'It's not getting any lighter,' muttered Soneka as he drove.

'You noticed that?' Heniker replied.

'What's going on? What's a "black dawn"?'

'Something unexpected. Something vile. The Nur-thenes' last gift to you.'

'To me personally?'

Heniker laughed. 'To the Imperial expedition.'

'Interesting choice of words,' Soneka replied, fighting with the wheel as they shook over the uneven crust. 'It implies you are not Imperial.'

'I'm not.'

Soneka risked a glance at him. 'What the hell are you, then?'

'I'm human. At least, human enough for your needs. I'm not the enemy, you have to understand that. I'm fighting for the same cause as you.'

'Which is?'

'The survival of the species. My one wish is to save the human race from the slow and tormenting death that is about to overtake it.'

'It would be great if you started dealing in specifics,' said Soneka.

'There's a war coming,' said Heniker.

'We're at war all the time. It's the natural state of mankind in this era.'

Heniker looked out at the desert scrub flashing past. 'This is a special kind of war. It will make all others seem futile and small. The Imperium is simply not prepared for it.'

Soneka checked the chart display, and turned them a few points west, along the edge of a great sink, where the wind was lifting white sand off the rim like steam.

'Can I ask you a question?' Heniker said.

'You can try.'

'Is Rukhsana alive?'

Soneka hesitated before answering. 'Yes, I think so. She was when I last saw her.'

'The Astartes got you to deliver her to them, didn't they?'

'Yes,' said Soneka, 'for her own safety.'

'If that's what they said,' Heniker remarked, 'it must be true.'

'She–' Soneka began. 'I'm sorry. I was reluctant to bring her to them, and I have regretted it since. Army Intelligence was close to taking her. They had discovered the link between you and her.'

Heniker nodded.

'Peto Soneka–' he said.

'What?'

'Nothing. It's funny. Not long ago, I'd almost decided to be you.'

'What does that mean?' asked Soneka.

'I'm talking about borrowing identities from the dead. But it turns out you're not dead.'

CR583 WAS A ruined Nurthene bastion on a sandstone crag overlooking a wide dune sea. The crag ran north in jutting steps, and joined the lip of the continental shelf where it dropped away into the Mon Lo coastlands. The dimpled expanse of the dune sea stretched away to the south, and had turned silver grey in the malevolent light, like a sheet of chainmail spread out and stretched as far as the eye could see. There was no heat, just a cold, restless wind.

Soneka brought the atav up under the shadows of the crag, and they dismounted. The bastion was one of a chain of ancient Nurthene watchtowers that had once guarded the threshold of the open desert, but it had been abandoned and left to ruin centuries before the expedition arrived. It was built of large hardstone blocks, sagging and crumbling in places. The upper levels were gone, and blank spyholes looked out over the dunes like empty eye sockets.

They clambered up the slopes of weathered scree and jumbled boulders. Many of the larger fragments were blocks from the tower that time had pulled down. The place was full of chilly echoes. As their boots disturbed loose pebbles and stones, the clatters repeated around them, spectral and hollow.

'This feels wrong,' said Soneka, drawing his pistol.

'They're just not taking any chances with me,' Heniker told him.

Soneka looked up at the crude walls of the bastion above them. He didn't seem convinced.

They clambered up a little further, to the foot of the bastion.

'There, you see?' said Heniker. 'This is the right place.' He pointed. A small but distinct mark had been heat-scored into the face of a loose block just ahead. The symbol matched the one branded on Soneka's flesh.

'Another house of the hydra,' Heniker muttered.

'What?'

Heniker pushed past him, and climbed up a bank of sand silt to the tower's open gateway. As he passed the marked block, he touched it. 'Still warm,' he called back. 'They haven't been here long.'

They walked under the heavy stone lintel of the gate and entered the tower. Its internal floors and staircases had gone, leaving an empty sleeve of stone open to the sky. It took a moment for their eyes to grow accustomed to the gloom. Through the window slots and open roof, they could see patches of cold, dull sky.

'Hello,' said Heniker.

'Hello, John.'

Two Astartes stood in the darkness, waiting for them. They were in full war plate, but their helmets were off. In the half-light, Soneka realised that he couldn't tell them apart. They were like twins.

'Herzog, Pech,' Heniker said, nodding to them.

'How–' Soneka began.

'John Grammaticus is a marvellously perceptive being,' said a deep voice behind them. A third Astartes came out of the shadows.

'Alpharius,' said Heniker. Soneka heard the confidence slip slightly from the spy's voice.

'Can you be certain?' asked the third Astartes.

Heniker recovered his composure slightly. 'Yes. I have heard your voice before, at the pavilion. I never forget a vocal pattern, and your build is appreciably larger than that of your captains. You are the Primarch Alpharius. Lord, it has taken a great deal of time, effort and trouble to meet you.'

'From the way you have evaded us, John, it would seem that you were keen to postpone that moment,' Alpharius observed.

'Things have changed,' said John Grammaticus. 'More than ever, I need to speak to you, and you need to listen.'

'Then let us withdraw and speak,' said Alpharius. The two towering captains stepped forwards and flanked Heniker, leading him towards the tower's doorway. Heniker looked back over his shoulder at Soneka. 'Thanks,' he said.

Soneka shrugged. The Astartes led Heniker out of the tower.

'Well done, Peto,' said the armoured giant.

Soneka holstered his gun, and made a solemn namaste. 'I must return to my unit, lord,' he said. 'The quicker I can resume my duties, the–'

'No, Peto. I'm sorry. You can't.'

'Why not?' Soneka asked.

'Peto, there is a question you haven't asked yourself.'

'And that is?' Soneka replied.

'How did Konig Heniker know that you were an operative of the Alpha Legion? How did he know how to find you?'

THIRTEEN

The last day on Nurth

IT WAS COLD underground. Soneka had believed the deserts of Nurth to be arid and waterless, but deep in the rock cisterns and chutes, moisture gathered on the walls and dripped off the ceiling like black saliva.

The tunnels they followed were fresh cut, no more than a few weeks old. The walls and floor displayed the tell-tale marks of fusion borers and rock cutters. How long had the Alpha Legion been here, Soneka wondered, and just how much careful preparation had they made before revealing themselves formally?

Quite suddenly, as it seemed to Soneka, they left the darkness of the tunnels and the echoes of their footsteps behind, and came out into the open air. He looked around, blinking.

They had emerged into a deeply scooped bowl of rock. A crown of fossil-dry cliffs rose all around. Overhead, the copper clouds bloated and knotted into tumorous shapes, and there was a foul reek on the wind. Even the Astartes seemed to notice the way the climate was rapidly deteriorating, as if the planet was sick and distempered.

'This world is unravelling,' remarked Grammaticus.

Alpharius cast him a look. It was Soneka's first opportunity to see the primarch's features in daylight. His face was handsome and strong, his scalp clean shaven. In the strange light, his dark skin appeared greenish grey and his eyes hard tungsten.

John Grammaticus was busy studying the details of their surroundings. He could not see Shere or any of the Alpha Legion's pet psykers, but he could feel at least two of them close by, watching him, ready to shut him down if he ventured so much as a millimetre outside his own skull.

In the rock bowl below, Grammaticus saw twenty Alpha legionnaires, the most he had seen in one place. They were armouring into their plate, checking their bolters, and uncasing support weapons from steel drop canisters. A dozen or so regular humans moved amongst them, assisting with the armour fittings, or fetching munition packs and tools. Most of the regulars were dressed in Army uniforms of various kinds, but some wore the shawls and robes of local desert costume. None of the Astartes or the operatives looked up as the party emerged from the cliff tunnel.

On the far side of the deep bowl, a heavy drop-ship crouched on thick claw-footed stanchions under dense camouflage netting. The drop-ship was of a non-standard pattern, or at least no pattern Grammaticus was familiar with.

John Grammaticus could feel the low throb and warble of powerful vox transmitters. He could smell communication all around him: encrypted flows, eddies of communication, estuaries of data flowing into information seas. The Alpha Legion was on a war footing, and this place had to be just one of many bolt-hole reserves preparing to mobilise.

Time was running out…

'My lord primarch–' Grammaticus began.

Ingo Pech shot him a hard look, and Grammaticus fell silent. Alpharius turned and walked away from them, down the stone litter of the slope to the floor of the basin where his warriors were making ready. One of them rose, half-armoured, and began to speak with him.

Grammaticus watched with mounting interest. They were too far away for him to overhear, and the angle was wrong for him to lip read, but he could discern their body language. Moreover, he could compare them. The warrior Alpharius had gone to talk to was big, even by the standards of hybrid vigour exhibited by Astartes. He matched the primarch in every dimension. Their body language duplicated, down to the slightest gesture. And their faces… they were like twins.

Grammaticus wondered if he had been wrong, or deliberately misled, in his identification. Who was the primarch here? Who was Alpharius? How many layers of deception had the Legion woven about themselves?

'Who is that?' he asked Pech.

'Who do you mean?' the first captain replied sullenly.

'The brother speaking with Alpharius.'

Pech looked at Herzog, who shrugged.

'Omegon,' Pech said.

'Omegon?' Grammaticus echoed.

'Commander of the stealth squad,' Herzog said. He and Pech laughed, as if at a private joke.

Grammaticus realised he knew what it was. His eyes widened. He knew he had to test this. He reached out with his mind.

A telekinetic scream tore into his head and blew the roof off his skull. He squealed, and fell on his face.

No, you don't, said a voice. The voice belonged to Shere.

Soneka started forwards in alarm. Heniker had suddenly convulsed and collapsed.

'It's all right, Peto,' said Pech calmly. 'He just got a little too inquisitive.'

'I don't understand,' said Soneka. 'He didn't do anything.'

'Nothing you could see,' Herzog advised.

Heniker lay on his face in the dust, twitching and moaning. Blood leaked out of his ears.

'Have you killed him somehow?' Soneka asked.

'It'll take more than that to finish the likes of him,' said Herzog. He raised his heavy bolter in a manner that suggested he knew at least one reliable alternative.

Soneka pushed past the massive second captain and bent down beside Heniker. Herzog laughed at the affront, and glanced at Pech. 'He's got some balls.'

'That's why I picked him,' Pech replied.

Soneka rolled Heniker over into the recovery position, and made sure his airway was clear. Froth drooled from the corner of the downed man's chewing mouth.

'Just breathe, Heniker,' he said. 'Just breathe slowly.'

'I know…' the man gurgled.

'Shush.'

'I know,' Heniker insisted, in a wet voice. 'I know how to recover from a psychic attack. Give me a moment.'

He opened his eyes. One had become very blood-shot. 'It's John, sir.'

'What?'

'My name, my real name, it's John. It always has been.'

Soneka nodded.

Alpharius and the warrior he had been talking with were walking up the slope towards them.

'Time to talk, then, John Grammaticus,' said Alpharius.

'He's hurt,' Soneka protested.

'He's sound enough,' said the Astartes at Alpharius's side.

Alpharius raised a hand. 'Your sympathy does you credit, Peto. Thank you.'

With Soneka's assistance, John Grammaticus rolled over and sat upright, wiping his mouth and looking up at the towering figures.

'You're so alike,' he said.

'It plays to our strength,' said Alpharius. 'Anonymity in shared identity. We all make an effort to look alike.'

Grammaticus chuckled and coughed. 'That's not what I meant.'

'To the eyes of non-heterosic humans, all Astartes look alike,' Herzog said.

'You cannot read our features, or distinguish our dis-similarities,' said Pech. 'To you, we are inhuman things stamped out of a single mould.'

Grammaticus shook his head. 'That's not what I meant either.' Leaning on Soneka, he rose to his feet. 'You're too alike. More alike than the rest. Face, voice, build, mannerisms. Like twins.'

'You cannot possibly read or distinguish the subtle differences in-' Alpharius began.

'No, I can. I really can. That's what I do,' said Grammaticus. 'Yes, you all look alike, to simple human eyes. They look alike to you, don't they, Peto?'

'Every one of them.' Soneka replied.

Grammaticus nodded. 'You look the same to Peto, but I can see. Him, he's three, maybe three and a half centimetres taller than the man beside him. He has heavier cheek bones. He has a thicker neck, and a propensity to grow hair. Those two are alike, except around the eyes, where it is telling.'

'Gene stock traits,' said Pech.

'No,' said Grammaticus. 'Cosmetic efforts to resemble one another. Except you–' he looked at Alpharius and Omegon. 'You really *are* identical.'

'The differences between us are simply too subtle for you to detect,' Omegon said.

'I doubt that. I really doubt that. Which one of you is Alpharius?'

'I am,' said Alpharius.

'Very well, let me rephrase the question,' said Grammaticus. 'Which one of you is the primarch?'

Alpharius smiled. 'I think it's high time we started asking the questions, John. You came looking for us, hunting for us, and you found us. Then you did everything you could to evade us. Now you come to us again. Why?'

'I was sent to broker terms with you, with the Alpha Legion,' Grammaticus replied.

'This would be by the Cabal you described?' Pech asked.

'Yes. They sent me. I knew the endeavour would be dangerous, and that you would resist me, so I was wary. However, matters have shifted, and I come to you openly.'

'Does the Cabal know of your change in tactics?' asked Herzog.

'The Cabal *ordered* me to change my tactics,' Grammaticus replied. 'Brokering of terms can come later. I'm here to warn you. This world has about a day of life left in it. You must flee before it overwhelms you.'

'WE'LL HEAD WEST,' said Bronzi. Tche nodded, holding the chart flat against the face of a boulder.

'West it is,' he agreed.

'The service track's probably–'

Tche shook his head. 'No, down the wadi and through there. The dry bed. Any further north and we risk getting caught up in this.'

'Oh, come on,' Bronzi said. 'It's all over, bar the body bagging.'

'Is it?' asked Tche. 'Have you seen the sky?'

'Fug the sky,' said Bronzi.

'Yeah, well, the wadi will keep us clear of any potential action, that's all I'm saying,' Tche retorted.

'Hm. I like that thinking,' Bronzi admitted. The elements he had gathered around him were too weak and unfocused to get swept up in the main brawl. If he could conduct them west as far as the palace, or at least its environs, the uxors could redeploy them properly to strengthen other sections.

'All right, we're moving out,' Bronzi told his senior bashaw. 'Wake 'em up and tell 'em where to go.'

Tche ran forwards, calling out instructions. The other bashaws became alert and started to relay them. The Jokers got to their feet obediently, gathering their kit and weapons. The Outremar troopers looked befuddled at the orders.

'Get lively and move!' Bronzi yelled at them. 'Come on, girls, it's time to go!'

Most of them, the Jokers included, had spent the last forty minutes watching a spectacle they would tell to their grandchildren. Titans and Hort armour, laying into the enemy with full military power, it was the stuff fireside tales were made of, the stuff that made grandpa or great-grandpa seem bigger than life.

An incredible sight, the Titans blasting all hell out of the landscape, slowly advancing into the vapour flume with the tanks of the Zanzibari Hort at their gigantic heels. Bronzi couldn't begin to guess how many thousand tonnes of munitions had been delivered into the enemy ranks. If there was a Nurthene left alive, he'd be surprised. The Imperial Army, combined with a Titan Legion from Terra's fraternal twin, Mars – *Emperor bless the Mechanicum!* – had done what it was designed to do. It had crushed, it had obliterated.

It had overwhelmed Nurth's last ditch effort.

The great show had disappeared from view. The Titans and their support line of heavy tanks had vanished into the vapour's haze. Bronzi could still hear them firing, still see the flash, and feel the distant over-pressure thump of their detonations.

The Nurthene storm, the veil that had so comprehensively overwhelmed the earthwork line at dawn, was folding back and dissipating. Bronzi imagined fields of burning sand, littered with dead Nurthene and exploded reptile carcasses, imprinted with the smouldering footprints of Titan monsters.

'Come on. Come on!' he shouted. 'Get off your arses, you idiots! Let's move! Down the valley and west!'

He looked up.

He suddenly realised how black and lightless the day had become.

'THE NURTHENE POSSESS a device known as a Black Cube,' Grammaticus said.

'Explain the term,' Pech insisted.

'I can't. I don't understand it. I only know what it does. It's a device, an ancient device. Older than you can conceive, a weapon constructed before the rise of man. The Cabal believes that they were used in ancient wars between the first-comer races, in the galaxy's youth.'

'Another portentous myth with no basis in–' Herzog started to say.

'Listen to me!' Grammaticus cried out. He was using his voice at its most formidable and persuasive. There was no longer any time for restraint. He had to make them listen and understand. Modifying his tone and pitch with a skill finessed over centuries, he made Soneka start, and the Alpha legionnaires stare at him. 'The Cabal believes there are no more than five of these infernal devices left in existence,' he said. 'It is a weapon of Chaos ritual. A Black Cube, once activated, manufactures a Black Dawn. From that point, no life on the planet is safe.'

'How is a Cube activated?' asked Pech.

'By blood,' said Grammaticus. 'By the sacrifice of blood. Don't you see, the Nurthene want you to kill them. They want you to slaughter them. That activates their weapon.'

A gust of foul wind swept around the rock bowl. Down in the bottom of the basin, the armouring Astartes and their operatives had stopped in the midst of their activities. Some had risen to their feet. They were listening too. 'How do we stop it?' asked Alpharius.

'You can't, not now,' said Grammaticus.

'Then what?'

'You must abandon this enterprise,' said Grammaticus. 'You must quit this world immediately and retreat to a point of safety. There is still a chance to save the Alpha Legion. Furthermore, if you are persuasive enough, there is still a chance to save the expedition forces.'

'Namatjira won't just–' Alpharius began.

'You're a primarch!' snapped Grammaticus. 'One of you is, at any rate. Use your influence, and even a Lord Commander will listen! Either that, or cut your losses and leave them to their doom. The important thing is… the Alpha Legion is far too valuable a resource to be lost in such a senseless manner.'

'You're here to save us, then, are you, John?' asked Omegon.

'Why do you care so much?' asked Alpharius.

Grammaticus sighed. 'Because I was sent here as an ambassador to open a dialogue between you and the Cabal. I've told you this already. I told it to Pech, I've said it until I'm sick of the words. The opportunity for subtle persuasion has gone. Come with me, flee this world, escape this doom, and I will take you to a place of revelation.'

'I don't run from a fight,' said Alpharius. 'I am committed. I don't just cut my losses and walk away when I'm oathed to a moment.'

'Don't you?'

Grammaticus and the Astartes glanced at Soneka.

'Did you speak, Peto?' Pech asked.

Soneka hesitated. 'Yes. I said… I meant… that's what you do. That's what I've seen you do.'

Alpharius's eyes narrowed. 'Peto?'

'Pragmatism, unsentimental pragmatism, seems to be your defining quality. I'm not, forgive me, I'm not questioning your honour or courage, but you do what you have to. You do whatever is necessary to accomplish the greater goal.'

Alpharius took a step towards him. 'Have you suddenly become an expert on the Alpha Legion's military ethics?'

Soneka shook his head. 'I only report what I've seen with my own eyes. Without qualm or reservation, you do whatever is necessary to win. The Dancers I left in the sand at Tel Utan will attest to that.'

'You make us sound clinical and ruthless,' said Alpharius.

'You are the most effective fighting mechanisms Terra has ever produced,' said Grammaticus behind him. 'Is that so bad a description?'

There was a long silence, broken only by the breath of the noxious wind. Alpharius stared at Omegon, then nodded curtly. He turned to Herzog and Pech. 'Signal the Legion to stand down and prepare for immediate withdrawal. Rapid evacuation pattern, unit by unit, standard reconstitution policy.' Alpharius glanced at Grammaticus. 'What is a safe distance?'

'The edge of the system would be prudent,' Grammaticus replied.

Alpharius turned back to his captains. 'Standard reconstitution policy,' he continued, 'in the heliopause. Do it now.'

They both saluted and moved off urgently, muttering streams of orders into their suit mics.

'Signal the Lord Commander, and tell him I will attend upon him in thirty minutes,' Alpharius told Omegon. Then he turned to face Grammaticus.

Grammaticus looked up into the primarch's eyes.

'If it turns out that you have played us in any way, John,' Alpharius said. 'If this proves to be a trick or a ruse, I will personally oversee your execution, and then I will hunt out and exterminate your precious Cabal.'

'That, sir, is entirely reasonable,' replied John Grammaticus.

PART TWO

THE HALTING SITE

ONE

**Vicinity of 42 Hydra, five months after the
fall of Nurth**

THE LOCK PLATE beside the hatch knew his hand, read it with a soft blink of light, and the hatch slid open. He picked up the heavy canvas satchel, slung it over his shoulder, and stepped through.

'Good day to you, John,' he said.

John Grammaticus smiled. 'Hello, Peto. Is it another day already?'

'Already indeed,' replied Peto Soneka, putting the satchel down on the steel table.

'One would hardly know,' said Grammaticus, true to form. It had become a refrain between them, varying only slightly from day to day, a shorthand of comradeship.

The cell was crude, but large enough for a man to waste hours in it pacing up and down. A cot, two chairs, the table, a basin in the wall and a chemical toilet were its only features. There were no windows, and the lights were on permanently. After weeks of quiet complaint, Grammaticus had been allowed an eye-shade so that he could simulate night.

Soneka never closed the hatch behind him. It remained open for the duration of each visit, tantalisingly open. A deliberate psychological effect, he presumed. Soneka did not close the hatch behind him, because he had been *told* not to close the hatch behind him.

With its recycled air, the lingering scent of the toilet and the bad lights, the cell was charmless and unpleasant, but despite the environment he was required to live in, Grammaticus was always clean and respectable. They gave him a change of clothes every three days, and he washed at the basin. His beard had grown out bushy and grey in a distinguished manner, like an old general's. They had not permitted him a razor.

Soneka opened the satchel and started to take out its contents.

'What do we have today?' asked Grammaticus, with false brightness.

'Cold meat and cheese,' Soneka told him, lifting out small parcels wrapped in waxed paper, 'a jar of pickled capers, a bottle of wine, a loaf of bread and the usual vitamin supplements.'

'A veritable feast,' said Grammaticus.

'The cheese is particularly welcome,' Soneka agreed.

They sat down, on either side of the table, and began to share out the food. Soneka took two plates, two cups, two bowls, two paring knives and two spoons from the bag, and set the bag on the floor. Grammaticus used one of the knives to slice the block of rindy cheese and share it out. Soneka pulled the cork plug out of the wine bottle, and poured measures into the waiting cups. They moved around one another, dutiful and relaxed, like a married couple that know each other's ways intuitively. Five months of shared meals would do that.

'Did you sleep well?' Soneka asked, passing one of the cups to Grammaticus.

'Peto, I haven't slept well in a thousand years,' Grammaticus replied, 'but I shan't complain. I have reason to believe my mission is about to be completed.'

'Really?'

Grammaticus took a bite of bread, sipped his wine as he munched, and placed the cup in the centre of the table between them. He pointed at it.

'What?' asked Soneka, adding a slice of cheese to his hunk of bread.

'The ripples, Peto, the ripples.'

Some distant vibration, too subtle to be felt, was being transmitted up through the deck into the table and the cup. Tiny, concentric ripples pulsed out across the surface of the wine like a sensor pattern.

'The drive rate has altered,' said Grammaticus. 'I think we're firing the engines to retard towards translation.'

Soneka put a couple of fat capers in his mouth and nodded back with a grin. 'We'll be translating in the next hour. Nothing much gets past you, does it, John?'

Grammaticus, chewing another mouthful, raised his eyebrows sardonically.

WHEN THEY WERE done with the meal, Soneka refilled the satchel and nodded goodbye to Grammaticus. As he closed the hatch behind him, he saw Grammaticus staring back at him from his seat at the table.

Soneka felt his profound loneliness return the moment the hatch had sealed. Though he could not, in all fairness, describe Grammaticus as a friend, the Cabal's agent was the closest approximation to real human company that Soneka had experienced in half a year.

Living amongst Astartes was a strange experience, and the novelty had long since worn off.

THE FIRST CAPTAIN was rehearsing close combat techniques in his chambers. Dressed in a sleeveless bodyglove, he stepped and turned smoothly through a sequence of passes, blocks and ripostes using a hardwood practice sword. Around him, eight operatives echoed his moves in perfect unison. The matching precision was impressive to watch. Soneka stood in the hatchway for a while, observing the session, until Pech signalled a halt with a brief nod.

The operatives filed out past Soneka. One of them was Thaner, the man Bronzi had taken him to on that fateful night. Thaner acknowledged Soneka with a slight tilt of his head.

There was no camaraderie between operatives. Each of them existed in his own quiet, driven world of service and duty. Soneka had not expected to engage with the Astartes, for they were a breed apart, and the distinctions between them and regular humans perfectly obvious, but the behaviour of the operatives puzzled him. They were all human still, humans drawn together for a common purpose, but they shared nothing. Soneka had never known a company of men to remain so disparate. The normal habits of military comradeship were missing. No one ever spoke of who they had been or where they had come from; no one ever shared a drink or a humorous story. In their way, they seemed less human than the Astartes.

Pech beckoned Soneka over.

'How is John today, Peto?' he asked, placing his practice sword back on the rack.

'Much the same as ever: contained, patient. He has deduced that we are at the point of arrival. That seems to have lifted his spirits slightly.'

Pech nodded. 'Anything else?'

Soneka shrugged. 'Yes, one thing. He didn't ask me about Rukhsana today.'

'No?'

'I can't remember a day in the last five months when he hasn't. I always tell him he'll be allowed to see her in time, but today, he didn't ask.'

'Well, at least you didn't have to lie,' Pech replied.

'There is always that.'

Pech began to buckle on a pair of heavy boots. 'I want you by my side for the next few days, Peto,' he said. 'Operations are about to begin, and I need you on hand to furnish me with any insight you might have concerning Grammaticus. You've spent more time with him than anyone else.'

'I don't pretend to know him,' Soneka replied. 'He hardly takes me into his confidence.'

'None of us knows him,' said Pech, pulling on a heavy, knee-length robe. He sighed. 'Sometimes I wish we'd just ripped the secrets out of his head. Shere might have enjoyed that.'

Soneka was aware that the Alpha Legion had strenuously debated the best way to handle Grammaticus. It had been decided that it wasn't prudent to risk damaging or killing their only link to the Cabal.

'We have come all this way,' Pech said, 'and we still don't know if he's lying.'

'He wasn't lying about Nurth,' said Soneka.

* * *

FIVE MONTHS BEFORE, Nurth had died, exactly as John Grammaticus had said it would. The final day, which had never properly dawned, had dragged out, darkening and thickening, into a primordial night. The atmosphere had congealed in a toxic caul of ash and soot, and hurricane winds that had flayed the surface of the world and boiled the oceans.

Lord Namatjira had at first categorically rejected Alpharius's instruction to abandon Nurth. He had laughed derisively in the primarch's face at the very idea of giving up on the hard-won victory presently in his grasp. His scornful laughter had grown hollow as conditions worsened, however, and it had become clear, even to him, that it would be suicide to remain. Gripped by a fury as fierce as the gathering damnation storms, Namatjira had ordered the retreat.

Turmoil had followed. No force the size of the 670th Expedition could be deployed or withdrawn easily, even under emergency protocols. Waves of landers and heavy lifters braved the vicious windshear to set down at makeshift extraction points where Army companies had hastily gathered. Imperial strongpoints and vehicles were abandoned. Entire units, struggling to make their way to evacuation rendezvous, were lost forever in the encroaching blackness. Some lift ships, fully laden, failed to make it back through the blizzarding atmospheric wrath to orbit. Others returned to the fleet with their holds empty, having been unable to locate a landing site or anything worth rescuing.

The panic-fuelled nightmare of evacuation had finally been called off after seventeen hours. Almost half of the expedition's strength failed to make it off Nurth alive. The logistical difficulties of extracting heavy vehicles meant that armour companies suffered particularly heavy losses. Princeps Jeveth openly denounced Namatjira. A lack of specialist super-lifters resulted in six of his Titans being left behind. A week after the fall of Nurth, Jeveth detached his force from the 670th Fleet and returned to Mars, warning the Lord Commander that he might never expect collaboration from the Mechanicum again.

No one in the Imperial expedition ever laid eyes on the object that slew Nurth. No confirmation was ever made of its size, construction, or process, nor even if it was actually a Cube at all. No one could account for its effect, or properly explain exactly the manner of the doom it unleashed, except that it was likened to some invasive disease, a plague that swept through organic and inorganic structures alike.

Imperial minds felt it, however. Its molten hiss escaped the failing edges of Nurth's atmosphere and bit corrosively into the astrotelepathic orders of the fleeing expedition fleet. It triggered madness and delusion. The uxors of the Geno Chiliad felt it less profoundly, but they felt it all the same. Privately, they agreed that it sounded like the mewling and squealing of some daemon, awakened and trapped in the lightless, broiling cinder pit that Nurth had become.

Peto Soneka still dreamed about the havoc of that day. He no longer slept well at all. When he wasn't dreaming about the roiling black clouds sweeping in to annihilate them all, he dreamed uneasily of diorite heads, and the verses lodged in Dimi Shiban's throat.

TWO

High anchor, 42 Hydra Tertius, the next day cycle

GRAMMATICUS WAS DRESSED and ready when Soneka arrived. He sat at the metal table, exhibiting a sort of anxious excitement.

'I imagine he's ready to speak with me,' said Grammaticus.

'He is.'

'Finally,' said Grammaticus, and got to his feet. 'We're at high anchor?'

'At high anchor above 42 Hydra Tertius. An interesting choice of location, John.'

Grammaticus smiled. 'It was selected very particularly, as a token of respect for the Alpha Legion's iconography. Do they approve?'

'I think the name just makes them suspicious. Then again, everything makes them suspicious.'

Grammaticus laughed, but Soneka could hear the nervous edge in it. 'John,' he said, 'I don't really understand what this is about, but if you want things to go

your way, if you want your mission to succeed, you
have to get yourself together. You've been in here too
long. You're wired. Try to calm down. Please don't be
hyper, or joke around with them.'

Grammaticus nodded and cleared his throat. He
took a deep breath. 'I understand,' he said. 'Thanks for
the advice. I am a little tense.'

They left the cell together. Grammaticus took one
last look back, as if he fully expected to see himself still
in it.

Soneka led him down the dull metal hallway of the
detention block, past the blank hatches of other cells,
and through two cage doors that slid open when he
waved his hand in front of the lock plates.

'How is the hand?' Grammaticus asked.

'Better than the old one,' Soneka replied.

They walked out into one of the battle-barge's main
spinal corridors. The deck was mesh, and the corridor
was so large that a tank might have been comfortably
driven along it. The gunmetal walls, banded with hor-
izontal bars of frosty mauve lights, seemed to stretch
away forever. Their footsteps echoed on the metal.
There was no one else around.

'They trust you,' Grammaticus remarked.

'What?'

'To send you to fetch me, with no escort.'

'This is an Astartes battle-barge, John, one of the
most fortified and secure warships in human space.
Where exactly would you run to?'

'Good point. They do trust you, though,' said Grammaticus. 'Did you ever wonder why they let you do
this?'

'Do what?'

'Fraternise with me? Eat lunch with me every day?'
Soneka made a sour face. 'I don't ask. In almost all
respects, I've been as much of a prisoner as you.'

'You must have thought about it,' Grammaticus
pressed.

'I suppose,' said Soneka, 'they believe you'll relate to
me better than to any of them, human to human.'

'Or whatever it is I am,' Grammaticus chuckled.

Soneka glanced at him. 'Actually, I asked their permission. They're not like me. They don't even eat, or
not that I've witnessed. For the first few days, I'd dine
alone, and then bring you your food. It seemed stupid
not to combine the two events.'

'And they said yes?'

'They said yes,' Soneka agreed. 'Of course, it quickly
occurred to me what they were really after. They
wanted me to build a rapport with you, the sort of rapport that none of them could fashion personally.'

'Didn't they worry that I might somehow... influence you?'

Soneka looked Grammaticus in the eyes. 'I think
they were actually hoping that might happen.'

'What do you mean?' asked Grammaticus.

'You wouldn't dare try anything with an Astartes, but
with a lowly operative? I believe they were interested
in what they might learn about you if you did try
something.'

Grammaticus pursed his lips. 'That's remarkably perceptive of you, Peto. So, do you think you've fallen
under my thrall?'

Soneka shrugged. 'How could I tell? I know you're a
dangerous man, John, and that you can achieve with
words what a Lord Commander couldn't with Titans.

My impression has been that we've always talked as friends. I doubt you'd admit otherwise.'

Grammaticus nodded. 'Of course I wouldn't,' he said.

A LITTLE FURTHER on, Grammaticus stopped and looked over his shoulder.

'What's the matter?' asked Soneka.

'I thought,' Grammaticus began. 'I thought I heard–'

'What?'

'I thought I heard her calling out to me,' he said.

'It was your imagination, John,' Soneka told him.

IN THE LONG walk from the detention block to the briefing chamber, they saw no signs of life, except for a pair of polished arachnoid servitors working at a wall panel and a busy cyberdrone that zipped past high overhead and vanished into the distance of the vast corridor.

The hatch was a huge blast shield, with the emblem of the hydra graven on its oiled surface. Soneka had seen many parts of the barge during his time on board, and all of them had been spare, functional and utilitarian. This was the only piece of decoration he had come across.

As they approached, the hatch opened, lifting a thick, toothed base up out of slots in the deck. It rose like the gate of a portcullis.

The chamber beyond was almost pitch black, but they could both sense how large it was. Twenty metres in front of them, illuminated by a single amber glowglobe, Alpharius sat on a heavy, undecorated steel throne. He was wearing his full armour, and his helm sat on the broad arm of the throne beside his right hand. He stared at them.

'Approach.'

'John Grammaticus, lord,' said Soneka.

'Thank you, Peto. Stay, please.'

Soneka nodded, and stepped to one side.

'John,' said Alpharius.

'Great lord,' Grammaticus replied.

'I believe there will be a reckoning,' said Alpharius. 'Your cooperation is expected.'

'And will be given, to the best of my abilities,' Grammaticus said.

'We stand at high anchor above the world you selected,' the primarch said. 'The expedition fleet is about nine hours behind us. As soon as it has arrived and recomposed, we will commence surface deployment.'

Grammaticus swallowed briefly. 'That suggests a war footing, as does your armour.'

Alpharius nodded. 'I don't venture into the unknown unarmed, John. You told me that this Cabal of yours asked you to bring me here. You say they wish to talk of weighty matters. I welcome discourse, and enjoy the stimulation of meeting new minds and new ideas, but I am no fool. The Imperial Army and my forces will assemble and make ready. At the slightest sign of disingenuity or betrayal, your Cabal, if it is really here, will face extreme sanction.'

'You must do as you see fit, lord,' said Grammaticus. 'In the spirit of cooperation, I would say that the Cabal does not find threat postures especially endearing. It would prefer to undertake its dealings with you without the duress of a military presence. However, I believe the Cabal will make allowances. They appreciate that you are a warlord, and that you will behave according to your nature. It is, after all, precisely your nature that interests them.'

Alpharius nodded again. 'Then we have a first measure of understanding.' He raised his left gauntlet.

There was a series of deep, mechanical thumps, and light began to shaft into the chamber, as the entire starboard wall began to retract into the roof. Soneka realised that a row of immense blast shutters was gradually opening to reveal a vast stellar observation port. The light, soft yellow but bright, like a summer's haze, poured under the opening shutters, and slowly flooded the chamber.

The briefing chamber was as large as he had expected, with a black grille floor, heavy bulkheads of bare metal, and a vaulted roof. Everything in it was bathed in the smoky golden radiance that streamed in from outside. Along the inner wall, behind Alpharius's spare, cyclopean throne, thirty-five fully plated Alpha Legion Astartes stood like monumental statues. They had been there all along, silent in the darkness.

They were all captains or squad leaders. Soneka recognised Pech and Herzog by their company marks, Omegon in his almost black armour, and Ranko in the monstrous plate of the Terminators. They were illuminated, in the golden light, like some elysian vision.

Grammaticus had seen them too. Soneka saw the pang of undisguised fear in his eyes.

Alpharius rose to his feet. The shutters ground to a halt, fully open. The view through the giant observation port was as impressive as the revealed post-human warriors. The vault of space, more profoundly deep than Soneka had ever seen it, was thick with distant stars that shone like motes of dust in sunlight. Radiant streamers of gas, as delicate and multicoloured as moth wings, lay across the star field like veils, causing some stars to glitter like faceted jewels, and others to fog and blur like uncut stones.

Nearby, perhaps only a hundred and fifty million kilometres away, lay a pale red sun, the local star and the source of the bathing yellow sunlight that made both the view and the chamber seem as if they were set in amber. Closer still, looming below them, was the night-side of a planet.

Alpharius pointed at the star. Hololithic graphics immediately lit up across the observation port, outlined the star, and contoured it. Numerical columns rapidly scrolled up the port, followed by block statistical data.

'Freeze there. Dim radiance and magnify by six,' said Alpharius. The hololithic projection blinked, and centred a glare-adjusted magnification of the star on the port display.

'42 Hydra,' said Alpharius. 'It's an old, population II star with poor metallicity. Its life is reaching an end. 42 Hydra, would you care to comment, John?'

Grammaticus looked lost for words.

'Lord?' said Soneka.

'Speak, Peto.'

'As I understand it, 42 Hydra was selected as a mark of homage to the Legion. An inside joke, if you will. I believe that, in hindsight, John possibly regrets the flippancy of the gesture.'

Alpharius nodded.

'That,' Grammaticus said, coughing but recovering some composure, 'that is the case, lord. No disrespect or mockery was intended. 42 Hydra was chosen because of your emblem.'

'Is this typical of the symbolism and nuance we can expect from the Cabal?' asked Pech.

'No,' said Grammaticus.

'Good,' said Omegon, 'because it's childish.'

'42 Hydra has six planets,' Alpharius continued. 'The third one, designated 42 Alpha Tertius, being the one you directed us to, John. We sit in orbit above it.'

'Above Eolith,' said Grammaticus.

'Repeat?'

'Eolith,' said Grammaticus. 'The Cabal's name for this world, 42 Hydra Tertius, is Eolith.'

'So noted. Isolate and enlarge.'

The graphics returned the star to its original position, and then surrounded the dark globe below them, sectioned it, and brought it up into the centre of the port. More graphics spooled across the projection.

'Small and unremarkable,' said Alpharius, 'it is wracked by pestilential weather and acid precipitation. Uninhabited, according to our vital sweeps, auto-probes detect only basic xenofauna.' He paused. 'Distinguish,' he ordered.

The display revealed the surface of the planet in terms of mottled topographic imaging, and then over-laid that with a graphic of striated weather patterns. The world looked like a grey, flecked iris.

'A backwater, in other words,' said Alpharius, 'and utterly hostile to human life. And yet…' He paused again. 'Enlarge.'

The display rapidly magnified a small section of the world and outlined it: a circular whorl of white vapour like an island in the streaked grey cloud mass.

'In the southern hemisphere,' Alpharius continued, 'we read a zone three hundred kilometres in diameter that possesses a rudimentary human bearable atmosphere. What are the chances of that?'

'What, indeed?' Grammaticus replied.

'Would you care to explain?' asked Alpharius.

Grammaticus took another breath to steady himself and remain calm. 'That is the venue. Elemental processors were activated there about five years ago, to prepare the area for your visit. They've barely had time to manufacture a decent micro-climate, but it's sustainable enough.'

'Atmospheric engineering?' asked Herzog.

'Yes, sir,' Grammaticus replied.

'Magnify specific,' Alpharius instructed. The boxed image of the white vapour blinked half a dozen times as the scale enlarged, resolving details of cloud masses, and then individual formations, until the view looked down through wisps of trailing white cloud at surface details. Soneka peered hard. He wasn't sure what he was supposed to be seeing: a range of hills, mountains perhaps, cold and grey, seen from directly above, and deep pockets of valley shadow. In the middle of the frame, nestled amongst the higher peaks, lay some sort of indistinct pattern, the outline of some structure.

'I find this particularly interesting,' said Alpharius. 'This structure reminded me of something.' He looked back at the port and raised his hand. 'Display and compare archive record N6371.'

A second graphic box appeared beside the first, showing another orbital image, taken under different conditions. It was clearly another world. A network of graphic lines rapidly linked areas on both boxes, until it was evident that hundreds of contextual similarities had been identified. The boxes then shuffled and overlaid. The surface structures matched with an unnerving precision.

'Archive N6371,' said Alpharius, 'is an orbital view of Mon Lo Harbour.'

There was a long silence.

'A structure of that type was the epicentre of an atmospheric deluge that almost annihilated us,' said Alpharius, 'and you take us to its twin on a world where atmospheric manipulation is already underway.'

'I can see how that looks bad,' Grammaticus admitted.

'John!' Soneka hissed.

Grammaticus glanced at Alpharius, and bowed his head respectfully. 'Forgive me, lord.' He walked across to the port and stopped when he was close enough to point out individual details.

'They are the same, because both worlds are halting sites,' he said.

'Define the term,' demanded Pech.

'Of course,' said Grammaticus. 'The Cabal is extremely old, and composed of various... what you would term *xenosbreeds*. They have no shared origin or homeworld. Since the earliest days, the time of their formation, they have been nomadic, moving from one world to the next, like the court circuits of the old kings of Terra.'

'How long do they stay in one place?' asked Omegon.

'However long they want, sir,' Grammaticus replied, 'however long they need. Over the ages, they constructed halting sites on the many worlds that formed their long, orthotenic routes. Landing zones, you see? On some worlds, Nurth being a good example, local populations later inhabited the sites in ignorance of their original purpose.'

'That implies a significant span of time,' said Pech.

Grammaticus nodded sadly. 'I need you to appreciate the duration and extent of the Cabal's activities.

The halting site at Mon Lo was constructed nearly twelve thousand years ago. The one here on Eolith is considerably older, about ninety thousand years. It was the Cabal's previous visits to Nurth, and their understanding of the culture developing there, that caused them to select it as a place to demonstrate to you the–'

'Wait,' said Alpharius. 'Did you just say ninety thousand years?'

'Yes, lord primarch.'

Alpharius seemed to consider this for a moment. 'Continue.'

'I… I've rather lost my thread, sir,' said Grammaticus. 'There is little left that I can explain. The Cabal has prepared the venue, and you have come to meet with them. I suggest…' He cleared his dry throat again, 'I suggest you get on with it. I'm your key, sir. You must take me to the surface and–'

'A moment,' said Omegon. He broke from the rank of watching Astartes, and walked over to the observation port. For a moment, Soneka feared that the warrior was intent on doing some harm to Grammaticus, but instead, he stared pensively down at the dark world below them. He uncoupled his helm and removed it.

'You've enticed us here, John Grammaticus,' he said, 'with vague stories of an impending cataclysm that threatens to engulf mankind and the cosmos, and the role we might take in preventing it. I would like to know a little more before this Legion commits to even a landing.'

Grammaticus laughed out loud.

Omegon looked down at him sharply.

'I'm sorry, Lord Omegon,' Grammaticus said, failing to stifle his giggles, 'but you have brought an entire, militarised expedition fleet across parsecs on the basis of my "vague stories". As I see it, you're committed fairly comprehensively already. Stop prevaricating.'

Omegon glared down at the human. 'First Captain Pech said you described the impending cataclysm as a war against Chaos.'

'I did, sir,' said Grammaticus, 'though the war against Chaos has been raging since the galaxy's infancy. However, the human species has now become the focus of the war, and the Imperium its chosen battlefield. The Cabal has far seen that what happens in the next few years will be pivotal to the destiny of all races.'

Omegon turned and looked back at the planet. 'Pech related something else you said, back in heathen Mon Lo. He said you called what was coming "a great war against yourselves". That would seem to describe a civil war, John Grammaticus.'

'Yes, it would,' said Grammaticus, still staring up at the giant.

'Civil war in the Imperium is an impossibility,' said Alpharius, walking forwards to join them. 'It simply could not happen. The Emperor's plan is–'

'Utopian,' Grammaticus cut in and finished boldly, 'and therefore predicated to fall short of its goals. *Please*. The Alpha Legion is the most pragmatic and subtle of all the Legions. You are not blinded by Imperial dogma like the others. You are not hidebound by Guilliman's ideals of conduct, or rooted in frenzied tribal tradition like Russ's warriors, nor are you stalwart lapdogs like Dorn's famous men, or berserk automatons like Angron's monsters. You think for yourselves!'

'That is the closest thing to heresy that has ever been spoken in my presence,' said Alpharius quietly.

'And that's why you're listening to me,' said Grammaticus, with a grin. 'You recognise the truth when you hear it. You only recruit the cleverest and brightest. You think for *yourselves*.'

He stood between the giants, rising to his scheme. Soneka smiled as he saw John Grammaticus's confidence return.

'The Emperor chases a Utopian ideal,' Grammaticus announced, 'which is fine as far as it goes. It ignites and drives the masses, it gives a soldier something to focus on, but perfection is only ever an ideal.'

'We have considered these issues,' said Pech quietly.

'And?' asked Grammaticus.

'We have come to appreciate that Utopian goals are ultimately counter-intuitive to species survival,' Pech replied.

'No power can engender, or force to be engendered, a state of perfection,' said another captain, 'because perfection is an absolute that cannot be attained by an imperfect species.'

'It is better to manage and maintain the flaws of man on an ongoing basis,' said Pech.

Grammaticus bowed. 'Thank you for that appraisal. I applaud you for your insight.' He looked up at Alpharius. 'Sir, the Imperium is about to implode. At the halting site on Eolith, the Cabal awaits to show you how best, as the first captain so eloquently put it, to manage and maintain the flaws of man.'

Alpharius let out a deep sigh. He gazed down at Grammaticus. 'I wonder, years from now, will I regret not executing you at this moment?'

'Civil war, sir,' Grammaticus cautioned, 'think of it.'

Alpharius shook his head. 'I am. John, my brother primarchs have their feuds and rivalries, they bicker at times, and fall out with one another, the way any close kinsmen might. I've come to that family only lately, and already I know the fashion of it. Roboute, for example, despises me, and I ignore him. It may lead to bruises at some stage, but not blood. For a civil war to ignite, primarch would have to be drawn against primarch in blood. That would never happen, John. It is simply inconceivable. Now that the Warmaster leads us, we–'

'Warmaster?' asked Grammaticus sharply.

'Horus Lupercal is Warmaster,' Alpharius replied.

'Since when?' Grammaticus asked. There was a queasy look on his face suddenly.

'Four months ago, after the Great Triumph on Ullanor. The Emperor retired from the Crusade and named his first son as Warmaster. I regret I could not attend the ceremony, but the retreat from Nurth and the business you presented to me was occupying my time. To be fair, I shun such occasions. I sent envoys.'

'Horus is already Warmaster?' Grammaticus whispered. He sat down heavily on the deck, and bowed his face. The massive Astartes looked down at him as if he was a child throwing a tantrum.

'What's the matter, John?' asked Omegon.

'Already,' Grammaticus murmured, shaking his head. 'So soon. Two years, he said, two years. We haven't got two years.'

'John?'

Grammaticus refused to look up at the Astartes around him. Soneka stepped forwards and scooped him back onto his feet. Grammaticus was trembling.

Wiping his mouth, Grammaticus looked up at Alpharius. 'Horus is the catalyst. Please, lord, escort me to the venue. Take whatever retinue you choose. I will be your shibboleth. I will conduct you to the presence of the Cabal, as intermediary, and vouch for you. This is the way it has to be done. There is no more time. Horus is Warmaster. Oh, glory, Horus is *Warmaster*.'

'Peto, conduct John back to his cell,' Pech said.

Holding Grammaticus upright, Soneka replied with a firm nod.

Grammaticus began to struggle. 'I have to go down first. I have to open the way!' he cried.

Soneka placed him in a tight arm lock, and led him towards the hatch.

'We will commit a landing party to the venue zone as soon as the fleet has arrived to support us,' Alpharius said.

'You're wasting time!' Grammaticus yelled, fighting with Soneka. 'You're wasting valuable time!'

'Remove him,' said Alpharius.

SONEKA PALMED THE lock of the cell open and threw Grammaticus inside.

'I don't appreciate the bruises, John,' he said, rubbing his arms.

'You don't appreciate anything, Peto,' Grammaticus growled, getting to his feet. 'Horus is Warmaster. Do you know what that means?'

Soneka shrugged.

'It means that our timing is out! It means the war has already begun for all intents and purposes. Peto, you've got to help me. I need to get down there, down to the surface. I need to pave the way. The Alpha Legion mustn't be allowed to go blundering in. It'll ruin everything. The Cabal will not respond to military intimidation. Please, Peto.'

'I can't help you, John.'

+ *Please, Peto!* +

Soneka recoiled as if he'd been stung. 'Ow! Don't do that again!'

'Sorry, sorry,' Grammaticus murmured. 'I'm sorry, Peto. Look, you have to help me get down to the surface.'

'The primarch has ordered otherwise. I can't do that.'

'Peto…'

'I can't!'

'For Terra's sake,' Grammaticus said, sitting down on his cot. 'The Alpha Legion has to be recruited before it's too late, and I have to open the way.'

'I have no leverage,' Soneka said.

'You hate it here!'

Soneka nodded. 'Yes, I fugging do. I've never been so lonely in my life. I trust the Alpha Legion less and less, and I positively despise my fellow operatives. I don't understand what I've become caught up in, but I loathe it, day after day.'

'So help me!'

'How?'

'You're in a position of trust! They *trust* you!'

Soneka shook his head. 'I can't. I'm sorry, John, I just can't.'

'Peto!' Grammaticus yelled.

Peto waved his new hand and the hatch slammed shut, cutting Grammaticus off.

SONEKA WALKED BACK down the grim iron corridors of the detention block. At the far end of the hallway, where he could no longer hear Grammaticus's angry shouts and pounding fists, he leant against the wall and slid down into a crouch.

'Peto?'

He hadn't heard the cage doors slide open. He sprang up, rubbing his eyes.

'Was he difficult?' asked Pech. 'Did he try his tricks on you?'

Soneka nodded. 'Yes, sir.'

'Are you all right?' Pech asked. 'Are you still up to the job? I can assign another operative to Grammaticus if you prefer.'

'No, sir,' Peto Soneka replied. 'I can do this. You've given me a duty to perform, and I'll see it through to the end.'

Ingo Pech nodded. 'Do it,' he said.

THREE

**High anchor, 42 Hydra Tertius,
fourteen hours later**

An automated voice was blaring out across the princi-
pal embarkation deck of the carrier *Loudon*. 'Move up
to designated markers! Move up to designated markers! Boarding by company will commence in thirty –
three zero – minutes!'

Buzzers sounded, and the announcement repeated,
fighting with the cacophony of machine noise and
shouts echoing around the vast platform.

Swathed in cascades of steam and fanfared by raucous sirens, the next bank of drop-ships rose up from
the service bays on the through-deck elevators. Flight
crews in russet overalls ran forwards to detach the
undercarriage bolts with power ratchets, and servitors
strutted up, tool limbs raised, to uncase and activate
the autoguidance arrays built into bulges under the
drop-ships' cockpits. Overhead, the hangar's primary
hoist system swung a brace of hook-nosed escort fighters down the length of the deck to the stern catapult

rails. There was a sudden, thunderous bellow of tank engines starting up. A row of forty, twin-barrelled assault tanks, drawn up along a line of thick yellow chevrons painted on the deck, began revving their turbines and snorting fumes from their exhausts, as service crews began to lower the cargo ramps of the massive bulk lifters.

'Move up to designated markers!' the automated voice repeated.

Hurtado Bronzi signed the data-slate with a flourish, and removed his biometric from the slot in its side.

'Your company stands certified, het,' the liveried weaponsmith said formally, taking the slate back. 'March in fortune.'

Bronzi made the old salute of the Unity fist against his chest, nodded, and turned back to his unit.

'You heard the call,' he yelled. 'Designated markers. Move your arses!'

'Designated markers!' Tche repeated.

The Jokers hoisted their heavy kit and weapons, and advanced from the check station onto the main platform. Shouting and waving their arms, the bashaws shepherded them into positions on the red-painted sections of decking.

'Request permission to furl the company banner for embarkation,' Tche said.

Bronzi nodded. There was a fire in his belly, for the first time in months. His appetite was back.

He looked along the length of the giant platform. His bashaws were lowering the standard, and the pikemen had temporarily set their long weapons on the deck beside them. Forty metres to his left, the Carnivales had drawn up along their markers, and beyond them, the Troubadours. To his right, the 41st Zanzibari

Hort were streaming forwards to their line. The air smelled of gun oil and engine smoke. Somewhere, diligently but futilely, a marching band was playing in competition with the general racket.

Honen Mu and her aides, all carrying small kit bags and dressed in foul-weather gear, advanced across the open deck towards him.

'Het Bronzi,' Mu said.

He made a namaste. 'My beloved uxor. You look especially fragrant and, uhm, waterproof, today.'

The aides sniggered.

'Operational?' she asked, remaining composed.

'We have just been certified,' he replied. 'We're ready to ramble, uxor. When do we get to find out where?'

'Any moment, Bronzi,' she replied. She appreciated his annoyance. Namatjira had kept the details of the operation close to his chest, a mistake, in her opinion. After the disaster of Nurth, the Lord Commander should have been working to rebuild morale. Instead, he had become even more poisonous than usual. The odium of defeat, she suspected, but there was no excuse.

The expedition fleet had reassembled at the edge of the Nurthene system twenty-eight hours after the final collapse of the evacuation effort. From there, they had made shift to Empesal for refit and recovery. A brief furlough had been granted in the souks and circuses of Empesal, but for nothing like long enough. Word had spread that Namatjira was in close discussion with the high officers of the fleet, and some new operation was already being planned. There was a rumour that the entire expedition might be despatched to Sixty-Three Nineteen, to support the Luna Wolves in the compliance war that they had undertaken there. That, Mu believed, would have suited well. All thoughts of failure and loss, the bitter smirch of Nurth, would have been quickly expunged by the glory of serving alongside the new Warmaster and his noble Legion.

However, Namatjira had evidently made other plans. He had declared that the expedition would be mounting an operation in concert with the Alpha Legion, and ordered immediate embarkation, an act so premature that nearly eight thousand Army casualties had to be left at Empesal, unfit for service, along with four carriers with refits and repairs still pending.

To remedy the diminished strength of the 670th Expedition, Namatjira hastily enfranchised two brigades of Lusitan heavy infantry and an armoured cavalry company from Pramatia, together with their carrier ships and tenders, and sixteen fleet auxiliary and fire support vessels. When the expedition departed Empesal, its strength stood at about two-thirds of the force that had begun the Nurthene compliance. Even with Jeveth's Titans gone, it was a considerable presence.

And, of course, there was an Alpha Legion battle-barge at the head of the convoy.

Namatjira had subjected his forces to a four and a half month shift to an undisclosed location. Onboard training continued as usual, but morale had wilted quickly. No one would say where they were going, or what manner of undertaking they would be expected to make. Namatjira seemed not to care. It was as if he had something to urgently prove, or wished to throw himself back into the field after the Nurthene debacle. Mu privately speculated that he was borrowing a little too much of the Alpha Legion's pitiless pragmatism.

A week before arrival, Namatjira ordered his forces to begin preparations for ground assault, and announced that the mission target had been designated as 42HtX.

This was greeted with general puzzlement. According to form, the campaign should have been officially labelled Six-Seventy Twenty-Six. Evidently, they were not heading for a compliance action. 42Ht was a planetary code, and the X indicated Extraordinary Operations. Namatjira informed his officer caste that he had committed the expedition to support the Alpha Legion in a classified undertaking, and that Alpharius had obtained direct permission from the Warmaster for Extraordinary Operations status.

Only the demands of deployment preparation, the daily routine of weapons certification and fitness tests, kept their minds, collectively, from wondering what the hell they were all getting into.

Mu turned to Tiphaine, who opened the black leather wallet she was holding, and took out a sealed packet of papers. Mu took it and handed it to Bronzi.

'Your operational orders,' she said.

'At last,' Bronzi said. He held the packet up to his ear and shook it experimentally. 'What does it say?' he grinned.

Mu resisted the temptation to grin back. 'I have no idea. We all get to read the details at the same time. You'll brief in transit. Get ready for last moment 'cept counsel as I get up to speed.'

'This is going to be fun, isn't it?' Bronzi asked.

'It rather depends on your definition of fun, Hurtado,' she replied.

He shrugged his heavy, armoured shoulders. 'Well, you know... dropping blind into a place we don't know, to go up against we know not what, with no advanced tactics? That sort of thing.'

She returned his grin with a mordant look. 'Then yes, this is going to be fun,' she agreed.

NAMATJIRA HELD OUT his arms, and the eunuch dressers slid on his full-length gloves and buttoned them around his shoulders and armpits. The gloves formed the sleeves of his dark tan leather doublet. He flexed his fingers to settle them into the gloves, as another dresser draped a cape of fur and zebra skin over his left shoulder, securing it with a golden fibula.

He extended his right hand, and the Warden of the Seal carefully slid the heavy signet onto his middle finger. The ring was gold, with table-cut rubies at the shoulders, and a large, square bezel that bore, in intaglio, the crest of the office of Lord Commander. The band of the ring contained a biometric authority. Until the moment Namatjira had been ready to put it on, the ring had been secured in a stasis box, carried by the Warden's men-at-arms. No chances were taken. The ring had legal force in and of itself.

Snare drums were rapping a tattoo in the stateroom beyond the lord's private wardrobe. Namatjira looked in the full length mirror, and then turned to his escort. One of the Lucifer Blacks carried the Lord Commander's ceremonial hand-and-a-half sword, another his golden cap helm with its high crinière.

Dinas Chayne entered the room, and saluted.

'Is he here, Dinas?'

'His ship has just docked.'

Namatjira snapped his fingers, and the dressers, the attendants and warden and his men hurried out through the servants' door.

The Lord Commander turned and marched through the ormolu archway into the stateroom, his companions in perfect step at his shoulders.

Namatjira's flagship had been named *Blamires* after a Concussion Age void Navy commander that the Lord Commander particularly admired. The *Blamires* was one of the best appointed and technically sophisticated vessels in the Imperial fleet. The stateroom he strode into was as long and broad as a cathedral's nave, paved in black and white tiles, and walled with gold caryatid pillars and tall crystal mirrors. The high roof displayed scenes from the Age of Unification in fresco form. The ceremonial band's tempo intensified at the Lord Commander's approach, and the honour guard of six hundred Outremar Lancers snapped to present arms.

Halfway down the stateroom, Major General Dev, in full dress uniform, stood waiting with Jan Van Aunger, the master of the fleet, and eight senior adepts in long emerald robes. Dev stood to attention as Namatjira came to a halt in front of him. The drumming ceased the moment Namatjira stopped walking.

'Lord Commander,' said Dev, 'the forces of the expedition stand ready for deployment. We await your authority.'

Namatjira nodded. 'Master Van Aunger?' he asked.

The venerable fleet master, robed in ermine and segmented mirror-steel, made a namaste. 'The fleet abides, Lord Commander,' he said, 'all components and sub-components report smooth running. The escort squadrons are ready for launch. Target solutions for the surface coordinates have been supplied to the siege frigates, rail gun platforms, and all long range ordnance. We can commence orbital bombardment at your discretion.'

'Thank you, Master Van Aunger. The bombardment will only be undertaken if necessary.'

Van Aunger frowned. 'As I have advised you, sir, the bombardment should precede the drop. We can't very well hammer surface targets if our troops have already–'

'*Thank you*, Master Van Aunger,' said Namatjira. 'You have your instructions.'

Van Aunger stuck out his chin bullishly, but said nothing, and stepped back.

'Lord Commander?' Dev said gently, indicating the small jade coffer that one of the elderly adepts was holding on a velvet cushion.

'A moment, major general,' said Namatjira. On cue, a fanfare of horns sounded outside the stateroom and the double doors at the far end opened. Alpharius, alone, in full war plate, gleaming and polished, strode through, and came down the stateroom towards them. His armoured bulk was so massive that the black and white tiles creaked like ice as they took each step.

'My lord primarch,' said Namatjira, bowing. 'Welcome aboard.'

'Lord Commander,' Alpharius responded, making the sign of the aquila, and then unlocking his helmet. He removed it, and held it under his arm. 'Your message said that you wished to speak with me.'

'Our business commences,' said Namatjira.

'Let us pray it is fruitful,' Alpharius agreed. In the silvery radiance of the grand stateroom, his eyes seemed as green as the jade coffer on the adept's cushion.

'I am about to issue authority,' said Namatjira. 'Is there any reason why I should not?'

'No, sir,' Alpharius answered. 'The objective must be sectioned and secured as rapidly as possible. You estimated three days?'

'Three days, lord primarch, unless we encounter unexpected difficulties of terrain or climate, or previously unidentified sources of resistance.'

'There has been no supplementary data suggesting that, sir,' replied Alpharius.

'Then we will proceed,' said Namatjira.

'For the Emperor,' said Alpharius.

'For the Emperor!' the honour guard barked with one voice.

At a gesture from the major general, the adept carrying the jade coffer brought it forward to the Lord Commander, and knelt down. A second adept opened the coffer's lid with a small silver key. As soon as the lid lifted, the receiver of the biometric scanner inside opened like a flower and dilated.

Namatjira reached in and pressed the bezel of his signet ring into the receiver. There was a whirr and a brief pulse of light.

'Authority confirmed,' the adept said. Another fanfare sounded and sirens began to blare in the depths of the flagship below.

Namatjira withdrew his hand, and the adepts closed the coffer and stepped back.

'Lord primarch, the forces of the 670th Expedition are deploying,' said Namatjira.

'Thank you. Now, what did you want to speak about?' asked Alpharius.

'Oh, that. Let us withdraw. Privacy, I think, would be best,' Namatjira replied.

ANOTHER BUZZER SOUNDED.

'Ten minutes!' Bronzi yelled above the hangar's uproar to his waiting company.

He looked at Mu. 'Our beloved lord general is cutting it fine. At this rate, we'll be making it up as we go along.'

She did not respond to his bait.

He tried again. 'I half expect to open the packet and find a note saying "Have a good time, see you soon",' he said.

Mu grinned, very slightly.

'Uxor?' said Jahni.

Mu turned. Genewhip Boone came jogging across the pad towards them. 'Authority has finally been issued,' he called as he approached.

'At last,' said Bronzi. He tore open his order packet with his teeth. Mu took hers from Tiphaine, and opened it rather more demurely. They were both silent as they read.

'Well?' asked Boone.

'Land and hold,' said Bronzi.

'It doesn't seem too bad,' said Mu.

'Open dropzone, mind, and the terrain looks ropey,' said Bronzi.

'It doesn't seem too bad,' Mu repeated.

'We're not far off the five-minute buzzer,' said Boone. 'Anything you want to catch before it's too late?'

Bronzi shook his head.

'Then march in fortune,' Boone said, and ran on to the next company.

Mu turned to her aides, who gathered around her, and began her 'cept briefing. Bronzi took another look at his orders, checked he hadn't overlooked anything, and ambled over to his men. They all turned to him. Those that had been sitting down on the deck got to their feet.

'Jokers!' he shouted. 'Today's benediction from his highness the Lord Commander comes in the form of an orbit to surface drop, into open country, for seize and hold purposes.'

There weren't too many groans.

'Terrain is said to be moderately contoured with moisture, which I think is Tactical's way of saying precipices with waterfalls.'

The men laughed.

'We'd better expect rugged geography, which means the drop is going to be tricky. Watch what you're doing, especially those lugging heavyweight kit. I don't want anybody coming off the ramp onto a slope or scarp and going over. No broken necks, please, no broken legs or ankles, not even sprains, I'm looking at you, Trooper Enkomi.'

More laughter.

'Full dispersal when we hit. Vishnu formation. Uxor Mu will 'cept your markers. Get down, get to those markers, and dig in. The object of the exercise is the seizure of territory. Once we've got our feet dry, we'll advance as per my instruction as the situation allows. Plan is, we'll be marching in country on this one, my lucky lads, so let's hope none of you skimped on the endurance training.'

More groans.

'Remember, my Jokers, a dropzone is like a woman. Land on her firmly, and make sure you have the vital parts located before you get going.'

The men laughed again.

'If the drop goes according to plan,' Bronzi continued, 'we'll have the Carnivales west of us, and a unit of light armour to our east. Of course, the drop will not go according to plan, because they never do, so expect to be facing the wrong way with your heads up your arses. All right, settle, it wasn't that funny, Zhou.'

The men quietened down.

'This isn't a ramble,' Bronzi declared, 'this is a serious operation. *Extraordinary*, don't you know? So no back-sliding, no idling, no thinking with your pants on backwards, no tarting about, and no mistakes. You're the geno's own Jokers, best in the Chiliad, so be sharp, be alert, and be what the trickster god created you to be. Which, in case you didn't know, is to be the best fugging assault infantry to ever come out of Terra. Questions? Lapis?'

'Will it be cold?'

'Fug me on a stick!' Bronzi shook his head. 'Yes, so bring mittens and a scarf, Lapis, you pretty little girl.'

The men laughed loudly, and Trooper Lapis fended off playful slaps and jabs.

'Calm down,' said Bronzi. 'In all honesty, it looks like it'll be pissy damp and cold. Scans show open land, little shelter, and steady precipitation, which is rain to you, Trooper Kashan. Hands up anyone who ignored this morning's standing order and didn't put on his boot liners and underglove, or sleeve his weapon? Better still, don't tell me. I don't want to know how stupid you decided to be when you got up today. If you get trench foot or crotch rot, if you freeze, or you find your fugging weapon won't actually fire, then it's your hard boo-hoo, and the genewhips will see you later. Anything else?'

Tche raised his hand.

'Tche? Is this going to be a sensible question, or something about the availability of local fruit produce like last time?'

'I like fruit,' Tche protested.

'Good for you. Your question?'

'The one thing you haven't covered, het,' Tche said. 'What hostiles can we expect to meet and greet?'

The Jokers whooped and roared aggressively.

Bronzi raised a hand for quiet. 'Excellent point, excellent point, Tche. There's a reason I haven't covered it. According to the specs, our target world is uninhabited. There are no hostiles.'

This provoked the rowdiest chorus of all.

'That's right, that's right… we're dropping dirtside for a nice walk in mountain scenery,' Bronzi yelled above it. 'Now shut up! That's better. What's the first rule of common soldiering? Trooper Duarte?'

'Always assume that anyone in a position senior to you isn't telling you everything?'

'That's my boy. There's more to this than meets the eye, so don't get slack.'

A buzzer sounded, crude and brazen, across the vast deck.

'That's it!' Bronzi yelled. 'The five-minute buzzer! Pick up your stuff, pick up your arses, and leave all your complaints and regrets on the carrier, they'll still be here when you get back. Jokers, are you with me?'

'March in fortune!' they yelled back.

'Company first, Imperium second, geno before gene!' he shouted. 'Now get the fug on with it!'

He strolled back towards Honen Mu. Her briefing had finished, and the aides had gathered into a tight huddle, discussing tactical variations in fierce, low voices.

'No hostiles?' he remarked to Mu. 'That's just got to be bad data, right?'

Mu shrugged. 'There's another alternative. This is a seize and hold. The Lord Commander is asking us to make a section of territory secure. I'm tempted to suppose there's something valuable down there, and we're being sent in to secure the ground so that it can be recovered.'

'Something valuable like what?'

'I don't know,' she said. 'Perhaps the Lord Commander's congenial side?'

Bronzi blinked.

'What?' she asked.

'You made a joke, uxor,' he beamed. 'An actual, proper, honest to goodness joke.'

She looked back at him. Her mouth wasn't smiling, but her eyes were. 'Yes, well, don't tell everyone, or they'll all want one,' she said.

The deck quivered and they heard the distant rumbling squeal of the plasma catapults at the stern end of the platform discharging.

'That's the first of the escort fighters away,' said Bronzi. 'It won't be long now. Nervous?'

'Why would I be nervous, Hurtado?' Mu asked.

He hunched his shoulders. 'It's not often that the uxors get to ride down with us soldier types at the sharp end of things. You usually follow on with the support lines.'

'Operational requirements,' she replied. 'We can't provide you with reliable 'cept coverage from orbit.'

'Uh huh. So, I was thinking… I could arrange to sit next to you, and hold your hand if it gets bumpy,' Bronzi offered.

'That won't be necessary,' she replied. 'I've made my share of combat drops. March in fortune, Hurtado.'

"Cept me well, Honen,' he replied.

She made a half bow and returned to her girls.

Bronzi took one last look around the vast carrier deck. An electric munition train clattered past. Four flight crewmen were frantically working to replace a faulty hydraulic on the nosegear of a nearby lander. Another pair of hook-nosed escort fighters whined by overhead on the primary hoist. The tanks had finally started loading, and more armour pieces had drawn up on the ramp from the lower deck, waiting to advance to the wait line for boarding.

He did what he always did before a drop, his private ritual. He pressed his fingertips to his lips, and then bent down and touched his fingertips against the deck.

'Let us all see you again,' he whispered. 'Let us all come back safe.'

He rose. He pulled his order packet out of his pocket, and made one final check to make sure he hadn't missed anything.

It turned out he had.

Tucked inside the vellum sleeve, along with his sheaf of orders, was a small green sliver that he at first assumed was a leaf.

He realised that it was a wafer-slim piece of metal machined to resemble a lizard's scale. On it, in Edessan, was written a brief, whimsical phrase, which translated as 'Your father cheers, your mother cries, that is the lot of the soldier'. Beside the phrase was the embossed brand of the hydra.

Bronzi stroked his thumb across the raised image. He put the green scale in his pocket and walked towards the waiting drop-ship.

NAMATJIRA LED ALPHARIUS into the forward lookout of the flagship *Blamires*. Vast petal-form ports glazed the side walls of the triangular chamber and met in a sharp apex overlooking the kilometre of prow projecting ahead of them.

'Give us the room,' Namatjira snapped, and the servants and ensigns hurried out. Chayne closed the hatch behind them and stood guard, his hands behind his back. Alpharius turned and looked pointedly at the Lucifer.

'He goes where I go,' Namatjira explained, helping himself to a flute of frost wine from a side cabinet. 'Dinas has the highest clearance.'

Alpharius nodded. 'Very well,' he allowed.

'A toast, lord primarch? Or is that contrary to your regimen?'

'Why not?' the primarch replied.

Namatjira poured a second glass, and handed it to Alpharius. The sub-servos of the primarch's gauntlet hissed and whined as they adjusted to the subtle act of gripping the flute without shattering it.

Namatjira walked towards the starboard side of the ports. His thylacene lay snoozing on the bank of seats under the windows. 'That's the *Maskeleyne*,' Namatjira said, pointing with the same hand that was holding the glass. 'A heavy carrier, very versatile. That, behind it, you see, is the *Tancredi*, an Outremar vessel.'

Alpharius came and stood behind him. The view from the lookout was humbling. The plates of the ports had self-tinted to reduce glare, and diminish the blaze of the local sun. Space fell away beneath them and soared away above. A trillion, trillion stars glimmered in that endless night. To the starboard side of the *Blamires* lay the eclipsed target world, a massive globe with a peal of light just slipping off its shoulder. Off to the flagship's starboard, a formation of mainline vessels hung, gleaming, in the target world's shadow, laid out in a chain astern, across several thousand kilometres.

'That's the *Agostini*,' Namatjira went on, 'and behind it, the siege frigate *Barbustion*. Behind that, the carrier *Loudon*–'

'I know the names and indicatives of all the fleet vessels,' said Alpharius.

Namatjira smiled and turned to face him, taking a sip of his wine. 'I'm sure you do, sir, but, oddly, I cannot name your great barge.'

He glanced back at the ports. 'That's it there, isn't it?' he asked, pointing towards a dark blur seven hundred kilometres off the *Blamires*'s starboard bow. 'That shielded object?'

'We do not name our ships,' Alpharius said. 'We simply designate them with serials.'

'Oh, and what is that barge's designation?' asked Namatjira.

'*Beta*,' replied Alpharius.

'Ah. I am forced to wonder what *Alpha* is doing this day,' Namatjira grinned.

'It is occupied elsewhere,' Alpharius replied.

Namatjira turned back and looked the giant figure up and down. 'Well, to business. My lord primarch, I summoned you because I find I have some misgivings.'

'Misgivings?' Alpharius asked.

'You made a firm commitment to me, sir, at Empesal. You swore that this undertaking would absolve the shame of the Nurth fiasco. You promised it would present me with the opportunity to make reparations for that loss, and restore my dignity and reputation in the eyes of the Council of Terra.'

'I stand by that promise,' Alpharius said.

Namatjira wandered over to one of the window couches, and sat down. He took another sip of his wine.

'As you explained it to me,' he said, 'the purpose of this mission is to acquire information vital to the continued security of the Imperium. The Emperor, you said, will thank me and reward me for securing this valuable intelligence, and bringing it to his attention. I might even expect a place on the High Council. I can only speculate as to what this information could possibly be.'

He paused. 'And that's where my misgivings begin. I can only speculate, because you won't tell me. I think it's high time you let me a little deeper into your confidence.'

'I see,' said Alpharius.

'You just watched me issue my authority and mobilise my forces in your service, Lord Alpharius,' said Namatjira, with a slight tone of menace. 'I deserve to know more.'

Alpharius pursed his lips, and set his flute down, untouched. 'You were willing enough,' he said, 'when I co-opted your expedition for this venture. My word was sufficient guarantee then.'

'Well, it turns out, it isn't any more,' said Namatjira.

'That's a pity,' said Alpharius.

'What is the nature of this information?' asked Namatjira. 'What does it concern? Where is it, and how do we secure it? Who has it? How did you learn of its existence and its location? What could possibly be so important, so valuable, so revelatory, so damn *secret*, that the fate of all human culture depends upon it?'

'You will know precisely what I choose to tell you, Namatjira,' said Alpharius.

'My Lord Commander said he needs to know more,' Dinas Chayne stated quietly, but firmly. He took a step forwards.

Alpharius slowly turned his head and looked at Chayne. 'Or what, companion? I hope for your sake that you don't presume to threaten me.'

Chayne did not move.

Alpharius ignored him and looked down at Namatjira. 'I had heard that the Lucifer Blacks were remarkably brave. I didn't realise they were clinically insane.'

'Step back, Dinas,' said Namatjira with a casual flick of his hand. 'My Lord Alpharius understands the burden of command. He knows full well that the paramount responsibility of a man in my position is the security and welfare of his forces, and it is his solemn duty to disengage those forces from any undertaking that he deems unwise or reckless. Isn't that right, my lord?'

Alpharius said nothing.

'I will not put my soldiers in harm's way without a very good reason,' said Namatjira, 'a very good reason, and a reliable source of intelligence. I would be derelict in my duty otherwise.'

Alpharius gazed through the ports for a moment, and contemplated the dark world below. 'In the course of the Nurth campaign,' he said quietly, 'my infiltration networks encountered the agent of a xenoform faction. The faction calls itself the Cabal. The agent claimed that the Cabal was in possession of certain information vital to the Imperium of Man. No evidence or provenance was offered, but the Cabal had clearly put a great deal of effort and ingenuity into making contact with me. They extended an invitation to meet with them, so that this information could be transmitted. 42 Hydra Tertius is the site chosen for that meeting.'

'Are you saying that this whole endeavour was inspired by the baseless tattle of some xenos spy?' asked Namatjira. 'Dear me, sir, I thought you were shrewd.'

'I never said I believed him,' Alpharius replied. 'While there's even a chance that his story is true, we cannot afford to ignore it. If it's a lie, then we're here, in force, to locate and suppress a dangerous xenoform power that has the means and skills to attempt manipulation of the Imperium. This is how I presented it to the Warmaster, and it is on this basis that he granted this expedition Extraordinary status. Lord Commander, we may be about to save the Imperium, or go to war to exterminate an insidious alien menace.'

Namatjira rose to his feet. 'And which do you suppose it is, sir?'

Alpharius shook his head. 'I make no guesses, lord, but there is one significant fact. It was the agent who first warned me of the Black Cube. But for that warning, we would all be dead.'

'And this agent?' asked Namatjira.

'He was operating inside the Imperial Army in an extremely capable and efficient manner. He got remarkably close to the centre of things.' Alpharius looked over at Chayne. 'He slew one of your men, companion.'

'Konig Heniker,' whispered Chayne.

'That's right,' said Alpharius. 'That was one of the identities he adopted, at least. My operatives captured him on the last day of Nurth's existence. He's in my custody.'

'Well,' murmured Namatjira. He lit up a very careful and benevolent smile. 'I feel my misgivings ebbing away. Thank you for your disclosure. This will, of course, remain entirely classified.'

'I expect no less,' Alpharius replied. He turned and walked towards the hatch. 'I take it our conversation is done?'

'One last thing,' Namatjira called to him. 'If the story is true, and this meeting takes place, I will, naturally, be there at your side.'

The Lord Commander didn't wait to see how Alpharius might respond. He turned to the windows. 'Oh, look. There they go!' he cried out jauntily, and pointed. Bright sparks, like meteorites, had begun to sear down out of the carriers behind them.

Alpharius opened the hatch and left the lookout.

'Dinas?' Namatjira said. 'In the light of the primarch's comments, please re-examine all the data we have on Konig Heniker.'

'Yes, sir.'

Namatjira took a sip of wine and tilted his head to one side reflectively, watching the drop-ships fall. 'I believe it will be instructive to learn how the picture fills in now that we have more pieces of it,' he said, 'particularly in terms of the Astartes and their manipulation networks.'

'Yes, sir,' Chayne replied.

THE DROP-SHIP lurched and fell. Metal spalling from the release claws showered backwards in a glittering tail behind it.

They began to pull two Gs, three. The airframe began to vibrate. Bronzi held out his hand and Mu took it. She squeezed it.

'Here we go,' Bronzi said.

FOUR

Orbital, Eolith, continuous

SONEKA OPENED THE cell hatch and stepped inside. He put his satchel down on the steel table.

'What? More cheese?' asked Grammaticus snidely. He was sprawled on the cot, dispirited.

'Get up. Quickly,' Soneka said.

'But we haven't eaten our lunch,' said Grammaticus.

'Shut up and get up,' Soneka told him. He looked back at the open hatch and the corridor beyond it. 'Hurry.'

Grammaticus sat up, frowning. 'What's going on, Peto?'

'Just follow me.'

Soneka turned towards the cell door and peered out cautiously. Grammaticus rose to his feet.

'Peto? What is this? Has the primarch agreed to let me drop with him and–'

Soneka looked back, his eyes narrow. 'Will you shut up? I'm doing what you asked. Keep a lid on it. Shere is everywhere.'

Grammaticus blinked in surprise. 'Oh,' he managed to say.

'Just follow me and keep quiet,' said Soneka. He opened the satchel over his shoulder and drew out a laspistol.

Grammaticus looked at the weapon as if he'd never seen one before. 'Oh my word,' he murmured. 'Peto, Peto just stop for a moment and look at me. Look at me. Control word *Bedlame.*'

Soneka turned and faced him. His eyes were vacant.

'What's your name?' Grammaticus asked.

'Peto Soneka.'

'What are you doing right now, Peto?'

'Your bidding, John.'

'Glory!' said Grammaticus. He stepped back, his hand to his mouth, staring at Soneka. 'I didn't think it had worked,' he said, laughing in surprise. 'I really didn't think it had worked. All those lunches, five months of casual lunchtime conversations, dropping a weighted tell word in, now and then. I thought you were resistant.'

Soneka remained blank.

'Peto, I'm truly sorry to have abused you this way,' said Grammaticus solemnly. 'I want you to know that. We're friends, I'd like to think. You have shown me great kindness. I hope one day, you will see the broader picture, and forgive me for doing this to you. Do you hear me?'

'Your voice, I can't fight it,' growled Soneka, glassy-eyed. 'Every day, I could feel you doing this, and I couldn't fugging fight it. You took advantage of my dis-affection. You're a bastard, John Grammaticus.'

'I know. I'm sorry. Can you get me off this barge?'

'I can do my best,' replied Soneka.

'Thank you, Peto, thank you. Control word *Bedlame*.'

Soneka blinked awake and steadied himself against the cell wall. 'What the fug was that?' he asked. 'I was dizzy for a moment.'

'You were saying something?' Grammaticus cued.

Soneka shook his head. 'Come on, I was saying. We've only got a small window. The fleet is deploying.'

'Already?'

'Come on, John.'

They hurried down through the quiet detention block to the cage shutters. Soneka waved his hand and the cages withdrew.

'What's your plan?' whispered Grammaticus. 'How do we reach the surface?'

'Drop-pod,' Soneka replied. 'They're all primed and certified for the Legion's landing. We'll head for the bay on underdeck eight. I checked the deployment schedule, and they have been assigned for the second landing wave in six hours' time, so it should be quiet. But there's something we have to do first.'

'What?' asked John Grammaticus.

'Something you'll thank me for. Something I need to do,' Soneka replied.

They turned onto the vast spinal corridor, and came face to face with a maintenance servitor. The servitor jolted, whirring as it studied them, upper limbs raised in query.

'This section is monitored and private. Show me your authority,' the servitor's vox speaker rasped.

Soneka shot it through the head. The servitor issued a thready whine, and clattered sideways against the wall, smoke trailing from its exploded cranium.

'Run,' Soneka said.

THEY RAN UNTIL they were hoarse and out of breath, and cut away from the main spinal corridor into a maze of sub-halls and gloomy compartments. The strips of mauve lighting made it feel like twilight in an empty city. No alarms sounded, but the air was pregnant and still, as if it was about to explode with noise.

'Where is everyone?' Grammaticus asked.

'In the arming chambers, preparing for deployment,' Soneka replied. He beckoned Grammaticus towards a heavy hatch shutter.

'Here,' Soneka said.

Grammaticus put his hand to his temple. An expression of pain, wonder and realisation filled his face.

'Oh!' he said. 'I hear her.'

'I know,' said Soneka.

'She *was* calling out to me, all the time, wasn't she?'

'Yes.'

'Thank you, Peto,' Grammaticus whispered. He looked as if he was close to tears.

Soneka faced him, and put a steadying hand on his shoulder. 'John, listen to me, this will be a shock. The Alpha Legion interrogated her, and damaged her in the process.'

Grammaticus looked at Soneka. 'I understand.'

'I hope you do,' said Peto Soneka, and waved his new hand in front of the shutter's lock reader.

The hatch opened. In a corner of the small dark room beyond, something stirred and whimpered.

Grammaticus pushed past Soneka and crossed the room, holding out his hands reassuringly.

'Hush, hush,' he said. 'It's all right. It's me.'

Snivelling and trembling, Rukhsana looked up at him, with wild eyes. She was pressed into the corner, her legs pulled in, and her arms wrapped around her body. Her robes were tattered. She looked at his face and cried out.

'Rukhsana, Rukhsana, it's just a beard. I've grown a beard.'

She put her hands over her eyes.

'Rukhsana, it's all right,' Grammaticus whispered. He touched her gently, and she recoiled. 'It's all right,' he repeated.

'Please be quick, John,' Soneka hissed.

Grammaticus embraced Rukhsana and rocked her. She buried herself against his chest and began to cry.

'What the fug did they do to her, Peto?' he asked.

'They let Shere have her. He went into her mind, looking for you and for any information on the Cabal,' Soneka replied. 'The process shattered her sanity. She's been like this since Nurth, five months ago. I've brought her food every day, and tried to keep her clean and healthy, but she's little more than feral.'

'Oh, Rukhsana,' Grammaticus whispered, hugging the uxor to him and tenderly stroking the lank blonde hair that had once glowed like spun gold.

'John, please, we haven't got much time,' Soneka urged. He stood in the doorway, watching the corridor outside. Grammaticus coaxed Rukhsana to her feet, and led her across the dark chamber, keeping her tight against his side.

'I've got her,' he said. 'Lead the way.'

* * *

Underdeck eight was an extensive space of industrial metal, thick pipe work, violet lighting and oily shadows. There was a constant background murmur of engines and the barge's heavy atmosphere plants. Every now and then, a distant sound of tools or machine shop activity echoed back to them. So much pipe and duct work ran along the roof space, the access ways felt low and claustrophobic.

Soneka brought them to a long hallway that had eight massive blast hatches in its left-hand wall. Gigantic rotor fans turned lazily in the roof cage.

The identical blast hatches, each one large enough to accept a large transport vehicle, all stood open, waiting. They stopped outside the first of them, dwarfed by the hatch frame, and looked inside. Four armoured drop-pods sat in an oily black launch cradle, like bullets loaded into a revolver's drum. The chamber was lined with greasy black hydraulics. Feed lines were attached to the pods, and steam wreathed up slowly from the cradle mechanism.

'This'll do,' said Soneka quietly. He nodded towards the adjacent hatches. 'They're all the same, four in each.'

'Whatever you say, Peto. This is your plan.'

Soneka led them over to the far side of the hallway. Rukhsana remained clenched against Grammaticus's side. He watched as Soneka woke up a large cogitator system built into the bulkhead. Soneka called up several pages of data, touch flicking through them, moving from one menu to the next.

'What are you doing?' Grammaticus asked.

'I'm checking that the navigation systems are programmed for the venue zone. Yes, that's good. Set. Right, I just have to countermand the launch notice.'

'What?'

Soneka gestured at the waiting pods behind them, and then carried on moving through screens and data scrolls. 'When one of these launches, a notification will flash up immediately on the excursion monitor on the bridge. I'm cancelling that instruction. They're going to know we're gone soon enough, and it won't take them long to realise a pod's missing, but I'd like to postpone discovery for as long as possible.'

'You can do that?' asked Grammaticus, impressed.

Soneka smiled and held up his new hand. 'They trust me, remember? They've given me the highest clearance, built in.'

'More fool them,' Grammaticus grinned.

'This should only take a couple of minutes,' said Soneka. 'Down on the right, there's a locker store. We're going to need three sets of foul-weather gear. See what you can dig out.'

Grammaticus nodded and hurried to oblige, as fast as Rukhsana would let him. They came back after five minutes with a bundle of suits tailored to fit operatives. Soneka was ready.

Together, the three crossed back through the huge blast hatch and clambered into one of the pods.

Soneka waved his hand. The massive blast hatch began to close. Hazard lights started to flash around the chamber, and a low electrical hum filled the air, mounting in intensity.

FIVE

Eolith

THE FIRST THING that hit them was the stench. It was vile and unexpected, like wet rot, like liquescent decay. It permeated the cold wet air. As soon as they had spread clear of the fumes from the howling drop-ships, it was all they could taste.

The Jokers ran forwards, fanning out across the slick, wet rocks. Some were gagging, or complaining about the reek.

'Don't be babies! Get on with it!' Bronzi yelled. He sniffed. 'Fug me, that's awful,' he said to himself.

The banner was up. The company was extending in a line away from the landing zone where the drop-ships waited, lifting spray from their idling jet wash.

Bronzi got his bearings.

They were in a flat-bedded valley between two lines of rock hills that were curiously regular, like plinths or flat roofed towers. It was cold, but the dampness was worse. The air seemed wet, less than rain, less than drizzle, just a swirling, particulate moisture. He could feel it on his skin like cold sweat. The Jokers were already soaked. Capes had gone lank, and armour gleamed with droplets.

The sky was low and dense with squally clouds. The terrain was grey rock, a hard stone rendered slippery by the accumulating wetness. The stone seemed to have a natural propensity to split and shear in quadrilateral plains, forming blocks and steps that looked unnervingly like they'd been cut by a stone mason rather than geology. Bronzi realised that the rock's planar property explained why the hills looked so much like cubic buildings. He'd never seen such a geometrically rigid landscape. It was dominated by straight verticals, hard edges and flat surfaces. He felt like he was standing in the jumbled heap of some giant child's building blocks.

To the west, more drop-ships were whining down out of the cloud cover. Tche signalled that the Jokers were clear, and Bronzi sent an instruction to the pilots. Hatches began to slide shut, and ramps retract. The sound of the engines rose in pitch as the drop-ships prepared to lift off.

Bronzi moved forwards through his extending ranks, mindful of planting every step carefully. Underfoot, the flat stone felt as spongy as bone marrow. Cavities had filled with black water, like rock pools.

'Some order please, ladies!' Bronzi barked at the Jokers. A couple of them had already slipped over, much to their chagrin.

'What isn't this?' Bronzi roared.

'A fug-fingered ramble!' they chorussed back.

'Could have fooled me,' he muttered.

Men began to call out as they pushed forwards into the lower levels of the cubic hills. They'd found things.

Bronzi went to look, and Mu and her aides followed him, stepping from block to block as if they were paving stones.

There were dead things amongst the stones. Drooling black matter, putrescent jelly, and bits of bone and quill lay in pool cavities or on flat blocks. Some were as large as men, some as small as rats. It was impossible to tell what they had been in life. No real structure remained, no anatomy. Local xenofauna, Bronzi presumed. It was as if some great tide had rolled out and left strange marine life forms behind to rot. That's what the stench reminded him of: beached fish, decomposing on a rocky shore.

Mu bent down to examine a few of the congealing horrors.

'Any thoughts?' Bronzi asked.

'The brief said this zone was an artificially generated climate,' Mu said. 'I suppose these are the remains of fauna types abundant in the planet's natural climate. They died here as the air, pressure and chemistry changed.'

The aides had all pulled up the hoods of their foul-weather suits, and buttoned collars up over their mouths and noses. Bronzi saw the anxiety and revulsion in their eyes. Huddled in their hoods, they looked like a scholam outing that had ended up in entirely the wrong place.

The Jokers advanced steadily into the hills, ignoring the litter of organic decay. Signals came in reporting that their supporting units were on the ground and advancing. No scan by eye, device or 'cept could detect any contact ahead. So far, the humans were the only living things on that abyssal shore.

'Keep scanning,' Bronzi called as he puffed and climbed up the blocks. A man behind him slipped over on his arse with a hard thump.

'I'll pretend I didn't see that, Tsubo,' Bronzi growled. 'Oh, fug!' he added. Reaching for a handhold, he'd dipped his fingers into something slimy and gristly. He shook the gloop off in disgust. The fish gut reek was noxious.

'Is it turning out to be as much fun as you hoped?' Mu asked him.

'Ha ha,' he replied.

THEY COULD SEE a good distance from the tops of the hills. A jumbled valley of grey blocks and glinting black pools fell away below, and stretched north, into the shadows of a great, dark wall of monolithic cliffs, split by gorges. The scale of the child's building blocks had increased. In places, they could detect the long, white ropes of cascades falling down rock faces. At the feet of the cliffs, vapour gathered like white smoke.

'When you said precipices with waterfalls, I thought you were joking,' said Tche.

'So did I,' Bronzi replied glumly. He checked his locator against the maps from the order packet. Mu did the same.

'The notation says they're called the Shivering Hills,' Bronzi said.

'How long to get up there?' she asked.

'A day, if we find a decent gorge or vent to follow.'

'Well, that's where they want us, so we'd better get going.'

He nodded. 'Are you 'cepting anything?' he asked.

'No,' she replied, 'but I'm cold and uncomfortable, and that doesn't help. This is… a difficult circumstance.'

'I'd prefer a good, honest war,' said Bronzi. 'You know where you are when someone's shooting at you. This is just getting creepy. Waiting for something to happen, that's just going to rack up the spooks. See what you can do to keep the men level.'

'Understood,' she replied.

'Tche!' Bronzi called.

'Yes, het?'

'Ten-minute halt here. Then we're going to head out across the valley. Tell the boys to have a drink, and a pinch of peck if it makes them feel jollier.'

'Yes, het.'

Bronzi wandered along the rocks away from the main group. He slipped the green metal scale out of his pocket and studied it again. It bore a code, standard Alpha form. The phrase 'Your father cheers, your mother cries, that is the lot of the soldier' had been written in Edessan to make it personal to him. He quickly substituted each letter for its numerical place in the alphabet, combined them as he had been taught, and ended up with two, seven digit channel codes.

Bronzi clambered up a line of blocks to the nearest vox officer, and borrowed his field set. He slipped on the headset, tapped in one of the codes and waited.

'Speak and identify,' said a voice.

'Argolid 768,' Bronzi said.

'Are you deployed, Hurtado?'

'I'm on the surface.'

'You are not alone. You were given the codes so that you could remain in contact during this event. Check in every two hours. We will inform you if you are required to take any specific action. Consider yourself on standby.'

'Understood.'

The signal finished. Bronzi erased the code from the vox-set's log, and carried the device back to its owner.

THEY LEFT THE drop-pod in the clutch of the scorched rock that had caught it, and moved west along a line of grey, buttress hills in the wet murk.

Rukhsana seemed to have recovered a little composure. Grammaticus believed that seeing him again had settled her mind slightly. She insisted on staying at his side and holding onto his hand.

The foul-weather kits were bulky and cumbersome, but they were glad of them. Stones dripped, and every surface shone with liquid. The place stank of rot and organic decay.

Soneka had brought a locator. 'How far do we have to go?' he asked.

Grammaticus took the device from him and activated it. He watched the display resolve, and turned slowly, checking other readings.

'Two hours, maybe three,' said Grammaticus. 'We'll keep heading west.'

Soneka looked at the chart display. 'You know where you're going, right?'

'Pretty much,' said Grammaticus. 'The Imperial landing forces will be concentrating on the Shivering Hills.'

'Why?'

'Because that's where the halting site is, and they'll assume the Cabal is there.'

'Isn't it?' asked Soneka.

Grammaticus laughed. 'Peto, the Cabal is as cautious about this meeting as the Astartes are. The Cabal is all too aware of mankind's propensity for shooting first, especially when it comes to xenoforms. Until the

members of the Cabal are certain that the Alpha
Legion hasn't simply come here with the sole purpose
of exterminating them, they're not going to show
themselves. Would you wait in the open for a stranger
whose intentions were unclear?'

'Not really,' said Soneka.

They scrambled down a slope of loose rocks onto a
series of wide, cubic blocks. Grammaticus helped
Rukhsana all the way. Every now and then, he reached
out with his mind, and looked into hers in an attempt
to monitor her wellbeing. There was nothing there,
nothing he could read, just a blizzard of thought noise
and panic.

'So the Cabal is staying out of the way?' Soneka
asked.

Grammaticus looked back at him. 'The halting site is
just an inert structure, a series of well-founded platforms and deep stone pilings designed to support the
mass of the Cabal's vessel when it visits. Alpharius
showed us the scans, and there was no vessel there, a
slight logic flaw that he didn't seem to appreciate.'

'So?'

'Alpharius should have listened to me,' Grammaticus
said. 'He should have come down here with me, instead
of landing a full military expedition. I'm the passport,
you see, Peto, the matchmaker. I make contact, bring
them together, and make sure both parties are comfortable. Then they talk. That's how it was supposed to go.'

'But Alpharius is far too wary?' mused Soneka.

'Exactly. He doesn't like unknowns. If he doesn't
know something, it means he can't trust it. He likes to
be in control all the time.'

They ascended a slope through scrolls of drifting
vapour.

'On the other hand, the Cabal is very circumspect when it comes to humans,' added Grammaticus. 'I'm afraid to say they have a fairly poor opinion of mankind.'

'Why?

'Humanity is a young race, a barbaric upstart child in the eyes of the Old Kinds, but, by the stars, it's vigorous and massively successful. It is spreading out and annexing the galaxy faster than any race has ever done before. It thrives like weeds, and finds purchase in even the harshest climes. The Cabal has been forced to recognise that mankind is a serious player on the galactic stage, and can no longer be ignored or sidelined, and, of course, they've seen what's coming.'

'This war you talked about?'

Grammaticus nodded. 'A civil war. It will tear the Imperium apart. The Cabal doesn't especially care about that. What matters is that a civil war in the Imperium will unleash Chaos. The Primordial Annihilator, the power they have fought to deny since the start of all ages, will use humanity's terrible conflict to gain final ascendancy.'

'They want the war prevented, then?' said Soneka.

'It's too late for that. They want the war won the right way.'

'Let's rest for a minute,' said Soneka. 'The uxor looks tired.'

Rukhsana looked especially pale. She was trembling from the cold. Grammaticus sat her down on a stone block. 'It's all right, Rukhsana my love. Everything is going to be all right.'

She looked up at him. 'Konig?' she asked.

'Yes, yes! That's right, Rukhsana. It's Konig. It's me.'

'Konig,' she repeated, and then gazed out over the misty rocks.

'You know where the Cabal's hiding?' asked Soneka.

'Yes,' said Grammaticus.

'We go to them, make contact…'

'We go to them, make contact, reassure them that the Alpha Legion means to listen, and then I'll go back to Alpharius.'

'Go back?' Soneka asked, incredulous.

'And bring him here.'

'He might just execute you, John.'

Grammaticus shrugged. 'I can't worry about that. This is too important. This is about deciding what the future will be about for everyone.'

SIX

Carrier *Loudon*, orbital

'WHICH OF YOU men is Franco Boone?' Chayne asked.

The six Chiliad genewhips standing in conversation in one of the hangar deck's check stations turned to look at him. Alarm flashed across their faces for a second as they realised that the question had come from one of the Lord Commander's companions. Chayne had shuttled to the *Loudon* in full Lucifer Black armour.

'I am,' said Boone.

'We will converse,' said Chayne. 'Come here.'

'Begging your pardon, sir,' said Boone, 'but I'm a little occupied. We're marshalling the second wave for drop. Come back in a couple of hours.'

Boone turned back to his fellow genewhips, and they continued to compare and check their data-slates.

'I believe,' said Chayne, 'that you understood my instruction to be optional, Franco Boone. It was not. We will converse. Come here.'

Boone tensed. His men looked on in concern, as Boone turned and walked across to the Lucifer Black.

'What?' Boone asked. He was a big man, but he had to look up into Chayne's visored face.

'We will converse, Franco Boone.'

'So you keep saying. What about some courtesy, sir? Remove your helmet so that I can see your face.'

'Why?' asked Chayne.

'Because that's what men do when they converse.'

Chayne didn't move for a moment. Then he raised his hands, unlocked his helm seals, and took the helmet off. He tucked it under his arm. His face was drawn and hard, and his eyes chilled Franco Boone's soul.

'Thank you,' said Boone. 'Your name? You seem to know mine.'

'Chayne, bajolur, companion guard.'

'Well, Chayne, bajolur, companion guard, how can I help you this day?'

'You can walk with me for a moment, you can answer my questions, and you can dispense with the verbal sport.'

Boone shrugged. They began to walk along the edge of the vast deck, past shouting flight crew and rattling tools. An autoloader cart zipped past them.

'This is a busy day for us, bajolur,' said Boone. 'Get on with it.'

'What can you tell me about Peto Soneka and Hurtado Bronzi?'

'Why?'

'I simply require you to answer the question, genewhip,' replied Chayne.

Boone frowned. 'They're two of the Chiliad's most respected hetmen. One's downstairs on 42 Hydra Tertius, the other was lost on Nurth.'

'During the last week of operations on Nurth,' said Chayne, 'both came under suspicion of treasonous behaviour.'

'They did,' Boone replied. 'I was gunning for the pair at one point, and I believe you arrested and questioned both of them. They were clean. We both found that.'

'I am reviewing the case material,' said Chayne.

'Why?' asked Boone. 'One of them's five months' dead, for fug's sake.'

'New data has been gathered,' Chayne told him. 'It casts doubt on the stories they told us.'

'Look, Chayne...' Boone began. He paused. 'One moment, bajolur.' Boone took a step aside. 'You. You men there!' he yelled out across the deck. 'Pick up your kit, you idiots. It's blocking the service strip. Come on, you gee-tards. You know the drill. Stay behind the cue line!'

The men from Mannequin Company hurried to oblige.

Boone turned back to the Lucifer. 'You were saying? New data?'

'New data,' Chayne replied.

'What sort of new data?' asked Boone.

'That's classified. It's beginning to appear that Het Soneka and Het Bronzi were not so innocent after all.'

'Listen to me,' Boone growled, looking the companion in the eye. 'You'd better have some fugging watertight facts before you come down here dragging the reputations of two of my hetmen through the gutters.'

'Ah, the famous Chiliad loyalty,' said Chayne. 'How does it go? "Company first, Imperium second, geno before gene"? I was told to expect that you'd close ranks.'

'We look after our own, companion, and I'm not sure I like what you're implying,' Boone answered.

Chayne nodded. He knew when to be forthcoming with a morsel of information. 'There were spies at work on Nurth, Boone. We assumed they were Nurthene agents. It now appears that they were part of the Alpha Legion Astartes infiltration network.'

'Hurt and Peto? Never!'

'Why never?'

'I'd have known. I knew them both,' Boone exclaimed.

'I have identified the spy at the heart of the business,' said Chayne. 'He was using the name Konig Heniker, and operating under the guise of an Imperial agent. Uxor Rukhsana Saiid was running him during the Nurthene operation. Bronzi and Soneka were arrested after an attempt to remove her from the palace. Was that the Chiliad covering itself, I wonder?'

Boone felt his mouth drying up. He breathed deeply, and steered the Lucifer Black out of the path of a trundling servitor truck laden with ground attack missiles. He led Chayne into a nearby repair shop where crews were working on service parts.

'Get out,' he told the men.

They withdrew, puzzled.

Alone, Boone turned to Chayne. 'Of course the Chiliad covers itself. We see a weak link, we clean house. Saiid was in bed, literally, I believe, with the spy. Soneka and Bronzi were simply covering our arses. I sanctioned them. You can't blame the Chiliad for that. We cleared up our own dirty laundry.'

'I won't blame you, Boone,' Chayne replied. 'Tell me about Strabo.'

'Fugging Strabo?' Boone asked, raising his eyebrows. 'Why is he called that?'

'I dunno. It's a long standing joke. Do you Lucifers make jokes, Chayne?'

'Never,' Chayne replied.

'Why am I not surprised?' Boone replied. 'All right, what's Strabo got to do with anything?'

Chayne walked away towards the shop's workbench and inspected some of the tools idly. 'He made a report, after the extraction from Nurth.'

'I think he may have,' Boone said.

'Don't be coy, Franco Boone,' Chayne said. 'With the Lord Commander's personal authority, I have accessed the Chiliad's private record base.'

'That's illegal,' Boone spat. 'You've no right!'

'Council of Terra edict 1141236a, powers of search and inquiry, as governed by the martial process,' Chayne responded. 'During war operation, the authority of any Lord Commander, or commander holding a position of equivalent authority over an expedition or similar task force, or equivalent mandate, may be allowed, under suspicion or general threat of insurgency, to seize, audit, copy, access and otherwise examine any data files compiled and stored by any military section of a regiment under his purview. *That's* my right. Tell me about Strabo.'

'It was nothing,' said Boone, miserably. 'Strabo was head bashaw of the Clowns. They'd lost their het. Soneka was sent in as proxy, to see them through. As Strabo reported it, Soneka left the Clowns on station under bashaw command during the last few hours of the Nurth campaign.'

'Why?' asked Chayne. 'Isn't that rather unusual?'

Boone shrugged. 'According to Strabo, Soneka just took off. Strabo, and bashaw Lon, who's a much more reliable source, said that Soneka had taken a spy into custody, and was personally escorting him to us genewhips. Then Nurth came down around our ears and no one ever saw him again.'

'Thank you,' said Chayne.

'That's it?' asked Boone.

'One last request,' said Chayne. 'Supply me with the surface drop coordinates of Het Bronzi.'

'Why?'

'He is not working for us, genewhip,' said Dinas Chayne, 'and he hasn't been for a long time.'

SEVEN

Eolith, continuous

THEY SCALED A steep slope of jumbled rock littered with decomposing residue. Soneka saw poking ribs and split fatty blubber, filled with liquid putrescence. The stench was intolerable.

'Come on, just a little further,' Grammaticus urged. He had become imbued with a boyish vigour. Soneka and Rukhsana followed on behind him, Soneka clasping the uxor's hand now.

'Down here!' Grammaticus called. They followed him down into a depression between leaning stone blocks. A cave of sorts lay before them, its basin flooded with black liquor between the scattered slabs.

The cave was cold and had an odd echo. Grammaticus leapt from stone to stone to avoid the stagnant water, hopping from one raised block to another as if they were stepping stones in an ornamental water garden. Soneka and Rukhsana followed him.

The cave opened out into the most enormous chapel of stone. Moisture dripped and trickled down out of the arched roof. There was a wide stone shelf in the centre of the space, like a stage, The wet rock shone like glass. Grammaticus helped Peto and Rukhsana up onto it.

'This is it?' asked Soneka, looking around at the ominous shadows, dubiously.

Grammaticus nodded.

'What happens now?'

'Wait, Peto, wait,' Grammaticus replied. He turned in a slow circle, gazing up at the walls. He seemed to be listening for something. 'I can't feel them,' he murmured. 'Where are they?'

'I may have to flect,' he decided after a moment.

'You may have to what?' asked Soneka.

'Flect! Flect!' Grammaticus said, as if everybody understood what the arcane term meant. He jumped off the stone platform and bent down beside a rock pool. He skimmed the surface of the water with his fingers. 'Please, please,' he mumbled.

Nothing happened.

'Come on!' he snapped, flicking his fingers across the water.

It suddenly went very cold.

Rukhsana pulled herself against Soneka.

+ There is no need to flect, John Grammaticus. +

Grammaticus looked up at the cave roof. 'You hear me? You're here?'

+ We've been here all along, John. +

'Show yourselves!' Grammaticus called out.

'Oh fug me,' Soneka breathed, holding Rukhsana close. She was crying and agitated.

Shapes were beginning to appear around the platform of rock, alien forms cohering into place.

Soneka swallowed hard as he saw the inhuman nature of the things solidifying in front of him: ghastly shapes, mockeries of creation, a gathering of the most disturbing xenosforms. Some were pallid, multi-limbed entities, others whispered their respiration through fluttering mats of gelatinous pseudopods. Others were stalk things, or crouching vulpine shapes, or asymmetric insects. Some were horned, or boneless, or armoured in bizarre environment suits. A giant mollusc uncurled, glistening, from its vast shell. Two spavined avian creatures hopped forwards and peered with bright, curious eyes. Something mechanical rose up on four, club-footed limbs. One entity seemed to be nothing more than a beam of discoloured light. An imposing eldar in pearl white armour, somehow the most terrifying thing of all with its oh-so human shape, walked to the front of the congregation.

Grammaticus opened his arms wide, and bowed. 'Hello, my masters,' he sighed.

An insectoid scuttled out in front of the mighty eldar and writhed its mouth parts.

'Greetings, John,' G'lattro announced in perfect Low Gothic.

'My friend, hello,' Grammaticus replied.

'Who have you brought with you to this place?' asked G'Lattro.

'Rukhsana Saiid, who is my heart love, and Peto Soneka, my friend,' said Grammaticus. 'I have come to arrange the meeting. The Alpha Legion awaits. I'm tired, sirs. This has been a long and punishing task, but it is done, and the Alpha Legion, though painfully cautious, is ready to hear what you have to say.'

Slau Dha, the autarch, murmured something.

'The autarch wishes to understand why you have brought mon-keigh things with you,' G'Latrro piped. 'Where are the envoys of the Astartes Alpha Legion?'

'I had to improvise,' Grammaticus said. 'The Alpha Legion is not easily manipulated. I could not allow suspicion and mistrust to debase this meeting. I did not want a misunderstanding to lead to bloodshed. Now that I have vouched for their intent, we can contact them directly and–'

'Mon-keigh!' Slau Dha boomed abruptly.

Grammaticus turned. Peto Soneka was aiming his laspistol right at him.

'Peto?' Grammaticus said, incredulously. 'Control word *bedlame. Bedlame*!'

Soneka laughed. 'You really thought that had worked, didn't you, John?' he asked. He tossed the locator to Rukhsana.

'Got it, Peto,' she said. She activated the beacon setting.

'Rukhsana?' Grammaticus stammered. '*No!*'

Stained light blinked and flickered all around the cave. There was a chorus of rapid, harmonic chimes. One by one, around the edges of the chamber, Alpha Legion warriors appeared in the shivering light display, weapons already trained. The teleport delivery left a dry, gritty scent in the air. In less than four seconds, fifty Alpha legionnaires were covering the Cabal from every angle. The members of the Cabal jostled and quivered, and jabbered in consternation. Slau Dha glared and reached for his weapons.

'Stand where you are and make no attempt to resist,' Omegon ordered, bolter aimed. He adjusted channels. 'We're secure.'

Light wafted. Alpharius materialised, with Shere at his side.

The primarch walked forwards. 'Cabal,' he said. 'We meet at last, on my terms.'

EIGHT

Eolith, continuous

'THERE'S A SHIP approaching,' said Mu. Bronzi called the company to halt and looked up into the saturated cloud cover. He couldn't see anything.

'There's no drop due,' he said, 'and we haven't been notified of air support. I can't see anything.'

'It's there,' she insisted, staring up into the sky. Her 'cept had caught its approach.

A dot appeared out of the clouds, and swooped down across the block valley, trailing vapour. It was a Jackal gunship.

'What does he want, I wonder?' asked Tche.

The gunship made two passes over the Jokers' position, and then banked in and hovered down to settle on the flattest patch of rock in the immediate vicinity.

As soon as its claws bit into the ground, figures dismounted from the side hatch and ran towards the waiting geno company.

'Lucifer Blacks?' Mu murmured uneasily.

Bronzi felt a shudder of panic. 'No, no,' he whispered.

The three companions, armed and armoured, covered the ground sure-footedly, and reached the Jokers. They came to a halt in a row, apparently oblivious to the surly glares of suspicion that they were getting from hundreds of big, genic soldiers.

'Hetman Bronzi,' said the lead companion. 'Identify Hetman Bronzi.'

A murmur ran through the company. Bronzi realised that he was trembling. There was absolutely no way he could run or hide from this. He did the only thing he could.

'That's me,' he called, walking out of the huddled troops to face the Lucifers. One of them immediately stepped forwards and disarmed him. Bronzi didn't fight.

'What the fug do you think you're doing?' Tche exclaimed.

'Hetman Bronzi,' the lead companion announced, 'you are detained by order of the Lord Commander. You will come with us.'

The Jokers started to yell and protest, spilling forwards out of their lines in outrage.

'Keep your places!' Bronzi yelled. 'That's an order! Keep your places! This is just a misunderstanding, and we'll get it cleared up!'

'You will come with us now,' the lead companion demanded.

'No,' Honen Mu snapped, striding out to stand beside Bronzi. 'I can't allow this. You cannot remove my hetman during an operation.'

'Your objection is noted, uxor,' said the companion, 'but it is overruled. Step back.'

'This is a disgrace!' Mu yelled. 'How dare you–'

'Step back, uxor,' the companion repeated.

'Don't provoke them, Honen,' Bronzi told her gently. 'I'll get this sorted out and be back as quickly as I can.'

'What is this about, Hurtado?' she asked, horrified.

'I don't know.'

'Bronzi, what have you done, you silly old dog?' she pleaded.

'Nothing,' he insisted. 'I've done nothing.' He clasped her hands in his and looked down into her eyes. 'I'll come back, Honen. Look after my Jokers for me, all right?'

'Hurtado…'

He bent and kissed her cheek, and then let go of her hands and allowed the companions to walk him back to the gunship.

He never looked back.

As she watched him walk away, Honen Mu had the most profound feeling that she'd never see him again.

'THIS IS NOT how it should be!' Grammaticus roared.

'Be quiet,' said Alpharius.

'No!' Grammaticus spat, turning to face the primarch. 'This is exactly the sort of confrontational duress I was trying to avoid. This is no way to deal with the Cabal. You cannot turn your guns on them and force them to–'

'I can do anything I want,' said Alpharius, 'and what I want is to be in control of this situation. Your Cabal has persistently and covertly schemed to manipulate the Alpha Legion. That is no basis for trust. I'll hear them out, but I will not let them use my Legion, or lead it into a trap.'

'It's not a trap!' Grammaticus wailed.

'Not any more it isn't,' Omegon agreed.

Grammaticus put his head in his hands and backed away. He looked up, and saw Soneka and Rukhsana.

'You used me,' he sighed in disbelief.

'No more than you thought you were using me, John,' Soneka replied, 'and you did try very hard to do that.'

'But–' Grammaticus said.

'This is what my lord wanted, and this is what I delivered for him,' said Soneka. 'He wanted to see where you would go, given the chance.'

'And you too,' Grammaticus murmured, looking at Rukhsana. 'It was all a sham.'

She opened the throat of her protective gear and revealed the pendant hanging there. 'Psionic scrambler, Konig,' she said. 'It made my mind seem as if it were out of joint.'

'Oh, Rukhsana, why?' he begged.

Playfully, she continued to unbutton her suit, and pulled the seam aside to show half of her right breast. The hydra brand appeared like a beauty spot on her pale skin.

Grammaticus looked away and sank to his knees.

'Who speaks for the Cabal?' Alpharius asked, advancing across the platform towards them.

'They will all speak through me,' clicked G'Latrro. 'Lord Alpharius, our agent is correct. This is no way to conduct business. The Cabal deplores your aggression.'

'But they want to talk to me, so they'd better get used to the situation and begin,' Alpharius replied. 'I have limited patience. What is so important that you'd go to such lengths to draw me here?'

The Cabal's interpolator did not reply. Behind him, in low, odd tones, the Cabal members consulted one another.

'Stay sharp,' Pech said to Shere, his boltgun trained on the aliens. 'Any sign of trickery…'

Shere nodded. 'There is psychic activity, but it is purely communicative. None of it is active.'

'Let me know if that changes,' said Pech.

The buzzing, mumbling stir of alien voices ceased. G'Latrro looked up at Alpharius.

'The Cabal will speak, though it resents the position you have placed it in,' it said. 'It is typical of human zeal and belligerence.'

'Begin,' said Alpharius.

'The Cabal will deal directly with the primarch of the Astartes Alpha Legion,' G'Latrro stated.

'You are,' said Alpharius.

'With the *entire* primarch,' said the insectoid.

Alpharius paused. 'You are,' he repeated.

'A show of trust is perhaps in order on your part, seeing that you hold us at gunpoint?' said G'Latrro. 'A token to signify that true secrets can be shared between us?'

Alpharius glowered for a moment, and then nodded. Omegon, in his gleaming, blue-black infiltrator armour, walked slowly over to stand at Alpharius's side. Soneka and Rukhsana exchanged brief glances of confusion. Grammaticus looked up, fascinated.

'Cut off one head and two shall grow in its place,' said G'Latrro. 'Alone amongst the genic sons of the Terran Emperor, you are the only twins. You are both the primarch, one soul in two vessels.'

'The fact is not known outside our Legion,' said Omegon.

'It is our most closely guarded secret,' said Alpharius.

'How did you know?' asked Omegon.

The insectoid's mouthparts twitched. 'Through a careful study and comparison of the known primarchs that has lasted for decades. It became clear to us that the oldest and the youngest sons were the most significant of all. Horus, for what he will do, and you for what you will undo.'

'What will Horus do?' asked Alpharius.

'He will let the galaxy burn,' said G'Latrro. 'He will ignite the civil war.'

'You speak heresy!' Omegon growled.

'Exactly so,' the interpolator replied.

Alpharius shook his head. 'This is futile. Like your agent before you, you speak of a coming war and a great doom. You describe a division that could not possibly happen. Horus Lupercal is Warmaster. He is the Emperor's right hand, and the most loyal of all. What he does, he does for the Emperor.'

'I believe you intend to sow the seeds of dissent with these wild tales,' Omegon told the interpolator. 'You wish to undermine the foundations of the Imperium.'

'They are not wild tales,' said G'Latrro.

'They are baseless and offensive to us!' Omegon snapped. 'You supply no specifics, you deal in vague pronouncements.'

'It has been farseen,' said G'Latrro.

'Again with this!' Alpharius laughed. 'Some vision, some shamanic dream? A worthless prophesy, a hollow auguring! It all means nothing! You cannot know the future, and therefore you cannot show us any proof.'

'Yes, we can,' said G'Latrro. 'If that is what you need, we will share the Acuity with you.'

'How exactly is that done? asked Omegon warily.

'It cannot be accomplished here,' said G'Latrro. 'We must first bring our vessel to the halting site, and transfer to it with you. As a matter of trust, we will allow you to escort us, under guard. We need you to know, Alpharius Omegon. We need you to see.'

'Do it,' said Alpharius and Omegon simultaneously.

NINE

Orbital, Eolith, three hours later

THEY TOOK HIM to a cell in the brig deck of the *Blamires*, and had him strip. Then they made him watch as they shredded his clothing and dismantled every piece of his equipment.

After that, they locked him in an iron restraint chair.

They did not speak once the entire time. After a while, when he realised that they weren't ever going to answer him, he stopped asking questions. From that point, the processing continued in silence.

The hatch opened. Dinas Chayne entered the cell, accompanied by a burly officer of the brig and two assistants in floor length plastek aprons. Chayne conversed quietly with the three companions who had brought Bronzi in and processed him.

He turned to the painfully restrained hetman.

'Hurtado Bronzi.'

Bronzi said nothing.

'You are detained on suspicion of being a covert operative of the Astartes Alpha Legion,' said Chayne. 'The Lord
Commander takes a dim view of spies, and of internecine
espionage. If you are found to be working for the Astartes,
it will be considered a gross act of disloyalty to your regiment, the Imperial Army, the expedition, and the Lord
Commander. Do you have anything to say?'

Bronzi flexed his throat and jaw against the iron bars
trapping them. 'This is a mistake,' he said. 'This is
wrong. You've got the wrong man.'

Chayne remained impassive. He walked across to the
metal side table where the debris of Bronzi's clothing
and kit sat in boxes. He reached into one, and produced the green metal scale. He held it up to make sure
Bronzi could see it.

'I don't know what that is,' Bronzi said. 'You've
planted it there.'

Chayne returned the scale to the box and walked
back to his prisoner. He pointed his right index finger
at the brand mark on Bronzi's right hip.

'And that, hetman? Did I plant that too?'

Bronzi scowled.

'You are in no position to equivocate, Bronzi,' said
Chayne, 'Tell me. Tell me your secret.'

Bronzi gritted his teeth. Very slowly and deliberately
he said, 'My name is Hurtado Bronzi.'

He looked at Chayne, and winked. 'There, I've said
it,' he smiled. 'I've said it and I can never take it back.
The secret's out.'

'Don't annoy me, Bronzi,' said Chayne. 'Tell me the
rest.'

'Ah. The rest?' said Bronzi. 'Well, if I *must* sir…'

* * *

ALL THE DEEP range scopes began to sound contact alerts. Van Aunger, master of the expedition fleet, got up from the leather throne in the middle of the *Blamires*'s wide main bridge and strode across to the tracking station.

'What's this?' he asked.

'Contact echo, sir,' the tracking officer replied. 'An object just appeared on the scopes, inbound to 42 Hydra Tertius.'

'Appeared?' Van Aunger repeated.

'I don't understand it, sir,' the tracking officer replied, adjusting his control panels with fast, expert hands. 'There are no energetic or magnetic profiles that would suggest a real space translation. The object just appeared. I speculate that it was previously cloaked.'

'Track it and project, full assessment,' Van Aunger ordered.

'Yes, sir,' replied the officer.

'General quarters!' Van Aunger called out. 'Shields and batteries to stand by!'

A klaxon started to sound. The bridge staff, over a hundred officers, bustled to their stations, their voices overlapping as they exchanged data and instructions.

'Trajectory projection!' the tracking officer announced.

'Main display,' Van Aunger replied.

The primary hololithic display lit up with a complex graphic diagram of the planet, the position of the fleet components, and the sweeping vector of the object.

'That will take it directly to the venue zone,' Van Aunger murmured. 'Have you identified vessel type or designation?'

'Negative, sir,' the tracking officer replied. 'It doesn't even read like a vessel. It's inert on all scans. It's... oh Terra...'

'What?'

'I'm marking it in excess of point eight superluminal, and it's big, sir. It's at least as big as we are.'

'Battle stations!' Van Aunger cried. 'Raise shields!'

The klaxon changed tone immediately. Van Aunger activated his vox-wand.

'My Lord Namatjira,' he said.

'What's going on, fleet master?' the Lord Commander's voice came back.

'An unknown craft of significant displacement is about to cut right across the fleet inbound to the planet.'

'Mobilise the picket,' Namatjira ordered. 'Interdict it now.'

'It's moving too fast, sir,' Van Aunger said. 'I've never seen anything like it.'

'Fleet master, I want you to–'

Namatjira's voice was lost in a wash of static. Every screen on the bridge stations suddenly milked out, and the main lights died. In the darkness that followed, a violent vibration shook through the mighty flagship for a few seconds.

The lights came back on. One by one, the screens came back to life.

'–an Aunger? Van Aunger?' Namatjira's voice blurted from the vox. 'What in the name of the Emperor just happened?'

'It went past us, sir,' replied Van Aunger. 'Whatever it was, it just went right past us.'

HONEN MU CRIED out. When Tche turned to look, he thought she'd slipped over on the wet rock. Then he saw that her aides were down too. He ran back over the flat topped rocks to reach her.

He began to feel it too, through the 'cept. All the men felt it, and they had come to a halt.

'What is it? What is it, uxor?' he asked.

She was down on her hands and knees, shivering with pain. 'I don't know,' she gasped, shaking her head. Huddled on the ground behind her, her aides were sobbing and wailing.

Thunder rolled. Tche and the Jokers looked up at the overcast sky and the thick banks of cloud.

'Is it a storm?' asked one.

More thunder, deep and heavy, shook out. The echo it left rolled down the wide valley that the Jokers were still only half way across.

A wind began to pick up, strong and lusty, and wet cold. Their banners and capes flapped. Spray lifted off the puddles and pools in the rocks around them.

Thunder sounded again, as if the sky was splitting. This time, Tche and his men saw lightning flare above the clouds, back lighting them. The pulsing discharges made it look as if the clouds were on fire inside.

The men started to point at the sky and cry out. 'Holy fug,' Tche mumbled.

A city was falling out of the sky on top of them.

At first, it was a great copper dish, half as wide as the visible sky. Streaks of luminous white and blue pulsed out from the centre of the dish, to its rim and back. The rim was turning like a spinning top, and flashing with iridescent patterns. The dish passed overhead, plunging them into shadow. It made an infrasonic murmur that quaked their internal organs and made them involuntarily squeal in fear. There was a smell of ozone, and sizzling bolts of forked lighting seared down from the clouds all along the length of the valley.

The copper dish, so vast that the very size of it was terrifying, swung in over the monolithic black cliffs of the Shivering Hills, and slowly descended. Now, they could see its upper surface, where giant copper structures resembling fans and leaves bloomed like a cyclopean, abstract water lily from the top of the dish.

It sank lower and lower, until the spinning dish was obscured by the cliffs. There was a colossal boom that shook the ground under them, and caused splinters of rock to topple over and come crashing down the face of the black cliffs. The dish had set down somewhere beyond the hill line. They could see the golden fans and petals of its upper structure rising above the Shivering Hills like the spires and monuments of some heavenly city.

Stray lightning continued to spark and flicker in the clouds, but the wind dropped as quickly as it had risen.

Tche helped Mu to her feet. Blood was seeping from her left nostril. They gazed in silent awe at the gilded shapes of the new skyline.

'What… what is it?' Tche asked.

Honen Mu had no answer for him.

NAMATJIRA SLOWLY STUDIED the orbital pictures.

'It's huge,' he murmured.

'A xenosform vehicle of some kind,' nodded Van Aunger. 'I'm afraid we can't determine any details apart from its size. It is resistant to our probes.'

'It has landed precisely at the location Alpharius instructed me to secure,' said Namatjira.

'Yes, sir,' said Van Aunger, 'inside the Shivering Hills area, at the heart of the atmospheric anomaly, and directly upon structures that our scans identified as artificial.'

'So,' the Lord Commander mused, 'the Cabal has arrived and shown itself.'

'My lord?' asked Van Aunger.

Namatjira looked up from the pictures. 'Return to the bridge, fleet master. Set the fleet to a war footing. Charge all main battery weapons, and target that object. You will only commence bombardment on my instruction.'

'Sir, we have significant ground troop deployments adjacent to that craft,' said Van Aunger. 'They would most likely be caught in any orbital bombardment we unleashed. I told you this, Lord Commander, before the day began. I told you that bombardment tactics would—'

'Charge all main battery weapons and target that object,' hissed Namatjira. 'Is that too complex an order for you? Should I break it down? Target that object! If that's beyond you, expect to be stripped of your mastery with immediate effect. I understand Admiral Kalkoa is eager to rise to fleet command.'

Van Aunger glared at Namatjira, made a sullen namaste and left the lookout.

Namatjira sat down on one of the window couches, and stroked the flank of his gene-bred pet.

Chayne entered the lookout, and dismissed the companion on duty.

'Did you see?' asked Namatjira.

Chayne nodded. 'The Cabal is clearly more potent than we feared.'

'They're not playing by Alpharius's rules either,' said the Lord Commander. 'This is not the schedule the primarch told me to expect. He anticipated that our ground forces would have the area surrounded and in our control before–'

He paused.

'Sir?' asked Chayne.

'Unless he lied to me,' said Namatjira. 'Unless he is already making contact with the Cabal and learning their precious secrets for himself.'

Namatjira rose. He crossed the lookout and poured a flute of wine, sipped it, and then dashed the glass against the window ports with a snarl of fury.

'He plays us!' he growled. 'He plays us and uses us! Everything he promised me, the honour, the glory, the Emperor's gratitude, was that all lies too?'

Chayne shrugged. 'I have not trusted the Astartes Alpha Legion from the start, sir. They do not practise the codes of nobility and honour shown by the other Legions Astartes. I believe their operation and conduct should be reported to the Council of Terra, pending censure or dissolution. It wouldn't be the first time a Legion Astartes has overstepped the mark, after all. They must be stopped and held accountable before they become too powerful.'

Namatjira nodded, thoughtfully. 'Agreed, and I will be the one to bring the matter directly to the Emperor's attention. Perhaps then I can salvage some of my reputation. We need to find them culpable, Dinas. We need firm evidence of their miscreant nature. I need to know precisely what they're doing, and what infernal compact they are making with these xenoform bastards.'

Chayne poured another drink, and handed it to his master. 'Thank you, Dinas,' Namatjira replied. He began to pace.

'We already have evidence of their espionage, sir,' said Chayne. 'I have detained an officer of the Geno

Five-Two Chiliad, and have manifest proof that he has been working as an operative of the Alpha Legion.'

'In our own damn ranks?'

'The man is Bronzi, sir. It is shocking to discover that the Alpha Legion has infiltrated at the highest operational level.'

Namatjira nodded. 'That's a start. Good. You have interrogated him?'

'He is resisting us, my lord, stoically, but my men are very skilled and patient. I do not know how much longer a man, even a man of Bronzi's considerable constitution, can withstand such levels of pain.'

'Get me a link to the primarch, Dinas,' Namatjira said, 'person to person. Let's see what new lies he chooses to spin me, and see if we can't establish his location while we listen to them. Prepare the Lucifer Blacks for teleport assault.'

Chayne saluted.

'And Dinas?'

'Yes, sir?'

'Show this Bronzi no mercy,' said Namatjira. 'Break him mind, body and soul, and pluck his secrets from him.'

'Yes, my lord,' replied Dinas Chayne.

TEN

The Acuity

SONEKA HAD NEVER travelled by teleport before. It
wasn't an experience he'd care to repeat. It made him
feel sick and disoriented, as if he'd been put back
together the wrong way around.

The Astartes showed no sign of being remotely dis-
comforted.

The teleport arrays of the battle-barge had relocated
them all, Imperials and Cabal aliens alike, from the
dank cave to a wet rock platform at the halting site, just
below the gilded lip of the Cabal's parked vessel.

The landing at the halting site had churned up the
local atmosphere. It was raining hard, and a vapour
like steam was rising from the cubic blocks and the oil
black pools. The encircling cliffs of the Shivering Hills
surrounded them in a ring forty kilometres in diameter. The water particles in the air had created a fabulous
half rainbow over the steaming bowl of the halting
site.

The Cabal's immense vessel, dazzling with gold and copper reflections, was too vast to comprehend. Soneka looked at it for a while, seeing it as a budding flower, opening its fimbriate petals to the sky, or a crown of oddly twisted thorns.

He realised at length, that it was simply too big, too alien, too unparalleled, for his mind to accommodate without collapsing into madness. He looked away. He'd seen enough of the extraordinary for one lifetime.

'It's…' Rukhsana mumbled. 'It's… simply…'

'I know,' Soneka said, and gently turned her aside to look at the rim of black cliffs through the rain. 'It's best not to look at it for too long.'

'What have we got ourselves into, Peto?' she asked.

He smiled. 'I really don't know any more. We've played our parts. I don't believe we matter at all now. A great destiny is being shaped, I think. Can't you feel it, the weight of future ages hanging over us?'

She nodded, and hooked her rain-plastered hair off her face. 'Absolutely,' she said.

'This is a task for stronger minds,' said Soneka, 'post-human minds, not our weak brains. We have to trust the Astartes to do what they were created to do. We have to trust them to keep our species safe.'

'Do you trust them, Peto?' Rukhsana asked.

'We both carry their mark, uxor,' he said. 'I think it's far too late to ask that question.'

She looked around. A considerable way away, down the rainswept platform, Grammaticus sat hunched under the guard of an Astartes.

'He hates us,' she said.

'Of course he does,' said Soneka, 'we betrayed him.'

'That was hard to do,' she said. 'To use him—'

'He's used everybody, every step of the way,' Soneka replied. 'He'll get over it. It may not have gone the way he'd have liked it to, but we got him what he wanted.'

'No, you have to understand, I loved him,' she said, 'or I thought I did, and I thought he loved me. I didn't understand what he was, even when he told me to my face. I didn't understand the scale of it all.'

'You were never supposed to,' said Soneka. 'Pawns are never supposed to perceive the game as a whole.'

A golden ramp, like a curving tongue, had extended from the rim of the Cabal vessel to meet the edge of the stone platform. The Astartes, bolters ready, had begun to steer the huddle of alien sentients up into the craft. Some whimpered or murmured as they were herded along. Slau Dha, the great autarch, walked with his crested head up, ignoring the trained bolters.

'Signal relayed from the battle-barge,' Herzog said to Alpharius.

'Content?'

'Lord Commander Namatjira requests personal vox audience. He worries that you have begun the meeting without him.'

'Tell him I can't be reached at this time,' said Alpharius. 'Tell him to maintain position and keep his forces on standby.'

'He won't like it,' said Herzog.

'That's his problem,' Omegon replied.

'I probably shouldn't tell him that, though, should I?' asked Herzog.

'Tell him I appreciate his patience, and I will contact him directly,' said Alpharius.

THEY BOARDED THE copper craft. Its internal compartments bore no relation to a ship of human design. Odd spaces opened out into curious chambers, or turned back on themselves like a maze. The walls glowed softly with inner radiance. In places, the ceiling seemed to soar away forever. Soneka felt muddled and uncomfortable.

The air smelled like burnt sugar and fused plastek.

They were left alone for a while in a chamber formed from three golden petals.

'What's that noise?' Rukhsana asked.

'I don't hear anything,' said Soneka.

'It's in my 'cept then, like a swarm of bees.'

First Captain Pech appeared and strode over to them. 'The primarch has called for you, Peto,' he said.

'Me?'

'He needs you. Follow me.'

Soneka glanced at Rukhsana. 'Go on,' she urged.

Pech led him through the luminous halls of the Cabal vessel to a chamber where Alpharius, Omegon and Shere were waiting.

'My lord?' asked Soneka.

'The Cabal is about to display the Acuity to us, Peto,' Alpharius told him. 'As far as we can tell, it's a perception device, a means of temporal lensing, based on eldar principles of farseeing.'

'Yes, lord. I don't really understand anything you just said.'

'We are about to have the future revealed to us,' said Omegon.

'Sirs, why did you send for me?' asked Soneka.

'I need to determine, as accurately as I possibly can, the viability of what they are about to show us,' said Alpharius. 'I have suggested that the witnesses should be Omegon and myself, Shere from the psyker perspective, and you as an unmodified human. Do you consent?'

'Sir, I–'

'Do you consent?' demanded Omegon. 'We haven't got time to waste.'

Soneka nodded. 'I will do whatever I can, my lords,' he replied.

'Thank you, Peto,' said Alpharius. 'We're ready,' he called out.

A wall that had seemed solid parted like smoke. The four men walked into the chamber beyond, side by side.

It was dark, and lit by a ruddy glow that seemed to come from everywhere and nowhere. Ahead of them, a monolithic slab of silver light shivered in the darkness.

+ I am Gahet. +

'I am Alpharius, primarch of the Twentieth Legion Astartes,' Alpharius replied.

+ Welcome. Let us know the others, and your other self. +

'I am Omegon, primarch of the Twentieth Legion Astartes,' said Omegon.

+ Welcome. Den Dang Keyat Shere, welcome. +

Shere bowed.

+ Peto Soneka. Welcome. +

'Hello,' said Soneka. 'You're inside my head.'

+ I am. +

'That's not entirely pleasant,' said Soneka.

'Oh, get a backbone, het,' snapped Omegon.

+ You are prepared to observe the Acuity? +

'Yes,' said Alpharius. 'Any tricks will result in our bolters dismantling this vessel piece by piece. Are we understood?'

+ Yes. You are a violent species, human. You threaten quickly. The violence will come later, and will be entirely your business. +

'Get on with it,' said Omegon.

+ We have battled to deny the Primordial Annihilator for longer than you have been evolved. Chaos cannot be permitted to gain control of the galaxy. +

'This fact has already been established, Gahet,' said Alpharius.

+ The human race is virile. It thrives, unruly and edacious. It is, in its ignorance, especially susceptible to the influence of Chaos. The Primordial Annihilator has buried its fingers into mankind, intending to turn it into a weapon. +

'Mankind will resist,' said Alpharius.

+ You will not know how to resist. The Primordial Annihilator is cunning. It will trigger civil war within the Imperium of Man, and bring all creation crashing down. See. +

The slab of silver light trembled and opened. They saw what was inside it. It felt as if they were falling from orbit onto a burning world. Shere began to weep.

+ This is our veridical testimony. This is the future as it will happen. The great war will erupt across the firmament and engulf the human race. The stars will go out. The Annihilator will rise. +

'No,' said Omegon bluntly. His eyes were wide.

+ You cannot deny it, Omegon. It is a process already underway. +

'You damn liar!' Omegon roared, and looked away from the Acuity's vision.

+ I cannot lie. I do not lie. The human race will become the absolute masters of teratogeny. They will create the greatest monster of all: Horus! +

Soneka's mind was numb. What he had witnessed made the sight of the giant copper craft seem unremarkable.

'How… how do we stop this?' he asked with a trembling voice.

+ You don't, but the Alpha Legion Astartes is perfectly placed to control and direct it. +

'Explain!' Alpharius demanded.

+ The civil war brought against the Emperor by Horus Lupercal will end one of two ways. Either Horus will win, and Chaos will triumph, or the Emperor's forces will prevail and drive Chaos into retreat. +

'The Alpha Legion has always, always, been for the Emperor,' Alpharius stated.

The slab of silver light flickered.

+ Regard, then, the future. Horus wins, and Chaos triumphs, a terrible prospect, but likely. The Cabal sees a scintilla of honour remaining in bright Lupercal. He will secretly hate himself for the atrocities committed in his name. If he wins, his fury will accelerate, along with his self-loathing. He will immolate the human species inside two or three generations. The self-destructive, redemptive urge in Horus will drive him to exterminate mankind in shame. Even his closest allies will war against him in a final armageddon. Chaos will burn brighter than ever before, and will then be extinguished. Its great victory will flare, and then gutter, as the dying Imperium takes it to the grave. The races of the galaxy will be spared, through the sacrifice of the human race. +

'Horus will not be allowed to win!' Omegon retorted.

+ Consider the alternative, Omegon primarch. This is what we have farseen. The Emperor will give his life to achieve victory. He will fall, at Terra, striking Horus down. This will be his destiny. See. +

The silver light shimmered. They saw the magnificence of the Golden Throne, and the howling rictus of the wizened cadaver locked inside it.

'Oh my lord!' Soneka cried.

+ If the Emperor wins, stagnation will seize the Imperium. It will seek to perpetuate itself, over and again, across thousands of years, but it will decay, slowly and surely. It will decay, and gradually allow Chaos to seep back in and consume it. +

'Victory... is defeat?' asked Alpharius softly.

+ If the Emperor wins, Alpharius, Chaos will ultimately triumph. Ten, twenty thousand years of misery and rot will follow, until the Primordial Annihilator at last achieves ascendancy. +

'This is the choice?' asked Omegon. He laughed bleakly.

+ The slow, inexorable conquest of Chaos, or a brief period of terror and frenzy. Creeping damnation, or a bloody century or two as the human race rips itself apart, and expunges Chaos from the galaxy. This is the choice we present to you. The human race is a weapon. It can save the galaxy or destroy it. +

'This is hardly a choice at all, Gahet,' said Alpharius.

+ I pity you, human. It is not, but you are pragmatic, that is your abiding virtue. You see the long view. You make the hard decisions. Alpharius, the stagnant future must be denied. +

'How do we do that?' asked Omegon. 'How do you propose we do that, you alien bastard?'

+ It is perfectly simple, Omegon. The Alpha Legion must side with the rebels. You must ensure that Horus wins. +

'Never!' snarled Omegon.

'It is unthinkable!' Alpharius yelled.

+ Then see the result. See it. See it for yourselves. +

The silvery glow shivered again. They flinched. They saw it all, in the space of a moment.

The Acuity showed them everything.

Omegon and Alpharius staggered backwards, screaming.

Shere burbled furiously, and then fell down, stone dead, his mind destroyed.

Soneka sank to his knees and wept.

ELEVEN

42 Hydra

THEY CAME BACK out into luminous halls that would never seem so bright again. The future came with them, like a shroud. Alpharius and Omegon were silent and expressionless. Ashen, broken, Soneka carried Shere's corpse in his arms.

The Astartes were waiting for them, their bolters still covering the furtive, whispering members of the Cabal.

'My lord?' Pech began. 'What did—'

Alpharius raised a hand for silence. He looked at his twin, and they stared into each other's eyes for a long time.

Soneka set Shere's body down on the deck. Rukhsana came over to him.

'Peto? Your face!' she whispered. 'What was it? What did you see?'

Soneka shook his head. He couldn't speak. She put her arms around him.

'He saw the Acuity.' John Grammaticus was standing behind them. 'It is a terrible thing, isn't it, Peto? Quite terrible, and wonderful too.'

'Wonderful?' Soneka burst out, pulling away from Rukhsana. 'How can you call it that?'

'Because in all the horror, it offers a chance,' said John Grammaticus. 'One pure, simple chance to save, to spare, and to protect.'

Soneka stared at him. 'I don't think much of the chance, John,' he replied.

SLAU DHA STEPPED forward to face Alpharius. The Astartes followed him with their weapons, but he ignored the threat.

'Well?' he asked, in halting, thickly accented Low Gothic. 'What is your response, mon-keigh? Do you have the strength to make this choice, or are you just as weak and self-serving as the rest of your vermin species?'

Alpharius gazed at the autarch levelly. 'I stand for the Emperor,' he replied. 'In all things, I am loyal to Him, and I cannot break that bond. He has many great ambitions, and the noblest of intentions, but I know that above all else, He is determined to stand firm against the rise of Chaos. He has always known the truth of it. The overthrow of the Primordial Annihilator is His greatest wish. So what I do, autarch, from this moment on, I will do for the Emperor.'

Slau Dha nodded. He turned and walked away.

'Lord Namatjira continues to plague us with demands,' said Herzog. 'He is becoming quite agitated. He insists that you report to him immediately and make full disclosure.'

'Does he indeed?' Alpharius replied.

Herzog nodded. 'He's beginning to make veiled threats too, my lord, accusations of treason or worse. I believe we must make some kind of response before he loses all patience and embarks upon a regrettable course of action.'

'We will make a response,' said Omegon.

Alpharius glanced at his twin.

'If we are to prevail in the task ahead of us,' said Omegon, 'we must be secure and committed. We cannot let our hand be seen too early, or have our undertaking betrayed. Secrecy is, as always, our most potent weapon.'

'Agreed,' said Alpharius. He bowed his head, and was silent and pensive for a moment.

'So?' asked Omegon.

Alpharius looked up him. 'Do it,' he said.

'STILL NO RESPONSE from the primarch or any of his officers, my lord,' announced the master of vox. 'His barge also refuses to acknowledge our repeated hails.'

Namatjira nodded. The bridge of the *Blamires* had grown increasingly quiet. The tension was palpable.

'Repeat the message,' Namatjira ordered.

'Yes, my lord,' said the master of vox.

The Lord Commander turned to Van Aunger. 'I'm going to withdraw to my chambers,' he said, 'and compose a statement of censure regarding the Astartes Alpha Legion. If we have not received a satisfactory reply by the time I'm done, you will send the statement directly to Terra.'

'Yes, my lord,' said Van Aunger.

'At that time, I will issue one final notice of intent, and if it is not answered, we will begin total bombardment of the surface zone.'

'Sir, I–' Van Aunger protested.

'Shut up and listen, Van Aunger!' Namatjira growled. '*Total* bombardment of the surface zone. Furthermore, you will position appropriate heavy cruisers to challenge and cripple the battle-barge.'

Van Aunger shook his head in dismay. 'They are Astartes, my lord. What you're proposing amounts to war against our own.'

'The Lord Commander does not believe they *are* our own any more, fleet master,' said Dinas Chayne.

Namatjira turned to leave the bridge, but a call from the tracking officer stopped him.

'Sir, the Astartes battle-barge has just slipped high anchor.'

'What?' demanded Van Aunger, hurrying to the station. 'Show me.'

'It's coming about, sir,' the tracking officer gabbled. 'It's turning in towards the fleet formation.'

'Those duplicitous bastards,' murmured Namatjira.

'That's an attack vector!' Van Aunger cried. 'Full shields! Battle stations!'

'The barge has opened fire, sir!' a deck officer shouted. 'The *Cantium* has taken direct hits! The *Solar Wind* too! It's open to the void!'

'Return fire!' Van Aunger ordered. 'All vessels with a viable target solution on the barge *Beta* fire at will!'

'The carrier *Loren* has gone, sir! The *Tancredi* and the *Loudon* both report damage!'

'It's just one ship,' barked Namatjira.

'It's an Astartes battle-barge, you cretin!' Van Aunger spat at him. 'It's ploughing through the centre of the fleet like a hot knife!'

The deck shook as the *Blamires* began to fire its primary batteries.

'Eight direct hits recorded on the target vessel,' the master of ordnance sang out.

'Yes!' crowed Namatjira, clenching a fist.

'The *Beta* is not slowing down,' said the tracking officer. 'Function does not seem to have been impaired.'

A shrill siren began to sound, slicing through the battle klaxons.

'Teleport signature!' a bridge officer howled. 'Full spread of teleport flares throughout the midsection! We're being boarded!'

INTERNAL HATCHES BLEW open in a welter of flame and flying metal. Bolter rounds ripped out of the smoke choking the hallway, and cut down crew personnel as they tried to flee.

The Astartes appeared, striding relentlessly out of the fire, their purple armour reflecting the rippling flames. Their bolters roared as they switched left and right methodically, covering every side tunnel and passageway.

'Repulse! Repulse!' shouted Major General Dev, sword in hand, trying to rally two platoons of Hort infantry. 'Open fire!'

The troopers began to blaze shots down the length of the hallway. Dev thought he glimpsed a purple figure staggering back, but bolt rounds seared out of the swirling smoke and destroyed two of the troopers beside him. Covered in their blood, Dev tried to pull his men back to cover. 'Keep firing!' he yelled. He grabbed his vox. 'Repulse squads to decks eight and nine! Heavy weapons! We need heavy weapons!'

They drew back along the hall, and into an assembly chamber. Bolt rounds chased them, and cut down three more men. Forty Outremar heavies were running forwards through the chamber to support them.

'Up! Up! Up!' Dev yelled. 'Come on! Hold the fugging hatchway! Keep them back!'

The deck shook with a series of loud blasts from somewhere below.

'Give me that fugging launcher!' Dev screamed, throwing down his sword and snatching the heavy weapon out of the hands of one of the Outremars. He began to pump rocket grenades out through the chamber hatch.

Light blinked and flickered in the chamber behind them. Coalescing matter swirled, and twisted the eddying smoke. Six Alpha Legion Astartes materialised, their weapons firing on full auto. The major general and his men perished in seconds.

'SOMETHING'S HAPPENING,' SAID Tche urgently. 'Something bad.'

Honen Mu gazed up at the sky. The bright flashes and sparks beyond the cloud cover were not lightning. It was orbital fire. The fleet had engaged.

'I can't raise the carrier, or the flagship,' the Jokers' vox officer reported.

'Keep trying,' she ordered.

'What is it?' asked Tiphaine. 'What's happening up there?'

'I don't know,' Mu replied.

Everyone winced suddenly. 'Cept pain shot through the uxor and her aides. Its iridescent rim turning slowly, the giant copper disk rose up behind the crags of the Shivering Hills, and ascended straight up into the sky. It vanished into the low cloud.

Mu sat down on a flat block of stone. It had begun to rain, fierce and cold. She could already smell the minute change in the air. Whatever purpose the atmospheric zone had been created for was done with. It was no longer needed, and it was being allowed to dissipate. She had no idea if the process would take minutes, days or weeks, but the caustic atmosphere of 42 Hydra Tertius would flood back and restore climactic equilibrium.

Honen Mu perceived that no one would be coming for them. The Jokers, and all the other ground assault units, would still be in the zone when the poison storms of 42 Hydra Tertius reclaimed it.

Then other decomposing remains would be left, drowned and scattered, across the lonely cubic rocks.

TWELVE

Blamires, orbital

DINAS CHAYNE PLACED a firm hand on Namatjira's arm.

'Now, my lord,' he insisted.

'No, Dinas,' Namatjira snapped, pulling away.

'The security of the flagship can no longer be guaranteed,' said Chayne. 'The companions must escort you to the safety of your sanctuary launch.'

The bridge was shaking. Every man at every station was shouting above the wail of the sirens. There was a distinct smell of smoke.

'Target it again!' bellowed Namatjira. 'Again!'

'We cannot break its shields,' Van Aunger yelled back.

'We just lost the *Barbustion*!' someone yelled.

'The *Loudon* is reported as on fire and drifting!' called another voice.

Namatjira walked up to Van Aunger and slapped him hard across the face. 'Destroy that barge, you piece of shit!'

Van Aunger recoiled, spitting blood from his lip. He balled his fist to swing back. Chayne took him by the throat. Van Aunger gagged.

'You will not raise your hand to the Lord Commander,' said Chayne. 'Complete your orders.'

He let go. Van Aunger fell to the deck, gasping. 'All weapons,' he coughed. 'All weapons, sustained fire. Everything we've got, damn it, before–'

'Contact!' the tracking officer cried. 'A second contact!'

They stared at the jumping graphics on the main display. A vessel was shown tracking towards the rear of the fleet mass.

'Where did it come from?' Van Aunger asked.

'It just appeared on the scopes, sir. It was concealed behind the planet.'

'That's another barge,' said Van Aunger in a low voice. 'That's another fugging battle-barge!'

'The *Alpha*,' whispered Namatjira.

'It has opened fire!' the tracking officer yelled.

'Now, my lord,' said Chayne.

This time, Namatjira allowed Chayne to lead him away.

'Noisy... out there...' Bronzi muttered through the blood oozing out of his mouth.

'Shut it!' ordered the officer of the brig. He exchanged a worried look with his two assistants in their blood-spattered aprons. The thump of explosions and the crackle of gunfire was impossible to ignore.

Bronzi began to laugh, but it turned into a wet, ragged cough.

'They're coming... they're coming for me, you see? I knew... I knew they would.'

'Shut up!' the officer snarled, and viciously tightened one of the cage screws.

Bronzi screamed.

He coughed out more blood. 'My name... my name is Hurtado Bronzi...' he wheezed. 'That's... that's all you're getting...'

The cell door slammed open. Two figures in black bodygloves burst in. Peto Soneka shot the officer of the brig twice through the heart with his laspistol, and then pumped several more rounds into his twitching corpse. Thaner decapitated one of the assistants with an expert slice of his falx, and then drove the long blade through the other's belly.

He tugged the weapon out. The man collapsed.

'Get him out of the restraint,' said Soneka. Thaner started to undo the heavy clasps and bolts.

'Peto?'

'Hang on, Hurt. You're a mess.'

'You... came for me...'

'A personal favour granted by the primarch,' Soneka said.

'You... came for me...' Bronzi repeated.

'We look after our own,' said Thaner.

They pulled him out of the cage. He couldn't stand, so they carried him between them, his meaty arms, blood-soaked, around their shoulders.

'Hurry,' said Thaner.

'Signal the teleport,' said Soneka.

Thaner nodded.

'We're going to get you out, Hurt,' said Soneka. 'We'll get you to the barge and patch you up. Just hang on.'

'It's... good to see you, Peto,' Bronzi murmured.

'And you, Hurt.'

'If it's so good… to see me… why do you look… so fugging grim?'

'Later,' said Peto Soneka. 'I'll tell you later.'

ONE END OF the flagship's vast carrier deck was ablaze. Chayne and a squad of six Lucifer Blacks ran Namatjira through the smoke and across the wide deck space towards the armoured sanctuary launch.

'Prepare for immediate departure,' Chayne cried into his vox. 'The Lord Commander will be aboard in twenty seconds!'

'I don't believe he will,' said Alpharius.

The primarch had emerged from the dense smoke pouring down the carrier space. He stood, gladius drawn, between the companions and the launch.

The Lucifer Blacks were armed with laspistols and sabres. Without hesitation, they rushed him, firing as they came.

Las-rounds pinged and flashed off Alpharius's armour. Some left scorched and dented holes. He drove in to meet the charge. One swing of his sword broke the back of the first Lucifer. Alpharius wheeled and crushed another's skull with his left fist.

Blades sawed at him from all sides. He blocked with his sword, and the gauntlet of his left hand. A sabre shattered. The gladius stabbed clean through the chest of a companion, and ripped free. Blood spattered out in a wide arc across the deck.

Blocking another sword stroke with his gladius, Alpharius delivered a crushing punch with his left hand that sent one of the remaining Lucifers flying backwards. He grabbed another, and broke his neck with one twist of his armoured fingers.

Chayne swung his sabre in, and it was barely blocked by the primarch's sword. He altered his attack dynamic. Alpharius had to take a step backwards to defend against Chayne's extraordinary swordsmanship. The primarch parried and thrust, but Chayne dodged the strike, and ran his sabre into Alpharius's side. The tempered blade, as strong and sharp as any metal known to man, punched under the side of the power armour, through the segmented layering, and deep into Alpharius's torso.

Alpharius looked down at the wedged blade. A tiny amount of blood oozed out.

'Hmh,' he murmured. He stared at Chayne, who knew he could not pull the sword out.

'That's all you get,' said Alpharius, and split him in half.

Alpharius sheathed his gladius, and dragged the sabre out of his torso. He tossed it away, and walked through the litter of bodies to where Namatjira was kneeling on the deck.

'Please! My lord primarch! Please, I beg you!' Namatjira pleaded, his hands making a desperate namaste.

Alpharius drew his boltgun.

'Why?' shrieked Namatjira. 'Why are you doing this?'

'For the Emperor,' said Alpharius, and pulled the trigger.

EPILOGUE

Cabal

THE COPPER DISH spun out through the darkest part of the void. John Grammaticus walked its silent halls for the last time.

'Where are you going?' asked Slau Dha.

'Away. It's over. I'm done.'

'There will be other tasks.'

'Not for me,' said John Grammaticus.

'The Cabal is grateful for your efforts,' said Slau Dha.

'I bet that was hard to say,' Grammaticus replied, scornfully.

He walked away from the autarch.

'You were successful, mon-keigh,' said the eldar lord. 'Why do you not seem satisfied?'

'Because of the measure of my success,' said Grammaticus. 'I successfully signed the death notice of the human race.'

'John?' Slau Dha called out. 'You are heading in the direction of the external hatches. John?'

John Grammaticus ignored him and kept walking. He felt he deserved it.

It wouldn't be his first death, but he hoped it would be his last.

ABOUT THE AUTHOR

Dan Abnett lives and works in Maidstone, Kent, in England. Well known for his comic work, he has written everything from Mr Men to the X-Men. His work for the Black Library includes the best-selling Gaunt's Ghosts novels, the Inquisitor Eisenhorn and Ravenor trilogies, and the Horus Heresy novel, *Horus Rising*. He's also worked on the Darkblade novel series (with US author Mike Lee).

THE BLACK LIBRARY

THE HERESY REVEALED!

These incredible books take you back 10,000 years and tell
the complete epic story that underpins the entire history of
the Warhammer 40,000 universe!

978-1-84416-294-9

978-1-84416-370-0

978-1-84416-202-0

978-1-84416-549-4

978-1-84416-476-9

978-1-84416-508-7

Visit *www.blacklibrary.com* to buy these books, or
read the first chapters for free! Also available in
all good bookshops and game stores.

READ TILL YOU BLEED

I AM HORUS. I AM THE WARMASTER
I AM THE MASTER OF ALL MANKIND

THE HORUS HERESY
Collected Visions

978-1-84416-424-1

THE COMPLETE COLLECTED VOLUMES OF THE HORUS HERESY ARTBOOKS

In this amazing omnibus, all four volumes of the popular Horus Heresy artbook series are brought together for the first time. It is the complete story of this pivotal period, in which the arch-traitor Horus betrayed the Emperor of Mankind. The epic tale is described by Games Workshop Loremaster Alan Merrett and illustrated by masses of fantastic art from the finest Warhammer artists, and includes a new short story by *False Gods* and *Fulgrim* author, Graham McNeill.

Visit *www.blacklibrary.com* to buy these books, or read the first chapters for free! Also available in all good bookshops and game stores.

THE BLACK LIBRARY

THE NEXT INSTALMENT

Enjoyed *Legion*? Look out for the next book in the Horus Heresy series

THE HORUS HERESY

Ben Counter

BATTLE FOR THE ABYSS

My brother, my enemy

978-1-84416-549-0

In stores from August '08

Visit *www.blacklibrary.com* to find out more and read the first chapter for free!

READ TILL YOU BLEE